Praise for *A Dying Breed*

Sunday Times **Thriller of the Month**

'Thoughtful, atmospheric and grippingly plotted' *Guardian*

'The multi-layered plot moves excitingly and entertainingly but also raises serious current issues . . . Hanington has true talent'
The Times

'A deeply insightful, humane, funny and furious novel. This is both a timely reflection on how Britain does business and a belting good read' A.L. Kennedy

'A tremendously good debut with characters who leap to life . . . I have not read anything that has taken me anywhere near as close to Afghanistan as a place – amazingly gripping' Melvyn Bragg

'Shot-through with great authenticity and insider knowledge – wholly compelling and shrewdly wise' William Boyd

Praise for *A Single Source*

'Topical, authoritative and gripping' Charles Cumming

'Tight, pacy and strong on atmosphere' Michael Palin

'Peter Hanington has a gift for fast-paced narrative, atmospheric location and authentic, often hilarious dialogue . . . [he] draws you in from the first line and keeps you guessing until, literally, the very last' Allan Little

'A fascinating, atmospheric read . . . Will keep you up till the early hours' Kate Hamer

'If you love le Carré, were gripped by *Homeland* and couldn't get your nose out of *A Dying Breed*, here's another thrilling read for you' Dame Ann Leslie

Praise for *A Cursed Place*

'An intriguing, timely and unsettling new thriller' Sam Bourne

'A panoramic thriller . . . chockful of vivid characters'
Sunday Times

'Crackles off the page' Allan Little

'As important as it is unputdownable' Amol Rajan

'Catapults you from first word to last . . . a pacy, sinister and timely read' Alan Judd, author of *A Fine Madness*

'Another page-turner from a writer who can take you into gripping worlds, real and virtual' Mishal Husain

'Vivid, quick-witted and dynamic, crackling with energy, dread and rage as it crosses continents and digs down into the human heart'
Nicci Gerrard

'Carver is a marvellous creation' *Shots Mag*

'Will have readers cancelling meetings and postponing dinner plans so as to read just one more page, just one more chapter'
Seb Emina

'A fast-paced and vividly written thriller' Rory Cellan-Jones

'Astute, pacy and possibly too true for its own good'
Gillian Reynolds

'A true page-turner . . . highly recommended' *Tortoise*

THE BURNING TIME

Also by Peter Hanington

A Dying Breed
A Single Source
A Cursed Place

PETER HANINGTON

THE BURNING TIME

BASKERVILLE
An imprint of JOHN MURRAY

First published in Great Britain in 2023 by Baskerville
An imprint of John Murray (Publishers)

2

A CIP catalogue record for this title is available from the British Library

Hardback ISBN 9781529305265
Trade Paperback ISBN 9781529305258
ebook ISBN 9781529305272

Typeset in Fournier MT by
Palimpsest Book Production Limited, Falkirk, Stirlingshire

Printed and bound in Great Britain by Clays Ltd, Elcograf S.p.A.

John Murray policy is to use papers that are natural, renewable
and recyclable products and made from wood grown in sustainable forests.
The logging and manufacturing processes are expected to conform
to the environmental regulations of the country of origin.

Carmelite House
50 Victoria Embankment
London EC4Y 0DZ

www.johnmurraypress.co.uk

John Murray Press, part of Hodder & Stoughton Limited
An Hachette UK company

For Tom, Lucia, Honor and Patrick

REUTERS . . . COP 21 – PREVIEW

With the 2015 United Nations Climate Change Conference just three months away, the organising committee has made its objectives clear. Executive Secretary Christiana Figueres says the Paris summit will deliver a binding and universal agreement on climate, the first in over twenty years of UN negotiations. It is a lofty ambition, but with President Obama and General Secretary Xi Jinping recently agreeing to limit greenhouse gas emissions and Pope Francis' encyclical letter demanding immediate action to tackle climate change, campaigners believe the political wind is blowing in their direction and hopes are high.

Prologue

MONTSERRAT, THE LEEWARD ISLANDS, 2 SEPTEMBER 2015

'I've got good news and bad news, which d'you want first?'

'Er . . .'

Christopher placed his coffee cup down on its saucer and considered the question. He glanced around the empty dining room, he and Collins were the Grand View's only guests and Christopher's landlady was in the back, frying up some eggs for Collins' breakfast. '. . . I guess, the good news?'

'Right you are.' Collins took his phone from his jeans pocket and put it down on the Formica table. 'I got an email overnight . . .' He pointed at the phone. '. . . telling me that Christopher Baylor's proposal is green-lit and good to go.'

'They've agreed the funding?'

'They have.'

'All of it?'

'Yep.'

'That's . . . incredible. Awesome. I don't know what to say.'

'You could kick-off with a *thank you.*'

Christopher's face flushed red. 'Yes, of course, I'm sorry.' He looked across the table at Collins. Met his gaze. Or tried to.

'Boss-eyed' – that's how the Brit described his disability, if it was a disability. Christopher wasn't sure. He'd googled the term, read about it, learned its medical name, and tried to work out the best, most sensitive way to deal with it. Christopher focussed on the eye that appeared to be looking at him and tried to ignore the other, misaligned eye, which was doing its own thing, dancing up and down in its socket while looking in the general direction of the kitchen. Christopher wished that Collins would put his fancy-looking sunglasses back on; he wore them most of the time. Just not this morning. Collins acknowledged the young American's obvious discomfort with a smile.

'You don't really need to thank me. The big bosses wouldn't be saying yes if they didn't think the work you're doing here had potential. They don't do charity.'

'It has got potential. Huge potential. Once we scale it up, I can get ten times the gigawatts anyone else gets. More.'

'I don't doubt it. But listen, you haven't had the bad news yet . . .'

'Oh, yeah, right.'

'You're going to have to put up with a Brummie hanger-on for another day or so.' Christopher shook his head and shrugged apologetically. He was still having trouble with the Brit's accent. 'The company have asked me to stay on a day – take another look at the set-up, more photos. They also want the very latest numbers – what the heat readings are and what you're harvesting.'

'That's okay. We can get all that up at the observatory.'

'Think of me as a glorified electricity meter reader.' Christopher saw the hint of a smile on Collins' face. He smiled too.

'No, you're doing yourself down. You know a bunch of stuff about the science.'

'I know a lot more about volcanoes now than I did the day before yesterday; I'll give you that.'

'Yeah, I'm sorry. I've probably bored you; I bore most people.'

Once Christopher got going, he could talk about vulcanology

and geothermal energy for as long as the person sitting opposite him was willing to listen. His favourite facts usually went down well . . . the earth is just a big lump of burning rock, floating around in space and it's trying to cool down. Volcanoes are part of how it does that. The tectonic plates beneath us are always on the move, but slow. They move at the same speed that our fingernails grow – people seemed to like that fact. It was after that, once he got into the detail of how much geothermal power a volcano could produce and how much energy we were wasting by not doing it more effectively – that was when he tended to lose his audience. Not Collins, he had stayed focussed, interested, asked the right questions. He'd soaked up every piece of information that Christopher had given him like a sponge. And he'd obviously presented it to the company effectively as well because they'd agreed to fund him. Five hundred thousand dollars to start scaling up the whole Montserrat project.

'I should call my mom and dad. I need to tell my supervisor back in Oregon too, she'll be stoked.'

Collins nodded.

'Sure, but how about we go up to the observatory and get the boys with the big chequebook what they need, then you can make those calls later?'

'Sure, of course. Let's go.'

Christopher Baylor's office was not neat. He had too many machines for the space that the observatory had allocated him, that was the problem. He liked the old-fashioned equipment just as much as the new digital kit and had rescued and repaired an ancient-looking seismograph soon after arriving on the island. This machine with its pendulum, pen and drum of yellowing paper had pride of place in his office and Christopher studied it first, crouching close to the paper and studying the wiggles and waves.

'Looks like she's been pretty quiet the last twenty-four hours.'

Collins nodded but said nothing, just watching while Christopher worked, checking the other, more accurate digital seismometers and seismographs before moving to his computer. Logging in, he went to the piece of software he'd written that would compare heat readings across the half-dozen different well heads that he'd drilled as close as possible to Soufrière's many domes.

'That's weird.'

'What?'

'I'm not getting any readings from two of these drill sites.'

'Which ones?'

'Epsilon and Zeta. The two closest to the crown.'

'Turn it off and on again?'

Christopher shot Collins a look.

'That won't work.'

'What then?'

'I'll need to go up there and see what's going on . . .' He went to check the monitoring machines once more. 'Hazard level's only at one. You want to come?'

'Why not? What was it you said . . . the volcano's effusive?'

'She's effusive, not explosive. We'll be fine.'

They drove down the hill from the observatory then up, through some stretches of lush, green tropical forest and on into the exclusion zone. They went past several signs warning of pyroclastic flows and threatening hefty fines but there were no police around and the Montserrat Observatory sticker in the front of the yellow jeep meant they were legit anyway. They parked as far up into Gages as they could before the terrain got too rough to drive and got out to hike the rest. The crown of the volcano was clearly visible, a halo of cloud and ash hovering above it. Montserrat and the rest of the Leewards were experiencing an unusually hot and humid late summer and it wasn't long before Collins was dripping in sweat. This close to the crown, it felt as though you were being ironed. He was uncomplaining and kept pace with Christopher well enough, the young American only having to stop once or twice to allow the Brit to catch up. He found it much easier to talk to Collins now that he had his Ray-Bans back on.

'We're nearly there. I'm sorry about this.' He smiled. 'At least you can get some good pictures I guess? Proper close-ups of the well heads. And maybe some of Soufrière too?'

'Good idea.'

Collins had no intention of taking more pictures. He'd taken plenty when he'd been up here earlier that morning. He looked around to get his bearings. Almost exactly here in fact. The kid was right. They were getting close.

Christopher reshouldered his bag and began walking again.

'I'll fix the kit super-quick and then we can find some shade? I brought enough iced water for the both of us.'

'Great.'

Collins followed the kid up the mountain, keeping no more than ten feet between them. The rock beneath their feet was mainly pumice, hard to walk on and not what he needed. As they got closer to the well head – as it became increasingly obvious that the site had been vandalised – Collins saw what he was looking for. A chunk of hard black rock, the size of his fist and with a nice sharp edge to it. He picked it up and moved closer. The young American had stopped, he was crouching next to the broken equipment, attempting to understand what had happened and working out how to fix it. Collins adjusted his grip on the blunt end of the rock and raised his arm.

PART ONE

CIRROSTRATUS

cirrus – lock or tuft of hair
stratus – flattened or spread out

Cirrostratus are transparent high clouds composed of ice crystals. They form a veil that covers all or part of the sky. The movement of cirrostratus clouds can help predict subsequent weather patterns.

1

LA BARROSA, ANDALUSIA, SPAIN

A quick detour wouldn't do any harm, screw the company if they thought otherwise. She was an hour ahead of schedule and so close to the sea that she could smell it – that briny Atlantic air swirling around the cockpit, mixed in with the more powerful stink of aviation fuel. Alma pushed the control stick left, taking the old crop-duster across a field of giant white wind turbines and west – towards the ocean and a slow-setting sun. The Costa de la Luz was fully deserving of its name this early September evening. The ocean catching and casting light, painting the whitewashed seaside town of La Barrosa a rose gold. At the stone-built Torre del Puerco, she turned a lazy loop, slowed the plane right down and headed north, with the sun on her left, tracing the coast. She slowed some more, not much above stalling speed and brought the yellow and white Air Tractor low enough that she could see the faces of the people on the playa. Her beach. Down on the broad white sands, brightly coloured kites were snapping and somersaulting in the wind, small children were running around pulling those crudely cut, white polystyrene planes that the beach-sellers sold for a euro a piece. Alma realised she was flying at the same speed, altitude, and distance from the shore that she used to back when she was doing her old job – her first gig as a qualified pilot and still her favourite – pulling advertising messages up and down the beach. Carlos used to help her attach the supermarket ads and birthday greetings to the back of the 'flying fried egg' as he called it and wave whenever she flew past the beachfront bar where he worked. She used to start work at noon, be finished by six and the rest of the evening and mornings were hers. All summer long. Maybe she'd go back to doing that?

The money she'd made working for the crazy Australian these last couple of years meant that the plane belonged to her; she could go back to doing beach work or crop-dusting. She'd had other offers too. She could do whatever she liked. The resignation letter she'd written, translated, and typed up so carefully was in the inside pocket of her denim jacket. She just needed to pluck up the courage to give it to her boss. Maybe she'd do it after this flight, at the debrief – if everything went well. And if he was there. Alma wanted to leave on good terms, but she needed to leave. Her relationship with the company had become too complicated. Her relationship with its owner, even more so. This latest mission was the loco Australiano's silliest project yet and another good example of why it was time to quit. Alma's instructions were to fly the crop-duster over a four-hectare area of Spanish military land, going back and forth half-a-dozen times, dumping not fertiliser, or insecticide – but four kilos of diamond dust.

'Loco.'

2

THE LONDON EYE, SOUTH BANK, LONDON

William Carver gazed skywards. He was trying to think of a worse place than this to meet a contact . . . he couldn't. There wasn't one. Who in their right mind would arrange to have a confidential conversation inside a glass pod at the top of the flaming London Eye? Suspended several thousand feet above London? The queue shuffled forward, and Carver read the information board underneath the ticket office window.

'A trip of a lifetime! Soar through the air at a height of 440 feet above London . . .' Okay, not thousands of feet then but still too high and much too public for Carver's liking. Plus, it felt like the wind was beginning to blow. He checked his phone, half-hoping that the man he was due to meet might have messaged him to postpone or cancel. No such luck. Carver was busy and generally speaking that was good. With this much work on, he had little time left over to think of anything else and he liked it that way. But right now he had more leads and potential stories on the go than he knew what to do with. He was a victim of his own success – his last investigation had made waves, generated headlines and, as his long-suffering editor had put it, made Carver 'flavour of the month'.

If the message asking whether he might have time for 'a chat and a catch-up' had come from anyone other than Leonard Allen, then he would have made his excuses. But the senior civil servant had been useful in the past – never the source of a story, but on several occasions he had confirmed a fact or detail that Carver needed confirming. Off the record of course. Always off the record. It wasn't exactly that he owed Allen a favour – more a matter of honouring a relationship. This was why he'd agreed to meet, but he'd said yes before knowing that the man's preferred meeting place was up the top of a four-hundred-foot Ferris wheel.

Carver sighed. The young woman on the other side of the Plexiglas had long, bright, emerald-green hair. She was taking an inordinately long time to do something as straightforward as selling a few tickets; engaging every customer she dealt with in lengthy conversation. Eventually Carver arrived at the front of the queue. He saw that as well as a book of tickets and a can of Diet Coke, the girl had a hairdressing magazine open in front of her. She gave him a friendly smile.

'Hello, I'm sorry to have kept you waiting.'

'Right. I've been here nearly half an hour.'

Her smile slipped.

'How can I help you then, sir? A single ticket, is it?'

Carver ran a thick finger down the laminated price list. He'd looked in vain for an idea of how much this folly might cost him while he was waiting in line and seen nothing. Now he saw why. The font size was tiny, the prices were not.

'Twenty-six quid. They've got to be kidding?'

'I'm afraid not.'

He sighed.

'Is that twenty-six pounds per . . . rotation?'

'Per ride, yeah.'

'What if I need to go around several times?'

'If you need to? Well then, I suppose it'll be several times twenty-six pounds.'

'Bollocks to that.'

The woman studied Carver more closely. She'd had him down as another ill-mannered, old office worker – a tax inspector or paper shuffler of some sort. Now she wasn't so sure. The game was to guess the punter's job and then work out what you'd do with them if you found them sitting in front of you at the hairdresser's. This was how she stayed sane, while at the same time as doing some prep for her City and Guilds in cutting and styling. This bloke was old, but not ancient and reasonably respectable-looking, albeit in a rather creased way. He was thinning slightly on top and heavy in the middle. His spectacles needed a clean.

'You want to go round a few times then, do you?'

'I don't want to . . .' He hesitated. '. . . but there's a chance I might have to.' Carver wasn't sure when the civil servant would turn up, nor how long this meeting would last.

'I could sell you the all-day ticket if you like? That's sixty quid. People get it so they can go round once, go away, do a bus tour or something and then come back for sunset but there's no reason why you couldn't just keep going round and round with that ticket if you like.'

'Sixty?'

The girl nodded. 'Most people who buy it end up never even coming back for a second go. It's like with the bottomless prosecco . . .' She waved a finger at that option on the laminated card, under extras. 'No one ever manages to drink more than a couple of bottles. People think they can, but they can't.'

'I see.'

'Smart marketing, I guess.'

'I guess so.' Carver took his wallet from the inside pocket of his blazer and opened it. Inside was a thick wodge of notes, including a range of currencies – American and Hong Kong dollars, euros, roubles, and rand. He removed two fifty-pound notes and slid them through the letterbox-sized gap at the bottom of the Plexiglas.

'I'll have the . . . all-day ticket then. Please.'

'Right you are.'

He glanced up again at the slate-grey London sky. The glass pods were swaying in an increasingly blustery wind. Carver took another tenner from the wallet.

'And the bottomless prosecco.'

3

LA BARROSA, ANDALUSIA, SPAIN

Alma checked her watch. One more quick run back up the beach and then she'd need to take the plane inland and head for the drop point. This was her favourite time of the day. On the long paved promenade, running parallel to the sea and just a few steps up from the sand, the early evening *paseo* was underway. Locals and tourists, young and old, taking advantage of the cooler temperatures to walk the strip. To see and be seen. Alma noticed a gaggle of older ladies in their best dresses and embroidered shawls gathering close to the children's playground that marked the start of the promenade. She strained her eyes to see if her mother was among them. Maybe that figure at the back? In the blue? Setting up his easel nearby she saw the leather-skinned old man in the tatty black beret – Picasso de la Playa, Carlos called him and what he lacked in artistic ability he made up for in commitment. He laid out his materials in the same spot every evening – selling the gaudy yellow and gold pictures of sunsets to holiday-happy tourists or swapping them for beer in the local bars.

Further along the strip Alma saw the familiar green- and white-striped canopy belonging to the Che bar, where Carlos worked. A crowd of teenage boys in skinny jeans and ironed T-shirts were hanging around outside, kicking a tennis ball about and play-fighting while they waited for their female equivalents to arrive on the scene. A few seconds and another two hundred yards later Alma spotted the girls that these boys were doubtless waiting for. They were walking arm in arm, some also wearing jeans and T-shirts but others – those with mothers like Alma's – in brightly coloured polka-dot dresses and with flowers in their hair. What a spectacle. She wished she was down there with them, and she would be soon. A job like this usually only took an hour or so. Two hours tops – unless the debrief dragged on.

When she'd first started flying for this company, the Australian boss had been at every demonstration and led every debrief. He had tried to make these meetings as short as possible and for the first few months showed no interest in hearing from Alma. That suited her, her English was okay but far from perfect and certainly nowhere near the level required to take part in a technical, scientific debate about whether sulphur dioxide particles had been more effective at reflecting sunlight than the saltwater spray. Or how about the powdered aluminium? Or the titanium? She found the discussions increasingly tiresome and repetitive and on one occasion made the mistake of letting that show – stifling a yawn while the Australian was mid-sentence.

'I'm sorry. Perhaps I'm boring ya?'

'No.'

'No? Good, because I'm also fucken' paying ya.' He stared at Alma, checking her out and spoke again, friendlier now. 'You get a bird's-eye view of this work we're doing. Which of the payloads you've been dropping do you reckon's best at thickening the cloud cover and reflecting sunlight?'

Alma shrugged.

'I drop what you ask me to drop, where you ask me to drop it. These discussions are not for me, they are for . . .' She'd waved a hand in the direction of the dozen or more lab-coat-wearing men and women in the room. '. . . your *cerebritos*.' Her boss had turned to his translator for an explanation.

'*Cerebritos*? It means . . . you might say "boffins".'

This had tickled the Australian and after that he regularly referred to his team as *los cerebritos*. A collective noun they disliked and which they blamed Alma for saddling them with. This exchange had somewhat soured her relationship with the rest of the team. The next day the Australian texted Alma asking her for a drink. She'd messaged him back with a polite no thank you. She was busy that week. The Australian had persisted, asking if there was a date further down the line that she could do? There was this seafood place he'd heard about. A Spanish chef who'd won all kinds of awards and Michelin stars. Maybe Alma had heard of the place? Alma had. It was a restaurant that everyone in town knew of but that almost no one had been to. For one reason you had to reserve a table about six months in advance; more significantly dinner for two would cost the best part of four hundred euros and that was before you'd even had a sip of wine.

Alma had shown her best friend Loli the message.

'What's the problem? It's dinner. That's all. Tell Carlos it's a work thing.' In fact, she told Carlos nothing. Not about the first dinner, nor about the other drinks and dinners that followed, and her lovable, if somewhat gullible, boyfriend had noticed no change in her. Alma lost her bearings for a while. The Australian had an ego the size of a planet – but it was an interesting planet. She had to admit that it was flattering too, a famous person like this being interested in her and her opinions. Also it was fun. Until it wasn't. Until it became . . . complicated.

She'd give the Australian the letter this evening and if he wasn't there then she'd leave it with one of his several assistants. Just then Alma saw something. A physical representation of her employer's vanity and pride.

'*Mierda*.'

The clunky-looking camera drone was hovering off to her right, waiting for her. As she flew past it wobbled in the air a moment then followed. There was already one camera attached to the underside of the Air Tractor but clearly that wasn't enough. They wanted this evening's demo filmed as professionally as possible and from several different angles. This had happened a few times back at the beginning of the project, when the Australian wanted to show the world what he was up to and raise some more cash. Once that had been achieved, he focussed solely on the science, but now the drone was back. The diamond dust experiment was obviously a big deal. As she looped back around the stone tower for the second time, Alma noticed that there were more birdwatchers out than usual; binoculars slung around their necks and long-lensed cameras attached to tripods. She guessed there must be another big flock of spoonbills heading this way. The drone was alongside her now and accelerating to overtake.

4

THE LONDON EYE, SOUTH BANK, LONDON

Carver was halfway round on his first rotation and two thirds of the way through his first bottle of prosecco when he saw Leonard Allen waiting at the foot of the London Eye, dressed for the weather in a fawn-coloured mackintosh with a black umbrella. It took another fifteen minutes for Carver's pod to wobble its way down to terra firma. When it did, he greeted the civil servant with a handshake and a quick hello before negotiating with the attendant to exchange his now empty bottle for a fresh one and a second glass. As soon as the pod doors slid shut, he filled both glasses and handed one to Allen who gave a little bow of thanks.

'I suppose it's five o'clock somewhere.'

'It's almost five o'clock here.' Carver looked at his watch. 'Or four anyway. I'm not a big fan of heights, I thought a drink might help.'

'I'm sure it will.' The civil servant shrugged himself free from his coat and folded it carefully, placing it on the egg-shaped bench in the middle of the pod next to his umbrella. He was wearing a dark suit with a faint chalk stripe to it, a white shirt and knitted navy-blue tie. 'I'm sorry, I wouldn't have suggested we meet here if I'd known you were . . . it's acrophobic, isn't it? Sounds a bit like the spider one but isn't. We could press that . . .' He pointed at a big red emergency button next to the sliding glass door. '. . . and ask them to let us off.'

Carver shook his head.

'We're here now.'

'True. I thought this would make a nice change from those dingy little pubs and hotel bars where we've met in the past.'

'I see.'

'Plus, there's that hiding in plain sight thing, isn't there? What could be less suspicious than two fellows taking a ride on the London Eye?'

Carver could think of many things, but he let it go.

'What's this about then, Leonard? I haven't heard from you for a while.'

'No, well you haven't asked me to . . . clarify anything for you . . .' He took a tiny sip of his prosecco. '. . . and I haven't had anything interesting to say to you.'

'Until now.'

'Yes, until now.' He paused. 'Well, that sounds a little arrogant. I'll let you be the judge of whether what I have to say is interesting or not. I hope that it might be.' Allen smiled. He had old manners. It was one of the things that Carver liked about him. 'I'm aware, however, that you're a man in high demand right now and my timing is probably not ideal.' Carver shrugged. 'After that last scoop of yours, I imagine your phone is ringing off the hook. Figuratively.'

'I am busy.'

'And those bosses of yours must be pleased.'

'For now. I've been around long enough to know that you go in and out of fashion. Either they want to sack you, or they want to start calling you a special correspondent, make you do a podcast and that sort of thing.'

'But you're holding out?'

'So far. Being a reporter is good enough for me.'

'The only un-special correspondent?'

'Something like that. Enough about me, Leonard . . . why are we here?'

'Good question. Enough prevarication.' Carver watched and waited. It was clear that Allen was teetering on the brink of something unfamiliar. He'd been useful before, cooperative – but he'd never initiated anything. Never come anywhere near blowing a whistle or spilling a full plate of beans or whatever it was he was getting ready to do now. 'This concerns my political masters.'

'Of course.'

'I think they might be about to make a mistake . . . a consequential mistake.' Carver gave him what he hoped was an encouraging nod. 'What do you know about Clive Winner?'

Carver searched his memory.

'Winner? Is he that inventor come green businessman bloke? Australian. A bit of an oddball.'

'Oddball's an understatement.'

Carver shrugged.

'Wasn't it Winner who did that rescue job on the Great Barrier Reef a few years back?'

The civil servant grimaced.

'Yes. Mr Winner and his people span that story extremely well. His team temporarily revived a small section of the reef.'

'That's not such a good news headline.'

'No, I suppose not. Anyway, you know the fellow.'

'I'm aware he exists.'

'Take a look at this.' Allen reached into his inside pocket and produced a cream-coloured business card with the government crest on it. He passed it over with a rather theatrical flourish.

Mr. Clive Winner
Senior Adviser Prime Ministers Office

The civil servant watched as Carver read.

'What do you make of it?'

'Shouldn't there be an apostrophe in "Prime Minister's office"?'

'Probably. Good grammar has gone the same way as the ministerial code – all the way down the toilet and halfway round the U-bend.' He pointed at the card. 'You notice the email address?'

Carver had noticed it. He'd memorised it too, as it seemed unlikely that Leonard Allen would allow him to keep the card.

'C.Winner@no10.x.gsi.gov.uk . . . that's a legitimate Downing Street email, isn't it?'

'It is. The landline's legitimate too. It connects to an answerphone message, a very efficient-sounding American lady telling you how much Clive is looking forward to talking to you.'

'It's unusual, I'll give you that.'

'Access like this? A job title like that? It's more than unusual. It's unprecedented. We're used to all the management consultants and corporate restructuring experts that this generation of politicians seem to like to bring in . . .' Carver nodded. He'd had run-ins of his own with management consultants brought in to shake up or restructure various bits of the BBC. He didn't like them. '. . . but Clive Winner is something different. Giving a private businessman a senior adviser title and a seat at the table, it's . . . well it's outrageous.'

Carver smiled.

'Outrageous? You're sure this isn't a case of a few career civil servants getting their knickers in a twist because someone else has got better access to the prime minister than they have?'

Allen made a harrumphing sound.

'I'm absolutely sure. This isn't a question of petty professional jealousy. Far from it. Winner is a snake-oil salesman, allowing him this sort of access to the PM risks national humiliation. Or worse.'

'Worse?'

'Clive Winner is looking for friends and funding in some rather odd places these days.' Allen detected a flicker of interest in Carver. 'My colleagues at the Foreign Office tell me that he's talking to people who don't have the same fondness that we do for the rule of law, human rights – old-fashioned stuff like that. They say he's playing footsie with at least one Moscow-linked hedge fund. No doubt he's chasing Chinese money too.' The veteran civil servant took a gulp of his drink. His face was red. 'I'm sorry. I promised myself I wouldn't get too agitated.'

'Don't worry, I understand.'

'If it was just Downing Street's reputation on the line, then maybe I'd leave them to it. Sit back and watch the uppance come.' Carver nodded. 'But it isn't. You and I both know it'll be the poor bloody civil service that will get it in the neck when this goes south. As it almost certainly will.'

Carver drained his glass, then refilled it. If even a little of that was true, this was a good story.

'I'm sure you know several well-connected people inside Downing Street, what do they say?'

'They advise me to let sleeping dogs lie. Look the other way.' He paused. 'I'm not willing to do that, but I'm not sure what else I can do. I've written a memorandum . . .'

Carver smiled. He remembered Leonard telling him once that the real purpose of a civil service memorandum was never to inform the reader, but rather to protect the writer.

'A memorandum, I see. But you feel the need for even more protection?'

'Not protection – action. A proper investigation. Believe me, Clive Winner is what we used to refer to as a *bad egg*.'

5

LA BARROSA, ANDALUSIA, SPAIN

If it had been her call then Alma would have been flying inland now, back over the long sand dunes and pine forests towards the Spanish army base where the drop was due to take place in . . . how long? Alma checked her mobile phone which she kept visible and accessible inside a clear ziplocked bag on a cord around her neck. The demo was supposed to begin in twenty minutes. She'd be late even if she turned the plane around right now. She had her instructions. For as long as the drone was positioned out in front of the plane, she had to follow it at a steady speed, allowing the audio-visual people back at base to get some good clear shots of her and the Air Tractor in action. Once they'd got what they needed the drone would drop back and follow her.

The drone was taking her west again, back out to sea. She could understand why, the sun was sitting on the water now, a blindingly bright, golden coin balancing on its side above a blue-green sea. The sunset was going to be good, even by Costa de la Luz standards and the flying fried egg would look great against a backdrop like that. She kept her speed and altitude steady so the drone could get the pictures it needed as quickly as possible. Another minute passed. Two. Three. The thing was taking her further and further away from where she needed to be. This was ridiculous, they must have the shots they needed by now. She lifted her headset back into place and radioed to base.

'Flight One to home. You copy?'

There was a crackle of static and then a reedy, Spanish-accented English-speaking voice.

'Home to Flight One. We copy.'

'I'm tailing the drone, north north-west. If it takes me much further, then I'm going to miss the drop time. When will you have the pictures you need?'

There was a pause at the other end.

'Repeat please.'

Alma repeated her message. More silence, then: 'No one here knows anything about a drone or any film, Flight One.'

'What?'

'The drone you're following is nothing to do with us. Turn around.'

'*Puta.*'

Alma started to turn the plane. Then changed her mind. The drone was so close. Squinting through the screen she thought she could see some words, and perhaps a serial number stamped in white on the black metal? If she could get a little closer, then she could take a photograph with her phone and they could find the idiot responsible for this. She accelerated. As she drew closer, she saw that the drone wasn't a particularly dextrous-looking device, it was bigger than the other camera drones she'd seen, and its movements were jerky. She got her phone out from inside the plastic Ziploc bag but before she could select the camera function and frame the photo the drone picked up some speed and accelerated away. She followed. Anyone watching would have seen a crop-duster engaged in an odd-looking aerial display with some kind of flying suitcase. But there was no one watching, she was too far out now. Alma moved closer again. She lifted her phone, selected the camera function and waited while the lens found its focus. There it was – she could see the larger of the words clearly now – *Vapor* – and beneath that some smaller text and a serial number. Suddenly, the drone veered off to the left. It appeared to stop in mid-air before rotating 180 degrees and steadying itself.

'*Mierda.*' Alma saw what it was she'd been chasing now, but too late.

There was a burst of automatic gunfire. Alma watched her windscreen crack and splinter and heard a deafening, ear-hurting noise. She grabbed the control stick and pulled up, trying to take the plane out of the drone's line of fire. She felt her ears pop and watched as the broken windscreen began to peel away from the metal frame holding it in place. Alma slid down into her seat and watched as the last few rivets snapped and the shattered windscreen went spinning off into the blue. Using both hands, and with enormous difficulty due to the force of the onrushing wind, she pushed herself upright again, just high enough so she might get a glimpse of where the drone was now. There was no sign. Alma realised she was panting – hyperventilating – and tried to regulate her breathing. She levelled the plane and pushed the control stick right, steering the old Air Tractor back in the direction of land. She was halfway round – the nose of the plane pointing in the direction of the watch tower at the northernmost tip of the beach – when even louder than the sound of the wind and the plane's struggling engine, Alma heard a second burst of automatic gunfire coming from behind her crippled plane.

6

THE LONDON EYE, SOUTH BANK, LONDON

There was no more than a dribble left in the second bottle. Carver offered it to Leonard Allen who, much to his relief, refused.

'Why are you bringing this Winner thing to me, Leonard? There are any number of other journalists you could take this to.'

'I don't know too many journalists. I mean I've met a few of course and I suppose I could email one of the better-known names but you and I . . .' He paused. '. . . I know we're not exactly friends but . . . you've been to my house. You've met Henrietta and the boys.' This was true. It was going back a few years, but he remembered accepting the invitation to Christmas drinks and taking the train to Haslemere. There had been a work-related reason for the trip, that he couldn't immediately recall. He did remember the civil servant's wife and Allen's three, or maybe it was four, sons – variously sized carbon copies of their father. Carver remembered the trouble Henrietta Allen had taken to make him feel welcome at a gathering of the sort of people that he'd usually go out of his way to avoid. The guests were an odd mix of Leonard's civil service colleagues, elderly relatives and the great and the good of Haslemere. Carver had been cornered by the local schoolmaster, a ruddy-faced man with mutton chops who'd been responsible for educating several generations of Allen men and was in charge of the current crop too. He wanted Carver to do something about BBC bias. Henrietta had rescued him.

Leonard Allen took another tiny sip of the prosecco before putting his glass down on the bench in the centre of the pod. 'The reason I came to you is that I trust you . . . I'm sure I've bent your ear before about the "good chap" theory of government.' Carver nodded. Allen had. 'Well, I know you're not "in government" but you are, I believe, a good chap.' Carver shrugged. 'And, William, if I'm being perfectly honest, I'm hoping that once you start sniffing around . . .'

'If I do.'

'Of course . . . if you do. Then that alone might be enough to persuade Downing Street to put a more sensible distance between Whitehall and Clive Winner.' Carver finished his drink. He appreciated the civil servant's honesty. Allen picked up his coat and umbrella. 'I'm just trying to do the right thing. Keep my corner clean. Or as clean as it can be . . . in these times.'

Carver smiled. There weren't that many people left in Whitehall who cared enough about the public good to put their career on the line. Or who could quote Orwell so casually.

'I'll give it some thought. I'll help if I can.'

'Thank you.' Their pod was approaching ground level once more. 'It was actually Henrietta who suggested I speak to you.'

'Is that right?' The civil servant's wife had been good company at the Christmas party, easy to talk to and interesting with it. When Carver left, he'd attempted to compliment her but ended up doing it in the most ham-fisted way possible. He felt embarrassed even thinking about it. Perhaps she hadn't mentioned it to her husband.

'Is she well?'

'Oh yes, she's excellent. She said to say hello.'

'Please say hello back.'

Allen smiled.

'And to say that she's still trying her best to be the *least unbearable* person in any room she finds herself in.' Carver felt his neck redden.

'Oh yes . . . well, good. As I say, please pass on my regards.'

Allen smiled.

'I shall. What about you, William?'

'What about me?'

'Is there anyone in your life at the moment?'

'What? No. Nothing like that.' He glanced at his watch. 'Just . . . you know, the work.'

'Of course. You should come down and see us again. Regardless of whether you're able to help me out with this Clive Winner business. Come for dinner. Henrietta would love that.'

7

LA BARROSA, ANDALUSIA, SPAIN

The second burst of bullets from the drone pierced the fuel tank. The plane lurched forward and back, and Alma had to fight hard to steady it. From the clunking sound that the engine was making, it was clear there was damage, but somehow the old engine was still turning. The Air Tractor was doing its very best to stay airborne. But for how much longer? Craning her neck left and right she looked for the drone but could see no sign of it. What she could see was a steady trickle of fuel falling from the rear of the plane. Also – from the underside of the aircraft – her payload. Alma watched as a glittering torrent of diamond dust fell hundreds of feet through the air and into the blue Atlantic Ocean. She tried the radio again, more in hope than expectation:

'Flight One to home. Copy?' She tried this several times but got nothing but loud static in return. She needed to think. The drone had taken her so far out that it would be all but impossible to make it back to land with whatever fuel she had left. Even if she made it, trying to land with a broken tank was too dangerous.

'*Concéntrate Alma, concéntrate.*'

She had no option but to bail. Keeping the plane level with one hand, she reached behind the seat with the other and found her lifejacket. She was scrambling to release her seat belt when she felt a warm, viscous liquid on the tips of her fingers. She finished unbuckling the belt before looking at her hand. The blood was thick and dark. It was coming from the top of her left thigh. Alma wondered how she could not have noticed this. Felt it. Adrenaline perhaps? She peeled back the blood-covered tear in her jeans and saw the bullet hole. Then the pain came. It felt as though someone was pushing a burning hot poker into her leg. She felt light-headed. Scared. She let go of the plane's controls momentarily and the crop-duster bucked up and then down. Alma righted the plane and tried to concentrate. Lifejacket first; if she was still alive by the time she'd put that on then she could figure out how and when she might be able to get out of the plane before it hit the water.

She took the jacket out of its packet and put it on. She stared at the bright yellow bag that the lifejacket had come in then folded it into a tight square and stuffed it inside the tear in her jeans. It wasn't much of a bandage but it was better than nothing. That done, Alma felt around on the floor until she found her phone and slid it back inside the plastic Ziploc bag hanging around her neck. This was good. This made sense. The fuel gauge on the panel in front of her was ticking down as she watched, she was still miles from land and losing altitude fast. It was now or never. She checked her lifejacket, pulling the straps at her waist and shoulders as tight as they would go. Alma pushed herself up in her seat until she was half-seated, half-standing. The sun was in the sea now, somehow even brighter, even more golden now that it was setting.

8

WESTMINSTER BRIDGE, LONDON

Walking back across Westminster Bridge, Carver stopped and gazed down at the river. It was high and pushing hard against its banks – brown water sloshing up and almost over the lip of the jetty where a queue of evening commuters was waiting for the Thames clipper to ferry them home. He got his mobile phone out. He'd received another half-a-dozen messages while he'd been meeting with Leonard – all work related. In his saved messages there were at least as many again that required his attention. Another story lead was really the last thing he needed. Nevertheless, the tale that the civil servant had told interested Carver. He dug around inside his yellow plastic carrier bag looking for the spiral-bound reporters' notepad that he was currently using. He wanted to make a note of Clive Winner's Downing Street email and the phone number before they slipped his mind. He made some other notes too – a summary of everything Leonard had told him – then checked his watch. If he was quick, then he could do a little digging now – half an hour's research and he'd be better able to decide whether this Winner tip-off was worth his time or if he should advise Leonard Allen to look elsewhere. He continued across the bridge and up Whitehall, heading for one of his regular haunts, the Charing Cross Library. Centrally located, warm and, most importantly, well stocked with newspapers, journals and a roomful of computers that library members could rent by the half hour.

The old head librarian had died the previous year – cancer of the stomach . . . or something of the something else. Whatever it was, it had killed him – which was sad but also a major inconvenience as far as Carver was concerned. The new librarian was trickier to deal with. The last time he'd been she'd insisted that he renew his membership card, something the old librarian hadn't bothered with for years. Pushing through the heavy Victorian doors and approaching the reception desk, Carver pulled his wallet out and tried to find the new membership card. It wasn't there.

'I renewed it a week or two back. I'm sure you remember?' The woman shook her head and said nothing. 'It's most likely back at home, I'll bring it next time. Maybe we can take this one on trust?' The librarian was shaking her head so vigorously now that Carver was worried that she might put her neck out. He lifted his carrier bag up onto her table and tipped out the contents. Several reporter pads, a MiniDisc recorder, half-a-dozen pens, a variety of painkillers and a large bag of dry roasted peanuts . . . eventually he found the card tucked inside one of his old notebooks and handed it over. The librarian eyed it suspiciously before allowing him entry.

There were several free terminals in the computer room. Carver picked the one closest to the window and furthest from anyone else and set to work. He began by entering Clive Winner's name together with that of the prime minister; he scrolled through the results. The first piece that looked interesting enough to read was a two-year-old *Wall Street Journal* article. It was long, built around an interview that the editor had done with Winner and the PM together. In it the British leader described the Australian as 'his kind of green'. One of the only people he knew who came to him with 'solutions instead of problems'. The two flagged up Winner's future involvement in a new science park the prime minister was planning. He said he'd identified a shovel-ready site and that work would begin within months. Carver checked the date of the article again. A full twenty-six months had passed since the PM had made this prediction and so far no science park and as far as Carver knew no shovelling. The rest of the piece talked about their shared commitment to combating what they both kept referring to as 'catastrophic climate change'.

The piece was five hundred words too long in Carver's opinion but there was some interesting stuff in there. He made more notes. Both the article and the accompanying photograph – the PM and the Aussie entrepreneur standing in front of a thick-trunked oak tree, sleeves rolled up and smiling – suggested that the two men were close. But there was no mention of Winner's senior adviser role or him being given a Downing Street desk – not in this article, not anywhere else. This was encouraging – it meant that at least some of what Allen had told Carver was new information. Articles in other papers repeated the prime minister's promise that Winner's team would have a key role to play in the exciting, thus-far non-existent, science park. One thing linking the two men that Carver found concerned the Great Green British Business Bank. This was something he had heard about and it did in fact exist – a prime ministerial pet project that had been investing public money in a range of green initiatives. It seemed that significant amounts of this money had been channelled Winner's way but finding out exactly how much and what the cash was being spent on was more difficult. Too difficult and too time-consuming for him to get stuck into right now, sitting in an uncomfortable plastic bucket chair in a corner of the Charing Cross Library. He read a little more about some of Winner's other interests – a rich and varied collection that included pieces on carbon capture, cloud brightening and thinning and other quite dry-sounding environmental projects, alongside rather odd and frankly slightly ridiculous-sounding schemes. There was a piece about Winner's plans to alter the DNA of cats in an attempt to stop them hunting birds, something about making

Australian cane toads impotent and all sorts of strange stuff involving mice. A recent *New Scientist* article had him injecting jellyfish DNA into chickens so that the eggs containing male chicks would glow green in the dark. The same magazine reported on his plan to float a million white ping-pong balls in the Med to see how much sunlight they reflected.

For Carver, a lot of this had the whiff of publicity stunt rather than serious science. But what did he know? The most obvious success story, the thing that had made Winner famous and feted was his work on the Great Barrier Reef. Carver was surprised to see that almost three years had passed since this had been front page news pretty much everywhere. It had succeeded both as the mother of all publicity stunts but also – despite Leonard Allen's protestations – as an environmental initiative. Because of it, Winner had won the backing of several Western governments as well as a few well-known billionaires. But as he scrolled through the more recent news pieces, Carver got the impression that this source of funding might be running dry. There were articles in the business pages about Winner having to refinance parts of his operation. If that was so, then Leonard Allen's suggestion that the Australian was looking for money in some of the darker, dodgier corners of the world could also be correct. Carver felt something shift in his gut. A familiar feeling and one which, down the years, he'd come to trust. He reached for his mobile phone, found the number he had for Patrick Reid and dialled it. It rang. And rang. Just as he was about to hang up it clicked through to a generic answerphone message. Carver summarised what Leonard Allen had told him and the most interesting stuff that he'd learned subsequently in a way that he hoped might pique his former producer's interest.

'I know you're not . . . er . . . one hundred per cent yet, Patrick, but this is a good one, believe me. Anyway, have a think about it and call me back. Say hello to Rebecca for me.' He was about to end the call when he remembered something. 'Oh and say hello to . . .' Bollocks, what was the baby's name? '. . . say hello to the baby.' As he was hanging up, Carver felt a tap on his shoulder. He jumped. It was the librarian.

'No phone calls in the reading room. It disturbs other people.'

Carver looked around. 'There aren't any other people.'

'That's because we're closing. I need to ask you to leave.'

'Okay. I'm nearly done, I'll just—' He was interrupted by a loud ping from his phone. 'Sorry.' Carver started packing up his notebook, pen and papers; once the librarian was safely back behind her desk he got his phone out. There were no new messages, which confused him briefly until he remembered that Patrick never used the phone or regular text messaging these days. He checked his WhatsApp and sure enough . . .

> William. Thanks for thinking of me but I can't help. There are plenty of other producers who could work with you on something like this.

Carver sucked at his teeth. He was about to delete it when another message arrived.

> PS . . . Please use an encrypted service for messages like the one you left me – it's safer. For you. For everyone. Remember Hong Kong.

Carver thrust the phone into the pocket of his blazer.

'Yeah, yeah.' Patrick was right, but that didn't make the exchange any less annoying. He knew he shouldn't have called on an unencrypted line, he'd got overexcited, that was all. He also knew that Patrick wasn't the only producer at the bloody BBC. Carver shovelled the rest of his stuff into his plastic bag and headed for the door. The trouble, of course, was that Patrick was the only producer that Carver wanted to work with.

Out on the street it was raining steadily, a mix of homebound commuters, tourists and theatregoers shuffled past holding umbrellas.

Carver took shelter beneath the library's pillared portico and considered his options. His favourite falafel place was nearby, the owner was a good bloke, always willing to give Carver a table for one regardless of how busy they were. He could go there. Or he could head home; there was some food in the fridge and an open bottle of red that needed drinking. There was nothing wrong with either of these options but for some reason Carver felt like he might prefer to see someone – a friend of some sort. He got his phone out and scrolled through the contacts until he found the number for *McCluskey, Jemima.* It rang. Carver waited. And waited, until it became clear that McCluskey didn't even have an answering service that he could leave a message with.

'What is this? National Don't Talk to Carver Day?' Stuff them both, he'd go for a falafel and think over what to do about Winner and how to handle this surfeit of work solo.

9

OXFORD CIRCUS UNDERGROUND STATION, LONDON

Naz took the stairs at Oxford Circus tube two at a time, swished her Oyster card across the reader and made for the exit. She zipped up her tracksuit top and ran north up Regent Street, dodging pedestrians, prams, slow-moving tourists, and other assorted hazards as she went. The homeless blokes who slept on the steps outside All Souls Church were packing up their cardboard beds and sleeping bags. It was a cold, crisp morning, cloudless and bright and the glassy front of Broadcasting House was glistening in the sun.

'New Broadcasting House,' she corrected herself. William Carver hated it when she confused the original, old building and the new. He refused to refer to New Broadcasting House by name at all, preferring 'the glass and steel monstrosity' or 'that bloody place'. Naz couldn't and would not ever admit to her former teacher and mentor that she preferred the new building to Old Broadcasting House – all that stone, oak-panelled rooms, and the dimly lit, labyrinth-like corridors. Not to mention that naked statue they had up above the entrance, done by some bloke who was well dodgy. Naz had googled him. She exchanged a friendly greeting with the security guard outside the new building and walked in through the tall revolving doors.

Behind a wall of floor-to-ceiling glass, down in the newsroom – the pit of despair Carver called it – dozens of journalists were working away, monitoring news stories as they arrived from every corner of the globe. Naz loved to watch and would sometimes eat her sandwich sitting on one of the uncomfortable red sofas that overlooked the newsroom. The stories deemed to be most important and most relevant to all the various BBC programmes were displayed on a huge flat-screen television, an ever-changing list of radio and TV despatches filed by BBC correspondents across the world: Washington, Moscow, Tokyo, Sydney. The city and then the name of the reporter and the time the story was filed. Naz imagined what it would be like to see your own name on that list. Not that you would see it; you'd be in the place where the news was actually happening, waiting to tell the world about it.

She pulled her eyes away from the bustling scene and walked towards the lifts. She hadn't been late for a broadcast assistant shift yet and she wasn't about to start. The work was a little tedious, administrative mainly, and her colleagues, the proper journalists and producers and presenters, weren't always the friendliest, but that was because of the pressure they were under and because she was still new. The point was that she was in the right place. Like William Carver had said, she had 'a foot in the door' and no force on earth was going to make her remove that foot. No chance.

10

WASHINGTON STREET, BOSTON, MASSACHUSETTS, USA

Jennifer Prepas shooed the builders out of the half-built kitchen and set the laptop up in such a way that her backdrop appeared as unremarkable as possible. Ideally, she would have taken this conference call back at the office but the Boston traffic was a nightmare at this time of day and she wanted to spend as much of the evening as possible with her son. She'd bribed Ryley to stay in his room with the irresistible offer of an extra hour of Minecraft plus a bowl of microwaved popcorn. The buttery and faintly burnt smell pervaded the room and she opened the back door that led on to a deck and a small backyard to try to air it.

Jennifer did her utmost to keep her work and personal life separate. When the man you worked for was Clive Winner that was pretty much impossible but there were certain rules she tried to stick to. The most important of these concerned her son. Winner knew that she had a boy, he knew his name and age and it was obvious from past conversations that Clive was keen to know more but Jennifer had thus far resisted. She checked her watch, walked to the hall, and shouted up the stairs towards her son's room at the top of the triple-decker house.

'You all good, Ryley?'

'Yup.' This said through a mouthful of popcorn.

'Downstairs is mine for the next hour, kid, yeah?'

'Gotcha.'

'We'll have some fun after this is done, yeah?'

'Sure.'

She'd keyed in the meeting ID ten minutes ahead of schedule. Clive Winner disliked a lot of things but being kept waiting was the thing he disliked most. As she walked back to the laptop, she was startled to see her boss's face, grinning at her from the screen. She went to unmute herself and saw that she already was.

'Hey, Clive, I'm sorry.'

'No worries, Jen. How are ya? Back home already I see, I'm clearly not working you hard enough. How's Ryley?'

'He's . . . he's fine. Thank you.' She was flustered. 'I'm really sorry . . . the machine hadn't even asked me to join the call yet.'

Winner shook his head. 'No, I know. You've heard of the term super user?'

'Sure.'

'Multiply that by infinity.' The smile grew broader. Clive Winner was handsome. He had a square jaw, a full head of blond hair and a healthy, suntanned complexion. Despite this, there was something slightly disconcerting about her boss's good looks. The combination of very pale-blue eyes, blond eyelashes, and eyebrows – so blond as to be virtually invisible – as well as his thin lips gave Clive's face a peculiarly empty look. Winner was sitting in a bright, white-painted room, behind him was a wall of windows and beyond that Sydney Harbour and the familiar jaggy-shaped Opera House. Jennifer pointed a finger.

'It looks like you've got a nice day down your way.' Her boss swivelled around on his high-backed ergonomic chair and checked out the view. Jennifer noticed that the collar of his polo shirt was turned up slightly at the back – an imperfection. She considered pointing this out, then decided against it.

'Not bad, huh? You know how much I had to pay for this view?' Jennifer shook her head. 'Half as much as they paid for the thing I get to look at. The Opera House cost a hundred million, this place was about half that. Not that I own it . . . it's mortgaged up to the fucken' ceiling. Like everything else in my life.' He turned back to face Jennifer. 'A harbour view! I can't believe I fell for that one, you'd think I'd know better, given what kinda work it is we do. The way things are going this place will be underwater or burnt to buggery in a decade or two. Did you read about these wildfires we've got here?' Jennifer nodded. Nodding was all you could do when Clive went off on one like this. 'I should sell the place. Maybe I will. Although the new missus won't like it.' She saw Clive's eyes flick in the direction of a white picture frame standing on his white desk, presumably a photo of the latest Mrs Winner, an extremely attractive actress-stroke-model. 'I might do it anyway. What about you? I see that building work of yours is still going on?' Jennifer turned and noticed that there was a small square of blue tarpaulin visible. It was covering a gap in the granite counter where the induction hob was supposed to be.

'We're nearly there.'

'How long over schedule are yer now?'

'A few months.'

'How much over budget?'

'Err . . . around thirty per cent.'

'It'll be double that by the time your tradies are done building.' *Tradies*. Jennifer had noticed that her boss used more slang and sounded more Australian when back in his home country. When outside, his accent and even his vocabulary changed. Clive Winner was something of a chameleon. 'So what sorta penalties you got built in?'

'Penalties? I haven't.'

Winner laughed.

'Sweet Jesus, Jen. No penalties? You have to have penalties, otherwise . . .' He paused. '. . . well, you're finding out what happens otherwise. Hang on while I let Daryl in.' She sighed – a little too obviously. Daryl Tread was Winner's head of security and in Jennifer's opinion an unpleasant and intimidating individual. The number of boxes on her screen increased from two to three and there he was in all his shaven-headed glory. Clive pulled a face.

'Christ-sake, hell, Daryl . . . move your face back from the screen a little, will ya? I've just had my breakfast. You need to get yourself some sun, mate. Urgently. You look like Nos – fucken' – feratu.' Daryl did as requested, leaning back from the computer into a dimly lit and apparently empty room. The only thing visible on his screen was Daryl and on the desk in front of him a glass ashtray full of cigarette butts. He unmuted himself but said nothing.

'Right . . . that's us quorate.'

Jennifer gave her boss a questioning look. 'I thought this was going to be an all-teams meeting?'

'No, I've had to switch that. It's just you two mongrels and me. We'll do the teams thing Saturday.'

'Saturday?' Ryley's soccer match.

'Yeah, is that a problem?'

'No problem.'

'Super. I need to get an update from you both regarding damage limitation.'

'We're talking about Spain?'

'Yeah, we're talking about Spain. Unless the two of you have discovered something even more potentially damaging for my company in the last twenty-four hours.' She shook her head. 'So where are we at?'

Jennifer waited until it became obvious that Daryl was planning to say his usual nothing and started speaking.

'Well, you saw the statement I put out.'

'Yeah . . . it didn't say much.'

'It said what we agreed it would say . . . we don't know what happened yet, every effort is being made, we're in close contact with the police and the girl's family . . . etc. The deal was that either Daryl . . .' She pointed at the head of security who withdrew even further into his gloomy-looking room. '. . . or you . . .' She looked at Clive. '. . . would give me more information when you had it and then I'll update.'

'Right.'

'So? Is there more? Have they found anything?'

Daryl leant forward. 'No.'

My God! It speaks.

'No sign of the plane, no wreckage? No . . . body? Nothing?'

'No.'

'Okay. And do we have any clearer idea what might have caused . . . whatever happened to have happened?'

Daryl's two words had clearly taken it out of him. He remained silent leaving Winner to jump back in.

'We have no clue yet . . . technical snafu maybe? An act of God. Who knows?'

'Not us, by the sounds of it.'

'No. So how are we doing at keeping the media away from this one, Jen?' Here came the purpose of this meeting. Or the purpose of Jennifer's involvement in it.

'There's been a little pickup already.'

'I saw a couple of things. But Spanish newspapers only, that right?'

'Spanish and Portuguese.'

'I need you to keep this out of the international press, Jen – papers, radio, TV. I'm in the middle of some promising conversations with people about money . . .'

'I see. Are these existing conversations, Clive? Conversations with people I know about?'

Winner shrugged.

'Some you do, some are new. The point is we're at a delicate stage. We can't afford any bad publicity. None. You understand?'

'I'll do my best. *El País* has an English edition, if it pops up in there and your name or the company name get mentioned then the story will travel.'

Winner shuffled in his seat. 'Well, you need to try and stop it from travelling, Jen. I'm sure you know people at *El País*. Or people who know people. Persuade them to spike it.'

'I can try.'

'Thank you.' His eyes flicked up towards the corner of his screen. To the clock Jennifer guessed. Winner didn't like long meetings. 'We'd better let you go; you've got work to do. Plus, that boy of yours will be wanting his dinner. Man cannot live on popcorn alone. I'll see ya tomorrow.'

The line dropped. *Conference has ended* it read. Jennifer powered the laptop down and put it away in a kitchen drawer. She walked out into the hall and called up the stairs to Ryley who responded that he was fine. He'd be down soon. There was someone at *El País* she used to know who might be able to help. He owed her a favour. But this wasn't what she'd signed up for. Suppressing news stories. Back when she was interviewing for the job, Winner's pitch had been a positive, persuasive one – he and the many strange-sounding technologies he was involved in were going to change the world. Not just change it, save it. Jennifer's job was to help spread the good word. What's more, she was going to be paid a shedload of money for doing it. She remembered how much she used to enjoy telling friends and family about her work and about Winner himself – a little crazy, unpredictable, often blunt to the point of being rude but nevertheless one of the good guys.

She didn't talk about her work so much lately, not that she cared what people thought, it was just . . . different. After offering her the job, picking Jennifer over scores of seemingly better-qualified candidates, Clive had warned her: 'We're gonna be doing some madcap stuff these next few years. But remember, no matter how crazy it gets, we're on the side of the angels – you and me.' Jennifer went to the cupboard and took down a goldfish-bowl-sized wine glass, then to the fridge. Half a bottle of cold white chardonnay didn't look like that much at all once decanted into the huge glass. She topped it up and carried the drink out onto the deck at the back of the house. Whose side were they on now, Clive Winner and her?

Back on the conference call, Clive and his head of security sat in silence for a while as though the meeting they were having with Jennifer had been a physical one and they were waiting for her to depart the room and walk the length of a long corridor. It was Daryl who finally spoke.

'I guess you want to know what happened?'

'I know what happened, Daryl . . . you dropped a bollock, that's what happened. What I want to know is what you're going to do about it.'

11

STOCKWELL ROAD, LONDON

Carver made himself a strong coffee, sat down at his kitchen table and studied the list of potential stories he'd scribbled down at the falafel place the previous evening. He'd spilt chilli sauce over the penultimate item on the list and it was no longer legible, but even without whatever story that was, it was clear that he had more work than he could manage on his own. Something was going to have to give. He looked again at the list.

Cash for honours . . . again.

'That's a good story. It shouldn't take too long either.'

Saudi defence contracts.

'So's that.'

NHS contracts offered to American firms.

Whips' Office blackmail . . . more.

Ambassadorial posts . . . old pals' act.

Then came the chilli sauce stain. He tore the paper from his pad, turned it over and helped it up in the direction of the window.

ssapsert fo noitinifedeR

'Bollocks. "Redefinition of trespass" is a good story too.' If only McCluskey would answer his messages or pick up the bloody phone.

He knew he could make a good case for them working together on some of these and they were the sort of stories that would interest her. She'd taken redundancy after the BBC bosses had decided, in their wisdom, to shut down the Caversham monitoring station and move everyone from there into that glass and steel monstrosity next to Broadcasting House. She was retired but still sharp as a tack and much too good to be sitting around twiddling her thumbs and gardening. If she wouldn't answer the phone, then the only sensible thing was to pay her a visit and surprise her. She'd probably appreciate the company.

McCluskey's red-brick, two-up two-down house was on a small estate between the Italian baroque manor house where she used to work and the local golf course. You could tell which house was hers by the thicket of short-wave aerials poking from the eaves. Carver fancied that some extra things might have been added since his last visit. He wouldn't put it past McCluskey to have taken some of the kit that Caversham were getting rid of and installing it here. As he drew closer, he saw his friend on the other side of a low flint wall, trying to drag a large sculpture of some sort across the front garden without falling into her fishpond. Carver called out.

'Hello, McCluskey.'

'What are you doing here?'

'I thought I'd surprise you.'

'A surprise is something that somebody wants to happen. This is what's known as a shock.'

'You don't look very shocked.'

'No. I figured you'd pull something like this.' She stood and took a moment to catch her breath. Her white candyfloss hair looked dishevelled and her face flushed pink with exertion. 'Are you going to just stand there like an eejit, or will you make yourself useful?'

'Okay, sure. What are you doing?'

'I'm protecting my goldfish. The herons had three of them last week, the greedy bawbags.' McCluskey's Glaswegian accent grew thicker when she was agitated, which she was now. She was trying to manoeuvre the heavy abstract-looking sculpture to the far end of the pond.

'What is that?'

'What do you mean what is it? It's a heron.'

'It doesn't look much like a heron.'

'It looks like a heron if you're another heron. You're not a heron – you're a human . . . more or less. Grab the beak . . .' Together they shuffled the wrought-iron sculpture around the pond towards a paving stone that had been placed there for the pretend heron to stand on.

'So, if a heron sees what it thinks is another heron standing here eating your fish, it'll go elsewhere?'

'That's right.'

'Why doesn't it think – this place looks popular, I think I'll eat here. That's how *I* go about choosing a restaurant.'

'I refer you to my previous answer . . . you're not a flaming heron. Herons are intimidated by other herons. They went through it all on *Gardeners' Question Time* the other week.' This was the end of the matter as far as McCluskey was concerned. She stood up and brushed out the creases in her tweed skirt. 'I suppose you'd better come in – now that you're here.'

'Great. Have you got any of those colourful little cakes you sometimes get in?'

'No.'

McCluskey made a pot of tea and they had that, along with a plate of slightly stale shortbread while sitting in her living room. The old colleagues exchanged small talk: Carver asked about the garden and listened while McCluskey complained about the unseasonably wet weather and what it was doing to her hydrangeas. She asked him about the BBC and listened while he complained about incompetent bosses and what they were doing for his ulcers. That done, Carver glanced around the room, trying to work out how best to go about asking what he wanted to ask.

'You've rearranged your snow globes.'

'That's right.'

He surveyed the mantelpiece which was where McCluskey kept her favourite souvenirs. On display either side of her gold carriage clock were the Eiffel Tower, Sydney Harbour, Mount Fuji and – at the end nearest her chair – the snow globe that Patrick and Carver had bought for her on their last work trip together. It was the Hong Kong skyline at night. McCluskey noticed William looking at it.

'I'm fond of that one.'

'I'm glad to hear it, it cost a bloody fortune. We went halves.'

McCluskey took a slurp of tea.

'So, what is it you're wanting, Billy?'

Carver took a deep breath. 'I had this idea. We've worked together on and off before but never properly. I've got a load of really interesting stories on the boil right now – these are important stories I'm talking about—'

'Important stories, eh?'

'Er . . . yes. And I thought we might . . . you know . . . have a go at them together?'

McCluskey nodded. She took a handkerchief from inside the rolled-up sleeve of her cardigan and blew her nose.

'Patrick still won't play ball then?'

'Well . . . no.'

'After what happened in Hong Kong . . . it's bound tae take some time. How is he?'

Carver told McCluskey what he knew, which he realised wasn't much. Patrick was back at the BBC but not at the *Today* programme or any other news programme; they had him doing some sort of desk job.

'It's a complete waste. He's a field producer, a news man, he shouldn't be pushing bits of paper about.'

McCluskey shrugged. 'From what I heard, it was his choice. He asked for a change and they offered him a job at the BBC complaints department. He was happy to take it.'

'Nonsense. Who told you that?'

'Rebecca.'

'Really? Patrick's Rebecca? Well, I suppose she'd know.' He hesitated. 'How come you two are in touch?'

'I sent her and Patrick a card, congratulating them on the new baby and she phoned to say thank you. She's an extremely polite young woman, that girlfriend of his.'

'Oh right. Yes, very polite.' Carver had meant to send a card himself but he'd forgotten. He'd left a phone message, but that was a week or two after the event. And the message might've started out being about something else. But he was sure he'd mentioned the baby. At the end. 'What else did Rebecca say?'

Patrick had been signed off work for six months' sick leave after Hong Kong but opted to go back earlier than that. He'd been sent for post-traumatic stress counselling but dropped it after just one session.

'It doesn't sound like Patrick is his proper self yet. Far from it. Rebecca says he just needs a little longer; more time to recover and to process what happened to him. Physically, he's on the mend, but his head's not right.' McCluskey dunked a piece of shortbread into her tea. 'I'd have been more convinced if she'd sounded like she believed it herself. I wanted tae talk for longer, see if there was anything practical I could do but that little one of theirs started bawling and it wasn't the right time.'

Carver nodded. 'I should call her.'

'Aye, you should.'

'Speaking to Rebecca's probably the best way to go about persuading Patrick that he needs to get back on the job again.'

McCluskey sighed. 'Maybe. But that's not why you should be calling her.'

12

HIGHBURY FIELDS, LONDON

Rebecca couldn't wait much longer. Patrick had promised he'd be back in time to take the baby, so that she could go to her meeting. He was late. She messaged him.

Where are you?

Sorry. Don't think I'll make it. Got to work late.

Great. Thanks a million.

She understood how this could happen in his old job; it was par for the course in news. Politicians would screw up, governments would fall, wars and famines and natural disasters would occur and Patrick's job was to report on it. Long, unpredictable hours and sudden changes of plan were part of the deal. But that was his old job; what sort of unforeseen emergency could crop up when you were working for the complaints unit? She typed an angry message back. *What happened? You received an urgent angry letter?*

Something like that.

She couldn't be bothered to ask for more detail or to argue; she didn't have time. But she was damned if she was missing the meeting. She'd take the baby with her. Patrick was aware how important the Planet Action meetings were for her. A couple of hours each week that had nothing to do with feeding or changing or bathing or sleep-training. A chance to do something interesting, worthwhile . . . and alone. She went to find Leila's warmest all-in-one and the papoose. She put her phone and the black Moleskine where she kept her Planet Action notes in the changing bag. The baby was happy to be wrestled into the fluffy white snowsuit and strapped into the baby carrier; being taken out at this time of the day was a novelty and she appeared up for the adventure.

'Good girl.' She looked like a baby bear. Rebecca put on the brightest red lipstick she could find and gave first Leila's hair and then her own blonde bob a quick brush. She checked herself in the hall mirror. It would have to do.

She felt her mood improve the moment she walked through the tall school gates. The local secondary was huge compared to her own south London primary school but the gates and the Victorian red-brick building were similar enough to make her realise how much she was missing her work, her colleagues, her pupils. She walked past the playing fields, Leila strapped to her front, her chubby legs swinging around happily. The day's rain had turned the school's long-jump pit into a paddling pool, but the skies had cleared now and the air felt fresh. Rebecca heaved open the door to the main reception: there, standing behind a canteen table was a man in his mid-to-late thirties. He was smiling like he'd won the lottery.

'Hey there, Jeff.'

'Rebecca! And a guest. This must be the famous Leila? What a lovely surprise.'

'Yeah. Well, let's see if you still feel that way once the meeting starts.'

'I'm certain I will.'

Jeff had shoulder-length brown hair, he wore faded blue jeans and a blue linen shirt open at the collar. He looked like Jesus. In fact, he looked so much like Jesus that Rebecca had come close to calling him by that name. She'd made the mistake of mentioning this to Patrick who now referred to Planet Action's north London regional coordinator as *Jeffus*.

She waited patiently while Jeff cooed over the baby, pinching gently at her cheeks and tickling her chin. Leila usually objected to this but seemed on this occasion not to mind. Rebecca tired of this before her daughter did and told Jeff she should say hello to the other members of the group gathered in the hall and find a seat.

'Sure. I saved you a seat though. You're down at the front, next to me. I thought you might like to say a few words about our Paris plans and maybe the school strike stuff too?'

'Okay. Sure. I'm still not sure about Paris though, Jeff. I mean I'm happy to help with the planning but I'm not sure I'll be able to come.'

'Understood. No need to decide now. We've got a while before we need to book anything. Be a real shame if you couldn't come though.'

Rebecca went to say hi to the other members of the group. She introduced herself to the newcomers too. There were seven or eight new faces, an encouraging sign she thought. Leila was beautifully behaved – smiling and gurgling and charming everyone. Or almost everyone. One of the newcomers – a gothy-looking young man in black denim jeans and leather jacket proved immune to Rebecca and Leila's charm, responding to her cheery welcome with grunts and monosyllabic answers. Jeff tried too and had a little more success but not much. The guy took a seat in the very back row, closest to the door and sat there, arms folded. When it seemed like everyone who was going to arrive had, Jeff vaulted up onto the raised stage at the front of the hall and introduced himself.

'I'd like to welcome you all to this Planet Action meeting. Welcome especially all you new attendees, we're delighted to have you here. I also need to say hello to any spies and spooks who've been sent along tonight to see what we're up to . . .' There was some embarrassed laughter and people glanced around at one other. One or two pairs of eyes turned towards the rear of the room. '. . . you police folk know who you are of course. Unfortunately, we don't, so if you wouldn't mind putting your hands up or just turning around and leaving then that'd be great.' More chuckling but no mea culpas and so he continued. 'Okay, well, we're going to go ahead anyway. We have a planet to save and not a lot of time left in which to save it. If the political powers that be think that makes us a security threat, then I have to question either their intelligence or their allegiance.'

There was a portable whiteboard on castors nearby and Jesus wheeled it squeakily across the floor before taking a thick marker from his jeans pocket and writing on it in large blue capitals:

1. NEW MEMBERS INTRO.
2. UPDATE AND LOCAL ELECTIONS.
3. PREP FOR PARIS!

'I always start by asking each of our newcomers to say a few words about themselves . . . who you are, why you're here, that kind of thing.' There was nervous laughter. 'I know that sounds a little scary so I'm going to ask one of our more seasoned members to show you how it's done. Rebecca, would you mind doing the honours?' Jeff was grinning but the smile slipped when he glanced down at the front row and saw the apprehensive look on Rebecca's face. 'I mean, not if you don't want to, I can ask somebody . . .'

Rebecca stood. 'No, I'm happy to do it. No problem.' She glanced around the room, reminding herself that the school hall was a natural environment for her and that she knew exactly why she was there.

She told the group that before getting involved with Planet Action she'd been loosely involved in green causes for years, running the sustainable food group at her own school . . . voting green at local elections and so on but that she wanted to do more.

'And be more active, really.' She smiled at the assembled group. 'And of course, it has started to seem even more important, more pressing, since I've had this one . . .' She stroked Leila's head. 'So, I decided I needed to do something.'

'You did do *something*. You did just about the worst thing any woman living in the West can do.'

Rebecca swung around to see where the voice had come from. The gothy-looking guy at the back met her gaze.

'I beg your pardon?'

'That.' He pointed. 'Your baby. He or she's going to burn through around sixty million metric tonnes of carbon every single year. That's quite a carbon footprint, wouldn't you say?'

'She's a girl, and . . .' Rebecca was about to say that her and Patrick had tried using recyclable nappies and were buying second-hand clothes before realising how pathetic and defensive that would sound. Her voice trailed off to silence and the bloke at the back forced home his advantage.

'Having a baby here in the West is tantamount to environmental vandalism. It's selfish and irresponsible.'

'That's enough.' Jeff had jumped down from the stage and was standing next to Rebecca.

'What? We all know it.'

'No. We all don't. I don't. What's more, shaming people into silence for having a baby, eating meat, driving a car or whatever is exactly the opposite of what we should be doing.'

'I'm just telling it like it is.'

'No, you were being confrontational. And rude.'

The young man rolled his eyes. 'I didn't mean to be rude. I'm . . . I apologise.'

Jeff took firmer control of the meeting after that, thanking Rebecca for her excellent introduction and encouraging as many of the newcomers who wanted to say a few words. The young man at the back decided to pass. That done, they moved on to other business – a summary of what the group were planning to do around the forthcoming council elections, a call for volunteers to take part in various actions. Rebecca put her hand up for a couple of things in addition to the Paris prep that she was already working on – a lobby of the local council to call for more traffic calming and pedestrianisation, leafletting at local tube stations. Jeff said that the group were also planning some more 'active actions' and that anyone interested in those should stay behind and speak to him about that. Finally came the discussion about Paris. Everyone in the room was aware that there was another big United Nations climate conference coming soon; some of the newbies had mentioned this as the reason that they'd decided to get involved.

'Paris is the big one. We all know what we're dealing with. If the planet were a whistling kettle, then it would have been whistling like a bastard for years now. The trouble is we haven't been listening. There are some hopeful signs . . . the fact that Obama and Xi Jinping are at least talking about greenhouse gas – that's something. The Pope's what-do-you call it . . .'

'Encyclical.'

'That's the one. That was a nice surprise. But we all know that the only way that the political leaders gathering in Paris will do anything meaningful is if we keep the pressure on. That includes our own prime minister. Paris is our last best chance. It's also a chance to put our little group well and truly on the map. With that in mind I'm going to hand back to Rebecca who's doing the groundwork for us on this and who, fingers crossed, will be leading the delegation.'

Rebecca shot Jeff a look before getting her Moleskine notebook out from the changing bag and talking through the plan so far. A group of ten or twelve would travel to France and work alongside green groups from right across Europe. Various actions were being planned but Rebecca was keen to hear other people's ideas both for events in Paris and in the lead-up. She also wanted the group's thoughts regarding the school strike idea. There'd been school walkouts before, both in Australia and the UK, but ahead of Paris, students of all ages and a range of countries were trying to organise a mass walkout. Did Planet Action want to get involved?

She handed back to Jeff who was very keen on the whole school strike idea. He talked enthusiastically about recruiting a whole new generation of green campaigners. He was a charismatic speaker, and looking around the room Rebecca saw new members hanging on every word. It was amusing to watch, but it was getting late, and she could sense Leila becoming restless. As the conversation continued, she caught Jeff's eye, mouthed an apologetic goodbye, and snuck away in the direction of the door. He caught up with her as she was walking through reception.

'Rebecca. Sorry, I just wanted to say goodbye properly. And to thank you for all the Paris work you've done, it's brilliant. Thanks for bringing Leila too.'

'No problem. I thought it was a good meeting. Well . . . most of it was good.'

'Oh yeah. I'm sorry about that new guy. I'll speak to him some more, let him know that's not how we do things.'

'It's fine. No biggie. At least we know he's probably not one of those spies or spooks that you're worried might have infiltrated us.'

Jeff laughed.

'That's true. They usually prefer to keep a lower profile than that guy managed and not pick fights.' He paused. 'There was one other thing . . .'

'Sure.'

'I know we've got your email.'

'It's on the members' list.'

'Yeah. But I wondered, maybe I could get your mobile too? Or I could give you mine?'

13

CAVERSHAM, BERKSHIRE, UK

Carver over-dunked the last shortbread finger. It collapsed into the mug of tea halfway between cup and lip.

'Bollocks. So I'll speak to Rebecca. Then hopefully to Patrick . . .' He took his spoon and set about retrieving the tea-soaked biscuit. '. . . but in the meantime, what about it?'

'What about what?'

'You and me working together on some of these stories I've got.'

McCluskey shook her head. 'I don't think so.'

'Why not?'

'I'm busy.'

'But these stories I'm talking about are—'

'Important; so you said. What makes you think the work I'm doing isn't?'

'Erm. What are you working on?'

McCluskey hesitated. Brushed a few crumbs of shortbread from her skirt into her hand.

'I'm not supposed to talk about it.' She tipped the handful of crumbs into her empty teacup. 'It's proper secret squirrel stuff.'

'Secret squirrel?'

She nodded. 'Aye.'

'Come on, tell me. You're itching to tell me; I know you are.'

McCluskey shifted in her armchair.

'I suppose I could let you have a quick look. A glimpse. I've got it all upstairs . . .'

'In the spare room? Your famous command and control?'

'If you're going tae take the mickey, you can forget about it.'

'Sorry.' He smiled. 'I'm sorry. I'd like to have a look.'

McCluskey pushed herself up from her chair and walked to the door. Carver drained the biscuity dregs of his tea and followed.

The single bed, pine wardrobe, and side table in the spare room had been pushed against the window to make space. The back wall and almost the entire floor had been given over to the 'secret squirrel' investigation. Carver tiptoed past some precarious-looking piles of newspapers and box files to take a better look. Sellotaped to the wall were lists of telephone numbers, hundreds of them, printed in large type and double-spaced to allow room for notes underneath. McCluskey had ringed some of these numbers with red marker pen and drawn a line between them and a seemingly haphazard patchwork of photocopied newspaper articles or pieces of agency copy also taped to the wall, either side of the list of phone numbers. Around a dozen numbers had been lassoed in red Sharpie in this way, some were attached to just one news article, some to several. The newspaper stories were in a variety of different languages – Carver recognised Spanish, French, Arabic, Russian – he couldn't remember exactly how many languages McCluskey spoke – six or seven. He stepped back from the wall and tried to figure out what it was he was looking at.

'I give up. What is it?'

'It's called Pegasus.'

'Like the horse? That's the name of your . . . investigation, is it?'

'The investigation doesn't have a name. Pegasus is the thing we're investigating. It's new. New, and worrying.'

McCluskey explained. 'An old Caversham colleague got in touch. Not one of the monitors – a tech type but a good man. He's helped me out in the past with various bits and pieces.'

'Retired now too I take it?'

'Aye. Retired, but keeping busy.'

'And he wanted your help with some kind of freelance thing?'

'No, he wanted to warn me.' McCluskey's anonymous mate had been doing his monthly regular deep clean, sweeping his home computer, laptop and phone for bugs and malware when he spotted something he didn't like the look of. 'This fellow knows everything there is to know about bugs and backdoors and the like, but he hadn't seen anything like this.' The new malware gave the attacker access to all text messages, conversations, photos, the microphone, geolocator . . . basically everything. Her friend had done the decent thing and contacted the people he'd been in regular contact with during the previous few weeks to warn them their phones could also have been compromised.

'Regular contact? Is this fellow a close friend then? Like a boyfriend?'

McCluskey glared at Carver.

'No, he isn't. Not that it's any of your business.'

Having been told that her phone might have been bugged, McCluskey hadn't taken any chances. Changing phones was annoying, but not as annoying as having someone eavesdrop every time you picked up your mobile. Or even when you didn't – her friend had transferred some of the contents of his infected phone, some apps and the spyware itself onto a burner phone so he could study it more closely. He found that the new malware could access the device even when you weren't using it. The phone's camera and microphone occasionally switched themselves on and started to record without him touching them.

'He got the impression that whoever it was that infected his phone figured out that he was onto them. A week after he'd found the spyware, it sort of . . . self-destructed.'

'Patrick and I saw some pretty sophisticated phone hacking happening in Hong Kong, but I've not heard of anything like this.'

'Nor had he. He got a tad too attached to this malware if you ask me. But he made the most of the time he had.' Her retired tech genius had managed to send a bug of his own back in the opposite direction. 'It copied what it could find. A wee bit random but better than nothing.' This was where McCluskey's list of phone numbers had come from.

'At first we thought they might'a been contacts for the toerags who bugged him in the first place. But it looks like these numbers belong to other folk being spied on.'

'So, you're trying to work out who they are and warn them?'

'It's not as simple as that. This Pegasus thing is being used properly by some folk . . . legitimate security services are using it to keep an eye on terrorist cells, drug cartels, a range of genuinely nasty bastards. But that's not what the lot who infected my friend's mobile are up to. They've got something altogether different in mind. We're trying to figure out what it is.'

Carver would have liked to have studied the wall and the links that McCluskey had so far managed to make for longer, but he could sense that his friend was getting fidgety.

'I promised my pal I'd keep this close to my chest.'

'Course, I understand.'

Back downstairs, Carver had one more go at persuading McCluskey.

'You could help this mate of yours out and help me at the same time. I bet we've been friends for longer. At least have a look at what I've got.'

He showed McCluskey the list he'd made. She read it.

'Cash for honours, defence contracts, Whips' Office blackmail, ambassadorial posts . . . it's all good stuff, Billy, right up your alley. What's this last one?'

'Trespass?'

'No, underneath that . . . Winner? Is that what it says?'

'Clive Winner. That's the latest thing I've had land in my in-tray. The straw that'll break the proverbial.'

'Interesting.' She paused. 'It's all interesting, Billy, and I'm flattered that you thought of me, but I'm up to my eyes.'

'You know the saying . . . if you want something doing, ask a busy person.'

'Yes, well, you're going to have to find a different busy person to ask. What about your woman . . . what's her name? Naziah. She's been helpful before, hasn't she? Pretty smart too as I recall. What's she up to?'

'Naz. I fixed for her to do a couple of broadcast assistant shifts on the programme . . . days and nights.'

'Lucky her.'

'She's a quick learner but she's still only half-fledged. She hasn't even finished her training yet.' Carver explained that Naz was studying for the National Certificate. McCluskey nodded approvingly.

'That's good, too few of this generation are learning the basics.'

'Exactly what I said. So, I'm helping with that, but she's not the finished article. Not yet. If you can't help me then it will have to be Patrick. I'll speak to Rebecca. Maybe the two of us can talk some sense into him.'

14

NEW BROADCASTING HOUSE, PORTLAND PLACE, LONDON

Naz sat in the programme meeting, cursing her luck and her limited wardrobe. Naomi hardly ever came to the evening handover meeting, sometimes she dialled in, listened, and offered advice but she almost never attended in person. Naz knew for a fact that her boss had been in the office since five a.m. that morning, Naz had booked her car. It was almost nine p.m. now. A sixteen-hour working day was long, even by *Today* programme standards but Naomi Holder still looked good – or a lot better than any of her employees anyway. Naz in particular. She pulled herself straighter in the chair and tried to tuck her feet and the scuffed trainers she was wearing a little further under the seat and out of Naomi's eye-line. There wasn't anything she could do about the tracksuit. At least it was the black Adidas and clean.

Naomi was her usual well-groomed self in flat shoes, navy-blue roll-neck sweater and black cigarette pants. Naz loved how her boss dressed. Classy. She wondered whether she might ever be able to pull off a look like that. It seemed unlikely. The conversation continued around her and Naz kept half an ear on what was being said while at the same time checking through the list of what she'd done already. She'd developed an ability to tune in halfway during these meetings, remaining aware of what was being said but only engaging if and when the subject matter directly concerned her. Paul, the pouchy-eyed day editor was talking the assembled journalists through the prospects – half-a-dozen pages of double-sided A4, which amounted to an à la carte menu of news stories, correspondent names, political heavyweights, features, and fillers from which the night editor – tonight it was Tracey – would construct her programme. Much of the discussion revolved around a pre-recorded interview with the Foreign Secretary, which, provided it didn't date, would probably be the 8.10 a.m. lead the following morning. Paul had listened to it.

'It turned into a bit of a love-in between the Foreign Secretary and Nick. It's over half an hour long and we only want seven or eight minutes. It's a simul-rec – Nick's at home and Hammond was in a boomy-sounding airport terminal, so it's in two pieces. I'm not going to lie, it's a horrible edit.'

'I'll do it.'

The sound of Naz's voice surprised everyone, including herself. She looked around the group.

Tracey was unconvinced. 'That's a kind offer, er . . . Naz. But I think it's probably best you concentrate on the studio and line bookings. There are a load of taxi and radio cars that need sorting too.'

'I've booked them.'

'All of them?'

'Yep.'

Naomi made a snorting sound, the assembled journalists turned in her direction.

'If Naz has the time, then go ahead and let her take a run at it. She did the best quick turnaround edit I've heard in a long time the other morning. That interview we did with the culture minister?' The team nodded. 'Tongue-tied Tina came out of the radio sounding like Cicero. I got a message from her press guy asking how on earth we'd done it.'

*

As soon as the meeting wound up, Naz found an empty workshop studio, logged in to the computer, downloaded the raw interview and set to work. She was leaning forward, elbows on the desk, her hands holding the headphones hard against her ears, listening for glitches. She didn't hear the soundproofed door being pulled open, nor her boss enter. When Naomi tapped her on the shoulder, Naz jumped. The programme editor smiled.

'Sorry, I didn't mean to startle you.'

'My fault. Miles away.' She gestured at the computer screen and the jagged soundwave on display. She had already made a dozen small edits. 'I thought I'd get cracking on this while I was still fresh.'

Naomi nodded.

'Fresh. Yes, I vaguely remember what fresh felt like. A distant memory.'

Naz smiled.

'You've had a silly long day.'

'You're right. Both long and silly.' She paused. 'I spent most of it in an overheated room with overpaid management consultants trying to explain to them what a news programme is.' Before she knew it, Naomi was telling her most junior employee all about the Director General's plan to save money by bringing in external consultants. Naz was easy to talk to.

'It's very clever. We give a big chunk of public money to people who have no idea what it is we do. They hang around and watch us work for a few weeks and then they tell us how we should change things, how many jobs we should cut, stuff like that.'

'Does it work?'

'Depends what you mean by work. My guess is that this consultation will end up costing as much as the savings we make. But the point is we're showing willing; our political masters don't like us much right now, we're in the firing line, so employing the same consultants that they use to do a job on us does make some sense. Political sense, anyway.'

'Political sense?'

Naomi brushed a non-existent crease from her jumper and smiled.

'Never mind. It's bad enough that I need to think about all this . . . nonsense, I shouldn't burden you with it too. I wanted to talk about something else, something altogether cheerier.'

Naomi pulled a spare chair from the corner of the little studio and sat down facing Naz. 'Despite these consultations and cuts and what have you, there are going to be a couple of jobs coming up.'

'Here? On the programme?'

'Yes.'

'That's good news.'

'Yes.' She paused, waiting for Naz to draw the obvious conclusion. Waiting in vain. 'And so, I'd like you to apply.'

'Me?'

'Yes, you. Would you have a problem doing that?'

'Well, the thing is, I haven't got my National Certificate yet. I mean I'm studying for it, I'm doing the work at the same time as working here. Not literally of course but I'm studying and hopefully I'll pass but I don't have it yet, so . . .'

Naomi smiled. 'There's no doubting whose journalistic prodigy you are is there?'

'Sorry?'

'The certificate's a good qualification.' Naz nodded enthusiastically. 'And it's good to have, no doubt about it. But it's not essential, not any more. You could apply for one of these journalist jobs I'm talking about without the certificate.'

'Really? Mr Car . . . I mean, William said that—'

'Let me guess. Carver told you that the certificate's a basic requirement?' Naz confirmed this with a nod. 'Maybe it was; once upon a time. But not any more. William is one for the old ways and a lot of the time that's a good thing. But not always. And maybe not in this case. The job advert goes live later this week. Take a look and then we'll talk.'

15

LA BARROSA, ANDALUSIA, SPAIN

Francesca woke, choking, unable to breathe. She shoved the sheet and quilt away from her body and pushed herself up in the bed; her nightdress was wet with sweat. It was the same nightmare that had woken her every night since her daughter went missing. In the dream Alma is little – five or six years old – she's playing on the beach, her hair in a ponytail, wearing a swimsuit with sunflowers on it. She is running up and down the shoreline, turning cartwheels, walking on her hands.

'The girl is as happy upside down as the right way up.'

She smiled, remembering her husband's words. But he was not there in this dream. It is just Francesca and her daughter and a strangely empty beach – the sun is brilliant, the water bright blue, but they are the only people there. Alma takes her mum's hand and pulls her towards the sea; they wade a little way in. They jump the waves together – gentle waves. Alma wants to go deeper but her mum won't allow it. They stay in the shallows, stepping over the small waves, Francesca lifting Alma up now and then when the wave is bigger, so that her daughter's toes skim the water and Alma whoops with pleasure. Then, from behind them, back on the beach, Francesca hears someone calling her name. She turns to find out who it is, what they want, but can see no one. The beach is empty. She's still holding Alma's hand; she's sure of this. She can feel her daughter's hand in hers. But when she turns back towards the water and looks down, Alma has gone. Francesca's hand is empty and holding nothing. She shouts her daughter's name – first quietly, then louder. She scans the sea around her and then further, out towards the horizon. Francesca starts wading around frantically but she can see no sign of her, and the water is gradually changing colour, from clear blue to an increasingly inky black. She plunges her arms into the sea and grasps left and right trying to find Alma. She thinks she feels some skin – an arm, or maybe it's her leg but then it's gone, and the current is growing stronger, tugging at her legs.

Francesca sat up higher in the bed, the back of her sweat-dampened nightdress cold against the wooden headboard. She folded her hands in front of her and tried to slow her breathing. After a couple of minutes, she had recovered enough to take in her surroundings; a ribbon of bright light on the wall beneath her curtains told her that she'd overslept. She looked at the bedside table, squinting to read the faint green numerals on her alarm clock. Almost eleven a.m. She'd slept long, if not well. Her mobile phone was alongside the clock; she reached for it and saw there was a message. She felt her pulse quicken again before checking the number and seeing that the message was from Alma's friend Loli, who had taken to calling her every morning and evening. Francesca listened to the beginning of the message then pressed delete. She'd call her back later. She went to put the phone back on the bedside table then stopped. She looked around the room, as though there might be someone there to pass judgement. Then she dialled her daughter's number. She waited, knowing that it would not ring, knowing that it would transfer straight through to Alma's answer-phone message – just as it had the last hundred times she'd called it. It didn't matter. The point of the call was no longer to wonder or wish that the phone might ring, to hope that somehow Alma would answer – it was simply to hear the sound of her daughter's voice.

'*Hola! Esta es Alma . . .*'

Francesca remembered chiding her daughter for this silly message – '*I'm in the air or on the beach or drinking at the Che bar with Mr Carlos. Leave a message and I'll call you back.*'

Francesca hung up before the beep and put the phone back on the table.

Carlos. She'd seen him just once, briefly, the day after Alma disappeared but not since then. She understood why he hadn't visited again and why he didn't call. It was painful. What's more, words would be required. Words were not Carlos' strong suit. When he and Alma visited each Sunday, her daughter would often speak for him and Carlos would sit and nod and smile, clearly happy that there was someone who could read his mind and translate his thoughts into words that other people might understand.

Nevertheless, they needed to speak. The longer she left it, the harder it would be.

16

THE YORKSHIRE GREY, FITZROVIA, LONDON

Rebecca had seemed pleased to hear from Carver; she'd been friendly on the phone and genuinely enthusiastic when he'd suggested that they meet. The conversation had left him feeling guilty for not having contacted her sooner. Sitting at the bar of the Yorkshire Grey drinking a pint, reading the newspaper and waiting for her to arrive, he began to wish that he'd offered to buy her lunch somewhere nicer than this. Two bar-stools down, a guy was bending the landlord's ear about something to do with George Soros and artificial diseases.

'His organisation claims it's promoting democracy but that's a cover story for what Soros and his rich mates are actually up to. Not that the mainstream media would ever tell us that.'

The pub was a stone's throw from Broadcasting House and given how many of Bernard's customers were hacks – radio reporters like Carver, presenters, and producers – it occurred to Carver that he might've been a little more full-throated in his defence of journalism. Perhaps that was unfair, the landlord's main purpose was to provide a patient ear and a never-ending supply of booze. Still this bloke Bernard was talking to was getting on Carver's nerves.

If you're going to have batshit-crazy ideas about a global conspiracy of some sort, at least have them quietly. He'd moved on to the subject of chemtrails. Apparently, the water vapour that drifted from the back of planes wasn't water vapour at all, it was a drug designed to sterilise and depopulate the world. . . it was obvious, there was evidence, yet the newspapers and the BBC wouldn't go anywhere near it. This was too much for William, he turned to face the man.

'You're right, the mainstream media is a vast conspiracy . . .' The bloke's eyes brightened. '. . . aimed at making you a little less stupid.' He drank the last of his beer. 'And it's bloody hard work.' He put the glass down on the bar, picked up his newspaper and his plastic carrier bag and walked towards the door that separated the two halves of the pub. Chances were that Rebecca would prefer the saloon bar anyway. It was quieter.

Carver was reading about a forthcoming cabinet reshuffle . . . 'Deckchairs on the *Titanic* . . .' when he heard the pub door behind him being pushed open and felt a draught of wintery air on his ankles. When he turned, Rebecca was standing there, a baby strapped to her chest, kicking away vigorously inside an elaborate-looking sling. She had a fancy-looking pram with her too.

'Hey there, William.'

'Hello. I didn't know you were going to bring, er . . .'

'A baby?'

'Er. Yes. I didn't know you were planning to bring . . .' He hesitated. 'I'm sorry, I've forgotten . . . the name.'

'Her name?'

'Yes, I've forgotten her name.'

'Leila.'

Carver nodded.

' "Layla"? As in Derek and the Dominos . . . ?'

'You've lost me.'

'Never mind. How do you spell it?'

'L. E. I. L. A.'

'Ah, Leila with an E. And an I. It's good – Leila. A nice name for a girl . . . Leila.'

'You're doing that thing, aren't you?'

'What thing?'

'That thing you taught Patrick. Saying someone's name three times so you remember it. He does it at parties. It's weird and a little annoying.'

'It works. I've remembered little Lisa's name, haven't I?'

Rebecca smiled. 'Very funny.' She loosened some of the many straps that were connecting her to the baby and sat. Rebecca looked around. 'God, it feels weird being back inside a pub.'

'Weird as in not good?'

'No . . .' She paused. '. . . weird but very good.' She took her phone from her pocket, checked it for messages before switching it off and dropping it into the empty pram. 'This place is looking a little fancier than when I last saw it.'

'Bernard is trying to persuade people that it's a gastropub. Hence the new soft furnishings and all the kale on the menu. Unfortunately, the food is still, largely speaking, not good.'

'Are we not eating here then?'

'No, we are. I just didn't want you to get your hopes up. Shall I go and ask them if they've got a children's menu?'

Rebecca laughed.

'She's not on solids yet, William. Still a long way away from that . . . just bottles and boobs.'

'Oh, er . . . right. Course, I'll just get the regular menus then. What'll you drink?'

Rebecca had a wine spritzer, Carver stayed on the beer and they both ate a passable pie and chips. Steak and ale for Carver, sweet potato, and other various vegetables for Rebecca. He marvelled at how she was able to feed herself, feed, burp and comfort the baby, all while simultaneously making interesting, entertaining conversation. It made him feel tired just watching it.

'Have you been getting out and about like this much? You and Leila?'

She shook her head.

'You've got to be joking. We've been working ourselves up for this great adventure for the last two days. Most of the time I'm at home, wandering around in a daze, with pieces of toast stuck in my hair.'

'What about Patrick?'

'Toast doesn't seem to stick to him in the same way it does to me.'

'Are the pair of you . . . three of you . . . doing all right?'

She shrugged. 'We're managing.'

'Right. Well, that's better than not managing.'

'True.' She picked up a charred bit of pie crust, dipped it in mustard and ate it. 'I know you want to talk about Patrick, William. I know that's why we're here.'

'That wasn't the only reason I wanted to see you.'

'Don't worry, I understand. I want to talk about him too.'

They talked. Or Rebecca talked and Carver listened. The situation was pretty much as McCluskey had described, Patrick was back at work but doing a job that was as far removed from front-line news and the work that he and Carver used to do as was possible to imagine.

'He's doing this complaints job. Answering angry emails and very long letters written in green ink. It sounds dreadfully boring, but maybe boring is what he needs . . . for now.' She gave Carver a questioning look and he shrugged. 'They told him he could work from home if he wanted to, but he said he'd rather go into the office.' She glanced across at her daughter, lying happily in her pram. 'Me and Leila are trying not to take that personally. I've been telling myself he just needs a little longer, more time to process things, but I'm starting to wonder exactly how long. I found myself googling "post-natal depression in men" the other night.'

Carver shook his head.

'I don't know if Patrick's depressed or not, but I know that if he is, it won't have anything to do with you. Or Leila. It'll be because of the accident.'

Rebecca put her wine glass down – harder and more abruptly than she'd meant to. The sudden noise was loud enough that the baby began to cry – the first unhappy noise she'd made since arriving.

'The accident? You're as bad as he is, William. What happened to Patrick wasn't an accident. He was attacked . . . stabbed. He almost died.' She paused. 'If it wasn't for you, then he would've died.' She picked Leila up and comforted her.

Carver shook his head. 'If it wasn't for me . . .' He left the thought unfinished.

Rebecca said, 'Patrick needs to talk to somebody. A psychotherapist or post-traumatic stress counsellor.'

'I thought that work had sent him to someone?'

'He went once. Said it didn't help, that it wasn't the right thing for him. That was that.'

'Well, maybe I could talk to him.'

Rebecca's face brightened.

'Really? Would you? That'd be so good. If you could persuade him to give counselling another go. Recommend someone?'

'Yeah, I guess I could do that. I know some people; people who've helped me after . . . various things.'

Rebecca knew better than to push Carver for any more detail than this.

'Amazing. I'll persuade Patrick to meet up with you. The only reason he's been so reluctant is that he assumes you'll just try to talk him into going back to his old job. Back to the rough and tumble of news before he feels ready.'

'What? No, of course not.'

Rebecca leant forward and squeezed Carver's arm.

'Thank you, William.' She glanced around the pub. 'I'm desperate for a wee. I don't suppose you could look after this one for me for a minute?' She looked down at Leila, calm and quietly happy again.

'Okay . . . sure.'

'Great. If you stand up . . .' Carver stood. '. . . and kind of cradle your arms.' He did as she instructed, and Rebecca passed the baby over. 'That's perfect, you're a natural.'

'I doubt that.'

Rebecca was grinning.

'You wouldn't believe how exciting this is. I'm going to the loo all by myself. I might be in there a while. If I forget to come back just give parenting your best shot.'

'Ha, right. But seriously . . . don't be too long.'

Carver cradled the baby for a while. She had an interesting smell to her – like fresh laundry but also something else, less tangible – a smell particular to small babies he guessed. When she started to wriggle, he tried a few other cradling positions before holding her out in front of himself, his arms straight and bobbing her up and down. She seemed to like that. The bobbing up and down was interrupted by Rebecca's phone which began to vibrate inside the pram. Glancing down, Carver saw the screen light up and the caller's ID: *Planet Action Jeff.* It rang for a few seconds but then stopped before Rebecca's message clicked in. He continued lifting Leila up and down until eventually she made a soft burping sound and looked up at Carver, an odd-looking expression on her pudgy face. He turned and saw Rebecca standing just behind him, watching.

'That's a smile. She likes you.'

Carver handed the baby back.

'She doesn't really know me.'

'Not yet.'

'Your phone rang.'

'Really? I thought I'd switched it off.' She took it from the pram, checked the screen. 'It's been playing up a bit recently, I should probably get a new one.'

They decided to have a pudding – 'Not even Bernard can bugger up a chocolate brownie' – and one more drink. After they'd finished and Carver had paid the bill, he offered to walk with Rebecca and the baby back to the tube.

'That'd be lovely. You've been so amazing. All of you.'

'All of us?'

'You . . . McCluskey . . . Naziah . . .'

'Naz?'

'Yeah. She sent us a card after the baby was born and a message offering to help if there was anything we needed fetching and carrying. Really sweet, especially since she hasn't known Patrick that long and we've not even met. Thoughtful.'

'Very.' He paused. 'That reminds me, the congratulations card. I meant to send one, or flowers, it was just that—'

'Don't worry about it, William. It's fine. Today, plus you offering to help make Patrick better, that's more than enough.'

They stopped several times on the way to Oxford Circus Underground. Carver looked after Leila while Rebecca went to buy some things from the chemist, then from a newsagent, finally the Whittard teashop for some herbal tea.

'Do you actually need any of these things?'

'Probably not. But it feels great.'

'Shopping?'

'Doing something that adults do.' She took Leila and laid her down gently in the pram. 'She's been a little coldy. Her nose is bunged up.' Carver took a handkerchief from his blazer pocket and once he'd established that it was reasonably clean, passed it to her. She shook her head.

'Her nose is too small for a hanky. You have to suck the bogies out of their noses.'

'With what?'

'With your mouth.'

'Right . . .' He retrieved his yellow plastic bag from the little hook on the pram handle. 'I should probably get going.'

Rebecca smiled.

'Okay.' She stepped forward and gave Carver a hug which he

managed to hold still for. 'Thank you, William. I had a really nice time.' She glanced down at Leila. 'We both did.'

'I'm glad. Me too.'

Carver walked through Cavendish Square, heading west. The air was heavy with rain but it hadn't started yet and it would do him good to walk off some of the pie and pints he'd consumed. He hadn't got what he'd hoped to get from his lunch with Rebecca, but he felt good about their meeting anyway. He felt responsible for what had happened to Patrick and so it was only right he take some responsibility for making him better. As far as the work was concerned, Rebecca's mention of Naz – first McCluskey, now Rebecca – had given him a new idea. A work in progress she may be. 'Half-fledged', that was how he'd described her to Jemima. Still, she was keen and the only way to find out whether a pair of wings work, is to give someone a chance to flap them.

17

WASHINGTON STREET, BOSTON, MASSACHUSETTS, USA

Jennifer stared at the screen – there was something wrong with the picture, but she wasn't sure what. It looked like Clive had placed some kind of sepia filter over his floor-to-ceiling windows. Perhaps he had? He'd done much stranger stuff than that. The harbour and Opera House glowed a peculiar yellowy, orange colour. When his face reappeared on screen, a glass of iced water in hand, Jennifer unmuted herself.

'What's up with the Opera House? It's changed colour.'

Winner turned and looked.

'Megafire. It reached the city limits late last night and we woke up to this. Crazy huh? Who knew that the end of the world would be so pretty? I need to let all these other drongos in, hold tight.'

Clive Winner's weekly all-teams meeting was a marathon run at a sprinter's pace. The purpose of the meeting was to update Winner on progress or problems with any of the dozens of scientific projects that he or his subsidiary companies were involved in. It was a three-ring circus and he was the ringmaster. Jennifer watched as her computer screen subdivided into a dozen smaller boxes, then twice that and more.

'What have we got? Twenty-seven items of business it says here. Okay – piece of piss.' The Clive Winner that appeared in front of the weekly all-teams was a more amenable, less abrasive version of the man that Jennifer and the rest of the executive team dealt with on a day-to-day basis. There was an element of performance here and even some rough-edged charm.

'We've got an hour. Let's start with the science and we can get to the money, public affairs and all that boring crap at the end.' It seemed that this charm would not extend to Clive's financial adviser or to Jennifer and her press and public affairs team. She muted herself and sat back in her chair; she was missing the first half of Ryley's soccer match for this.

'Martha, how 'bout you go first.' Winner lifted a finger to his screen and the collage of thirty-plus postage-stamp-sized faces disappeared, replaced by a whole screen image of Martha Tobi – a thin-faced, dark-haired woman in a spotless white lab coat with Winner's logo on the top pocket. She was holding a wad of notes with both hands and appeared nervous. There were beads of perspiration visible on her upper lip. Tobi ran Winner's laboratory in Melbourne. The Barrier Reef work had originated here as well as several of Winner's other more outlandish experiments; it was his pride and joy.

'Are you all right there, Marth? You're sweating like a pig. Open a window for God's sake.'

'We can't open windows; we are a sealed unit. As you know.' The accent was eastern European – Romanian to be precise. She dabbed her upper lip dry with a handkerchief and gathered herself. 'Where shall I begin?'

'Run us through the latest DNA work for starters.'

She shuffled her notes, they were carefully ordered with the key sections in each area of research highlighted with handwritten addenda in the margins.

'Crispr is a gene-editing technology aimed at subtly altering the DNA of—'

'I know what Crispr is. I've been doing it since I was knee-high. I'm bloody Mister Crispr.'

'I'm aware of that. But at the last meeting you asked me to begin each section with a short explanation for others, so they didn't . . .' She glanced down at her notes. '. . . die of boredom.'

'Fine.'

Tobi and her team of gene-editing scientists were working to create pigs with a resistance to swine flu, a new variety of heat-resistant coral spores, detoxified cane toads, burp-free cows, American chestnut trees that could shrug off blight . . . the list went on. Winner listened, rapt and clearly delighted.

'You've seen what's happening over this way, Martha?' He pointed back across his shoulder towards the pall of yellowish smoke shrouding Sydney Harbour.

Tobi nodded. 'I've seen.'

'We might need to start work on fireproof koalas.' Tobi nodded again. Unsure whether this was a joke or a new project. 'We can talk about that when I come see ya. I haven't seen the team in action for weeks and, as every sensible person knows, time away from the lab is . . . what is it, Jen?'

Jennifer unmuted herself.

'Time away from the lab is wasted time, Clive.'

'Dead on. Was there anything else, Marth?'

Jennifer watched the woman glance beyond the screen and towards – she guessed – her fellow scientists.

'Yes, we need to talk about funding, basic supplies here are—'

'Hold up, Martha. Fuck me dead! Were you not listening?' Tobi's face flushed red. 'I told you we'd do the money stuff at the end.' She glanced up at her unseen colleagues and then down towards the floor. 'Make a list of what you need, and you'll get it. No worries. Okay . . . what next? Let's do the geoengineering. Who's got good news?'

Winner got updates from his carbon capture project in Iceland, then from a team of Oxford-based researchers who were looking at ways of placing reflective sun-shields in space. After that he jumped across the Atlantic to a New Mexico-based project examining whether enormous propeller-driven balloons could be used to carry a calcium carbonate mix into the stratosphere and distribute it there. The moustachioed man leading the team had concerns.

'Our modelling has it working half the time. But if it doesn't work – or rather if it works too well – then we shut down the Indian monsoon system.'

Winner nodded. 'That's not ideal. I'm going to come and visit and take a look at the balloons and go over the numbers in the next week or two.'

Jennifer made a note; that made four projects in four different countries that Winner had promised to visit in the next week or so.

'What's next? Let's do renewables. We need to pick up the pace.'

The German team working on wind and wave power gave Winner their summary.

'Sounds good. Better than last time. And you're sure these numbers aren't shonky?'

The German team were sure.

'Okay. What's next?'

Next was solar.

'Those are good numbers too. Where next?'

The only place left to go was Spain and Winner's cloud-altering projects. Jennifer was interested to see how her boss would play this. The Spanish team leader, a handsome Andalusian who for some reason Clive had nicknamed 'Señor Cerebrito' was there on the screen, waiting patiently.

'Oh yeah, of course, Señor . . . Romero. What you got for us?' A look of confusion clouded the man's face.

'Well, as you know, we are closed down at this time because of the . . . accident.'

'Sure . . .' Winner glanced down at his notes. '. . . but regardless of that we haven't had a decent result from these trials of yours for a while now, have we?'

'Er . . . not a definitive breakthrough, no.'

'Thought not. And we're nowhere near the proof of concept you promised me way back when.'

'Not yet, no.'

Winner shrugged. 'I reckon that project rain in Spain went down with that fucken' plane.' He was smiling.

The Spanish scientist shifted uncomfortably in his seat.

'A young woman is missing, Mr Winner.'

'I know that. You think I don't fucken' know that?'

Winner was about to speak again when Jennifer unmuted herself and jumped in.

'We're all absolutely devastated about the accident, Mr Romero, and all our thoughts are with you and the team. I'm in touch with Alma's family, but as you know we've asked everyone to maintain a respectful silence until we learn more.' The man nodded. 'I know Mr Winner won't be making any hasty decisions about the project's future until we have all the facts.'

'Thank you, Miss Prepas.' Romero gave a dignified bow of the head.

Winner reappeared, nodding, and seemed temporarily subdued. 'What she said.' He scratched at his stubbled chin. 'But while we're waiting and being respectfully silent and all of that I'd like you to collect all the cloud data together and send it across to Edith Walston. If anyone can make a silk purse from that sow's ear you've got there, then it's her.'

'She will say that it is incomplete.'

'Don't try to second-guess Prof Walston. Just send it and we'll see.' He glanced at the clock. The hour had come and gone. 'We're outta time, people. I'm afraid we'll have to have the money chat offline . . .' Jennifer saw the looks of frustration and exasperation on the faces of the assembled scientists, and Winner clearly noticed too. '. . . there's no need for anyone to go spitting the dummy.

We've got the money. Just send me and Tony a list of what you need and when and we'll sort it. You've got my word.'

The meeting over, Jennifer threw some snacks and her son's waterproof jacket into a bag. She was halfway down the hall when she felt one of her two mobile phones vibrating inside her pocket. It was the wrong phone – the one she couldn't ignore. She checked the message.

Jen . . . do us a favour and join Mr Money and me for a quick post-match, will ya. There was no question mark. It wasn't a question.

Now?

Sure.

Mr Money's real name was Tony Yeoh – a Malaysian-born, Melbourne-based accountant who according to Winner cooked the books for every 'gold standard greedy billionaire bastard you can think of'. Clive had made it clear to Jennifer that he considered Yeoh more a necessary evil than a key member of the team. So logging back into the laptop it was a surprise to see the two men sitting alongside each other in Winner's plush apartment. Tony was an unattractive man, both in the flesh and on a computer screen. Sitting there, rotating to and fro in an ergonomic chair, his girth was more than sufficient to block out the Opera House and most of the rest of Sydney too. When Winner greeted Jennifer, Tony leant forward in the chair and gave her a wet smile.

'Always a pleasure, Miss Prepas.'

'Good to see you, Tony.'

Jennifer was reminded of the Australian cane toads that Clive and his team had been trying to detoxify. They'd have their work cut out with this man.

Winner cleared his throat.

'I'll make this quick, Tony's pilot wants to fly him out of Sydney before this megafire turns into a gigafire or whatever it is that's bigger than that.'

Jennifer nodded. She wasn't in love with her job right now, but at least she didn't have to fly Tony Yeoh around the world in his private jet, with who knew what going on in the back; that had to be a contender for the worst job in the world. She checked the time. The second half of her son's football match would have started by now. At least her ex-husband was there. That was something.

'A quick meeting suits me.'

'Good, first off, I wanted to thank you for jumping in between me and Señor Romero back there.'

'No problem.'

'I was about to lose my temper and sack the fucker.'

'I think he's just upset about the accident.'

'Yeah? I think he's just a little prick trying to show how hairy-chested he is in front of his team. And in front of mine.'

'Well—'

'I've never been Romero's biggest fan – a little too up himself for my liking. More importantly, he told me we'd have proof of concept on that cloud-brightening project within a year. He's had twice that and so far he's delivered proof of fuck all.'

Tony Yeoh laughed, open-mouthed, his huge shoulders rising and falling. It appeared to Jennifer like his head was being slowly but steadily eaten by his neck. Winner ignored him. 'It's Spain I wanna talk to you both about.' He paused. 'I need to know what you reckon the compo's going to cost us, Jen.'

'The what?'

'The compensation. I'm sure it's crossed your mind; I hope it has anyway. What are we going to have to pay her family?'

'Alma Galinda's family?'

'Yes.'

'Assuming that she is dead?'

'Yeah. It's been a week, the Spanish police and coastguard have found nothing. I think we have to assume that she's dead.' Another pause. 'Tragically.'

Jennifer let the word tragically hang in the air for a moment before answering.

'It's going to cost a lot.'

The words 'as it should' were in her mind but she didn't say them. She'd had her team look at industrial accidents in Spain going back five years – in particular any cases involving fatalities and life-changing injuries. Not the same as the case they were dealing with here, but similar enough. 'I'd say we're talking somewhere in the region of six or seven hundred thousand.'

'Dollars?'

'Euros. If it had happened here in the States, then it would be ten or twenty times that.'

'Sure, and also we're insured against this sort of shit.' He turned to face his accountant. 'Over to you then, Tony. Did you finish going through that policy my secretary sent across? The most recent one?' Jennifer saw the photo-booth-sized version of herself on the screen frown. Most recent, what did that mean?

'Yup, I've got it here.' Tony tapped a fat knuckle on the pile of papers in front of him. 'I've had the fine-tooth comb out. Been right through it.'

'So, what's the payout likely to be?'

'The insurers might try and push back a bit . . . the ink's not long dry on this and obviously they won't like that.'

'They'll fight it?'

'I'm sure. But this insurance covered the entire Andalusian project, reputational damage as well as loss of life. More to the point, they've got a bunch of tenderfoot wankers and . . .' Yeoh flashed another smile. '. . . well, you've got me. So sooner or later, they'll pay and I reckon it'll be somewhere between nine and ten million dollars. American, not Australian.'

Clive absorbed this.

'Okay, so if both of you are right then we're looking at a pretty significant . . . er . . .'

Jennifer saw her boss reaching for the right word. Or for Mr Money to say it. When it was clear that they wouldn't, she did.

'Profit.'

18

OLD SANCTI PETRI, ANDALUSIA, SPAIN

Loli had spent the morning walking in and out of every café and bar in Barrosa; it was almost noon before she found Carlos. His beaten-up old motorbike was propped against the wall outside La Ola – a bar in Old Sancti Petri, close to the port and frequented almost entirely by local fishermen. The terms of La Ola's licence seemed to reflect the irregular working hours of customers, either that or the police simply turned a blind eye. The local cops certainly wouldn't be interested and even the Guardia Civil might think twice before trying to shut down the fishermen's favourite drinking spot. Walking in, Loli felt a catch in her throat; she coughed and almost turned and walked back out again. The place stank – old booze, dead fish and male sweat plus a few other smells she didn't want to think about. She already regretted promising Alma's mum that she'd track Carlos down. She wondered whether she'd have time to go home and change between doing this and starting work.

La Ola was a bar for serious drinkers, dingy and dark. A gold-flecked mirror ran the length of the room, doubling the already impressive range of spirits the place had to offer. The bottles were arranged by group: a dozen different rums, the same number of vodka brands and gin and tequila and then maybe three dozen different whiskies – the local fishermen's favourite and so the bar's speciality. Loli weaved her way between the small round tables, sticky to the touch, arriving at the back of the bar where five men were sitting around some pushed-together tables, next to a wall-mounted cigarette machine and close to the toilet. Here came another smell that Loli could have done without. The table was a mess of shot glasses, espresso cups and half-eaten plates of food. Carlos had seen Loli walk in and was making himself busy, spreading fatty-looking pâté onto a torn-off chunk of bread. While he did this, the other men checked Loli out. One stood and offered her his chair.

'I'm not staying. Carlos . . . I need to talk to you.'

'I'm busy.'

'Busy doing what?'

'We're putting something together. A fresh search.'

'I see. A fresh search.'

'Yeah. The boys here have been telling me about an Indonesian guy, a fisherman, he survived in the water for fifty-four days.' Loli shot the men at the table a look. 'Alma's only been gone a week. You see? So, this *hombre* here . . .' He squeezed the shoulder of the reprobate sitting next to him. '. . . he's going to take me out on his boat later. I'll work for six hours and then he'll give me an hour at the end. I've got an idea where to look. I've been studying the tide tables.'

Loli stared at him. Her look a mix of disbelief and despair.

'The tide tables? You're a barman, not a fisherman. When Alma took you on that boat trip for your birthday, you were back within the hour. You chucked your guts up.'

'That's not true . . .' He looked at his new friends and shook his head. 'It wasn't like that.' He pushed his plate away and looked up at Loli. 'Why don't we talk outside.'

'Good idea.'

Outside the bar they stood alongside Carlos' motorbike. He idly kicked at the machine's tyres while Loli took several welcome breaths of fresh air.

'Do you know how far these guys go out to find the tuna and the other fish they catch?'

'Course I do. That's the point. We need to go further. The search and rescue – it didn't look hard enough.'

'It wasn't just search and rescue, Carlos, you know that. The navy patrol and the police helicopters were out there too – for hours and hours over several days. They told Alma's mum that there was an army spotter plane up there too . . . everyone has been looking.'

'Not for long enough and not in the right places. She was flying up and down the beach, we know that. Then she headed west.' He pointed out towards the horizon. 'What if she headed south after that? Towards Morocco or further down the African coast.'

'Why would she do that?'

'There could be any number of reasons. She had engine trouble and Morocco was within reach. Or perhaps she came across one of those migrant boats and they were in trouble . . . one of those overloaded dinghies and she tried to help. You know what Alma's like, she's . . .' He stopped and turned away. 'Absolutely anything could have happened.'

Loli put her hand on his arm. 'Alma's mother needs to see you.'

'I've seen her.'

'You saw her across a roomful of other people, she said you only stayed five minutes and you didn't even speak to her. She wants to see you properly. To talk to you.'

He gave the motorbike's back tyre another pointless kick.

'I can't. Not yet.' Carlos looked away.

'Why?'

'I don't want to go and sit around being sad with Alma's mother, Loli. I don't want to be consoled.'

'You could go and console her.'

He turned back to face her, his eyes glistening.

'No, no! Everyone else might've given up on Alma, given up trying to find her or finding out what happened . . . but I haven't.'

19

NEW BROADCASTING HOUSE, PORTLAND PLACE, LONDON

Carver reread Naz's message – *LMK when you're there*. What the hell did that mean? He looked around the room, it was fish-and-chip day in the BBC canteen and the smell of vinegar and chips was overwhelming. It was making him hungry. If Naz didn't show up soon, he'd be forced to have a second lunch. He messaged her back – *I'm in the canteen. Waiting*.

The huge flat-screen TV on the wall close to where he was sitting was showing something odd. It was a live broadcast from Westminster Bridge where a couple of dozen protestors dressed in grim reaper costumes had handcuffed themselves, first to each other and then to either side of the bridge, blocking traffic. BBC news bosses had decided, in their wisdom, to send a helicopter up to cover this and Carver watched for a while. Not very much happened. A number of policemen were on the scene, milling around trying to work out what to do. That was about it. To be fair, this wasn't the most pointless use of the so-called news copter that Carver had seen. There'd been worse. Someone had told him that the BBC had paid the helicopter company a large sum of money in return for a certain number of flights per year. It had turned out that not that many stories needed a helicopter but in order to keep the price per flight down the bosses were always looking for reasons to use it. Hence the bird's-eye views of the prime minister's car travelling from Downing Street to the House of Commons every Wednesday – as though viewers might learn something by looking at the roof of a Rover travelling a quarter of a mile.

'Hey there, Mr . . .' She stopped herself. '. . . William.' He had told Naz to ditch the Mr Carver thing and call him by his Christian name, but it still didn't feel quite right. What's more Carver always appeared a little put out when she used his first name.

'Er . . . hi. How're you?'

'All good thanks. Excited to know what this is all about.'

'Yes, okay. So I've decided it might be time to push you out of the nest.'

'Eh?'

'I'll explain, but before I do, I need to know where you are with your National Certificate work. Are you on top of it all, completely up to speed?'

'Absolutely. I've got two pieces of course work due in soonish but it's under control.'

'How soon is soonish?'

'Tomorrow.'

'And you're doing a programme shift today.'

'Only a short one. I can do *this* too. Whatever *this* is.' Naz knew she wouldn't have been Carver's first choice to help, but she didn't care.

'It's a story . . . it could be a good one. But I need someone smart and with a good news head on her to get across it and put in some calls.'

'I'm your woman.'

'Have you got your notebook?'

Naz pulled a rolled-up reporter's notepad and pen from her track-suit pocket and held them up for Carver to see.

'Fine.' He talked her through his rendezvous with Leonard Allen at the London Eye. 'The information this contact has provided in the past has been reliable. Rare but reliable. So, the source is good, which . . .'

'. . . is absolutely crucial.'

'That's right.'

Naz took notes in her own home-made shorthand – it was effective enough but also a painful reminder that she needed to practise her Teeline. It was one of several weak points that urgently needed addressing if she was going to pass the National Certificate exams. She reread her scribbled notes, making sure they contained the cues she needed to write a fuller version of what Carver was telling her once he'd gone: *Clive Winner – green genius – PM's ear – desk in Downing Street – dodgy friends.*

'I know you know a lot more about this stuff than I do, but is it really that unusual for business blokes – billionaires and all that – to have this sort of access?'

'Access isn't unusual. But this sort of arrangement is.'

'Okay. But I guess it's only really an issue if your man Clive Winner is dodgy.'

Carver shook his head.

'No, there are principles involved – accountability, democracy – old-fashioned stuff like that.' He paused. 'But you're right – it's a bigger deal, a bigger story, if Clive Winner is a bad 'un.'

'And we think he is?'

'We don't know yet. I've only read what others think. He doesn't do many interviews – almost none in fact. He divides opinion, depending on who you read. He's either Doctor Moreau or he's the Second Coming of Jesus Christ. That's one of the first things we have to work out.'

'Who's Doctor Moreau?'

'Google it.' He watched as Naz got her phone out and did exactly that. 'You can check that one on your phone but I'd prefer it if you did the rest of the research on a public computer.'

Naz nodded.

'Sure, I remember. There's half-a-dozen different internet cafés on the same street as my parents' place. I'll go to the busiest one I can find. I'll not talk to anyone and pay in cash and all of that too.'

'Okay, fine.' Naz's excitement was palpable. Her eyes shone.

'So, this is like a genuinely deep-cover, secretive investigation we're doing here, isn't it?'

Carver shrugged.

'We don't know what it is yet. But it's good to do things properly. For now, we're just doing a bit of digging, seeing what we find.'

'Okay.' Naz's phone vibrated in her hand, she checked the screen. 'One of those climate change protestors has just thrown herself off Westminister Bridge.'

Carver looked across at the flat-screen TV and the live news feed. There was no sign of this having happened.

'How do you know?'

'Twitter.' Naz looked over at the screen. 'They always get stuff before the BBC.'

'Right. But remember . . . it's better to be *right* than to be *first*. While you're having a look at Winner I'm going to try to clear the decks a little. I'll write up some of these other stories I've got on the go as online pieces and put some of the longer-term stuff on the backburner. Let's catch up in a couple of days, see how we're doing.'

20

PENTHOUSE SUITE, THE EPIC, SYDNEY HARBOUR, AUSTRALIA

Clive stood at the window and stared out. It appeared as though someone had taken a giant rubber and was slowly erasing the Sydney skyline. He turned to face Tony Yeoh.

'This smoke's getting thicker, mate. You'd best get a move on. Your pilot won't fly if it gets much worse.'

'He'll do what he's told. Pity about this bloody fire though, I'd have liked to have hung around for a little while, we could've gone for a gargle.'

'Yeah. Shame.'

Winner hoped this sounded more convincing than it felt. He watched as Tony pushed himself, with difficulty, out of the office chair and shuffled over to the long white sofa. He fell back into it with all the grace of a three-hundred-pound bag of potatoes. The springs of the sofa complained under his weight.

'I'll bugger off shortly, but I did want a quick word. Mano a mano.'

'Go ahead.'

'You understand that this insurance payout – good as it is – won't buy you a lot of time, old son. You should know that. A few months if you're lucky.'

Clive put his hand to the back of his neck and tried to massage away the dull pain that had been troubling him for days.

'I know it doesn't fix the problem, but it'll pay some of these red bills that've been piling up.'

'True.'

'And I reckon it could help persuade the banks to bear with us. Maybe even lend us a little more?'

His accountant shook his head. 'No way they're lending more. But they might extend.'

'That's all I need – a bit more time. In the medium term, it's all fine. Several of these projects are starting to come good. You heard what Martha said about the work we're doing with DNA . . .' Winner was pacing up and down the room, talking as he walked, running Tony Yeoh through all the exciting stuff happening in his beloved Melbourne lab; climate-friendly cows, disease-resistant trees, the latest coral reef work. When he'd finished going through the list he looked back at his accountant.

Tony Yeoh was checking his phone.

'Sorry, mate. Just staying on top of this flight. Plane's on the apron.'

'No worries.'

'I'm gonna level with you, Clive. The DNA stuff . . . The genetic rescue and all of that, it was only ever supposed to be the icing on the cake – a way for your fragrant Miss Prepas to win you some nice little headlines. Right now, it looks to me like that's the only thing that's working. In other words, old son – you're all icing and no cake.'

'There's the renewables work. You were in the meeting; those numbers are even better this month than last.'

'Yeah, and that's fine as far as it goes. But you're forgetting your USP, mate.'

'Go on then. What's my USP?'

Tony Yeoh pushed himself out of the sofa and onto his feet and met Winner's eye.

'You're Mr Miracle . . . you're the guy who saved the Barrier Reef, the guy who said that climate change was just an engineering problem. And that you were the bloke to fix it.'

'Yeah, well . . .'

'It's the geoengineering stuff that people want to hear about. That's what they want to invest in. Carbon capture, sun-reflecting mirrors, chemical shields in the stratosphere, magic fucken' clouds . . . that's the stuff that has them licking their lips and opening their wallets. So . . .' Tony retrieved his briefcase from Winner's desk. '. . . give the people what they want.'

'Which people are we talking about here, Tony?'

His accountant frowned.

'Don't play the wet-behind-the-ears wanker, Clive, the part doesn't suit you. You know which people.'

PART TWO

ALTOCUMULUS

altum – height
cumulus – heap

Altocumulus clouds are mid-level layers of clouds formed by the break-up of altostratus or as a result of turbulence. They take various forms, most notably altocumulus castellanus, a tower of cloud – taller than it is wide – and are a reliable indicator of instability.

21

CAMP KARLSEN, THE NORTH GREENLAND ICE CORE PROJECT, GREENLAND

Carla pulled the top of her T-shirt up to nose-level and took a sniff. Not good. She tried to remember the last time she'd washed – not just a soapy flannel to the armpits and other bits, but a proper hot shower and a clean change of clothes. She couldn't. A week ago? Maybe two. The shower block was on the other side of the research station – a twenty-minute walk in sub-zero temperatures from her bunk room and the drill site where she spent between twelve and sixteen hours a day. She hadn't had a lot of spare time this past week and she certainly didn't have a single hour to spare today. The man her sponsors were sending to see her would have to put up with it. He hadn't visited Camp Karlsen before, so the chances were he'd be too busy being amazed by the place and staring at snowflakes dating back to the time of Plato to worry about a little body odour. Carla put on a couple more layers of clothes followed by her purple snow jacket, matching ski pants, two pairs of thick woollen socks and the Adidas sliders that her brother had sent her for her birthday.

The email from the company had asked her to meet their

representative off the Herc and give him the tour. That was all it said – no comment at all about the draft report she'd sent through, no comment on her findings or when and where they might want to publish them. That's if they wanted to publish them at all. Carla had given this a lot of thought. They'd paid for the report; paid for her to do the work she'd been doing for the last two years. Technically speaking the report and her findings belonged to them. Therefore, she knew that if they wanted to then they could just bury the whole thing – take it and put it in the dustiest filing cabinet in the darkest room they could find. They had the right to do that. A *moral and legal* right according to her little brother who was busy acing every exam that the Copenhagen University School of Law could throw at him. But Carla had a plan B; the company owned the report, but they didn't own her. She would take what she'd learned and build on it, find another sponsor, do some more research, and write a second paper . . . she'd publish it herself if she had to.

The Hercules landed half an hour ahead of schedule – a rare occurrence – and so when she arrived at the airstrip the company rep was waiting close to the plane. He wore dark-blue ski pants and jacket, Ray-Bans and had a small rucksack on his back. Carla had expected a more officey-looking individual. This man didn't look like that.

'Carla Jensen?'

She nodded.

'I'm Collins.' He looked at his watch – somewhat theatrically in Carla's opinion. 'I thought you scientist types prided yourselves on accuracy. Reliability?'

Carla shrugged.

'I'm here right on time. Your plane arrived early. Do you want me to apologise for that?'

'You clearly don't intend to, and I don't care much whether you do or don't. How about we just go?'

'Fine.' Carla noted that the man's Midlands accent grew more pronounced when he was riled.

They had got off on the wrong foot and for most of the time they stayed there. On the walk from the airstrip to the camp, Collins took in his surroundings. Huge expanses of white, flat ice – the same in every direction and for as far as the eye could see.

'Must get depressing, being surrounded by all this nothing.'

Carla shook her head.

'I think it's beautiful. More than beautiful . . . sublime.'

'Each to their own I guess.' He gave Carla a questioning look. A look she ignored. She had resolved to stop trying to please or placate grumpy, middle-aged men several years ago. They were within sight of the camp now – a dozen bright-red tents arranged around a large dome-shaped structure. Collins pointed at the dome. 'I'd like to eat before we do anything else, I'm starving.'

'Okay.'

Relations deteriorated further over food. They had the camp canteen to themselves, which felt awkward, and once inside Collins removed his Ray-Bans and gave Carla what felt like a challenging look; daring her to comment. She took the dare.

'My brother was born with a squint like that. He had it corrected.'

'Right. Bully for him.'

'I suppose ophthalmology probably wasn't as advanced when you were at an age when they can realign the eye.'

'I suppose so.'

'I'm sorry. I didn't mean to offend you.'

'You haven't. I'm thick-skinned as well as boss-eyed.' Carla watched as Collins worked his way through a heaped plate of scrambled eggs and heavily buttered white bread. Once finished he wiped his mouth with his sleeve and stared across at her. 'Shall we start with the tour? You remember that your sponsors asked you to show me around, do you?'

'Of course.' She was really beginning to dislike this man. The tour of the research station that Carla gave him was cursory. '. . . Camp

Karlsen sits on top of two miles of solid ice . . . it's one of the most remote scientific stations in the world . . . we have fourteen scientists working here right now and five support staff – caretakers, cooks . . .'

'A bartender?'

Carla shook her head. 'Drinking is discouraged. You wouldn't think it, given the amount of snow around here, but dehydration is a real issue.'

'If I lived here, I'd need a drink.'

'There's a bar in Kangerlussuaq.'

'Where's that?'

'About five hundred miles in . . .' Carla looked around to get her bearings and then pointed. '. . . that direction. Perhaps we should skip the sightseeing and go straight to the drilling room.'

'Suits me.'

'After that, maybe we can talk about the report that I sent through.'

'Sure.'

The drilling room was the centrepiece and main purpose of Camp Karlsen. To reach it you had to walk down an eighty-foot-long tunnel that had been constructed with chainsaws and ice picks. Before they entered, Carla explained that the tunnel was a fragile thing, the ice encroached on every side and from above, and thick beams of wood were used to reinforce the roof. It was a losing battle. Every now and then one of the thick pine beams would shatter or splinter under the weight of the snow and ice. She warned Collins not to touch anything and to be especially careful to avoid the wooden beams. This was easier said than done, the icy walled tunnel was barely six feet in height and poorly lit. Collins took his time, following Carla, but keeping some distance and walking with deliberate strides – as though he was measuring the tunnel's length. Eventually the tunnel opened out into a larger central chamber kitted out like a laboratory but with a huge, silvery drill at its centre. A couple of geeky-looking glaciologists were sitting either side of the drill, crouched over their laptops and tapping away. Collins noticed that their computers were sitting on heat pads designed to stop the machines seizing up in the cold.

'It's bloody freezing. How long do you lot spend in here at any one time?'

Carla answered: 'For as long as it takes. You get used to the cold.' The other two scientists looked at Carla with what appeared to be a mix of admiration and disbelief.

A kid in black-rimmed glasses spoke.

'Carla stays down here for longer than anyone else. She is like one of those fish that they found living at the bottom of the Mariana Trench – oblivious to dark or cold.'

'Is that right?' Collins said and smiled. 'So, which of you two wants to tell me about this work you're doing then?' It was clear that he would rather hear from one of the junior glaciologists than from Carla herself. They glanced at her again and she nodded, giving them permission to speak. Together the two explained how the twelve-foot-long core drill was slowly lowered down through the borehole – first hundreds, then thousands of feet. Once they reached the desired depth the drill was switched on via remote control and it started to turn. The silvery drill bit was allowed to spin until its centre had filled with compacted ice; the team then brought the huge drill back to the surface and studied what had been collected. The bespectacled scientist led Collins over to a glass-fronted cold storage cabinet.

'The deeper you drill, the further back in time you are travelling; one hundred and forty feet and the snow you're studying dates to the American Civil War, at two thousand five hundred feet you're seeing snow that Plato might have seen floating overhead in cloud form.'

Carla interrupted. 'That is incredibly unlikely and not very scientific.'

'Sorry, I've been working on new ways to explain it to non-experts.'

Collins laughed. 'I get the point. And these . . .' He pointed at the rows of icy cylinders on display inside the cabinet. '. . . are your samples.'

The kid nodded. 'In this sample you can see volcanic ash from Krakatoa . . . here, lead pollution from the Roman smelters. If you know how to read the samples then these are a history of the world – earth and sky. And Carla . . . Miss Jensen . . . really knows how to read them.'

'I'm sure. But it's not just a matter of reading the ice, is it? You have to work out exactly what it is telling us.'

Carla joined the two men. 'Of course. And I have, if you'd read my report . . .'

'I *have* read the report; several people have read the report. What's more, they've compared it with the original proposal that you sent them. The one that persuaded them to give you all the money they gave you. It's not a happy comparison.' Collins jutted his chin in the direction of Carla's colleagues. 'Perhaps these chaps here should take a break and we can talk?'

Once Carla's colleagues had gone – the sound of their footsteps and nervous whispered voices disappearing as they walked down the icy corridor – Collins took one of their seats. He flipped the laptop that the glaciologist had been working on back open.

'Lots of data in the report you sent back . . . impressive stuff.'

'Glad you noticed.'

'Whole new perspectives on the ice age, Greenland's temperature shooting up and down by fifteen degrees in a decade, really crazy swings. Not just here but in other places too – Italy, China.'

'Yes. And after that, ten thousand years of stability.'

'What do you call that again? What's that section title in your report?'

'The tranquillity that made civilisation a possibility.'

'Good stuff. Very good stuff.' Collins stood and wandered around the lab. 'It's only when you get to the conclusion that you really balls everything up.'

Carla laughed. 'What don't you like about the conclusion?'

'Don't play dumb, it doesn't suit you. The pitch you made, the proposal that got you this gig and the financial backing – remember that?'

Carla remembered it well, looking back it was a source of some embarrassment to her. 'I thought that given the history of climatic instability – the rapid warmings and sudden freezes – then perhaps a case could be made that climate change might help ward off the next big freeze.'

'That's right. So, what happened?'

'I was wrong; completely wrong. I can explain . . .' Carla talked Collins through her change of mind. It all boiled down to the fact that once you worked out that the climate was inherently unstable – the last thing you should do is mess about with it. 'I know that's not what you, or rather the people we both work for, want to hear, but it's the truth.'

'The truth? Okay. So, here's another truth. You need to rework your report. Keep all the excellent research, keep all the instability stuff, just change the conclusion.'

'I can't.'

Collins smiled. 'Of course you can. And you should.'

Carla shook her head. 'This report is more important than me getting more funding or my next career move.'

Collins laughed. 'I'm not talking about your career, Carla.' He shook his head. 'You know what never ceases to amaze me in this job? It's how *pig-shit thick* people can be. Clever people like you.' Collins glanced around the room. 'I'm going to stretch my legs, give you some time to think things over – an hour or three. Where'll you be?'

'I'll be here.'

Collins walked the perimeter of the camp; the sky and snow were a blinding white. After a while he started to understand what Carla Jensen and others might see in this place. What was the word she'd used? Sublime. He wasn't sure he'd go that far but there was certainly a special quality to it – a peacefulness. Shame it was all going to melt to fuck and drown the world while it was at it. Still, that would be long after Collins was gone. Seize the day – that was his motto.

On the walk back he saw no one. It was getting late now, and he guessed most of the other scientists were either at dinner or enjoying some R&R. The place felt deserted. At the entrance to the tunnel there was a toolbox, inside it a range of chainsaws and ice picks. He took one of the ice picks. Inside the underground laboratory Carla Jensen was examining an ice sample, peering at it through an electron microscope. She was aware that Collins had returned but she didn't look up.

'You made up your mind, Carla?'

'Yes. I won't rewrite the report. Not one word.'

'That's a shame.'

'The company can do what they like with it – bin it or bury it or whatever. They paid for it. I won't put up any fuss.'

Collins smiled. 'No, you'll move on to that Plan B of yours.'

Carla glanced up from the microscope. She looked first at him and then at the ice pick he was holding at his side.

'What the hell are you doing? Get out.' She reached for her mobile phone but Collins was faster than seemed possible for a man of his height and weight. He strode across the floor and grabbed the phone from her hand.

'You cross-eyed goon. You're going to lose your job for this.'

Collins laughed. 'This is my job.' He delivered a back-handed slap to the side of Carla's face, knocking her from her seat and onto the floor.

'The ice pick wasn't meant for you, but it can be. You're coming with me.' He grabbed the back of her ski jacket and pulled her kicking and screaming towards the tunnel. When her screaming started to grow louder, Collins hit her again. 'What did you think was going to happen when you sent that report through? Did you think the people you work for would just accept it?' He glanced down.

'I can rewrite the report.' They were a few feet inside the tunnel now. Collins tightened his grip and dragged her more quickly.

'Too late for that.'

'Where are you taking me, you ugly fucker?'

Collins stopped. 'Here'll do.'

They were halfway down the tunnel. He let go of Carla's coat and hit her again, sending her sprawling. 'I wasn't going to tell you, but now I think I will. After I'm done here. After they dig you out and everyone's finished saying how sad it is, what a tragedy and a waste and all of that bollocks . . . after that, they'll put me on a plane to Denmark to go and kill your little brother too. Because they know you sent him the report as well.'

Carla opened her mouth to yell but Collins was too fast. The punch to the side of her head had a concussive power. Once he'd knocked her out he positioned her directly underneath one of the thick pine beams. He used the ice pick to chip away at the ice at either end of the beam; first the beam directly above Carla and then – one by one – all the other beams between there and the tunnel entrance. Outside it was dark and the temperature was dropping. He could hear the ice inside the tunnel moving, contracting. And soon after that, another sound – the sound of wood beginning to split and splinter.

22

SERGIO'S CAFÉ, GREAT TITCHFIELD STREET, LONDON

Outside the fogged-up café window, the rain was turning into snow. Carver shook his head.

'What's with this weather? It's bloody September. Not December.' He pulled his shirt cuff down over his hand and wiped a porthole-sized circle in the condensation. He peered out onto Great Titchfield Street. He didn't know if Naz had been to Sergio's before. Not many BBC types seemed to come here any more, preferring the newer, slightly more upmarket eateries nearby. Still, the café was a local landmark, and its bright shop front, painted in the colours of the Italian flag, was hard to miss even in the rain and the snow. Most likely the post-programme meeting had overrun. Carver had a full English breakfast in front of him and a plate of warm buttered toast on the side. He liked to keep the toast until he'd eaten everything other than the scrambled eggs and beans. He stared at his food. There was no point waiting, it'd only get cold. He was enjoying a mouthful of black pudding, bacon, and sharp English mustard when Naz arrived, shouldering her way through the café door holding her rucksack over her head as an umbrella. An icy blast of wind followed her in, and Sergio hurried from behind the counter to push the door shut. She thanked him and they exchanged a few words; it seemed like she had been here before. Carver watched her shake the sleety snow from her bag before plonking herself down in the seat opposite.

'Hey there . . . William.'

She looked tired.

'Hello. Are you all right? A tough night shift, huh?'

'Insane. We ended up throwing most of the programme out and remaking it from scratch when the news broke.'

'Yeah, that can happen. Who was it that resigned? Environment secretary, was it?'

'Yep. That's the department's top minister and their most senior civil servant gone in the space of a week.'

'Interesting. Maybe she jumped before she was pushed; ahead of this reshuffle?'

'Could be. None of the main players are talking, not on live radio to seven million people anyway.'

'I can understand why that might not appeal. You want a cup of tea? Some grub?'

Naz shook her head.

'D'you mind if I just run through what I've found so far . . .' She pulled a bundle of notes from deep inside her rucksack. '. . . then head home to bed? I'm knackered.'

'Course . . .' Carver glanced around the café. An old fellow in the corner had fallen asleep reading his copy of the *Sun*. Glasses on but eyes closed. A young couple at another table were much too tied up in each other to be paying any attention to anyone else. '. . . go ahead.'

'I ended up spending hours in the internet café. I moved to another one down the road actually, cos I thought it might look suspicious that I was staying there so long.' She glanced across at Carver.

'Good thinking. So what did you find?'

Naz went through her notes as clearly and concisely as she could manage in her sleep-deprived state. She turned the photocopied articles and sheets of scribbled-on A4 face down after she'd been through each one, anxious that Carver didn't get too good a view of her embarrassing shorthand.

'In a nutshell it looks like we . . . or rather you . . .'

'It's we . . . we're working on this together now.'

'Okay.' She smiled. 'We seem to be the only people outside Whitehall who know about Winner's Downing Street office, his adviser title or any of that. No newspaper or agency or website I've found has even a mention of it.'

'That's good . . .' William had finished the meatier main part of his breakfast and was spooning the beans and scrambled egg onto his toast. '. . . but it won't stay that way for long, not if the senior civil servants are unhappy. That place can get leaky quickly when it wants to. We need to make sure we stay ahead of the pack; have you tried Winner's email address and phone number yet?'

Naz nodded. 'I also called the regular Downing Street press office and asked them to clarify exactly what his role was.'

'Any response?'

'They said they'd get back to me about my specific question, but they sent a holding statement in the meantime – you want to hear it?'

'Sure.'

'Mr Winner is an internationally respected scientist and entrepreneur. He and his team are at the forefront of numerous cutting-edge green technologies. He is a valuable ally in the prime minister's mission to—'

'Don't tell me . . . save the world from catastrophic climate change.'

'That's it.'

'What about that phone number? The one on his business card?'

'I tried it a few times, no one ever picks up; it clicks through to a message with some stiff-sounding American lady asking you to leave a message. I did that yesterday.'

'Saying what?'

Naz read the verbatim note of the message she'd left; it was simple and straightforward. Faultless in fact.

'Whose phone number did you leave?'

'I left my Auntie Meena's number.'

'What?'

Naz stared at Carver.

'I left my number. Who else's number would I leave?'

'Fine.' He paused. It was more than fine, she'd done well. He made a mental note to tell her as much before she headed home. 'We need to work out what's going on here. Why the special treatment? Why give Winner the Downing Street desk and the adviser title? What's in it for them?'

Naz could feel her tiredness beginning to lift, replaced by a feeling of excitement.

'He makes them look good. He's a bit of a rock star this guy – in that whole weird green science world I mean.'

'I guess that's true. Every prime minster for the last sixty years has wanted to be Mr or Mrs White Heat of Technology. So, the PM gets to be interviewed sitting next to your fellow – the rock star – and talk about green solutions and science parks, things like that.'

'And he's always been well keen on this stuff, right back to when he was in opposition. I was reading about that trip he took to the Arctic – riding sledges, cuddling huskies.'

'Oh yeah, that whole husky-hugging episode. I'd forgotten about that.'

Carver was drawing circles on the waxed cotton tablecloth with his teaspoon. 'But I'm not sure that any of this is enough to risk annoying your top civil servants and every other inventor or entrepreneur in the country. Let's park that one . . .' He put the teaspoon down. '. . . perhaps it's the second half of this question that's more interesting. How does Winner benefit from this arrangement?'

They were interrupted by the rap of a knuckle on the café window. It was the *Today* programme editor, Naomi, dressed for the inclement weather in a gabardine raincoat and holding a thin, bamboo-handled umbrella. She smiled and gestured towards the café entrance, indicating that she was coming to join them.

Carver sighed. 'What the hell does she want?'

Inside the café Naomi swapped a few words with Sergio before walking over to join them. She unbuttoned her coat, shook her umbrella dry and smiled at the pair.

'I thought it was you two . . . the archetypal odd couple.'

'Hey there, boss.'

'Hello.'

Naz got the strong impression that Naomi was waiting for William to ask her to join them. The invitation did not arrive. Naomi looked at Naz. 'Good work from you overnight, Naz. Again. Both that last-minute editing and the briefing work you did. It was like having an extra producer on board . . . a good one.'

'Thank you.'

There was an awkward silence.

'So . . . what were you two talking about in such a serious-looking manner just then?'

Glancing down, Naz saw that Carver had somehow managed to remove her notes from the table and stow them somewhere. He picked up his mug of tea and took a noisy slurp before answering.

'We were just going over the journalistic definitions of slander and defamation. Naz has a couple of bits of coursework due in for the National Certificate.'

Naomi nodded. 'That's very thoughtful of you, William.'

'Least I can do.'

'You're still going ahead with that then, Naz?'

Carver answered. 'Course she is, she—'

Naomi raised a hand. 'I wasn't asking you; I was asking Naz.'

The young journalist's glance darted between the two.

'Well, yeah, I think so, boss. It's a good qualification and I'm a good way through the course.'

'Fair enough. But you shouldn't be working on this or anything else at the end of a fourteen-hour night shift and with no sleep . . .' She looked at Carver. 'You need to let this young woman go home to bed. She's been up all night; I know you're used to working those kinds of hours, but she isn't.'

'Of course, we're nearly done here . . .' He started digging through his plastic bag, looking for nothing other than a further clumsy hint that she should leave them alone. 'Good seeing you, Naomi, we should catch up soon.'

'We should.' She patted Naz on the shoulder. 'You make sure you head home soon. You look like death warmed up. Sleep well.'

As soon as he was sure she'd gone, Carver retrieved the notes from beneath his left buttock and started flicking through them again. He saw the questioning look on Naz's face.

'We'll tell her all about this when the time's right. For now, the fewer people know about it the better.'

'Including our boss?'

'Including her. Where were we?'

'The second question.'

'Oh yeah. So, Clive Winner gets a desk and phone, neither of which he gives a tinker's toss about. So, what else is he getting? Have you worked out how much taxpayers' money that Green Bank thing has been sending his way?'

'No luck with that yet but I'm still looking.'

'You might need to put in a Freedom of Information request. Have you done that before?' Naz shook her head. 'Doing it for real is the best way to learn.' Naz nodded although the thought of adding this to the ever-expanding shopping list of things she was already meant to be doing made her feel slightly panicked. She took a breath, in through the nose, out through the mouth. She was sure she'd be fine; it was all manageable – she just needed a good night's sleep. Or rather a good day's sleep and then she could start work on this and the National Certificate studying later this evening. Carver was still talking. 'Whatever the total sum of money is, we know Winner's getting cash but what else is he getting?'

'Access?'

'Yes, access to everyone from the prime minister on down. But maybe access to information too. My source implied that this might have national security implications too.'

'Could your source be more specific?'

'I can ask him. I'll arrange another meeting. We've got plenty of questions to put to Winner himself as well; what are the chances of us being able to do that, do you think?'

Naz shrugged.

'Everything I've read suggests that Winner's a hard man to get to meet. He hasn't done a proper one-to-one interview in years. Just that sit-down alongside the prime minister in the *Wall Street Journal*.'

'I read that.'

'More of a puff piece than a proper interview.'

Carver nodded. That was exactly what it was.

'But there is one route to him that I thought might work.'

'Go on.'

'She's called Edith Walston. She's like . . . the world's number one expert on clouds.'

'Clouds? Are you talking about, er . . . cloud computing? That sort of thing?'

'No. I mean clouds, clouds. Those white fluffy things that bob about in the sky.' Naz handed William a smudgy-looking photocopy from something called the International Meteorological Report. It was a list of contributors, and a name at the foot of the alphabetical list had been highlighted in Day-Glo pink.

'Edith Walston's advised Winner for years – on and off. First it was this crazy-sounding rain-making project he was working on but more recently it's been all about cloud alteration – cloud brightening, thinning. Did you read about that?' Carver shook his head.

'It's well weird. He talks about counteracting global warming by putting a dimmer switch on the sun.'

William spluttered into his tea.

'Christ on a bike . . . if that's not a God complex, I don't know what is.'

'According to Winner, Edith is a card-carrying genius . . .' Naz checked her notes. 'His role model, muse, hero. Bear in mind this is a bloke who hardly ever says anything nice about anyone.'

'And they're in regular touch these two?'

'I don't know how regular. But they see each other, and they work together. Edith was given some sort of honorary degree from her old college at Cambridge University a few years back and Winner turned up unannounced at the ceremony – this was just after he'd done that work on the Great Barrier Reef. He was one of the most famous blokes in the world and I'm sure he had other places to be – but he showed up anyway. I read about that in the *Cambridge Evening News*.'

'You found that in the *Evening News*' archive?'

'Yeah. They've got a good system for a small paper . . .'

Naz hadn't just checked the national and international newspapers; she'd been through regional and local newspaper archives too . . . looking for anything related to Winner. Carver was impressed.

'But the best thing about Edith is she's still living and working in Cambridge.'

Carver nodded. 'Okay. So, we try to get to Winner via Edith Walston.' He put his mug of tea down on the empty plate and pushed it to one side. He looked across at Naz. 'I've got a feeling about this story. One of those old-fashioned gut feelings . . . do you know what I mean?'

Naz shrugged. 'I think so. Maybe. To be honest, I mainly just feel tired.'

'Of course, yeah . . . you should go home and sleep.'

'Thank you.'

'Before you do, I wanted to say . . . well just like Naomi said before.'

'That I look like death warmed up?'

Carver laughed. 'Not that bit. The bit about you being a journalist. And not a bad one either.'

23

LA BARROSA, ANDALUSIA, SPAIN

Carlos was late for work. He'd suffered from occasional bouts of insomnia since his early teens, but the last few nights had been something else. He'd gone to bed exhausted at ten p.m., then lain there, wide awake, for most of the night. He'd listened to the bells in the nearby church announcing the hours and half hours and had grown increasingly desperate. Midnight. One a.m. Two. Three. The three-thirty chimes were the last set he remembered hearing and his alarm woke him at seven. It wasn't enough sleep, but it would have to do. He had enough to worry about without getting fired by the Che bar's owner.

He picked through the pile of clothes on the floor, sniffing at various items, trying to identify the trouser and top combination that smelt least of vomit and fish. The trawler outing that he'd invested so much hope in had been a waste of time – worse than that, it had been an embarrassment. He'd promised to lift nets, check the catch or do something useful for six hours in return for a couple of hours at the end of the shift. The trawler captain and the rest of the crew had agreed to take the boat south in the direction of the North African coast in the hope that they might find some sign of Alma or the plane.

In the event Carlos had spent the six hours he was supposed to work doubled over with his head between his knees or leaning over the side of the boat throwing up. He had been surprised by how much vomit he had in him, it seemed to go on forever. He'd felt marginally better by the time the four-man crew were hauling the nets back in and tidying up but too ashamed to argue much when they said they were heading back to port, not further out to sea. He was sick and they were tired. Maybe some other time.

Carlos picked a few strands of stringy-looking vomit from the front of an otherwise clean T-shirt and gave it a good blast of deodorant. Loli had been right, the unofficial search had been a stupid idea.

He boiled the kettle and made himself a strong cup of instant coffee; he walked to the window and pulled the blinds up. His shoebox-sized top-floor flat looked across the town towards the beach and sea. On most mornings the view was a good one, but not today. The town and the Atlantic beyond it were hidden beneath a blanket of white sea mist; only some thickets of dark television aerials and a handful of the town's irregular-shaped white chimneys were visible above the mist. He checked his phone. He had three missed calls from Loli and another voice message from Alma's mum that had arrived the previous day but that he still hadn't summoned up the courage to listen to. Maybe later.

He finished his coffee and left the flat, pulling the door shut behind him. Down on the street he climbed onto his bike and turned the key. The motorbike's old engine coughed into life, then died again. He tried a couple more times but with the same result. The old bike didn't like damp weather. Carlos jogged down through the town, acknowledging the occasional shouted greeting from fellow locals with grunts and waves. He arrived at the Che less than an hour late and with no sign of the owner. A few people were taking their morning constitutional, but the cloudy weather meant most of the tourists and therefore most of the bar's morning trade were still in their hotels or holiday apartments.

He unlocked the metal shutters and pushed them open, they clattered noisily, and the sound carried in the mist. As he was winding down the green- and white-striped awning, he surveyed the beach. There was a familiar-looking figure standing down at the shoreline – a lone fisherman casting into the swell in the hope of mackerel or red snapper. As he was staring the man turned his head, saw Carlos and raised his free hand and waved. The wave became a beckoning gesture, the bow-legged angler was ushering Carlos over and something about the way he was doing it suggested urgency.

Pepe was a regular at the Che bar, a leather-skinned old man who was related to Alma's mother in some distant, second-cousin sort of way. Alma referred to him as uncle and insisted Carlos keep him well-provided with free beer and food whenever he was in charge of the bar and the boss wasn't around. As a result Pepe had come to know Carlos' work rota at least as well as Carlos himself knew it. The old man had made some sort of living from the sea for over fifty years. He'd crewed boats – trawlers, fancy yachts, even long-haul shipping containers – but these days he mainly just fished from the shore or the shallows with his collection of ancient-looking rods and nets. As Carlos got closer, Pepe smiled a gap-toothed smile.

'You okay, *hombre*? You look a little green.'

News of Carlos' humiliating fishing trip had clearly reached Pepe's ear.

'I'm fine.'

'What were you hoping to find? Out for a day trip with those scoundrels?'

Carlos reluctantly repeated the details of his plan to Pepe. How he'd studied the tide tables, how he'd hoped he might stumble across some evidence of the flying fried egg if he was able to search further afield.

'Which direction?'

'South. Closer to the Moroccan coast.' As he was speaking, he realised how ill-thought-out the plan must sound. He came to a stuttering halt. 'I guess it sounds stupid to you. The police helicopters have looked, the coastguard too.'

Pepe nodded. 'I'm sure they have.' He had laid down his fishing rod on the beach alongside a large cool box where he kept his catch. He took a pipe from his pocket and a box of matches from the other. 'But then, the coastguard couldn't find their arses with both hands. I've been waiting for you. I wanted to show you this.'

He kicked the side of his large, polystyrene cool box with his foot while trying to light his pipe. Carlos bent down and removed the lid, inside was a huge fish.

'It's a . . . tuna?'

Pepe guffawed. 'There's no getting anything past you, is there? I can't imagine why you and the boys on the trawler didn't get along.' He struck another match and cradled the flame. His hands were shaking, and the match kept missing the pipe. Carlos pretended not to notice.

'It's a good-sized fish. Er . . . are you going to sell it?'

Pepe shook his head. 'It's an okay-sized fish, I catch much bigger. But it is interesting anyway. I will show you.' He passed his pipe and matches to Carlos. 'Hold this for me, will you? My hands aren't working well today.'

The old fisherman bent down and grabbed the tuna, lifted it, planted a thick thumb either side of a foot-long cut he'd made down the belly of the fish and pulled it open. A fishy stink hit Carlos in the nostrils, and he gagged.

'Look closely.' Pepe held the fish up in front of Carlos' face. 'You see that?'

Carlos looked, unsure at first what it was he was looking for.

'I don't understand.'

'Fish usually glisten on the outside. Not on the inside as well.' And now Carlos saw. There was a bright, sparkling line running the length of the fish's insides. Carlos squinted and guessed.

'Mercury?'

'Not mercury. Diamonds. This tuna has a bellyful of diamond dust. That's what my little Alma had on board her plane, wasn't it?'

Carlos nodded, speechless.

Pepe put the fish back, carefully folding it so it would fit back inside his cool box. He pointed at the pipe and the matches which Carlos was still holding. 'Do me a favour and light that for me, will you?' Carlos nodded. 'I'm going to tell you where I caught this fish and I'll bet you a beer that it's a hundred miles from anywhere the coastguard or the cops have been looking.'

24

CANONBURY SECONDARY SCHOOL, HIGHBURY, LONDON

Rebecca was stacking chairs in the corner of the school hall when Jeff came bounding up.

'A few of us are going to pop round the corner to the Compton Arms for a drink before closing, can you make it?'

Rebecca shook her head. ''Fraid not.'

'I thought your other half was on Leila duty?'

'Yeah, he is, but . . . I need to get back anyway.'

'That's a shame, I was going to buy a round. It might never happen again.'

Rebecca smiled. 'Let's call it a rain check. Good meeting tonight.'

'Very good. Great that everyone's on board with the school strike and Paris coming together nicely.' He paused. 'I don't suppose you . . .'

'I don't know yet. I'd like to come, I will if I can.'

'Sure. Don't mean to hassle you.'

'It's not hassle. I'm flattered that you think me being there would make a difference.'

'It'd make all the difference in the world.' He grinned. '*In the* world and *for the world*, geddit?'

'That's dreadful. No wonder you're not allowed anywhere near the placard-writing workshop.' She smiled. 'I'll see you next week.'

Arriving home Rebecca found Patrick sprawled on the sofa, asleep and snoring. The TV still on but with the volume down. On the screen, a presenter and a couple of suited and booted former players were standing by the side of the football pitch still analysing a game that must have finished an hour or two ago. The glass-topped coffee table told the story of his evening – Patrick's work laptop was still open, there were four empty cans of Stella and a tube of salt and vinegar Pringles.

Rebecca went to check on Leila. She was fast asleep in the white wooden cot next to her parents' bed. She too was snoring, although in a quieter and significantly more endearing way than her father. Back in the kitchen, Rebecca removed the bag from the kitchen bin, took it through to the sitting room and swept the debris from the coffee table into it. Patrick woke, bleary-eyed.

'Oh, hey. Sorry, I was going to do that.'

'Not a big deal.'

'How was your evening? The meeting? All good?'

'Really good. I'll tell you about it tomorrow.' She turned towards the door.

Patrick cleared his throat.

'Oh, er . . . yeah. I meant to say. I've gotta go in early tomorrow, like half-six. The head of news wants to go over our response to a letter of complaint from Downing Street.'

Rebecca shrugged. 'Sounds important.'

'Er, yeah. It's climate-related, actually.'

'What was the complaint?'

Patrick cleared his throat again. 'I kind of promised I wouldn't talk to anyone about it. Not until it's public.'

'Including me?'

'Well, including anyone.'

'I see.' She looked at Patrick. His face was grey, the whites of his eyes slightly bloodshot. 'Have you called William yet?'

'Not yet, but I will. Tomorrow.'

'That's what you said yesterday. And the day before. And the day before.'

'Tomorrow. I promise. A pinky promise.' He proffered his small finger.

Rebecca ignored this but smiled.

'Tell me a little bit about the meeting. I'm interested. If you're not too tired? What's Planet Action's latest plan? Rewilding the North Circular?'

Rebecca sat. Not on the sofa but the armchair opposite.

'The meeting was mainly about the delegation we're sending to the climate conference in Paris. I've been doing a lot of the planning and Jeff is keen that I go.'

Patrick nodded. 'Been hearing a lot about Jeffus recently. You should ask him over. Him, and Mrs Jeffus.'

'I don't know whether he's got a partner. He hasn't mentioned one.'

'No. I bet.' There was a silence. Neither wanting to speak first.

Eventually it was Patrick who broke. 'So, he . . . they . . . want you to be part of the delegation, that's cool . . . how would it work? You'd take Leila? Or we'd all go?'

Rebecca shook her head.

'I'd be working, so I guess it would work like your work trips. I'd go and you'd look after Leila.'

'Right.'

'I'm going to bed.' She stood. 'Will you switch everything off?' She gestured at the TV and lights.

'Sure.'

Patrick stayed on the sofa, listening to the noises from next door. He heard Rebecca washing her face and brushing her teeth. He heard Leila make a half-hearted crying sound and her mother comfort her. He heard the door to their bedroom close. After a while, he stood up and looked around for the TV remote; he noticed Rebecca's phone, poking out between the cushion and arm of the chair where she'd been sitting. He picked it up. Stared at it. Then he did something that he'd never done before. He typed in Rebecca's security code and started scrolling through her messages.

25

WASHINGTON STREET, BOSTON, MASSACHUSETTS, USA

Winner climbed out of the black SUV that had collected him from the VIP exit at Boston airport and driven him into the city. He stood on the pavement and looked up at the wooden, triple-decker house. It was painted a bright powder blue with white window frames and there was a tall ash tree growing out the front. He remembered Jennifer mentioning that they sometimes shot movie and TV scenes on this street and Clive could see why. The residential neighbourhood would be many people's idea of the American Dream made real. He walked up the path and rang the bell, waited. He counted to five. Then rang again.

'I'm coming . . . Christ a'mighty.' Jennifer answered the door wearing a kimono-style dressing gown, her hair wet from the shower. 'Clive? What the hell?'

'Surprise.'

'What are you doing here?'

'I was in the neighbourhood . . . well, vaguely in the neighbourhood. I was in North America. You gonna let me in or what?'

'Huh? Oh, sure.' Jennifer led Winner down the hall and into the kitchen-cum-dining room. There were several boxes of breakfast cereal on the table, a half-finished bowl of Froot Loops and a litre carton of milk and one of orange juice.

'I see your builders still aren't done.' He gestured at the gap in the granite counter where there was a square of blue tarpaulin where a cooker should be. 'You should sue the fuckers, I'll lend you one of the corporate lawyers.'

'We're nearly there. Just waiting for the right-sized induction hob to arrive.'

'Waiting for fucken' Godot. At least threaten to sue them.'

'Why are you here, Clive?'

'Apart from to check on your tradies?'

Jennifer smiled. 'Apart from that.'

Winner told her. He was on his way to New Mexico; he'd spend a day or two with the team who were trying to work out whether you could cool the planet by placing a calcium carbonate screen between the sun and the earth. 'It works like a fucken' dream on paper, we just need to make it work in real life.' From there he was going to California to – in his words – shake the can in front of some of the big philanthropic types who'd reached deep into their pockets in years gone by. 'I wanna talk to you about that. We need to get some good press out west before I arrive. Plus there's some other things I need to brain out with someone. Someone with a medium- to large-sized brain.'

'And that's me?'

'You'll do.' He glanced around the kitchen. 'Have you got any coffee-making facilities in this half-finished house of yours?'

'What? Oh yeah, sure let me . . .'

'Just point me in the right direction. I'll make it while you get dressed.'

By the time Jennifer had dressed, dried her hair, and returned to the kitchen, Clive was sitting at the counter eating a bowl of Froot Loops and drinking black coffee. He poured her a cup and gestured at the seat opposite his.

'Have it while it's hot. I made it strong. The coffee on the plane was piss weak.'

'Even the fine people up in first class have to drink crap coffee, do they?'

'Even there. It could be the altitude . . . second law of thermodynamics.' He cupped the mug with both hands. 'Although if they . . .' He glanced back up at Jennifer and smiled, shaking his head. 'I'll chew that one over later.' Jennifer nodded and watched as her boss took a gulp of the coffee and ate a couple more mouthfuls of cereal. 'This stuff is good. Ryley's favourite, is it?'

She nodded.

'Is he around?'

'What? No, he's at school.'

'Oh yeah, school. That's good. Tell him I said hi.'

'Okay.' She paused. 'Have you ever thought about kids? You and Cindy?'

'What?' He met her eye. 'Nah. Well, thought about it, but the way the world is going right now. It seems a bit . . . selfish, bringing a kid into this shit show.'

'Right. I guess.'

'So, there's that.' He took another mouthful of cereal. The milk had turned a pale purple colour. 'Plus there's the fact that my dick is crook.' He smiled. A different smile from the one Jennifer was used to. 'So . . . no kids for me.' He pushed the cereal bowl to one side. 'Let's talk about what I came to talk about. I need you to try and get me some positive press out west before I have this round of meetings.'

'So, in—'

'Two or three days from now. I need a fair fucken' wind of some sort. What are the chances of you getting me some of those "Clever ol' Clive" or "And the Winner is . . ." headlines? Or another *Time* magazine cover.'

Jennifer sighed. Clive mentioned the *Time* magazine front cover regularly – her finest hour he'd called it. It featured Winner's face, smiling broadly from behind the glass of an old-fashioned, square red fire alarm. Written across the alarm in bright white capital letters was the legend – 'In Case of Emergency Break Glass!' The headline underneath the image asked the question: 'Can geoengineering genius Clive Winner save the planet?'

The idea for the cover hadn't been hers – a clever sub or picture editor at the magazine had come up with it, but Jennifer had gladly taken both the credit and the hundred-and-fifty-thousand-dollar Christmas bonus that Winner had given her by way of a thank-you.

'I can't think of anyone who's had two *Time* magazine covers in the space of a couple of years, Clive.'

'It's been three years, Jen . . .' He paused. '. . . not that anyone's counting.'

'Let me make some calls, I'll speak to the *San Fran Chronicle* and the *Times* and see what they say.'

'Good.'

'Have you got time to write an op-ed if one of them will run it?'

'An op-ed about what?'

'A look ahead to the Paris conference?'

'Sure.'

'And how about an interview?'

Winner shook his head. 'No way. No interviews. I'm desperate, but not desperate enough to submit myself to an hour-long chinwag with some wooden-headed hack.'

Jennifer nodded. 'Fine. I had to ask the question – an interview is what every editor I speak to will want.' She paused. 'While I'm asking unpopular questions, you say we're desperate for cash – why? What about Spain? The big insurance payout that Tony's negotiating for you.'

Clive heard the disapproving tone in Jennifer's voice but chose to ignore it.

'It buys us time, but not much. Turns out that amounts to sticking a Band-Aid on a big fucken' arterial bleed.'

'Ten million dollars.'

'Between nine and ten. And arriving who knows when. I know you're still pissed about the whole Spanish thing.'

Jennifer met her boss's eye and held it.

'I'm not pissed, Clive. I feel guilty. And sad.'

'Right. I understand. So do I.'

'I asked our guy Romero to go and see Alma's mother; to tell her that if the worst comes to the worst there'll be significant compensation.'

Winner nodded. 'Did he say how she was?'

'He said Mrs Galinda still thinks we'll find her daughter.'

'Yeah? Well, she's wrong.' Clive slid off the stool he was sitting on, picked up his empty bowl and carried it to the sink. 'If there was anything to find – of the plane, or Alma. We . . . or they . . . would've found it by now.'

'They?'

26

DOS HERMANAS, CÁDIZ PROVINCE, ANDALUSIA, SPAIN

Pepe rode pillion, his bony hands clamped to Carlos' waist, holding on so tight that it hurt. At least he was sitting downwind. If he hadn't been then Carlos thought the combined stink of pipe tobacco, halitosis and fish that emanated from the old man could easily have caused him to ride the bike off the road. So, he was grateful for the strong headwind.

The Portuguese border was a three-hour ride with just Carlos driving, with Pepe on board it was closer to four. The bike wasn't really made to take passengers, he and Alma used to use it for trips – up into the mountains to go camping or inland to Seville to go partying – but they were both skinny as rakes and the bike didn't mind. Riding with Pepe on the back was a very different experience. Carlos could feel every bounce or bump in the road and the bike's engine complained at the slightest hint of a hill. To his credit, Pepe was uncomplaining. After he overcame his early nerves, he grew into the trip, increasingly enjoying the experience and leaning forward and shouting against the wind to tell Carlos the history of a ruin they'd just ridden by or a restaurant that served a speciality that he was fond of. The old man had a story or fact to accompany almost every village, river or farm they rode by.

'Before it was wind turbines this was a stud farm . . . biggest in Cádiz . . . the bulls that fought in Ronda and Seville used to be raised back there . . .' Carlos looked. 'Not there . . . there . . . the biggest freshwater fish I ever caught, I caught in this river here. It's half the size now that it was then and the only thing you'll catch these days would be a two-foot-long turd.' The old man laughed. He was having a good time and as long as Carlos held his breath whenever Pepe leant forward with another tale, he enjoyed it too.

Some of the stories seemed too tall to be true but you could never tell with Pepe. 'They filmed *Lawrence of Arabia* near to here. I was an extra in that film . . . and I helped look after the camels. We lost a couple and they went off and mated with the wild camels. So now we have wild, movie-star camels in Andalusia.' Carlos turned his head.

'There aren't any wild camels left in Spain any more, Pepe.'

'Yes, there are. It's like anything. You just have to know where to look.'

The waterlogged fishing village and nearby beach that Pepe had told Carlos about was only a few kilometres south of the Portuguese border and hard to reach. The road Pepe had put them on after the town of Lepe soon became a dirt track and then nothing at all. The bike took them a lot further than any car could have managed but when they reached the reed-covered nature reserve and beyond that, just sand dune after sand dune, it was obvious they'd have to walk the last part of the way.

Carlos' legs felt stiff from the ride, he was thirsty and the dunes seemed to go on forever, but he kept going, following Pepe. The old fisherman set an impressive pace and continued chatting away, although it was unclear whether he was talking to Carlos or himself. They were heading in the direction of the Atlantic, which in time Carlos was able to hear and smell if not yet see. Up ahead Pepe had stopped talking and was studying his surroundings, looking for something.

'It's around here somewhere. I'm sure . . . it was easier to see from the boat. No sand in the way.'

They walked a little further and the dunes levelled out and Pepe spotted what he'd been looking for. 'Ah, there you are!' It was a watch tower – or the top ten or twelve feet of a tower anyway. Built as a vantage point where locals could keep a look out for Barbary pirates, there were scores of these towers up and down the Andalusian coast. A small fishing village had grown up around this particular tower and, Pepe told him, flourished for most of the nineteenth and early twentieth centuries. 'It was called Bartolme. The men and women who lived here were scoundrels but they knew how to catch fish.' The tower was used to process the catch and manufacture garum, 'the best fermented fish sauce in Spain'. Now, however, the tower was barely visible and the rest of Bartolme was gone – buried under mud and sand.

'What happened?'

'The sea came in.'

Pepe pointed at the boggy-looking land. 'It is too muddy to walk that way, we would sink. We have to go around, but it is not far.'

They skirted the drowned tower and after just ten minutes more of walking they were there. Carlos blinked, scarcely believing what it was he was seeing.

'What on earth?'

Pepe nodded. 'It is like I told you – the sea is greedy, but sometimes it gives back.'

Pepe had tried to describe the small but significant shift in sea currents that he'd noticed this fishing season and Carlos had nodded along without really understanding much of what the old fisherman was telling him. Now he understood. The change in what Pepe called the Canary Current meant that this remote stretch of beach, no more than a hundred yards long, had become a destination for . . . well, everything.

'What is all this?'

'It's a beachcomber's wet dream. That's what it is.' Pepe pulled a black plastic sack from his jacket pocket and wandered off to see what he could salvage. Carlos headed off in another direction, his eyes glued to the debris-strewn sand. He saw scraps of broken fishing boat, a blackened tree trunk, bright white sand dollars, dead starfish of various sizes and colours and the most enormous seagull he'd ever seen, its body twisted and its eyes busy with flies. There were plastic bottles, plastic sandals, toys, cutlery, food trays – plastic pretty much anything you could think of. He counted half-a-dozen bright-white ping-pong balls, a few oranges, several hairy brown coconuts and an old wooden tea chest with the words HIGH GROWN KENYA TEA still legible on the side and its insides crawling with crabs. Pepe wandered back over; he was waving something – a set of dentures in its plastic case.

'What do you want with those?'

'Look . . .' He opened the case. '. . . there are three . . . no, four gold teeth in here. A man I know in Cádiz will give me a hundred euros for these.'

'What does he do with them?'

'He wears them.' Pepe laughed and poked Carlos in the stomach with an arthritic finger. 'He melts them down and sells the gold of course. What else would you do with them?'

Carlos nodded. He pointed further up the shore.

'How come there are so many life jackets? Do you think a cruise ship went down?'

Pepe shook his head.

'Refugees . . .' he said sighing. 'Human beings degrade, life jackets don't.' He dropped the dentures into his black plastic sack, it looked half full, he'd clearly gathered quite a haul. 'What about you, have you found any sign of the flying fried egg?'

Carlos shook his head. 'I'm going to keep looking.' He walked up and down the shoreline for an hour. If there was anything he thought might interest Pepe, he called him over. Another hour passed. It was beginning to get dark and more difficult to see. The ride here had been tricky enough, riding home in the pitch black and with Pepe and his sackload of stuff on the back would be positively hazardous.

Carlos was about to turn back in the direction of the sunken tower and walk away from the shoreline when he felt something, like a gentle tug on his sleeve. He looked down to his side and there, next to a chunk of dark-coloured driftwood, half buried in sand – something. Carlos dropped to his knees and stared at this triangular shape poking up like a tiny plastic pyramid. Then, very carefully, using the tips of his fingers, he started to dig. He looked like a man unearthing some rare and precious archaeological find. A Ziploc bag. Pepe had noticed and walked up in time to watch as he brushed the sand from the sides of the see-through bag. Inside, as clear as day – a mobile phone.

'It's Alma's.'

27

WASHINGTON STREET, BOSTON, MASSACHUSETTS, USA

Jennifer watched Winner rinse his cereal bowl in cold water before switching the tap to hot and cleaning the bowl and spoon with a squirt of dishwashing detergent and a J Cloth. He placed them carefully on the drying rack and then ran his hands under the water for a while. There was a meticulousness to the operation. She was reminded of the day, early in her employ, that Clive had invited her to spend some time with him inside the Melbourne lab. The idea was that she would gain a better understanding of the sort of work the company did, but the insights she got into her boss's character were just as interesting. Put Clive Winner in a white lab coat and surround him with centrifuges, Petri dishes, pipettes and all the other expensive-looking kit Jennifer had seen in that airlocked laboratory, and he was a very different person. Once the washing up was done to his satisfaction, Clive sat back down at the counter – calmer now.

'I want to do the right thing by Alma and her family. Maybe we could set up a scholarship in her name somewhere in Spain? Or we double the compensation we give her mum once the insurance payment comes through? Or both? I'm open to ideas.'

'Okay.'

'Course, we can only do that if the company's still fucken' solvent six months from now.'

'It's that bad?'

'You were in the all-teams meeting; you saw what's happening. I've got about a hundred and fifty hungry scientific mouths to feed. Thirty or forty different projects . . .' Jennifer nodded. 'They all need more funding, some of them need it pronto or else we're going to have to shut up shop.' He turned to face Jennifer. 'You're my consigliere. Go on – consiggle me. What d'you think I should do?'

'You should do less.'

Winner grimaced. His face suggested that Jennifer's words caused him real physical pain.

'How can I do less? What if the thing I do less of, is the thing that works? The thing that makes the difference?'

'That's the risk.'

He shook his head slowly. 'Nah, we're not there yet.'

'Then at least prioritise what seems to be working best, the projects with the most promise. Those numbers that the wind and solar people gave us in the all-teams meeting were brilliant, I think we're underplaying that work. I was gonna ask you if I could put some of it in a press release.'

Winner shook his head. 'Not yet.'

'Why?'

'It's too soon and . . .' He paused. 'It's just too soon. I need to keep all the plates spinning and to do that we need money. Lots of it. Let's hear some ideas.' Winner made another pot of coffee. Even stronger than the first. Jennifer made some suggestions and Winner listened.

'If we need money fast . . .' Clive nodded. '. . . then how about I organise a round of One-to-Ones with Winner?'

Clive groaned. 'Shoot me.'

'I know you don't like them, but they work.' The one-to-ones were effectively a series of meet and greets. In return for a significant sum of money, businesses of all sorts, cities, town councils, charities or whoever could bring an environmental conundrum to Winner. He would talk it through with them, take it away and try to work up a solution of some sort. The fact that he was willing to agree to do another day or two of these was an indicator of just how desperate he was. 'We can do them online. Although people would pay more if we did it face to face.'

'Don't talk about it, Jen, just arrange it. And whatever we were charging last time – double it. I want us to shake every money tree we can think of. Especially those bigger trees.'

Jennifer considered this.

'What about the UK?'

Clive shrugged. 'Maybe.'

'There's the Paris Climate Conference coming up. The PM will want to make a splash at that and maybe we can help. The timing's good. You've still got that adviser title remember, the Downing Street desk. He likes you. Perhaps we can persuade him to put his hand back inside that Great Green British piggy bank of his.'

'Perhaps. We've got along fine in the past.' Winner paused. 'Some of the people around him I'm not so sure about. I know what we'll do . . . you call them. Ask for a meeting. If they say yes – you go.'

'You want me to do the trip?'

'Yeah. See how the land lies.' Winner poured some more coffee into Jennifer's mug and the last dribble into his own. 'My California trip, another round of one-to-ones and some cash from the Brits and we might be all right.' He finished his coffee. 'If we're not I'll just have to go back to the dustier, darker corners of the Rolodex. See who else might want to give us a shitload of money.'

Jennifer shook her head. This was exactly where she didn't want the conversation to end up. The company had been approached by several smaller, more opaque-sounding hedge funds in the past. Hedge funds that upon closer scrutiny turned out to have links with China, Russia, even North Korea. Clive hadn't needed their money then. It had been easy to say no. But now . . .

'Money that comes from places like that comes with strings attached, Clive.'

'All cash comes with strings attached.'

'Yeah, but some of it tends to be more . . . entangling.'

Winner laughed. 'I'd love to spend the rest of the day discussing string theory with you Jen, but I've got a begging bowl to polish, and you've got a trip to London that needs planning.'

Jennifer sighed. 'It's part of my job to safeguard the company's reputation . . . your reputation. That's a hell of a lot easier if the people we're dealing with are respectable.'

Winner laughed. 'Jen, you're so smart. It's actually a relief to discover that you haven't figured everything out.'

'I don't understand.'

'It's the respectable people that you really need to worry about.'

28

CHARING CROSS LIBRARY, LONDON

Carver looked up from his laptop and surveyed the library. It had filled up while he'd been working. All the threadbare armchairs over by the magazine racks were taken – library-going regulars reading an assortment of local, national and international newspapers. The long line of white desks next to the window were busy with local school kids doing their homework. Half-a-dozen pensioners were gathered around a nearby computer terminal learning how to navigate the internet – the Silver Surfer Club it was called. Choosing to write up his online pieces here instead of the office had been a good idea. Firstly, no one here would bother him. Secondly, sitting in a library – any library – always left Carver feeling that there was, in spite of everything, still some hope for humanity.

Carver reread the pieces he'd written for the news website. There were four articles, each of them a tightly written six hundred words. He gave each a single-word title for easy reference – *Whips. Honours. NHS. Ambassadors* – before emailing them in a single document to the website editor. Margolis was an old-school hack who'd been at the BBC longer than anyone could remember. Carver had told him to expect something. While waiting for Margolis to read and respond, Carver took care of other business. First he sent Patrick a WhatsApp – *Rebecca told me you were going to be in touch, did I miss a message?* He knew very well that he hadn't. Next on his to-do list was Leonard Allen. He found the civil servant's contact and sent him a message too, he kept it deliberately vague – *I need another chat, couple of things to clarify. Same place is fine, send day and time.* He pressed send. Then he wrote a follow-up – *Hope you and Henrietta are well, please give her my regards.* Carver paused and reread the second WhatsApp message. He tutted to himself. 'Idiot.' He deleted it. Checking his email he saw Margolis had responded already.

Four pieces. What is this, my birthday? Quick call? If so it's ext. 6950.

Carver looked back in the direction of the door and the reception desk. The eagle-eyed librarian returned the look. He tucked his laptop under his arm and went outside to make the call.

'Hey, Margolis, it's me.'

'William Carver, my fairy bloody godmother.' Carver could hear the hubbub of the newsroom in the background.

'Are the pieces okay?'

'Better than okay. Just got a couple of questions . . .' Margolis went through the pieces one by one, confirming some dates and details. He asked whether Carver had double-sourced several of the more controversial claims. He had.

'Great. I don't mean to nit-pick.'

'It's not nit-picking, Margolis. It's good journalism, I'm glad someone's still doing it.'

'Okay, well, I think that's all. There are a few semicolon issues I need to sort out but apart from that we're good. If you tell me when the radio pieces are going out I'll run these on the same mornings.'

'There's no radio. Just the written pieces, for now anyway.'

'How come?'

'There's something else I need to work on. I just wanted to put a flag in these stories.'

'You've done a good deal more than plant a flag. So, how about we go with one piece a week for the next four? After that we have back-to-back climate pieces in the run-up to Paris.'

'Fine by me.'

'And Naomi's signed off on all these already, yes?'

'Well, not yet. We still need to jump through that hoop, do we?'

'You know we do, William.'

'Okay. I'll sort it.'

'Good man. I'll wait to hear. Before you go . . . one more question – this other thing you're working on, even better than the stuff you've sent me, is it?'

'Might be. I'm not one hundred per cent sure yet, but—'

'You've got one of those gut feelings of yours, have you?'

'Yep.'

'You really should see a gastroenterologist about those.'

Carver called Naomi next.

'Where are you?'

'I'm . . . down near Charing Cross.'

'That's convenient, I'm at Millbank. Tell me where you are and I'll come to you.'

'That's not necessary, I can—'

'Just tell me where you are, William. We'll talk about these articles of yours and clear a couple of other things up while we're at it.'

Carver bought himself a hot chocolate from the library's drinks dispenser and went to wait for Naomi outside underneath the portico. It was a dark and drizzly late afternoon. He'd barely taken a sip of his drink when a black cab pulled up and Naomi climbed out. She paid the driver and joined Carver on the stone steps.

'Are we going inside?'

'Probably better to stay out here. The librarian's pretty strict about talking.'

'I see. Why are you working here, William?'

'Well, it's got everything I need.'

Naomi turned her head and looked through the glass.

'Right. You know that we have desks and chairs and computers and all that kind of thing at our office too now.'

'I know.'

'It's been so long since I've seen you in the office I wondered if maybe you'd forgotten.'

'No, I remember the office.' Carver stared across the street at the rooftops opposite; a plume of slow smoke was rising from a red clay chimney.

Naomi cleared her throat and spoke. 'I'll read the online articles you sent. Once I've done that, we can discuss why there aren't any radio packages to go with them. At the very least I'll want bulletin pieces and early two-ways.'

'Sure.'

'You'll be able to manage that alongside whatever it is that you and Naz are cooking up, will you?'

Carver nodded, there was no point in denying it. 'Naziah's a talented young woman, a good prospect.'

'Yep.'

'You did a good job finding her.'

'Thanks.'

'So it'd be a real shame if we ended up burning her out before she even got going.'

'I've no intention of doing that.'

'I know you don't intend to, but I'm concerned it might happen anyway. Let's face it, it wouldn't be the first time you'd . . .' She stopped herself. Carver looked across at the thin, three-storey brick building opposite and then up at the top-floor window. He imagined someone sitting in that garret room warming their feet in front of an open fire. He wished he was doing the same, doing anything in fact, other than standing on the rain-drenched street talking to his boss. Or rather, not talking to her. 'The National Certificate is difficult enough, but now you've got her doing some other work on the side.'

'A little research. That's all.'

'It all adds up. You know that hardly anyone in radio or TV news has the certificate these days.'

Carver nodded. 'I know. You can tell.'

His boss smiled.

'You're impossible, William. All I'm trying to say is that there are other qualifications . . .'

'They aren't as good.'

'. . . And other ways for Naz to get to where she wants to go.' Carver shrugged. 'It's important that we don't – for whatever reason – stand in her way.'

'I'm not standing in her way. I'm showing her the way.'

Naomi stifled a laugh. 'You're aware how pompous that sounds aren't you, William?'

'What I'm aware of is that you've got a problem with how I'm mentoring Naz. I'm also aware that the reason you've got a problem is you want to poach her and put her behind a desk instead of doing some real journalism with me.'

'That's rubbish.'

'Is it?'

'I want Naz to be allowed to make her own mind up and I want you to give her the space she needs to do that.'

'Fine. Let's let her decide. She can do things properly . . . a proper qualification, proper preparation, proper journalism. Or she can do things your way.'

'That's incredibly unfair, William. And offensive. I don't believe you mean that.'

Two spots of anger had appeared just above Naomi's cheekbones, but Carver would not back down now.

'I mean every word of it.'

'Really? Okay, fine. It's agreed then, we let Naz decide. But in the meantime, I want you to promise . . . any work she does for you, it's straightforward stuff.'

'Sure.'

'Nothing dodgy. Nothing dangerous. Nothing Naz isn't ready for.'

William gazed down at his feet.

'Course not.'

29

JUBILEE STREET, HOUNSLOW, LONDON

Naz was late home and therefore late for the chores that she'd promised her parents she'd do. She ran from Hounslow Central tube, down the main street in the direction of the minimarket and family home. In front of the family shop, cramping the pavement, was a long wooden trestle table covered in green plastic grass. Naz stopped and heaved a relieved sigh. Her brother was standing over the table rearranging the dozen or more white plastic bowls, each of which contained a mixed selection of fruit and vegetables. He'd bailed her out – again. The bowls usually sold for two pounds apiece, but Satish was selling them for half that. It made sense – this late in the afternoon and with the weather how it was.

'One pound . . .' Her skinny brother was shouting to the passers-by in a loud London accent. 'That's your five a day and a couple more for one quid. Put your hands in your pockets fast, people – before I come to my senses . . .'

The banter was working well, and a small crowd had gathered, arranging themselves into a disorderly queue in front of the table and blocking the door to the shop. The boy stood at the head, pocketing coins, and tipping the contents of the plastic bowls into flimsy blue plastic bags as quickly as his thin-fingered hands could manage. He saw his sister approach.

'Make way please, people. Here she comes – the Queen of Sheba.'

'Get stuffed, Satish.'

'Get stuffed?' Her brother grinned. 'Who says get stuffed? You can't even swear proper these days, man. The BBC censor is inside your head.'

'At least there's something inside my head.'

'Be nice, *Apa*. Remember who should be selling this fruit and veg tonight. I'll give you a clue . . . it's not me.'

She smiled. 'I'm grateful. I'll pay you back. Promise.'

'Sure.'

A small brass bell on a curled spring announced her arrival inside the family shop. The place was empty, apart from her father who was at his regular post, standing on a raised box behind the till. A paraffin heater next to the counter was doing its best to keep the cold out. Her dad had his spectacles in his hand, cleaning them on his shirt tail. Naz saw the two indented triangles of darker skin at the bridge of his nose where his glasses usually sat. She walked swiftly past him and towards the back of the store.

'I saw you, Naziah.'

'How? You're blind as a bat without your glasses.'

'You are my daughter. I do not need eyes to see you.'

'Right.'

'And you are late.'

'I know, I'm sorry . . . I'll finish off a couple of quick work things upstairs then I'll take over from Satish. Promise.'

'Winning at flippin' life!' Naz put a line through the seventh item on her ten-item to-do list and paused. 'Flipping?' Her brother was right, she couldn't even swear properly these days. Several of William Carver's favourite expletives had found their way into her vocabulary . . . 'get stuffed', 'flipping', 'Christ on a bike' . . . she'd used all of these, much to the amusement of her brother and confusion of her parents. They'd been spending a lot of time together, perhaps it was inevitable.

She turned her phone over in her hand and considered whether she should call Carver now or wait. She wanted to tell him that she was up to speed with all the National Certificate coursework and that she'd filed the Freedom of Information request asking for a list of companies in receipt of monies from the Great Green British Business Bank. She was particularly pleased with how she'd worded the request – using the word 'monies' somehow made it feel proper. Like she really meant business. The only thing left outstanding from the work Carver had given her concerned Edith Walston. Naz had written an equally carefully phrased letter to the cloud lady but so far had nothing back. She decided to give the professor a few more hours before chasing it up. In the meantime, she could do her shop-related chores.

Down in the shop her father was dealing with a delivery. There were three trays of bright yellow lemons on the counter in front of him and he was examining them while the delivery guy stood waiting for him to sign the receipt.

'Ah, Naziah, it's good you're here. Satish left a couple of extra jobs for you. He said you would not mind. First, the storeroom.'

'Argh, Dad. Really?'

'Yes, young lady, really. You owe your brother several favours. And, anyway, hard work never killed anybody.'

Naz nodded. Between the two of them, William Carver and her father seemed determined to test this dubious hypothesis to its limit. She headed for the storeroom, leaving her dad prodding at the top tray of lemons while the delivery man watched on.

'Are you planning to check all of those, mate?'

'I am now, yes.'

Naz had almost finished making an inventory of the storeroom when a conversation between her father and a customer in the shop distracted her. There was something about the tone of her father's voice as he answered this man's questions that caught Naz's ear. She made a note of where she'd got to and walked into the shop to look. The customer had finished quizzing her dad; he'd bought what he wanted to buy, but he was still at the front of the shop and appeared in no hurry to leave. He was standing by the magazines, staring up at the top shelf while eating the egg sandwich he'd just bought. The guy's clothes were unremarkable – jeans, a blue hoodie with the hood turned up, Caterpillar boots. The only incongruous thing about him was the sunglasses. Naz strode down the shop to stand next to her dad. As she walked past the man, he stepped backwards, bumping against her. Naz stumbled before steadying herself against the shop counter.

The stranger turned and smiled. 'I'm so sorry. What a clumsy-clogs. Apologies.'

Naz glared at him. She saw twin versions of herself reflected in the dark lenses. And behind that something else. Something not quite right.

'Forget it.'

'I'm guessing you're Naziah?'

'Eh?'

'Naziah. That's your name, isn't it?'

Naz glanced across at her father who shook his head.

'My name's Naz.'

'I thought so.'

'Do I know you?'

The stranger shook his head.

'No.' He took another bite of sandwich. 'It's a lovely place you've got here.'

Naz tried to place the accent. Midlands maybe?

'Thanks.'

'A family business, isn't it . . . dad, mum, brother, sister. A good old-fashioned family business.' Naz said nothing. 'I was just telling your dad how much I like places like this. You can get anything.'

'What do you want?'

'Apart from an egg sandwich?'

'Apart from that.'

'Not much. I just wanted to say hello . . . put a face to the name.'

'My name?' The man nodded. 'Why? Who are you?'

'No one important. Not for now anyway.'

'Young man . . .' Naz turned and saw that her father was standing behind her, holding his mobile phone. There was a slight tremor in his hand. '. . . I am telephoning the police.'

The stranger smiled.

'No need. I'm leaving. Good to meet you, Naziah. Stay safe.'

30

LA BARROSA, ANDALUSIA, SPAIN

Carlos put the phone back in his jacket pocket. Then took it out again. How many chances did you get? Loli had asked around and seemed certain that this particular make and model of smartphone locked you out for good if you didn't get it right on the fifth try. If that was correct, then Carlos only had one more guess. He sat on the wall that separated boardwalk from beach and stared out at the horizon. It was grey and the sea and sky met without any visible join. He'd tried Alma's birthday. He'd tried Alma's mother's birthday. He'd tried 1 2 3 4 5 6 and Loli had cuffed him round the head when he'd told her this.

'It's Alma's phone you're trying to open, you idiot. Not yours.' But her suggestion – something to do with an American TV show they both used to watch, but with an extra zero on the end. That hadn't worked either. Loli had punched in 9 0 2 1 0 0 with great confidence and been furious when it failed to work. 'That was her password for ages, she must've changed it.'

'I guess so.'

Now he had one shot left. His instinct was telling him to try his own birthday although that seemed arrogant, and therefore wrong.

The problem was he couldn't think of anything else to try. Loli had suggested his date of birth too. 'It's worth a go. Obviously, you're an idiot and no one in their right mind would use your birthday as their password, but on the other hand . . . she loved you.'

'Loves. Not loved.'

Carlos carefully typed in the day, month and year of his birth. He waited. The phone did nothing at first and Carlos waited. One second. Two. Three. It was as though the device itself was making a decision. Eventually there was a soft, doleful-sounding bleep, the screen dissolved into black and the mobile phone shut itself down and Carlos out.

31

JUBILEE STREET, HOUNSLOW, LONDON

It took Naz a while to persuade her mother and father not to call the police.

'What would we tell them? That a man came in and bought a sandwich? Said he liked the shop?'

'He had your name, Naziah. How does he know you? Is he a stalker of some kind?'

'I don't think so, Ma, not a dangerous one anyway. More likely he's just some saddo who saw something about me online. On Facebook or Twitter.'

'Online, I see.' This explanation made sense to her parents. They believed that many of the most troubling aspects of the modern world originated online. Naz would have liked to have believed this explanation too. She didn't. As soon as she'd managed to calm her mum and dad she went upstairs to her room and called Carver. She told him about her encounter with the stranger. She half hoped that he might dismiss it as no big deal. Carver did the opposite.

'That's worrying. How long since you started digging into Clive Winner's affairs? A few days?'

'Three.'

'What did this idiot say to you? I know it's hard, but be as precise as you can.'

Once she'd gathered herself, Naz was able to recount the conversation pretty much word for word. After he'd absorbed that, Carver asked her to walk him through the work she'd done in chronological order.

'You did the original bit of research on a public computer yes?'

'In two different internet cafés.'

'Good. And your phone calls and messages have all been on WhatsApp.'

'Yeah. End-to-end encrypted so they're safe.'

'They should be. So, all that leaves is the phone call to Downing Street.'

'Two calls. The message I left on Winner's own number at Number 10 plus a call to the press office.'

'Right.'

'I screwed that up?'

'Not at all. You let them know that we were interested, that's all.'

'So where does the guy in the hoodie and dark sunglasses fit in?'

'I'm not sure yet. But it tells us that we're onto something. We're barking up the right tree.'

'The kind of tree that comes round to your house and scares the hell out of your family?'

'Well . . .'

'Is this kind of thing part of the job?'

'It can be, yes. Do you want me to come over? I could speak to your mum and dad, try to reassure them.'

'No, no, it's okay. They're fine.'

'And what about you?'

'I'm fine too.'

'I realise I've had you flying solo with this, Naz. That stops now. I've cleared the decks. From here on in we work on this together, okay?'

'Okay.'

32

WASHINGTON STREET, BOSTON, MASSACHUSETTS, USA

Jennifer Prepas' life had many moving parts. If the Prime Minister's man agreed to a Downing Street meeting then she would need to give him definite dates. She wanted the trip to cause as little disruption to Ryley's day-to-day life as possible. This meant negotiating with his father, her ex-husband, and that was always best done face-to-face. Ryley's dad had done the weekend soccer run – another game that Jennifer had had to miss. She'd texted him and asked if he could pop in and see her, instead of just dropping Ryley at the kerb, which was his usual modus operandi. He'd agreed while at the same time warning that the soccer match had gone badly and that their son was in a foul mood and hungry.

Jennifer put a pepperoni pizza in the oven and made a note of the dates when she thought she could catch the red-eye to London and back. It would only work if her ex was willing to pick up the slack. She resolved to be super-upbeat and super-friendly and not mention the fact that he was a useless bastard who'd half-starved their son.

Ryley arrived home still wearing his soccer kit, boots unlaced and socks around the ankles. He was red-faced, dishevelled, and sullen. He struggled free from Jennifer's attempt at a consoling hug, accepted the pizza without a word and stomped upstairs to his room. His mum waited for the inevitable door slam before opening negotiations with his father who was standing on the doorstep. The look on his face suggested that he was a man who'd scaled the very heights of the moral high ground. It was too much for Jennifer.

'It didn't occur to you to take some food for him. Or a drink. Or clean clothes?'

'At least I was there.'

Negotiations over whether and when Jennifer might be able to leave Ryley with his father took a while: 'If you take him here, I'll give you back a long weekend there . . .' Fifteen minutes of bickering and bargaining that left her feeling guilty and cross. The only consolation was that their son was three floors away and plugged into a computer game of some sort.

Armed with the dates that they'd agreed, Jennifer sent an email to the person she dealt with most often inside Downing Street, the prime minister's special adviser Jeremy Cunis. She read and responded to some messages from her team about the next round of one-to-ones with Winner that they were working on. Just as she was about to log out there was a digital swishing sound and a new email landed in her in-tray. It was the prime minister's man.

Hello. You callable?

Jennifer typed back. *Of course Jeremy, love to talk.*

The Downing Street switchboard called two minutes later, confirming her name, and asking if she would take a call from Jeremy Cunis. There was a loud click and then a booming, English-accented voice almost deafened her.

'A late-night missive from Jennifer Prepas. What a pleasant surprise.'

'I'm glad to hear it, Jeremy. You're working late.'

'No rest for the wicked.'

'Whatchu working on?'

'Everything; all at once. But this particular moment it's mainly

Paris. There's this little climate get-together on the horizon . . . you might've heard of it?' Jennifer acknowledged that she had. The fact that he'd mentioned Paris before she had to was an encouraging sign. 'So, your email was timely. In fact, perhaps you even felt your ears burning.'

'How so?'

The prime minister was considering setting up a 'brains trust' to help him write his Paris speech. Winner's name had been mentioned.

'The PM's got five years under his belt. He's getting to that point where political leaders start to worry about their *legacy* – God help us. He wants Paris to be part of that.'

'I sympathise. It'd make sense for the environment to be where your man leaves his mark though. The PM's commitment to green causes goes way back. Wasn't that how he first made his name – that Arctic trip and those lovely—'

'Please don't mention the huskies. They're something of a sore point right now.'

Cunis explained that the recently departed environment minister had suggested that she and the prime minister go back to the Arctic, that they might even try to track down the original pack of huskies. 'That idea plus the bottom-numbing speech that her team suggested the PM deliver in Paris are two of the reasons why she's no longer in post.' Jennifer had read about the reshuffle.

'There was a bit more to it than that, wasn't there?'

Cunis hesitated.

'A little more – tedious internal arguments, I won't bore you with it. The point is that the PM decided to put his foot down. I believe his precise words were "no more silly photoshoots and cliché-ridden speeches".'

Jeremy explained that his boss had read the Pope's encyclical in full, he'd been watching what the American President and Chinese General Secretary were saying. He wanted, in his adviser's words, to 'pick up the baton and run with it'.

'The PM wants this to be a "speech for the ages".'

'I see. Well, I think that Clive might tell you that we don't have *ages*. And that we need a lot more than speeches.'

Cunis laughed appreciatively.

'That's exactly the sort of thing we're after. Have you copyrighted that?'

'No, you can have that for free.'

'Excellent and what about this "brains trust" idea, do you think Clive might have the time? In theory?'

'In theory and in practice. We'd make time.'

'That's good to know.'

They spoke some more about the speech. It seemed that the long-promised but still unbuilt science park was back on the agenda. 'The PM likes the idea of announcing that in Paris – a British equivalent of the Frenchies' *grands projets* if you will. But it needs to be a park with a purpose.' He asked for an update on Winner's various geoengineering initiatives and Jennifer obliged with an upbeat thumbnail sketch of several. At the other end of the line she could hear Jeremy tapping away on a laptop, taking notes. Now was the time to ask.

'How about this? I put a few of these ideas together, a short presentation. Me and Clive will chat about the Paris speech too and work up a few lines. I fly over and talk to you and your team. If you like what I'm telling you, great . . . if you don't, you can tell me to go kick rocks.' There was a pause while he considered this.

'I'm assuming the reason you want to come and see us is that Mr Winner is looking for funding.'

There was no point denying this.

'Of course. Isn't every single individual that walks into Number 10 asking you for money or similar?'

Jeremy laughed. 'Tragically, yes.'

'We're looking for more funding for several of the projects I've mentioned, no doubt about it, but it's a quid pro quo. I think one or maybe more than one of these might work for you. Clive hasn't changed, he's still in the business of bringing you and the PM solutions not problems.'

'Still our type of green?'

'Absolutely.'

Jennifer waited.

'I'm going to be completely honest with you. The PM is still a fully signed up member of the Clive Winner fan club but there are other people who aren't quite so enamoured.'

'People in Downing Street?'

'People in and around government.'

'I understand.' Jennifer scribbled a note to herself – *in and around government.*

'That said, I think it's worth you coming to see us. Worth my lot hearing what you have to say. I'll need to do a little groundwork ahead of your visit but let's go ahead and arrange something.'

'Great.' She gave Jeremy the dates she could do, he told her he'd check them and confirm as soon as possible. The conversation was drawing to a close and she was about to say goodbye and salvage what she could of a free evening with her son when Jeremy cleared his throat and spoke. His tone somewhat changed.

'One final thing, Jennifer.'

'Shoot.'

'That Downing Street phone number that the PM gave Mr Winner way back when.'

'Yes.'

'I don't suppose you've had any out-of-the-ordinary messages left on that line recently?'

'Out of the ordinary?'

'Any interview requests?'

'I'd have to check. I'd be surprised.'

'But if you did get a request . . .'

'We'd refuse. We refuse all of them. The last interview Clive gave was that sit-down with your boss. He hates doing interviews, you know that.'

'Good, good.'

'I'll have one of my team check the tape.'

'Terrific.' He paused. 'And if anything . . . potentially difficult pops up, I do hope you'll share it with us?'

'Of course.'

It was clear to Jennifer that they had shared it already. Whether they'd intended to or not. As soon as she'd finished the call to Jeremy, she phoned her assistant.

'Get me all the messages that've been left on Clive's London line in the last fortnight and send them over.'

'Now?'

'Now.'

33

CHRIST CHURCH, HIGHBURY GROVE, LONDON

The row of brightly painted placards stretched from the door of the church, all the way down one wall and ending at the altar. Rebecca counted seventy-plus double-sided placards; as soon as they had dried, she and some of the older teenagers would take them up to the top of the church and a space that the vicar had cleared in a box room. He'd been very accommodating – offering Rebecca the use of the church after the secondary school where Planet Action usually met decided that hosting the school-strike placard-making project was a bridge too far. He agreed that a snapper from the local paper could come and take pictures. He'd even painted his own placard, which he carried carefully over to Rebecca for her approval.

She read it aloud: 'I brought you into a plentiful land to enjoy its fruits and good things. But when you came in, you defiled my land and made my heritage an abomination.' She gave an approving nod. 'Terrific, vicar, powerful stuff.'

'Not too esoteric?'

'I don't think so.'

'I plumped for Jeremiah over Revelation in the end. I know you said we want to shake people up a little with the placards, but there are limits.'

'Good call.'

'I could always do a quick Revelation one as well?'

Rebecca shook her head. 'I think we're nearly out of paper. And brimstone.'

The vicar's only request was that he be allowed to check the posters that would be on show when the photographer from the local paper arrived. He and Rebecca inspected the placards together, picking a dozen or so for the kids to hold:

We are skipping our lessons to teach you one.
You'll die of old age. We'll die of climate change.
Like the oceans – we rise

All of these were arranged front and centre. The vicar's hand went briefly to his dog collar when they were reading some of the older girls' placards:

Make love, not CO 2
I want a hot date not a hot planet

But Rebecca persuaded him that the older teenagers should be allowed to pose with the messages they'd written.

'I suppose you're right. I wouldn't want to suppress free speech. And if there's nothing too sweary or out-and-out blasphemous . . .'

He agreed to take part in the photoshoot himself, standing at the centre of the group of school strikers. The photographer took her time and seemed pleased with what she'd got, telling Rebecca that she wouldn't be surprised if it made the front page. As she was leaving and the packing-up operation had begun, Jeff arrived. Rebecca was tidying the paints away when she saw him chatting to a group of the older teenagers at the church door. He was wearing the same faded blue jeans and a dark-blue linen shirt he always seemed to wear along with a black Fred Perry bomber jacket. It was clear that one or two of the teenage girls were rather taken with him and there was a fair amount of hair-flicking going on as he admired the placards and talked to them about Planet Action. Eventually he managed to extricate himself and make his way over to the paint table.

Rebecca smiled.

'I thought I told you not to come to the placard-making workshop – it's not where your talents lie. Long speeches are your thing, not pithy phrases.'

'Ouch. I thought I could help you tidy up. I could also do one of my speeches if you need to clear people out of the church quickly.'

'I guess that could be useful.'

Jeff helped transport the placards up to the box room, he thanked the vicar and talked again with a few of the older school strikers. Almost all of them were Planet Action newbies. He asked Rebecca where she'd found them.

'Social media. I posted something pretty mundane about the placard-painting project. I figured I'd get a handful of local kids, but it got shared.'

'You went viral.'

'Hardly. But we did well. There are teenagers from right across London here . . .'

'So I see. This is the new generation of green campaigners I've been banging on about, they're right here.' He glanced over at the group of teenagers he'd been talking to. 'Have you got all their names?'

'No, this whole thing is pretty informal. I mean I know a few of their names but not all.'

'You know what'd be great? If before they go, we could get their names. So we can stay in touch and let them know about other actions ahead of Paris. Their names . . . and their mobile numbers too. I'll start with that lot over there . . .'

34

CÁDIZ, ANDALUSIA, SPAIN

The back streets of Cádiz were like a labyrinth. Carlos had been here dozens of times before but every time he managed to get lost. Alma used to tease him about it. 'Seaside boy. Can't even find your way around the smallest city.' This time was no exception. The friend that Pepe recommended was based in the heart of the old town, at the centre of the labyrinth. The shop front and everything on display suggested that it was antiques and religious relics that he dealt in, but Pepe assured Carlos that he did more besides. 'He bought those teeth I found, he deals in gold and silver and all sorts. His eldest son does the modern stuff – computers, phones, all of that. He'll be able to open Alma's phone and he'll keep quiet about it.'

By the time he found the shop and parked and locked the motorbike in a secure-looking spot, Carlos was almost an hour late for the appointment Pepe had made. The shop owner was dressed in an ill-fitting brown suit, matching waistcoat with silver pocket watch and chain. He was serving some customers – a German couple – and Carlos waited and listened in. The couple were interested in a weeping Madonna. A blue-robed, dusty, slightly cracked-looking piece that the shopkeeper said he'd rescued from a derelict monastery. When the couple asked him where the monastery was, he named a town Carlos hadn't heard of and which he guessed probably didn't exist. After the tourists' credit card had gone through and he'd wrapped the Madonna in old copies of *El País* and sent them on their way he turned his attention to Carlos.

'You're Pepe's little friend?'

'Yes, I'm sorry I'm late.'

'Makes no difference to me. I'm always here.'

Carlos had no trouble believing that.

'What was this about again? Not teeth this time?'

'No. It's a mobile phone.'

'Oh yes, Pepe said something.'

Carlos took Alma's phone from his pocket and put it down on the glass counter.

'I need it opening.'

'Fine. I'll tell my son. It sounds straightforward. Leave a number and he'll call you when it's done; you can pay when you pick it up.'

'He isn't around now?'

'No. He's away until the end of the week. I never leave . . . he often does.'

'I'd rather have him do this while I wait.'

'You don't trust us?'

'It's not that. It's just . . . personal. I'd like to be here when the phone's opened.'

The man grinned, it was not a pleasant sight; he should have taken some of the money from the gold dentures he melted down and bought a set of his own.

'I understand. There's some interesting stuff on the phone, is there? Photographs of your girlfriend maybe?' He looked Carlos up and down. 'Or your boyfriend?' Carlos shook his head.

'Nothing like that.'

'Pepe warned me you were an odd one. Well, suit yourself. Come back on Thursday, we open at ten. The boy will do it while you wait.'

Carlos first noticed the four-by-four on the road out of Cádiz, a long stretch of road that ran parallel to the sea. The Guardia Civil patrolled this road diligently and Carlos had been caught before. He didn't want any hassle, much less a fine and so he was cruising slightly slower than the seventy kilometre an hour speed limit. The silver Toyota was a few car lengths back and keeping pace. Once the motorway began and the limit rose, Carlos switched lanes and overtook several cars and a lorry; the silver Toyota did the same. He slowed again, squinting to get a better look at the car in the bike's wing mirror. He decided to come off the A10 early, at the Chiclana exit to see if the car followed. It did. At the next roundabout, Carlos waited at the junction, pausing long enough for the Toyota to be forced by the traffic behind it to come closer. It was a hire car, he could see the green Europcar sticker in the front window. He could see the driver now too. It was not a pretty sight. A shaven-headed, long-faced man – white as a ghost. The scowl on his face suggested that he knew Carlos had seen him. Carlos waited until he saw a stream of cars, clumped closely together driving out of Chiclana and towards the roundabout, almost certainly heading for the Cádiz exit. He waited until the line of cars was almost level with him before revving loudly and accelerating onto the roundabout. The Toyota tried to follow but couldn't make it in time. The first car in the line of Cádiz-bound traffic braked suddenly and the cars behind followed suit. There was the smell of burnt rubber and a chorus of horns and shouted abuse, but Carlos was away and gone and the ghost-faced man in the Toyota was stuck.

35

THE LONDON EYE, SOUTH BANK, LONDON

Carver had arranged to meet Leonard at the London Eye. They'd rendezvous there and walk – there was no way he was going back up in the bloody thing. He'd arrived early as usual and decided to spend the spare twenty minutes wandering the Waterloo Station branch of Foyles. He perused their poetry section which wasn't bad for a small-ish shop before asking about a non-fiction book he'd seen reviewed in one of the Sunday papers. It hadn't been published yet, next week. Outside the station Carver was relieved to see that the weather had improved – but not a lot and not for long judging by the slate-grey skies. As he was waiting to cross Waterloo Road, a bus passed close to the kerb, churning a gutterful of sleet into a muddy slush and sloshing it up onto the pavement. He stepped back just in time to stop his shoes from being drenched. He watched as the wave of slush swept up the pavement then back down into the gutter. When the green man appeared, Carver crossed and headed in the direction of the Eye. He was walking briskly past the ticket booth when the intercom crackled.

'Hello!'

It was the same young woman as last time sitting behind the

Plexiglas screen, although her emerald-green hair was now bright pink and shorter. She was wearing a paper crown with IT'S MY BIRTHDAY! written on it in bright, block capitals. She was waving at him; Carver walked over. He was, unsurprisingly, her only customer.

'I didn't expect to see you back again so soon.'

'I'm not going up.'

'I don't blame you. The weather's even worse than the last time you were here.'

'Yep.'

'You meeting that bloke again?'

Carver hesitated. She was observant.

'Er, yes. My brother.'

'Really?' She studied Carver more closely. 'You don't look that alike. And he dresses a lot smarter than you do.'

'Yeah, he got the dress sense; I got the brains.' Carver looked around for a change of subject. 'Is it really your birthday?'

'Yep. It's not as sad as it looks. I've got some mates coming down later for a drink.'

'That's nice.' Carver's eye settled on the hairdressing magazine, open in front of her. There were notes next to some of the pictures. She saw him looking.

'I'm taking a City and Guilds course in cutting and styling. This . . .' She gestured at the cramped ticket booth. '. . . it's just temporary.'

'I see.' There was an awkward silence. 'I think I'll go and wait over there, under cover.' He glanced up at the skies. 'Feels like it might start sleeting again.'

'Sure. Nice to see you.'

Leonard Allen arrived bang on time and sartorially correct as ever in his fawn-coloured mackintosh, black brogues and brolly. They shook hands before setting off along the river, walking east towards Waterloo Bridge and the Festival Hall. They talked as they walked,

Leonard falling silent if anyone passed even remotely within earshot. Carver also saw the old civil servant glance back over his shoulder once or twice. He seemed edgier than when they'd last met.

'Everything all right, Leonard?'

'What? Yes, all fine.' Allen had dead-batted or completely ignored Carver's first couple of messages asking for another meeting. Then yesterday he'd got back unprompted, asking that they meet as soon as possible. 'Things at my end have just hotted up a little.'

'In what way?'

'It's complicated. I'll try and give you the short version . . .' Leonard spoke in a manner befitting a man who'd spent his working life in Whitehall. Wordy to the point of being abstruse, they were past Waterloo Bridge and within sight of Blackfriars before the veteran civil servant managed to say something specific or useful.

'You remember I confessed my hope that once you had started sniffing around, that alone might be enough to persuade Downing Street to put a more sensible distance between themselves and Clive Winner.'

'Yes.'

'Well, that doesn't appear to have worked. I'm told that one of Winner's top people has been invited to London for a pow-wow. A meeting at Downing Street.'

'I see.' This didn't seem very complicated. It did however explain Leonard's sudden keenness to meet. 'Your contacts have told you this meeting's happening; do they know what's on the agenda?'

'Not in any detail, but one can guess. Clive Winner's timing tells you everything.'

'His timing?'

'He's obviously planning to use his peculiar access rights to the prime minister at the most opportune time. Opportune for him. Inopportune for us.' Carver glanced across at Leonard.

'I don't understand.'

'Paris . . . it's all about Paris.' Leonard explained how desperately keen the British prime minister was to make his mark at the upcoming climate conference. The way he told it, a good deal of other government business was being pushed off into the sidings in order that he could concentrate on this single event. 'The French have just released the provisional conference timetable. The PM is down to chair or co-chair a dozen different subcommittees and plenary sessions. He's not just turning up in Paris, he wants to try to steer the thing.'

'What's wrong with that?'

'I fear he might end up driving under the influence.'

'Of Clive Winner?'

'Yes. The PM has already sacked his environment secretary, he's shuffled a couple of other ministers and mandarins. Now he's decided to go outside Westminster and Whitehall altogether for guidance. Ergo – the imminent arrival of Clive Winner's consigliere.'

Carver sighed. 'Do you mind if we stop for a moment?' He needed a rest. The more aerated Leonard Allen became, the faster he walked. Carver had begun to feel like he was on an involuntary army route march. They stopped and went and stood at the waist-high wall overlooking the river. The choppy brown Thames rolled by. 'Let's assume Clive Winner does want to exert some influence over the prime minister—'

'Of course he does, he—'

'Let me finish. We assume that he has the PM's ear.'

'Not just his ear. One or two other more intimate body parts is what I hear.'

'Fine, whatever . . . tell me why that matters.'

'Well, there's a right way of doing things and a wrong way and . . .' Carver started to shake his head. Leonard paused. 'What is it?'

'That's not going to cut it, Leonard. At some point I have to sell this story to my boss; she has to sell it to hers. Tell me why a busy person, wolfing down their morning cornflakes before running out the door to work would stop and listen to a story about Clive Winner and the prime minister?'

'Okay, I understand.' He paused. 'I'll give you the best- and the worst-case scenarios.'

36

JUBILEE STREET, HOUNSLOW, LONDON

It took Naz and her dad a couple of hours to get the new security camera working. First, they had to find the right place to put it, eventually settling on a spot directly above the shop door. Naz drilled a couple of holes in the wooden door frame while her dad held the ladder. She attached the round, glassy-eyed camera just a few inches from the old brass bell on its curled spring and angled it so it would record what was happening at the shop counter and most of if not all the rest of the store. Once that was done, Naz installed the software, made sure the feed from the camera was connecting with the family computer and pressed record. She turned to her mum who was watching on in a way that suggested she was seeing a minor miracle performed.

Naz smiled. 'There we go. This will make us all feel safer.'

'Yes. That's good. Also, it will allow me to see when your father is flirting with those ladies from the hair salon.'

Her dad made a harrumphing sound.

'Good customer service is not flirting.'

Naz was sweeping up the sawdust at the front of the shop when she felt the phone buzz in her tracksuit pocket. She glanced at it and was about to let it click through to her answering service when she recognised the Cambridge dialling code. She propped the broom against the magazine rack and walked to the back of the shop to take the call.

'Hello?'

'Naziah Shah?'

'That's me.'

'This is Professor Edith Walston; you emailed me.'

'Yes, fantastic . . . thanks so much for calling.'

'Your email hovered somewhere between the deliberately vague and the completely vacuous. What is it that you want?'

37

RIVERSIDE WALK, LONDON

'The PM wants to announce something big in Paris. What better way to make a mark than by unveiling a *grand projet* in the home of *grands projets*?' Leonard Allen put his hand out, palm upwards. 'Raining again.' He popped his umbrella up and shuffled close enough to Carver that it covered them both. 'The prime minister's long-promised science park is the obvious thing, but he needs something big and clever to put in it – and he needs it fast.' Leonard turned to face Carver. 'My fear, my strong suspicion, is that Winner will try to sell him one of his madcap schemes. You'll have read about some of those . . .' Carver nodded. '. . . and what we'll end up with is a two- or three- or five-billion-pound *pup*.'

'Okay. So, it's about money.'

'Partly. Money and pride. Doing a deal with Winner risks national humiliation as well as billions of pounds of taxpayers' money being wasted. And this is my best-case scenario.'

'Okay, we'll come back to the money. What's the worst-case scenario?'

A nervous look clouded Allen's face. He stared out across the Thames, a tree trunk floated by, pursued by a chunk of polystyrene.

'There's this Downing Street meeting . . . but there are other meetings happening elsewhere. Meetings that Clive Winner himself is attending.'

'Where?'

'My contact at the Foreign Office either wouldn't or couldn't say. But he suggested that if I put a pin in a map of former Soviet republics then I might get close.'

'The sort of places where the less respectable hedge funds you mentioned tend to operate out of?'

'Exactly.'

Carver pondered this.

'I'm certain there's a story here and I want to tell it, but I can't just go on rumours and gut feelings – neither mine nor yours – we need facts and evidence. Let's go back to the money – money that Winner's already had I mean. Do you know how much this Great Green British Business Bank has given him?'

Leonard shook his head. 'I don't. I just know it's a lot.'

'Can you make enquiries?'

'Not without very obviously poking my head into parts of government that aren't in my bailiwick. I think a Freedom of Information request is your best bet there.'

'We've done that.'

'Have you? That's good. An enquiry like that will create a flurry in one or two official dovecotes, I'm sure . . .'

Carver glanced down at his feet. He realised he wasn't sure whose name and contact details Naz had used when she'd filed the FoI request. His hopefully. He made a mental note to ask her. When he looked back he saw that Leonard was still talking: '. . . It's probably too late to stop this initial meeting from taking place, but it might put a crimp in Downing Street's later plans.'

Carver ignored this.

'Winner's consigliere – who's he meeting with?'

'*She* not *he* – I'm told. I don't have her name. She's seeing the PM's special adviser Jeremy Cunis. He's another slippery character.

I don't know who else is supposed to be in the meeting, but I'll bet you a pound to a penny there won't be a civil servant in that room.'

The rain had eased. Leonard lowered his umbrella and the two men continued walking, more slowly now. They parted company at the Globe. Carver thanked him and asked that he get in touch immediately if any of his Foreign Office and Downing Street contacts told him anything useful. Any details at all about the meeting between Winner's woman and the prime minister's *spad* would be particularly helpful.

'Of course, I'll keep my ear to the ground. I want to be as useful as I can. I just need to work out a way of doing that without flushing a thirty-year career down the toilet. Henrietta's put up with a lot down the years but I'm not sure that she'd tolerate having a sacked civil servant with no pension for a husband.' He gave Carver a rueful-looking smile.

The pair shook hands. Carver had turned away and was heading back west when Leonard called him back.

'I nearly forgot. Before you go, Henrietta asked if you might be able to make it over to ours for a meal at some point soon? Nothing formal, just a little kitchen supper.'

'Sure. I'd like that.'

This answer and the enthusiastic way it was given took both Leonard and Carver himself by surprise.

'Excellent. I feared I'd have to beg or bribe you. Henrietta will be delighted. I'll give her your number, if that's okay . . .' Carver nodded that it was. '. . . and the two of you can talk about dates.'

'Okay.'

Leonard smiled. 'A good deed in a naughty world.'

'I beg your pardon?'

'That's what she calls you.'

'I see. Okay. Well, goodbye.'

It would be good to touch base with the civil servant again soon. It made sense – workwise that was. What's more, he liked Leonard

Allen. He liked his wife. And he couldn't remember the last time he'd been to anyone's house for dinner. Or rather for *a kitchen supper*. Carver really had no idea what that meant, or how one might be expected to dress for it. Perhaps he could ask Henrietta when she called him.

On the walk back Carver checked his phone. He had a few missed calls including two from Naz. He dialled her back and she picked up immediately.

'Professor Walston has agreed to meet us; day after tomorrow at her place in Cambridge.' The excitement in her voice was obvious.

'That's good.'

'It's great, isn't it? I was sure she was gonna say no. No one who has anything to do with Clive Winner seems to like to talk about it. Or about him. Anyway, I talked her into it. Or maybe I just kept talking for so long that she gave up and said yes. Day after tomorrow.'

'That's good work, well done. I've made some progress too, I'll tell you about that on the way to Cambridge. We'll go together, yes?'

'Great, we should do some more homework first.'

'Homework?'

'About clouds I mean.'

'It's clouds . . . how complicated can it be?'

'Really, really complicated. I was just reading one of the things I printed out for you from the International Meteorological Report . . . an article she wrote.'

'What's that like?'

'It's like a Harry Potter book – but not a good one. It's all spells and no story. *Cumulus congestus . . . altostratus duplicatus.* I began to get worried that I might turn myself into a badger or something.'

'Right.'

'Anyway, its complicated stuff, for instance . . .'

Naz's further examples were wasted on Carver who, as he arrived back at the London Eye, had been distracted by the pink-haired woman in the ticket booth. She was waving at him.

'Naz, sorry. There's someone here I need to talk to. Catch up later?'

'Sure, no probs.'

He ended the call and walked over.

'Hello again.'

'Hi. I just thought I should let you know that earlier . . . after you'd left, this bloke came up and started asking me questions about you. Who you were, what we'd been talking about.'

'What did you tell him?'

'I told him I didn't know you. You were just a punter. He said he was a cop but when I asked for ID to prove it he buggered off. Anyway, I thought I should let you know.'

Carver asked what did the guy look like, what was he wearing?

'A long khaki raincoat, blue hoodie under that and short hair – like an army cut. The weirdest thing about him was the sunglasses, expensive-looking – Ray-Bans maybe. Why would you need those in weather like this?'

Carver shook his head.

'And he only asked about me?'

'Just you.'

'Thank you, er . . .'

'Iris.'

'Thank you, Iris.'

'No probs.' She smiled.

Carver turned to go then changed his mind and turned back.

'Before I go, I wondered, do you still do that bottomless prosecco thing?'

'Sure. But I thought you weren't going up on the Eye?'

'I'm not. I'm going home. But I thought I might buy it anyway. For you . . . and those mates you've got coming. For your birthday.'

38

LOGAN INTERNATIONAL AIRPORT, BOSTON, USA

Jennifer walked a circuit of the business-class lounge at Boston airport looking for something she wanted to eat or drink. The problem wasn't a lack of choice – there was a seafood and sushi bar, a salad bar, an all-day breakfast station where a guy who looked like the Pillsbury Doughboy was standing, smiling, waiting to grill or griddle or fry you up some bacon, sausage, pancakes or pretty much anything else you could think of. Jennifer decided she wasn't hungry and headed instead for the juice bar where she ordered a Leafy Greens. It tasted horrible enough for her to be sure it must be doing her some good, and having finished it she was sure she deserved a glass of Gavi. Two glasses in fact.

She took these drinks to the far end of the lounge and found an empty seat and side table overlooking the runway. She reached into her Coach handbag for her laptop and opened it. Clive had sent through the summary of his various projects that she'd asked for but she'd only skim-read it. She looked at it again now to check there was enough raw material there for her to turn into a persuasive presentation. As she read, a couple of things surprised her.

Winner had promised a sunny-side-up assessment of how things were going – this document was hardly that.

'. . . huge potential but limited progress in the areas of space-based reflective sun shields . . . the risks of distributing calcium carbonate into the stratosphere are still unquantifiable . . .' Jennifer guessed that Clive's trip to New Mexico hadn't gone as he'd hoped. '. . . Several of the carbon capture projects have made progress but the costs of scaling up are significant . . .' Jennifer sucked at her teeth, she was going to have to completely rewrite this. The other surprise was Clive's decision to include a long section on the progress made in renewable research. He'd prefaced this with an NB: 'I know they'll want the sexy, geoengineering stuff Jen but make sure you chuck this in too . . . renewables are boring as hell but the work some of our teams have been doing is potentially game-changing if someone really gets behind it. Give it a go.'

Jennifer sighed. She was going to have to spend a good part of the flight trying to craft something that told Jeremy Cunis and his team about the geo projects they seemed most interested in but also gave them a bit of what Winner wanted them to hear. The third surprise came at the end of the email in the form of two postscripts from Clive:

P.S. Re. the 'Brains Trust' thing you mentioned – I'll do it if you think it could be worth our while. I'll send some Paris speech thoughts through ASAP.

P.P.S. On the cloud alteration work – I got something back from Edith. Not a ringing endorsement but not a bucket of shit either. She wants to meet up. Spain is a goner but maybe we can continue these experiments somewhere else? It could be the UK if the Poms will put their hands in their pockets?

Jennifer found herself nodding as she read. This was more like it. Perhaps she could make this work? She read on . . . 'Run the cloud thing by them. But keep it vague and make no promises – other parties also interested.'

'Fuck.'

39

THE 0914 LONDON KING'S CROSS TO CAMBRIDGE TRAIN

Carver had shaved before bed to save himself some time in the morning. It was a trick that Patrick regularly used and had suggested Carver try – a life hack he called it. The combination of having to catch an early-ish train to Cambridge and needing to look presentable for Edith Walston persuaded him to give it a go. It was just as well he did – a combination of insomnia and the irregular clanking sound of the hot-water pipes in the flat upstairs kept him awake until three. At that point he'd reset his alarm for seven and taken a sleeping pill. Four hours of sleep should be enough to get him through the day, so long as he kept himself regularly topped up with coffee.

The tube to King's Cross was a rush-hour-stuffed horror show but on the train to Cambridge he was travelling against traffic, and he had the carriage to himself. William stared out of the window, sipping at his double shot of espresso, and watching as a succession of terraced brick houses and small back gardens flashed by. He caught glimpses of trampolines, colourful plastic push-along cars, washing lines with sheets and clothes flapping vigorously in the wind. Naz was going to catch the bus from her house to Potters

Bar and join the train there, but there was no sign of her at the station or after the train pulled out. Chances were she'd made an earlier connection.

Carver took his reporter pad from inside his plastic bag and some of the photocopies that Naz had given him. He flicked through the articles before deciding to have a go at a piece Professor Walston had written called 'The Cirriform Conundrum'. He quickly realised why Naz had recommended some pre-meeting homework. The introduction to the article lauded the study, calling it the definitive piece of work on cirriform, cited more than any other study and responsible in part for Walston's unparalleled reputation and her many honorary degrees. He read a couple of pages before a combination of unfathomable Latin names and never-ending sentences defeated him. It needed an edit. He skimmed a couple of the other articles before turning instead to the notes he'd made after his meeting with Leonard Allen. He would run through these with Naz and work out what their next move should be.

If they didn't manage to meet on the train then the plan was to rendezvous at the coffee shop at the station, but as they pulled out of the last stop before Cambridge, Carver felt his phone vibrating inside his jacket pocket. He took it out and read the text: *William, v sorry but got a call late last night from Naomi asking me to cover for a producer who's gone sick. I'm in the office now. Crazy! Gutted to miss the Cambridge meeting, catch up later. Sorry . . . again. Naz.*

Carver shook his head. Since when did the editor of the programme ring round to try to fill a hole in the rota? This would be Naz's first full producer shift; her excitement was palpable, even in the short text message. He frisbeed his phone onto the empty seat opposite.

'Bloody Naomi.'

When the train reached the outskirts of Cambridge, he packed up his notebook and papers, retrieved his phone and went for a wee. Glancing at himself in the train toilet mirror Carver saw the obvious downside to shaving the night before instead of in the morning. He had five o'clock shadow at nine in the bloody morning. He splashed some water on his face, dried himself with a paper towel that felt like sandpaper and went to wait by one of the doors. His reasonably good mood had soured somewhat, but there was no point in sulking, he needed to get as much information as he could from this meeting with Clive Winner's favourite cloud expert. After that he would figure out how to win this stupid tug of war over Naz.

Carver handed the outbound half of his King's Cross to Cambridge return to the ticket collector at the station gates, walked out past the taxi rank and headed in the direction of the town centre. There were more boring-looking steel and metal buildings than he remembered seeing last time he was in Cambridge, but mainly around the station. As he approached the centre, more familiar landmarks began to appear. He navigated his way to Professor Walston's address via some of the famous and famously beautiful university college buildings as well as a couple of familiar pubs. He arrived at Victoria Terrace – a narrow street, lined with good tall straight trees – a few minutes early.

The brass plaque beneath her doorbell read 'E. R. Walston'. He rang the bell and waited, staring through the geometrically patterned stained glass into the corridor beyond. Before long a small shape appeared and moved briskly towards the door.

'William Carver?'

'Yes, pleased to meet you.'

The professor's eyes were so dark and deep-set that they appeared almost black. They studied Carver, top to toe, and left him with the impression that he'd been found wanting. Sure enough . . .

'Is it just you?'

'I'm afraid so.'

Her face was thin and bony, as was most of the rest of her. Her clothes were smart and slightly donnish – a white polo neck with gold glasses on a chain, a knee-length black skirt, woollen tights and sensible shoes. The only unusual thing about her appearance was the brightly coloured bobble hat she was wearing on her head. Maybe she'd just come back from a walk?

'I was expecting a young lady as well.'

'Oh yes, I'm sorry, but my colleague was called in to work on the programme late last night.'

'Poor her. Naziah wasn't it?'

Carver confirmed this.

'They work all night to put that show of yours on the radio then, do they?'

'Yes, fourteen hours.'

'Really? I always assumed you just turned up in the morning and gave it a good go.'

'No. There's quite a lot of preparation.'

'Interesting, I would never have guessed.' She looked past Carver, temporarily lost in thought. While she was doing this, he stared again at the bobble hat – it couldn't have looked more incongruous if it tried. Perhaps he should say something? 'Forgive me, leaving you standing there like a statue. Do come in, I've made coffee.'

'Thank you.' The walk from the station had left Carver parched and in urgent need of more caffeine.

Edith Walston led William down the corridor, ushering him into the first room they came to on the right, a strangely bright, high-ceilinged study. It had large picture windows and floor-to-ceiling bookshelves on every wall.

'This is where I work.'

It was the oddest-looking library, in fact one of the oddest-looking rooms, that Carver had ever seen. He stared at the shelves, uncertain at first what it was he was seeing. Every book in the room was turned towards the wall, with the white, cut pages facing outwards and the spine hidden. The professor let him take this in for a few moments before she spoke.

'I know it looks a little odd. I've heard that some silly interior designers have started doing this for aesthetic reasons. I assure you that's not why I do it. Although it does make the room feel nice and bright.'

'Why do you do it?'

'It's a game that I like to play with myself. A memory game. You have to stay sharp when you reach my stage in life. Some colleagues do crosswords or Wordles or whatever – I do this.'

'This being?'

'I'll give you a demonstration. What kind of books cross your mind when you consider my area of expertise?'

'Clouds?'

'Yes . . . clouds.'

William racked his brains. 'I don't really know what kind of books you'd read for your work, professor. Rather technical ones I would imagine.'

'Not always. Take a guess.'

Carver remembered the cuttings Naz had given him.

'I suppose you'll have a few copies of the International Meteorological Report here. I read that excellent piece about cirriform clouds that you wrote.'

'Did you? Poor you. I'm afraid that piece has been rather over-accoladed. It could have used a good edit . . .' She glanced around the room. 'I don't have those here. I read the Meteorological Reports of course, but I don't keep them. Try again.'

'Er . . .'

'Come on! Which book springs to mind when I say the word "cloud".'

Carver felt a little panicked.

'Shelley. Shelley springs to mind.'

Edith Walston lifted an eyebrow. 'Interesting. I did not expect you to say that.'

'Well . . .'

'Don't worry, I like to be surprised . . . that's why clouds are my thing. Endlessly surprising. You know Shelley's cloud poem, do you?'

Carver hesitated. Buying himself some time.

'I knew it once, a long time ago . . . "I bring fresh showers for the thirsting flowers" . . . er . . .'

'Go on.'

'I'm not sure I can remember much more. Something about "Orbed maidens and fleecy floors" . . . it all gets a bit purple as I recall.'

Edith Walston frowned.

'I think if you're Percy Shelley, then you're entitled to get a touch purple now and then.' She walked to the bookshelf closest to the window. William watched her right hand hover around the back-to-front books for a while before it plucked one from the middle shelf. She gave a satisfied little grunt.

'Not senile yet.' She opened the book. 'Although the irregular cut of the pages is a bit of a giveaway.' She turned the marbled end sheet and flicked through a few pages until she found the poem. She passed it to him. 'It's one of my favourites.'

She indicated with a gesture of her bobble-hatted head that Carver should take a seat and sat down herself in a large white leather armchair. It appeared that he'd passed some sort of test.

'What exactly did you want to talk to me about, Mr Carver? Your colleague Naziah said that it had something to do with Clive Winner, but not much more than that.'

Carver explained that he was interested in doing a story about Mr Winner, on the work he'd been doing on climate change with the backing of the UK government. In particular, Carver was interested in these geoengineering projects Mr Winner was involved in – notably the cloud-brightening and thinning work. He knew that the professor advised him on this and that she was the world's leading authority. He hoped that talking to her might help him understand cloud brightening and also what Mr Winner and the government were hoping to achieve. Carver was pretty pleased with the pitch he made – intriguing and unthreatening, reasonably flattering and suitably vague. He waited.

'I see. But you don't work for a science programme though, do you, Mr Carver?'

'No.'

'Nor a business programme either.'

'Not exactly, although we do—'

'You work for a news programme.'

'That's right.'

'Okay, I just wanted to be clear in my mind about that.' Professor Walston had her hands folded in her lap. She was staring at Carver as though he were a particularly troubling cloud. 'Why don't you go ahead and ask me some of your questions and we can see how we go.'

Carver nodded. Perhaps his pitch hadn't been as persuasive as he'd hoped.

'Of course.' He reached into his plastic bag for a pen and pad. 'Do you mind if I make notes?'

'I'd be concerned if you didn't. How else would you have an accurate account of our conversation?'

'Er, yes.' William wondered whether the professor had forgotten about the coffee, he really needed one. 'Perhaps I can start by just asking what it is you and Clive Winner talk about?'

'About clouds.'

'Could you be more specific?'

'I could be extremely specific, but I think I'd probably lose you within a minute. Or less.' This was a little insulting but also almost certainly true. 'Clive Winner comes to me because as you said I'm the foremost expert in the field.' There was nothing boastful to this, it was a simple statement of fact. 'He telephones me now and again. Sometimes he visits, especially when he needs someone to push his ideas against. He sends me data too, now and again.' The professor shifted slightly in her seat.

'You're sort of a one-woman peer review process?'

'Something like that. Although I'm not sure Clive Winner considers anyone his peer. Still, he finds me useful. And I find him interesting. He has a lively mind. I enjoy talking with him . . . even when he's talking nonsense.'

'Are his cloud-altering ideas nonsense?'

'Not at all. But it's complicated.'

'Putting a dimmer switch on the sun?'

Professor Walston met Carver's eye.

'You object to that term, do you?'

'I have no opinion.'

'Really? Are you sure you haven't already made your mind up about Clive Winner?'

'Not at all.'

'Okay, just checking. Well, whether you like the "dimmer switch on the sun" phrase or not, it's much easier to say it than it is to do it. You read, or attempted to read, that piece I wrote about cirriform?'

'Yes.'

'Well, they are part of the problem – high altitude, ice-particle-carrying clouds – thin enough to let the rays of the sun shine through but thick enough to hold the earth's warmth in. Shelley was a little off the mark with that one . . .'

'I beg your pardon?'

Edith gestured at the ox-blood-coloured hardback on the coffee table.

'"Sunbeam-proof, I hang like a roof" . . . it's a line from the same poem. Well cirriform clouds aren't. Sunbeam-proof I mean.'

'Poetic licence I suppose.'

'Partly. And partly ignorance. We didn't know much about clouds back then. The trouble is, I'm not convinced that we know an awful lot more two hundred years later. Clouds are complicated. Spraying them with seawater or sulphates or sprinkling them with diamond dust or Lord knows what else doesn't make their behaviour easier to predict. If anything, it makes it more difficult.'

Carver had been scribbling away in shorthand. Now he stopped.

'Did you say diamond dust?'

40

BA 212 BOS TO LHR

The main cabin on the red-eye to London was at capacity, and as a result a handful of economy passengers had been bumped up to business. Jennifer wasn't against this on principle, she wasn't a snob, she just wished that whoever it was that decided who to upgrade could do a better job of it. The young woman sitting diagonally across from her right now was a case in point. The girl had been practically vibrating with excitement from the moment she sat down – or rather didn't sit down. Seasoned Boston to London business travellers were easy to spot; they got on the plane, had one drink, and worked – some for an hour, some for longer. That done they put their seat into its fully horizontal position, put on an eye mask and some noise-cancelling headphones, covered themselves in a blanket and slept. The woman adjacent to Jennifer had phoned her sister and several friends before take-off to let them know she was travelling business; she'd wandered up and down the cabin for a while, drank four glasses of champagne and had long conversations with the stewardess about what she should have for supper and breakfast. After that she'd flicked through the in-flight entertainment options, announcing her movie choices out loud. Now she'd found the complimentary White Company Relax and Restore kit and was spritzing and moisturising herself while testing the hydraulics on her adjustable seat – trying out a variety of different positions, seemingly for fun. Jennifer was trying to work – to work and not to reach across the aisle and throttle her.

She'd rewritten the geoengineering update that Clive had sent her but with her own added and significantly more positive spin. The way she was planning to tell it, the space-based reflective sun-shields were showing potential, as was Winner's carbon capture programme. As far as the cloud-brightening work was concerned, the Spanish project was being phased out – there was no reason to give them all the whys and wherefores – the data gathered was being analysed by various experts in the field including Clive's favourite, Cambridge-based academic. The next stage of this exciting research could happen anywhere with the correct topography and coastline; Jennifer planned to drop Northumberland, Cornwall and the north Norfolk coast into this part of the conversation. She made a note to ask her team to identify a couple of other places where the UK government had promised . . . what was their phrase? – levelling up.

A shadow fell across her computer screen, and she glanced up. It was her annoying neighbour. 'Excuse me, I'm really sorry to bother you but can I ask if you're planning to use that?' She was pointing at the complimentary pampering pouch, sitting unopened on Jennifer's armrest.

'I'm not sure.'

'It's just that if you're not . . . or if you don't . . . I've got a mate who would completely die if I gave it to her.'

Jennifer handed the pouch over.

'Be my guest.'

She spent another half hour subbing down the renewable-related research that Clive had sent to a length that would not test the Brits' patience. It seemed clear that Downing Street's interest in waves and wind was limited – not cutting edge or exciting enough to build a new science park around – but her boss wanted it included and so . . . She checked the time. If she didn't stop soon and get some sleep, then tomorrow was going to be a nightmare. She had one more look at the suggestions that her and her team had come up with for the prime minister's Paris speech. They weren't bad but she knew that Clive would do better; with luck his ideas would arrive before the meeting, although knowing him it would be seconds before she had to knock on that Downing Street door. She closed her laptop.

'Sleep.'

Jennifer remembered that she'd promised to call her son before his bedtime . . . before her plane took off. Ryley would be asleep now and she was thirty thousand feet above the North Atlantic. She'd call as soon as she landed. She pressed the call button and asked the stewardess for one more glass of Gavi – a nightcap. How many was that? Three. Possibly four. She drank her wine. Adjusted her seat. Closed her eyes and tried to sleep. She couldn't. There was something else nagging at her. Jennifer retrieved the laptop from her seat pocket and opened it again, she went to her emails and found the message her assistant had sent through, it was titled: *No. 10 Ansafone CONFIDENTIAL*

She plugged her headphones into the computer, clicked on the audio file attached and listened again to the voicemail message that was troubling her. It was straightforward really: the London-accented journalist was asking for details regarding Clive's role in Number 10's climate change strategy. She also wanted to log an interview request. Her programme would be happy to talk to Mr Winner at any time and in any way that suited him – studio, ISDN line, phone etc. Jennifer had a stock press release that answered the first point. As regards the interview request it was a simple: Clive Winner thanks you very much for your interest, but take a hike. The message was unremarkable apart from the fact that no other journalist had ever got hold of this number or used this line. Jennifer wondered how the young, slightly nervous-sounding woman had happened across it. More than that she wondered why this message or the person who'd left it was so . . . what was Jeremy Cunis' phrase? – 'potentially difficult' – to Downing Street that they'd decided to raise it with her.

41

VICTORIA TERRACE, MIDSUMMER COMMON, CAMBRIDGE, UK

Carver was getting an unasked for but not uninteresting crash course in clouds.

'They're all excellent as far as I'm concerned but if you're interested in cooling the planet then some clouds are better at that than others. The trouble is how do you create the clouds you want and avoid the ones you don't? Get the brightening and thinning just right and maybe you can slow global warming, you win the Nobel Prize, they put up statues and everybody loves you. But if you get it wrong . . .'

'No more fresh showers for the thirsting flowers?'

'Exactly. Perhaps you overshoot a little and accidently shut down the Indian monsoon system – which is a real risk by the way. Even getting it a tiny bit wrong could mean less rain, less wheat, more famine, mass migration and tens of thousands of dead people.'

'You've told Clive Winner this?'

'He knows, or I think he knows. Every time I see him, I remind him what a very bad idea it is – rushing into a dramatic, world-reshaping technology in a huge hurry. There's still a lot of science to be done, numbers to be crunched. And of course, the numbers need to be reliable, the data sets have to be clean and complete. I'll tell him again when I see him next . . .' She paused. 'Forgive me, Mr Carver, I promised you coffee, didn't I?'

'Oh, yes. Thank you.'

'You stay right there, I'll fetch it.'

Edith Walston popped her bobble-hatted head around the door a couple of times to ask whether he took milk. Then sugar. He got the feeling that she was more interested in checking that he was still sitting where she'd left him than she was in finding out how he took his coffee. Carver sat and stared around the room; this combination of white walls with all the backward-facing books and Edith's huge white leather chair brought to mind a padded cell. Carver found it strangely comforting; he could hear some light birdsong from the garden and the sound of the kettle boiling in the kitchen next door but nothing else. It was also as neat as a pin. The only item out of place in the whole room was a magazine that the professor must have been reading when he'd rang the doorbell and was now lying on the floor next to her chair. The magazine was open and halfway down the right-hand column of the visible page was a story that somebody – Edith herself presumably – had found interesting. She'd drawn a neat square around the article in red biro.

He leant forward in his seat to get a better look; the text was upside down from where he was sitting, but he had always been able to read just as well that way round as the right way up. The problem was distance; he shuffled to the edge of his seat, mindful that the sound of a boiling kettle in the kitchen next door had been replaced by the sounds of crockery and cutlery. The magazine was the *New Scientist*. He squinted, trying to read the date and page number, shuffling forward until it was only one corner of one buttock that was still in contact with the chair. As a result, when the door suddenly swung open and the professor appeared, holding a tea tray, it was just one square inch of bottom and a degree of core strength that Carver didn't know he had that stopped him from toppling head-first onto the floor. He attempted to disguise the huffing sound of a big man overexerting himself as a cough and shuffled back into his seat, smiling. Edith smiled back, and on her way across to the coffee table casually pushed the magazine underneath her chair with the toe of her left shoe.

They drank coffee and talked about clouds. There was a plate of custard creams on the tea tray and Carver munched his way through those as well. Eventually he saw the professor checking her watch, it was clear that she was planning to bring the meeting to a conclusion before long. He picked up the penultimate custard cream and nibbled at it, buying some time.

'Mr Winner obviously has a reasonably good relationship with the government. With the prime minister himself in fact. I know he's received a fair bit of money from the Great Green British Business Bank and that several of his projects have been funded that way. I don't suppose he's spoken to you at all about that?'

'Not my area of interest. I know he speaks to the prime minister now and then. All sorts of other politicians too I imagine . . . poor man.'

'And to foreign governments and financial institutions I suppose?'

Professor Walston checked her watch once more.

'I have another appointment, Mr Carver. And quite frankly, this fishing expedition of yours has become a little too obvious. If you want answers to these sorts of questions, you should ask Clive Winner directly.'

'I would if I could. I wondered if maybe you could help me with that?' It was a last and somewhat desperate throw of the dice.

'I am many things, Mr Carver, but a diary secretary for Clive Winner is not one of them. I'll see you out.' She stood and waited for him to do the same. 'I enjoyed aspects of our meeting if not the entire thing.'

'I'm very grateful for your time. And I'm sorry to have been so . . .'

'Pushy?'

'I was going to say nosey.'

'Let's settle on pushy and nosey.'

'Fair enough.' William reached for his wallet. 'I know it's a long shot but just in case you think of anything else or if for any reason you find yourself in need of a boorish, nosey, news journalist . . . can I leave you this?'

The professor snorted. But she took Carver's business card and pocketed it. She walked him to the door.

'Goodbye.'

Edith Walston stayed staring out through the stained glass in the centre of her front door until her visitor had gone. She walked back into her study and retrieved the copy of *New Scientist* from underneath her armchair. She ripped the page with the highlighted article from the magazine and folded it in half. She would put it in the manila envelope, along with the others – more than a dozen news stories and feature articles now. She would ask Clive Winner about them when she saw him. The question was, what she would do if Clive either wouldn't or couldn't explain what on earth was going on. If that was the case, perhaps William Carver's business card might prove to be useful after all.

42

CÁDIZ, ANDALUSIA, SPAIN

The son of the Cádiz shop owner was no less creepy than his father. In fact, Carlos found him even more repellent. He turned Alma's phone in his hand, studying it.

'I charge forty euros to open this make of mobile – they can be tricky.'

'Fine.' It seemed like a lot, but Carlos had little choice.

'Okay, I'll get going. I don't have to worry about there being anything dodgy on this phone, do I? Nothing illegal or obscene?' The lank-haired kid didn't look worried.

'No, nothing like that.'

'Okay.'

Carlos watched him work. He removed the SIM first and put it into another phone, then attached that to his laptop via a cable.

'Can you talk me through what you're doing?'

'I'm opening your phone.'

'I know, but how?'

'If I told you that, then you'd be doing it and charging other people thirty-five euros and I'd be out of business.' He took the SIM card out of his phone and put it back into Alma's. He switched it on. 'Looks like that's worked.' Sure enough the phone was waking up. Carlos recognised the photo on the front of Alma's mobile. A snap that Loli had taken of the two of them outside the Che bar. Carlos was sitting on his girlfriend's lap, they were both grinning like fools.

'I need to open up the back to do the next bit.' He fumbled around in the drawer. 'I can't find my pliers. Do me a favour, go and ask my dad for the spare suction pliers, will you?' Carlos did as the boy asked but when he got back it seemed they were no longer required.

'Don't worry, I've found them. I've reset your password to six zeros.'

'Okay.'

'You can change it to anything you want.'

'Right.'

'Do you want to know what the old code was?'

'Sure.'

'For five more euros?' Carlos shot the boy a look. 'Just kidding. I'll tell you anyway. It was zero four, ten, ninety-nine.' Carlos took the phone in both hands and stared at it. At Alma's beautiful smiling face. When he looked back up the kid was staring at him. 'What's that pass code all about then? Your first date? First time you . . . you know . . . fucked?'

'Here's your money.'

He tossed two twenty-euro notes onto the boy's workbench and left. The date 4 October 1999 was Carlos' first day at school. His mum had moved from the mountains to the seaside town; they'd had to leave at short notice because of problems at home – problems related to his father. He and his mother had arrived in Barossa with two suitcases and the clothes on their backs. The local school was already halfway through the autumn term but they found room for Carlos. On his first day, the teacher had asked the seven-year-old Alma to look after this raggedy new arrival. 041099 was the first day that Carlos and Alma set eyes on each other and for Carlos at least it had been love at first sight.

On the ride back from Cádiz to home, Carlos had his mind on other things. On the past and not the present. He kept the bike in the right-hand lane and drove slowly. The shaven-headed man in the silver Toyota had no problem keeping an eye on Carlos from two, sometimes even three, cars back. Carlos led him all the way home. To the street that he lived on, right to his front door.

43

THE 1435 CAMBRIDGE TO LONDON KING'S CROSS TRAIN

Carver called Naz from the train. He called her several times before giving up and leaving what he subsequently feared was a rather short-tempered-sounding message. His train was pulling into King's Cross station when she rang back.

'Hey there, William.' She sounded sleepy.

'Where've you been?'

'Asleep. For an hour or two anyway. I worked last night, remember?'

'Oh yeah. Bollocks. I'm sorry. I can call back if you like, although—'

'Don't worry, I'm awake now. How'd it go with the professor?'

'So-so. She's an interesting character. She's got her own issues with Winner but she likes him and she's loyal. Something tells me that she might be willing to help us . . . just not yet.'

'Okay.'

'I'll bring you up to speed properly face to face but I needed to ask a quick favour.'

'Shoot.'

'Do you have the *New Scientist* at home? I mean do your parents sell it in their shop?'

'I think so, my mum and dad stock just about every magazine you can think of. Why?'

'Professor Walston had a copy in her study, and she didn't seem that keen on me seeing it.'

'So?'

'So . . . we need to see it.'

'And it was this week's edition?'

'I'm hoping so. Could you have a look and phone me back?'

'Sure.'

Naz climbed out of bed, pulled a jumper on over her pyjamas, and went downstairs to the shop in search of the magazine. She stopped briefly in the storeroom to see if there was anything there that she felt like eating – she'd skipped breakfast and now her stomach was rumbling but nothing took her fancy. In the shop, her dad was at his usual post, standing on the box behind the till.

'I thought you were asleep, did the bell wake you?' He gestured up at the brass shop bell on its curled spring. 'I can put some cotton wool inside there for the rest of the day, no problem.'

'No. Thanks, Dad, the bell's fine. I just remembered that I had some work I needed to finish.'

'It is sleeping that you need to finish.'

'I will. As soon as I've done this one thing . . .'

She went to the magazine rack and found the most recent *New Scientist* tucked in between the *New Internationalist* and *New Statesman*.

'Can I borrow this?'

'Of course.' Her dad gave her a sympathetic smile. 'Will you also check for me that the new camera is working?'

'Sure, Dad.'

On the way back up through the house Naz checked. It was working fine. She took the magazine upstairs to her room; sat down at her desk and called Carver.

'Did you get it?'

'Yes.'

'Great, hang on . . . I'm at King's Cross, let me try and find a quiet spot.' He disappeared for a time, Naz listened to the familiar sounds of a major train terminal. Platform announcements, bustle, the booming acoustic of a huge, high-ceilinged building with thousands of people moving through it. Eventually it started to fade and Carver was back.

'Where do all these bloomin' people come from? Or go to? I'm outside now. So if you have a look at page thirteen. And page eighteen. I think it was one or the other.' He waited while Naz looked. 'Is there anything there that jumps out at you? Anything about Winner or any of his projects?'

'Not that I can see. How about I WhatsApp you a photo of both pages and you have a look.'

'Good idea, yes.'

'If it's not there I can go online later and look at back copies.'

'Great, yes. So, when are we going to meet? You probably need a couple more hours' sleep so how about we say—'

Naz interrupted. 'William, I was about to tell you. I have to work again this evening.'

'What?'

'Naomi asked me to work again tonight.'

'Tell her to bugger off. I can tell her if you like.'

Naz stared down at her desk. The open magazine.

'The thing is . . .' She paused.

'What's the thing?'

Naz told him. After that morning's show had finished and the post-programme briefing, Naomi had offered Naz a full-time job as a producer.

'A desk job? You don't want that.' He hesitated. 'Do you?'

'The truth is I'm not sure. It's a good offer. A one-year contract, proper pay . . . it's pretty tempting.'

'What about the work we're doing? This investigation? What about the certificate? Any journalist worth—'

'I know, I know . . . any journalist worth their salt has got the National Certificate. I'd like to finish it . . .'

'You have to finish it.'

'Naomi said I don't. Or perhaps I leave it for now and come back to it later.'

'No. I've seen what happens . . . once you take a job inside that glass and steel monstrosity it's all but impossible to get out. You're not some desk jockey, Naz, you're an investigative journalist – or you could be. You've got the ability, the instincts . . . all of it. You just need to stick with it.' He paused, waiting for Naz to respond.

She was silent for a worryingly long time, then: 'It just all feels like a bit too much right now, William. The day job, studying for the exams, the Clive Winner investigation . . . I feel like I'm drowning.'

'I understand.'

'On top of that there was the visit from the goon in dark glasses . . . that's completely weirded my parents out.'

'Okay. I see. Let's think this through . . . what have you told Naomi?'

'I told her I needed some time. That I wanted to talk to you and to my mum and dad and that I'd call her after I'd done that.'

'Good. That's good. The important thing is not to make any kind of hasty decision. Especially when you're tired. You worked all last night; you should be sleeping really.'

'Yes, well . . .'

'How about this . . . you go and get your head down; you need at least four hours.'

'Naomi said seven.'

'Between four and seven, that's right. So you go and get some more sleep and then you call me when you're up and we'll talk it all through. We'll figure out a plan. Plus I need to give you chapter and verse about the meeting with Professor Walston. I really think there's a chance she'll take us to Winner, if we play our cards right.'

'Okay.'

'Good. Speak to you later and, er . . . sleep well, Naz.'

William pocketed his phone. He was standing outside King's Cross station, directly opposite the St Pancras hotel. He gazed up at the ornate spires and turrets and the rich red brick. In front, a tree, its branches dancing in the wind. He'd been a one-man band for years before Patrick came along. He guessed he could go back to working that way if he needed to. But that wasn't what he wanted. He realised that when he'd told Naz that she should *stick with it* what he really meant was that she should stick with him. They were a team. In which case he needed to be more supportive. And get her some help. It was time to call in the cavalry.

44

WHITEHALL, LONDON

'How does the prime minister get in and out of Downing Street when things like this happen?'

Jennifer's taxi driver shrugged. 'Back entrance maybe? Or I heard there's a tunnel that goes all the way from Number 10 right into Westminster. A mate of mine reckons he saw the door when he was doing the tour of Churchill's War Rooms. Might be complete bollocks of course.' The cabbie turned to look at his passenger. 'You might want to walk the last bit, it doesn't look like we're going anywhere soon.'

Jennifer paid and took the man's advice. The approach to Downing Street was well and truly jammed, the protestors had lain down in the road and traffic was at a standstill in both directions. Jennifer walked up Whitehall, past the Cenotaph and after a little pushing and polite apologising she managed to slalom her way through the thousand or more protesting students and get to the metal entrance gates at the top of Downing Street. She heard a few shouted remarks as she was allowed in past the first security check: *Are you part of the problem, or part of the solution? . . . Tell the prime minister we think he's a knob.*

She smiled. The demo was good-spirited, someone was playing Marvin Gaye through a speaker attached to the back of their bike and the placards were a cut above anything Jennifer had seen back in the States. It occurred to her that the prime minister might even want to take a couple of the gags and slogans and repurpose them for his Paris speech. It wasn't until she gave her name to the security guard and was told that she wasn't on their list that Jennifer had anything to worry about. She called Jeremy Cunis, who answered straight away, seemingly expecting her call.

'Don't worry, some bureaucratic cock-up no doubt. I'll come and get you.'

He came and got her, promising the security guard that he'd sign her in formally inside. They walked up Downing Street together. Jeremy wore a blue three-piece suit – the waistcoat uncomfortably tight – he'd put on a significant amount of weight since Jennifer had last seen him.

'You made it through the revolting hordes. Well done.'

'They seemed pretty friendly to me.'

Jeremy shrugged. 'I suppose so, I'd still prefer it if they were in school, rather than standing outside my office yelling. Judgemental little so-and-sos.'

'Perhaps we deserve to be judged . . .' She glanced across at him. 'Our generation I mean.'

'Good God, you sound like the PM when he's in full Paris mode. Probably not a bad thing, given the reasons that you're here. It's very kind of you to come all this way.'

'It's my pleasure.'

'Everyone's very excited.'

Jennifer nodded. She wondered who 'everyone' might be and how excited they really were. The famous black front door did its magical swinging-open thing as they approached. There was another security desk inside, but Jeremy walked them straight past that one as well and up the stairs. They climbed a couple of flights, then walked to the very back of the building.

'Here we are. I'll gather my little gang together and then we can get going. Coffee?'

'Tea. If you have it.'

'Tea? In England?' He turned and smiled. 'I'll see what we can do.'

A man in blue overalls was busy removing a piece of art from the wall outside the room where Jeremy had left her. The artwork consisted of two lines of messy handwriting, blown up into two-foot-tall, bright-white neon. The scribbled sentence read: *I cried because I love you.* Jennifer liked it. She wondered why the artwork was being taken down and asked the guy in overalls as much.

'All I got told was that the artist wanted it back. It was only here on loan.'

Jennifer suspected that it would take Jeremy a while to gather his people together; in the meantime she decided to call Ryley. He was eating his breakfast. Froot Loops no doubt.

'Guess where I am.'

'London?'

'Sure, London, but where in London?' There was a sighing sound but no words. 'Well, I'm in Number 10 Downing Street. Actually inside. That's the British prime minister's crib.'

'I know what Downing Street is, Mom. And please don't say crib.'

'Sorry. I'm just trying to impress you. Whatchu up to today then? It's a soccer day, isn't it?'

'There's no match. It got rained off. Dad says we might head over to the house of a friend of his. They've got billiards and an indoor pool.'

'Really? That sounds fun.' She switched her phone from one ear to the other. *Don't ask. Do not ask.* 'Who's the friend?'

'Um . . . like Lindy or Linda?'

'Cool. That all sounds really cool.' She looked down the empty corridor to her left then back at the closed door. 'Well listen, I've gotta go do this meeting. You have fun and I'll call again later, okay?'

'Sure.'

'I love you.'

'Yeah.' He hesitated. 'Me too.'

In the event it took Jeremy very little time at all to gather his people. Staring at them from her end of the unnecessarily long conference table Jennifer wondered whether this might be because the people he'd brought were unlikely to have been in great demand elsewhere. No Cabinet Secretary, no Permanent Secretary . . . no civil servants at all in fact. Just a bunch of kids. 'Meat in the room' was what they called it back home. Not a phrase Jennifer was fond of, but a lot of companies did it. Having a few folk nodding along while you made your argument was a must in American meetings these days and it appeared that like a lot of nasty business habits, it had spread to politics as well. Jeremy's team was made up of four ridiculously young-looking political researchers. Introductions were made, two of the kids fell over each other to pour her a cup of Earl Grey tea, Jeremy opened his laptop, and the meeting began. Jennifer launched right in with the good news.

'So, I ran your Brains Trust idea by Clive; he's ridiculously busy but he wants to be part of this, he's already had several thoughts about how we might make the prime minister's address . . .' She paused for effect. '. . . A *speech for the ages* was your description I think, Jeremy.' Cunis gave a half-hearted nod. 'We'll make time in Clive's diary so he and the PM can sit down and work through some ideas together. Paris is only a few weeks away so I assume you're thinking *asap*?'

Jeremy coughed. 'Yes, well, let's not get ahead of ourselves.'

'I'm sorry?'

'There are a few things we need to establish before we start planning face-to-face meetings and whatnot.'

'I'm sorry. I thought the Paris speech, this Brains Trust thing were your absolute priorities?'

'We have many priorities. And several things we need to clarify before we start organising prime-ministerial play dates.' He turned and smiled at his team who smiled back – that was their job. Jennifer did not smile. What was going on here? Jeremy glanced down at his laptop then at her. 'Let's rewind a little. Perhaps you could begin by updating us on Mr Winner's various projects?'

'Of course, happy to.' She'd had her hotel print out the notes she'd made on the plane, and she turned to those now. She'd decided to start with the geoengineering projects she knew Jeremy and co. were keen to hear about and get to the renewable stuff that Clive wanted mentioned later. Much later. She kept her voice bright and the energy high. The pitch went well.

'The headline is we're making good progress in all areas . . .'

The way Jennifer told it, the work that Winner's teams were doing on space-based reflective shields was exciting . . . his idea that you could increase the protective power of the stratosphere had been proven in theory and they were on their way to making it work in practice. Jeremy tapped away at his laptop, making notes while she spoke and chipping in with questions now and again.

'How about the various carbon-capture projects, Jennifer? I think a healthy-sized chunk of British money has gone into that work. The PM will probably want to mention it in the Paris speech.'

'It has indeed and absolutely; the prime minister should be shouting that from the rooftops.' She gave him a sunny-side-up assessment of this work too and promised to send further facts and figures. She was keen to get to the cloud-brightening work and dangle the carrot of more UK involvement that Clive had suggested. Jeremy beat her to it.

'How about the cloud-related research? We've heard rumours that the Spanish-based project might have run its course.'

Jennifer nodded. Something about his tone of voice suggested that Jeremy knew not just this, but significantly more.

'That's right. We're analysing the data collected so far – there's a lot of it – in fact we're using some excellent British-based brain power to do that work – and then we'll move forward.'

'Move forward how exactly?'

'Well, you understand the whole development process as well as anyone, Jeremy . . .' The prime minister's special adviser agreed that yes he did. '. . . but for the benefit of others, I'm talking about larger-scale tests until we reach the point where we have proof of concept. After that we'll start moving into development and production.'

'Of course.'

Now was the time to unsleeve what Jennifer believed to be her second ace card. She hoped it would go down better than the first.

'Mr Winner wanted me to use this meeting to sound you out on the idea of doing that here, in the UK.'

'All of it?'

'That's right.'

'The testing, the development, production . . . everything?'

'Testing first of course, but for that all we'd need would be a little more financial support and the right piece of coastline. We've been looking at north Norfolk, Cornwall . . .' She reeled off a recently updated list of English counties and seaside towns that all happened to have been promised a chunk of levelling-up money ahead of the next election. She had copies of the potential test sites for people to look at, and while she read they passed these around. Jeremy and his small gang of room-fillers nodded their approval. It was going well. The only thing troubling Jennifer was the amount of time that her opposite number was spending making notes or staring at his laptop. She'd stopped speaking and still he typed.

'Everything okay, Jeremy?'

He looked up. 'All good. This proposal of yours, bringing the whole show here. This would be, as you like to say on your side of the pond – a big deal.'

'It would. Ambitious in the extreme. The kinda project you could imagine, for instance, building a science park around.'

Jeremy laughed.

'Very good.' Jeremy glanced down at his screen again. He was in conversation with someone outside the room, Jennifer was sure of it now. The prime minister himself? Unlikely. Who then? When he looked back up from the laptop, he was all business.

'We should talk about money.'

'Of course. How about I give you some numbers, an idea of what we think would cost what, if we bring the whole show, or some of the show, to the UK? Bear in mind these are just Fenway Park figures.'

'Fenway P . . . oh, I get it.'

Sums of money were bandied about. Cunis seemed unphased by the big numbers that Jennifer opened with. Amounts of money that if agreed would make Clive Winner a happy man. Everybody was getting along and the energy in the room was good. Jennifer decided that now was the time to keep the promise she'd made to Clive and mention his renewable projects. The words had barely left her lips when Jeremy raised a hand and stopped her.

'Er . . . I know you mentioned you'd made some progress in that department, Jennifer, but I'm not sure we want to use this meeting to talk about that. As I think I said before, we've had every Tom, Dick and Harriet you can think of bending our ear about bigger wind farms, more solar panels and the rest.'

Jennifer nodded, although she could remember Jeremy saying no such thing.

'I understand.' At least she could say she tried.

Jeremy glanced at his screen again. It was like playing a game of good cop, bad cop but with the added complication that the bad cop was outside the room and communicating via an act of ventriloquism.

'We were actually hoping to get some reassurance from you in the other direction.'

'I'm not sure I understand.'

'Back when Mr Winner and the PM first struck up this relationship your boss used to tell us that climate change was simply a geoengineering problem.'

'Yes, I remember.'

'Do you think Mr Winner still believes that?'

'Of course.'

'Good to know.'

The remainder of the meeting was taken up largely with Jeremy's young colleagues discussing the list of possible test sites that Jennifer had given them. They were quizzing each other about the number of constituencies around a given area, their current political affiliation, and the size of the majority that the sitting Member of Parliament – their own or the other side's – had won last time around. Jennifer didn't fully understand what they were talking about, but she got the gist.

As the clock on the meeting-room wall clicked towards two, Jeremy removed himself from the political parlour game that his colleagues were playing, closed his laptop and offered to walk Jennifer out. He gave her a short, cheery, guided tour of the nooks and crannies of Downing Street. The Cabinet Room . . . the door to the prime minister's apartment. They walked past a portrait of Wellington and a couple of small Henry Moore sculptures; Jeremy listed the names of every prime minister featured in portrait form as they walked down the main staircase. He insisted on walking with her not only to the main front door but right out into the street. Standing on the pavement, with Jennifer on the point of saying goodbye, he spoke again, his tone different now.

'I'm sorry if I appeared a little . . . conflicted at certain times during the meeting.'

Jennifer shook her head. 'Not a problem.'

'Once we manage to get your boss and mine together in a room, all things will be possible. But I need to tiptoe around several elephant traps before that will be allowed to happen.'

'Okay.'

'You're an intelligent woman, I'm sure you noticed several ways in which this meeting differed from our previous Downing Street encounters.'

'Yes.'

'And I'm confident that you'll draw the appropriate conclusions – you and Mr Winner – once you have a chance to report back.' Jeremy glanced back over his shoulder. 'I should go. One last thing . . .'

'Yes?'

'If you could give Mr Winner our regards.'

'Of course.'

'And tell him to be careful.'

'Careful? Of what?'

'Just tell him that.'

45

NATIONAL PORTRAIT GALLERY, ST MARTIN'S PLACE, LONDON

Rebecca was having what she thought of as one of those good London days. A day when you feel lucky to live in the city, when the transport system works, the journey into town is a breeze, you feel grateful to live so close to somewhere as amazing as the National Portrait Gallery. The baby was increasingly interested in staring at people's faces and so Rebecca thought she'd give her daughter the chance to gaze into the eyes of a few famous and slightly weird-looking ones. The Portrait Gallery was one of Rebecca's favourite places, a significant location for her and Patrick and she wanted Leila to like it as much as she did. Rebecca checked the buggy in at security and carried Leila around the various galleries. Before long, inevitably they ended up standing in front of her favourite picture: Jane Austen as painted by her sister Cassandra in particularly watery watercolours. If you waved your hand or moved your head in front of the special display cabinet, then a light inside switched on and then off. Leila loved it.

'That's Jane at the disco.' Rebecca whispered the joke that Patrick had told her, to their daughter. That had been one of the first times he'd made Rebecca laugh out loud. She tried to remember the last time the pair of them had laughed out loud together and couldn't. Still, at least he'd finally got in touch with William and agreed to meet him. That was a start. After a quick nappy change in the loo next to the lift near the Pre-Raphaelites they went to the café and from there to the shop. She checked her watch, she wanted to get home before the evening rush but there was plenty of time to walk down to Whitehall and have a quick look if she wanted to. And she did want to. A couple of the kids from the placard-making workshop had messaged her saying that they were planning to be at the Downing Street demo. It wasn't going to be a big thing, more a dry run ahead of the nationwide school strike, which the various green groups involved had agreed would take place the day before the climate conference started. The teenage kids who'd contacted her weren't even sure who had organised today's event – it had been 'kinda organic' they said.

Wheeling the buggy down past Trafalgar Square and into Whitehall it became clear that – organic or not – it was big. The striking school kids had managed to block the traffic in both directions. Apparently, a large group of teenagers had sat themselves down in the middle of the street and were refusing to move; a few of the kids had handcuffed or even – it was rumoured – glued themselves to buses. Rebecca stopped at the point just before the crowd thickened. She and Patrick had talked about taking Leila on demonstrations; broadly speaking Patrick was against it. His main objection was safety, he'd seen how quickly demonstrations could turn violent. He'd been caught in the middle of this several times. Rebecca looked at the young school strikers, it looked more like a festival than anything else. This was London on a bright autumn day not Hong Kong or Cairo or any of the various other places where Patrick had seen things turn nasty. Just then she caught sight of one of the girls who'd been at her workshop, holding one of Rebecca's favourite placards. She looked down at Leila who was smiling broadly and apparently loving the whole experience. She headed in the girl's direction.

'Hey there, Ava.'

'Hey there, miss . . .' She was grinning. 'You made it.'

'Yep. Me and Leila thought we'd pop by and make sure the placards were doing the trick.'

'Sure are . . . people love my one.' She gave it a wave. 'I've had a few newspaper photographers take my picture.'

'I bet.'

'And I've collected about a dozen phone numbers.'

'Any of them *hot date* material?'

'One or two weren't bad. But I'm not letting it distract me from the demo. I promise.'

Rebecca smiled and stared down Whitehall at the crowds of kids. 'Not a bad turnout for a dry run.'

'Amazing, isn't it? There are more and more kids talking about it every day. The main Paris demo is going to be huge. We'll bring London to a standstill I reckon. And Manchester, Glasgow, Bristol. Everywhere.'

Rebecca talked to Ava and some of the other young people from the placard-making session for a while longer. One of them asked for a go at holding Leila and the baby was passed around for a while, which she seemed to enjoy. Eventually Rebecca decided it was time to go.

She was making her way back through the crowds when out of the corner of her eye, she saw another familiar figure. It was Jeff, dressed differently from usual. He'd swapped his open-necked shirt and jeans for a dark tracksuit and baseball cap. Perhaps this was his demo-wear? She was trying to work out the best way to manoeuvre the buggy through the groups of school kids to get to him when something made her change her mind. She stopped and looked. Jeff was standing with a group of other men, all similarly dressed. They were deep in conversation. Once or twice, he looked up and gestured in the direction of the crowd. He appeared to be pointing towards particular groups, or even individuals.

She turned the buggy around swiftly and headed back up Whitehall in the direction of Charing Cross tube. As she walked, she wondered what it had been about seeing Jeff in those clothes and in that company that she'd found quite so . . . wrong. She came up with several possible explanations, none of which she liked. She decided she'd ask him about it at the next Planet Action meeting. In the meantime, she was having the devil's own job getting through the crowd to the Underground station. More and more young people were arriving all the time. She wheeled the buggy off the crowded pavement and into the road in the hope of finding a path through the stalled traffic. This idea came a cropper when a gap between a bus and a black cab proved too narrow for the buggy. She was about to remove Leila from her straps, fold up the buggy and walk when the cab driver leant out of his window.

'Hold on a minute. I can shuffle a little closer to the bus.' He started his engine and did this. On the way past Rebecca stopped to thank him.

'No worries. Pain in the blooming arse this is, isn't it? I dropped someone off near Downing Street hours ago and I've hardly moved since.'

Rebecca shrugged. 'I guess they feel they have to make their point somehow.'

'Maybe. Although from what I heard a lot of them get paid for causing trouble like this.'

'Paid? By who?'

'Who knows? Radical groups and such.'

Rebecca shook her head. 'I know some of these kids and I can honestly promise you none of them have been paid to be here.'

'You know them? How come?'

'I'm a teacher.'

'A teacher? Well then all of this is your fault.'

'Why?'

'They should be in school, shouldn't they? It's your job to keep them there.'

She looked back at the young demonstrators, the stalled traffic. 'So all of this is the teachers' fault?'

'Why not? Who else? It's not my fault, is it?'

46

LA BARROSA, ANDALUSIA, SPAIN

Carlos wasn't sure what he'd hoped to find on Alma's phone. A message just for him. An explanation of what had happened. Or a clue of some sort. He'd found none of these. Not yet anyway. It would help if he knew what he was looking for, but he didn't. Alma was in the habit of deleting her text messages and emails with ruthless efficiency. He was pleased to see that she'd kept a couple of messages that he had sent her but there wasn't a lot else – a link to tickets she'd bought for a concert that had now been and gone, some boring-sounding work stuff and that was about it. The second thing he'd looked at on the phone were the photos. The most recent pictures she'd taken were just weird – a handful of strange, vaguely arty shots of an empty sky. If you enlarged them enough then you could see a few clouds in the distance but literally nothing else. Next, he'd listened to Alma's old voice messages but the only interesting thing there was the number of missed calls, dozens of them, from the same withheld number.

Carlos kept the phone close to him at all times in case the anonymous caller phoned back and he could answer it. But it was the other, older photos that held his attention most keenly. He'd spent hours lying on his beaten-up sofa with the phone inches from his face, staring at the hundreds – maybe thousands – of photographs that Alma had on her mobile. He studied each one, staring at the faces and locations, trying to work out where and when they'd been taken. He was in lots of the pictures – most of them even – but that didn't always help when it came to placing them. In many of the photos he looked a little drunk, either because he was, or because he seemed to appear a little drunk whenever he was around Alma.

'Love struck.' That was how Alma's mother described it. A kind way to explain his inarticulate mumblings, silences and general shyness whenever he and Alma visited Mrs Galinda for Sunday lunch. She'd recently left Carlos another message, asking him to come and see her so they could talk. He knew he couldn't put this off much longer. Part of him wanted to go but it would be so much better if he had something useful to say to her, something hopeful. Alma's phone was his last best chance of finding that. There would be something here; he was sure of it. He flicked back to the main screen and the image Alma kept as her screensaver – the two of them outside the Che bar. Carlos sitting on his girlfriend's lap, grinning like the man who'd won the biggest EuroMillions lottery prize ever awarded. He enlarged the image until just Alma's face filled the screen.

'*Dónde estás?*'

Down on the street, outside Carlos' apartment, the shaven-headed man in the silver Toyota used the last half inch of the cigarette he was smoking to light a new one and waited.

47

ST JAMES'S PARK, LONDON

Jennifer initially attempted to leave Downing Street the way she'd come in, but security told her that was impossible. The demonstration had grown too large; it had certainly grown noisier. She was redirected to the other end of the street and a short cut out into St James's Park.

She walked for a while to clear her head, then found an empty bench and sat. The clouds had cleared, and it was brightening. She liked London's parks, especially in the fall and in this kind of weather. She thought about calling Ryley again, just a quick call so she could hear his voice. She resisted the temptation; her son would think it was weird – two calls in the space of a couple of hours. Also she really needed to phone Clive while all the details of the Downing Street meeting were fresh in her mind. She dialled his number.

'Hey there, Jen.' Clive Winner sounded like he was speaking from inside a wind tunnel. 'How're things?'

'Okay.' She was tempted to launch straight into the details of the meeting but although they'd exchanged several messages she realised she hadn't actually spoken to Clive since his surprise visit to the house back in Boston. A brief enquiry into her boss's well-being was unavoidable. 'How've you been?'

'I've been going around licking billionaires' bumholes when I could be in the lab doing something interesting or useful. How'd you think I've been?'

'I see. Are any of our philanthropic Californian friends interested in giving you a huge amount of cash?'

Winner gave a frustrated sigh. 'They're not falling over themselves – not on the West Coast anyway. That op-ed you placed helped but I'm not sure it'll be enough. I've been finding out a lot about the fourth law of thermodynamics in the last few days.'

Jennifer racked her brains. She'd listened to Winner and his teams discuss a wide range of scientific laws, but she didn't remember this one.

'The fourth law?'

'Yeah. *Either you're hot . . . or you're not.*' The volume of background noise was impossible to ignore. Jennifer was having to strain to hear what Clive was saying.

'Where are you?'

'I am in a holding pattern, twenty or thirty thousand feet above your head. That is if you're in London?'

'I am.'

'Right, well so am I. I'm here to see Edith.' He paused. 'Her and some other people.'

'People I almost certainly wouldn't be happy about you seeing?'

'Maybe. There's a group of potential investors based in Minsk who happen to be in town.'

'Minsk as in Belarus?'

'You know another Minsk?'

A thought occurred to Jennifer. If Clive was in London then some of the meetings her team were working on – the one-to-ones with Winner – could happen face to face. She suggested this.

'No fucken' way.'

'Come on, it makes sense. Several of the people who've signed up are UK- or Europe-based. We could do those in-person, we can also sell more. We can charge more too.'

'How much more?'

'A lot. Double. Three times maybe.'

'Okay, I guess beggars can't be choosers.'

'No . . . but hopefully we won't be in the begging business much longer.'

'From your lips to God's fucken' ear, Jen. When're you due in Downing Street? Later today is it . . . or tomorrow?'

'The meeting just finished.'

'Really? My time clock's all turned around with the travel. Go on then, tell me.'

She told him. All of it. From the fact that Jeremy Cunis obviously didn't want a written record of her being in Downing Street to the underpowered nature of the people in the room.

'No Cabinet or Permanent Secretary?'

'No civil servant full stop.' She told him about Jeremy's odd behaviour in the meeting – knocking back the offer of Winner's help with the Paris speech when that was what he'd previously been most interested in. She mentioned her suspicion that Cunis was communicating throughout with somebody outside the room.

'So maybe the meeting wasn't so underpowered after all?'

'Maybe. Do you want the good news?'

'Please. Before I decide to push the plane door open and just fucken' jump.'

She told him how enthusiastic Cunis and co. had been about the idea of bringing the cloud-related research to the UK, and mentioned the sums of money discussed.

'This line isn't great, Jen. Did you say ten figures?'

'Yes.'

'That's not nothing.'

'Money like that would mean you could cancel any future day trips to Minsk. Or Moscow-on-Thames.'

'Maybe. What else did he say? The very nice stewardess lady is here, asking me to turn my phone off, Jen. Make it quick if you can. Did you talk about the renewable work?'

'I tried to. He didn't want to hear it, shut me down straight away. Jeremy responded by asking if you still thought climate change was a geoengineering problem. If you still believed that?'

'If I believed?'

'Yes. Weird huh? But then afterwards, on the street, he kinda rowed back on that. He said that once we can get you and the prime minister to sit down together, all things will be possible.'

'You finished the meeting out on the street?'

'Yeah.'

'What else did he say once you were outside the building?'

Jennifer could hear some sort of commotion at the other end of the phone and then Clive's voice. 'I'll turn the phone off in a second, sweetheart. I just need thirty more seconds. Go on, Jennifer.'

'He said to send you their regards. Him and the PM I took that to mean. And . . . well . . . he told me to tell you to be careful.'

There was a brief silence at the other end of the line, then: 'I've got to get off the phone now, Jen. Do me a favour and call Daryl, tell him to message me and tell me where he is.'

'Daryl? Why?'

'Because Daryl's job is security. And as of right now I'm not feeling very fucken' secure.'

48

STOCKWELL ROAD, LONDON

Carver woke. Something odd had happened to his legs during the night and they took a little bit of unfolding. He'd forgotten to close the curtains before falling asleep, and gazing out of the bedroom window he saw a bus rolling up Stockwell Road, the top-deck passengers at eye level. He reached over and pulled the curtains closed, turned on the bedside light and found his mobile phone. He wanted to see if McCluskey had returned any of his emails or calls yet. She hadn't. 'Calling in the cavalry' was proving to be a lot easier said than done. Without her and Patrick on board, the plan he'd hatched to persuade Naz to continue with her studies and stick with him instead of accepting Naomi's job offer was dead in the water.

He took a couple of painkillers from his bedside drawer and drank them down with what he assumed was water but turned out to be a watery whisky and soda. He must have brought his nightcap through from the living room and fallen asleep before drinking it. It didn't taste bad. Maybe he should have one of these every morning. At least Patrick had agreed to see him, albeit reluctantly and only because Rebecca had insisted. He'd go and meet Patrick, give him the contacts for the shrinks he'd promised and persuade him to lend a hand with Naz. If Patrick agreed then Carver could take that to McCluskey and put the other half of his plan in place. Except Jemima wasn't even returning his calls.

He'd asked Naz to give him a day or so before she made a decision; his time was up. Perhaps he should let it go? Let her go?

'Bollocks to that. Time to take the initiative.'

He called Naomi first. The conversation wasn't an easy one and he had to make a couple of promises and agree to do a couple of things he wasn't happy about in order to get her to agree. After they'd figuratively shaken hands on the deal, Carver called Naz. She picked up straight away. It was busy wherever she was and initially she sounded distracted.

'It's William, where are you?'

'I'm in Tesco Metro doing a price check for my dad.'

'Oh, okay.'

'I'm staring at a large bag of onions. One kilo for fifty p.'

'No kidding.'

'Yeah, and they've come all the way from Egypt. How the hell are they managing to sell them for fifty pence?'

'Where do your onions come from?'

'Essex, a bloke called Rix. My mum and dad like to buy local if they can.'

'Well, I'm not sure whether onions can have moral high ground but if they can, then yours probably have. Can I talk to you about work? I mean your journalism work?'

'Yeah, Naomi texted me last night, asking what was happening.'

'Right. I've just spoken to her; she wants to talk to you directly but here's where we are . . .'

Naomi was in between meetings when Naz got hold of her. They talked through everything that Carver had arranged – Patrick Reid had agreed to walk her through the whole National Certificate syllabus ahead of the final exam.

'That's really good news. If I remember rightly, Patrick did well in that.'

'He got ninety-one per cent. One of the highest-ever scores, Carver must have told me that about a dozen times.'

'I'm pleased Patrick's up for that. He's had a difficult time. Working with you could do him some good.'

'And at the same time William's mate McCluskey is going to help me get my shorthand sorted.'

'Yes. Have you met McCluskey?'

'Once, briefly at the College of Journalism, after one of William's classes.'

'She's a legend. But not easy. McCluskey and Carver are cut from similar cloth. Nothing you'd want to wear directly against the skin, but she's brilliant.'

'So, you're not pissed o . . . sorry. I mean you're not angry?'

'No, course not. You'll get a good qualification that's worth having, you're being taught by two of the best.' She hesitated. 'And this is a postponement of my job offer, not a cancellation. We agreed we'd pay you the producer salary but give you a couple of months to finish your studies and figure out what type of journalism is right for you. See if working with Carver is really a good fit. It's not for everyone.' She paused. 'Did he tell you what he agreed to do in return for me being so accommodating?'

'Er, no. He just said you'd chatted things over and reached an understanding.'

Naomi laughed. 'I thought not. William promised me he'll be more of a team player – to tell me more about this Clive Winner story you and he have been working on and about whatever else he has on the boil. He said he'll spend more time in the office. He even agreed to take part in the time and motion study that the management consultants are insisting on.'

'That's good, I guess.'

'It's more than good, Naz. It's borderline unbelievable. Keeping hold of you must mean a hell of a lot to Carver, for him to agree to all that.'

Carver was early for his meeting with Patrick. He waited outside Abney Park Cemetery watching a workman who was busy giving the tall metal gates a fresh coat of black paint. He was an old man, grey-haired, wearing paint-splattered overalls. He was humming quietly to himself as he worked. He seemed happy. When Patrick arrived, Carver realised that he was half-expecting him to have the baby with him.

'Hello. I thought you might bring Leila.'

'Oh. Did you want me to?'

'What? No. I just thought you might.'

'I see.'

'It's probably just as well. I heard the weather forecast on the radio this morning. It sounded pretty dreadful.'

Carver realised he hadn't held out his hand to shake or greeted Patrick properly at all really. Shaking hands or hugging or whatever would feel awkward now. 'So . . . shall we walk?'

'Sure.' They walked in through the newly painted gates and headed left. Patrick seemed to have a route in mind or at least a sense of where he was going. 'This is my regular walk.'

'I see.'

'I've come here with a few people. Family. A few other friends.'

'That's nice.'

'I've been trying to start seeing people again. Socially. I was getting a little reclusive before. Rebecca was worried I was turning into a hermit.'

'I always thought being a hermit could be a good job. Straightforward anyway.'

'I guess.' They reached a fork in the path and Patrick led them to the left. 'It's usually around now that people tell me how well I'm looking.'

Carver looked across at his colleague.

'Really? I was just thinking that you were looking a bit crap . . . tired. And you've put on weight around the middle. You want to watch that.'

Patrick laughed, he shook his head.

'You know, I had an idea that I was going to regret agreeing to see you, William. I didn't think I was going to regret it quite so quickly.'

'Yeah? Oh well, we're here now, might as well make the best of it.' Carver paused. 'What else do these other people you go walking with say? Maybe I can pick up some tips.'

Patrick shrugged. 'Let's see . . . what doesn't kill you, makes you stronger . . . that's a favourite. Quite a few people say that.'

'Is that right? In my experience, what doesn't kill you does not make you stronger. It just nearly bloody kills you.'

'Yes.' They walked in silence for a while. Eventually reaching a part of the cemetery where some kind of work was taking place. Reburials perhaps. There were tombstones stacked against the trunk of a large oak tree, each leaning against its neighbour like the pages of a book. Carver tried to make out the name or date on the gravestone closest to them, but time and weather had erased every detail. He turned to look at Patrick who was standing on the path.

'How are you feeling? Really?'

Patrick shrugged. Other people had asked this question. Phrased it in exactly the same way. But coming from Carver it sounded different. Maybe because he knew that Carver would only ask the question if he was interested in the answer.

'Not great.'

'No.' Carver hesitated. 'I can tell. And I'm sorry.' He reached into his blazer pocket. 'That reminds me. Rebecca asked me to give you this.' He passed Patrick a folded piece of paper. 'Those are the names and numbers of a couple of shrinks that helped me in the past. As far as I know they're still alive.'

Patrick took the paper; read the names.

'Thank you. I'll call them.'

Carver shook his head. 'No, you won't.'

'Huh?'

'You won't call them. Not yet. You're not ready to talk yet. But you might be, further down the line. That's what happened with me. You should keep hold of the numbers just in case.'

'Okay. Thank you, William.'

'No problem.'

Carver looked up at the sky. It was slate grey. 'Is this really your regular stroll?'

'Yes, why?'

'It's pretty bloody depressing.'

'I like it.'

'I suppose you've got to do something with all this time you've got on your hands. Although if you ask me, you're a bit young to be retiring.'

'I haven't retired.'

'Really?'

'You know I haven't retired, William. Becs told you what I'm doing, I'm working for the BBC complaints unit.'

'Oh, that's right, I remember.'

'It's more interesting than it sounds.'

'It would need to be.'

They walked on and talked. Carver bided his time, waiting for the appropriate moment to ask what he needed to ask. Eventually Patrick gave him the opening he required.

'What are you working on?'

'Lots of stuff. Spinning more plates than I can count. The thing I'm most keen on right now has to do with that bloke Clive Winner. I think I might've mentioned him; when I called you.'

'I remember. I also remember advising you to stick to encrypted lines when you're chatting about stuff like that.'

'Yeah, fair point. I have been. I just got a little overexcited. It's a good little story.'

'The five most dangerous words in journalism.'

Carver ignored this. 'I'm making progress. There's something there, I know there is, but it's complicated. It's the sort of story that has to be done properly, with the right people.'

Patrick sighed. 'I know what you're doing and it's no use, William.'

'What am I doing?'

'You're getting ready to ask me to work on this with you. About how I'm wasting my time at the complaints unit, and I should "get back on the horse" or something like that.'

'What? Not at all.' Carver paused. 'I didn't even know you had a horse. Where do you keep it?'

Patrick laughed. 'Okay, my mistake.'

'I know you're nowhere near ready to come back to work. I know it's too early. I've been through this sort of thing myself remember?'

'Right, I'm sorry.'

'There is something you could do though, if you did want to be helpful. Do you remember Naz?'

Patrick nodded. 'I do. Is *she* the new *me*?'

'Not at all. She's different. But she's good. She found a way to get to Winner. She could be key to telling the whole story. But she needs a little help.'

49

LA BARROSA, ANDALUSIA, SPAIN

The car stank of cigarettes. The chances were, the hire company would withhold his deposit; he didn't care about that but the smell of the car every time he got back in did make him think about his clothes. If the smell stank up the car's upholstery, then more than likely it did the same to his shirt and trousers and coat. If he'd known this job was going to drag on this long then he'd have brought more clothes. It should've been done and dusted by now but the Spanish kid didn't seem to want to leave his apartment and it was a busy block – lots of coming and going. Daryl glanced at his phone lying on the passenger seat; Winner was due to call any time now, no doubt to chew his ear off for still being there. The car was hot as well as smelly. He took a handkerchief from his pocket and dried the back of his neck and shaven head. That felt better. He was about to crack the window open and let a little air in when the phone started to buzz. It was Clive.

'Boss.'

'Where are you?' Daryl told him. 'You're still there?'

'Yes. Sorry.'

'Seems to me I hear you saying sorry rather a fucken' lot these days. What did Jen tell you when she called?'

'Nothing. Just to drop you a line. She doesn't like me much, that one.'

'Can't imagine why. I'll fill you in when you get back.'

'Once I'm done with this?'

'No, now. Soon as possible. If what I think is happening, *is happening* then I need you back here. And I need you to sort me some security between now and when you arrive.'

'Okay, no problem.' Daryl glanced out of the car window, up at the apartment. The curtains were closed. 'And what about . . . this?'

'You're going to have to subcontract the Spanish job.'

'Fine.'

'And Daryl . . . give it to someone reliable.'

50

ABNEY PARK CEMETERY, STOKE NEWINGTON, LONDON

Carver was starting to understand why Patrick liked wandering around the cemetery. It was peaceful, a good place to think. He decided to stay on and do one more circuit by himself after Patrick left.

He was happy with how the meeting had gone. They'd got on well and parted on good terms. Not the same as in the old days, but he guessed that was to be expected given they'd been out of touch for so long. It had been a step in the right direction. Just as importantly, Patrick had agreed to lend a hand with Naz. Or rather he'd said that he would if McClusky did. That was the next job. Carver stopped. He was standing next to a small, modest-looking stone marker, surrounded on all sides by significantly taller, more ostentatious tributes – most of them to the great and the good of the Salvation Army. He crouched down and read the name – Dorothy Brown. And the dates of her birth and death – 12 November 1887 to 15 November 1887. Underneath this was a poetic attempt at an explanation. 'Came in, looked about, didn't like it, went out.'

He stood up.

'Jesus. That's bloody tragic.' He was glad Patrick wasn't with him to see that. He was depressed already; this might've pushed him over the edge. He wondered whether Patrick ever came here with Rebecca. Or Leila. They certainly shouldn't see it. He made a mental note to warn Patrick next time he saw him.

'Right. Onwards and upwards.' He got his phone out. 'Okay, McCluskey, you awkward old bag. I'm not going to take no for an answer this time.' He realised he'd been talking to himself rather a lot while walking around the cemetery. Not that there was anyone around to either hear him or object. He got his mobile out and called Jemima's WhatsApp. It rang once then clicked through to a messaging service. He took a deep breath and launched into it.

'I know you're busy, Jemima. I know what you're doing is important, but I really need a favour. It's not a big favour. It won't be a load of work or take a lot of time and . . . well, I'd be very, very grateful if you could help. Er . . . that's it. Phone me back.' The machine gave him the option to erase this message and try again and Carver considered this but he wasn't sure he'd be able to do any better with a second try. He hung up. He was busy reading the largest of the several very large Salvation Army tributes when he felt his phone vibrating inside his blazer pocket. He took it out and read McCluskey's message: *Come round you eejit. Ask me your favour. But be warned, there's something I need in return. I'm in most of tomorrow, let me know when you'll be coming.*

First Naomi; now McCluskey. It appeared that doing deals was the order of the day. He wondered what his old friend might want.

51

THE COMPTON ARMS, COMPTON AVENUE, LONDON

Rebecca didn't feel great about lying to Patrick. But as lies went, it was about as small and inconsequential as you could get. That was what she was telling herself as she sat at the back of the pub, a glass of white wine and a packet of salt and vinegar crisps on the table in front of her. She was waiting, not for an old teacher-training college mate as she'd led Patrick to believe, but for Jeff. She'd been planning to wait and talk to him after the next Planet Action meeting but for some reason she couldn't get the image of Jeff and that strange group of tracksuit-clad characters at the Downing Street demo out of her head. She needed to ask him who they were, why Jeff was with them and what exactly they'd been up to.

She looked around the pub – half empty this early on a midweek evening. The last time she'd been here was with both Patrick and Carver – the three of them together. That seemed like a long time ago now – pre-baby and pre-pregnancy too because she remembered getting a little drunk listening to Carver regale them with stories about the pub and in particular one of its most famous former customers – George Orwell. William claimed it was the Compton

Arms that Orwell had had in mind when he was writing his essay describing the ideal English pub. Carver couldn't believe that Rebecca and Patrick hadn't read 'The Moon Under Water' and the next day a collection of Orwell's essays, including that one, landed on their doormat. Inside was an inscription to the pair of them from William. Rebecca was trying to remember what it was he'd written when Jeff arrived.

'Am I late?' He was back in his trademark jeans and open-necked blue linen shirt and smiling broadly. Rebecca returned the smile, shaking her head.

'Not at all, I was early.' She gestured at her glass. 'Half a glass and one packet of crisps early.' Jeff went and bought her the same again and himself a pint of slightly weak-looking lager.

'I was so glad to get your message. When you asked for a rain check before, I kinda assumed that meant thanks but no thanks.'

Rebecca shook her head. 'Not at all. Although I don't want you to get the wrong end of the stick. I thought we could have a social drink but also talk a bit about work too.'

'Course, yes. Completely. How're Leila and . . . I'm sorry, I've forgotten your fellow's name.'

'Patrick.'

'That's right. How are they?'

'Both good, thanks.'

'She's such a special baby that one. I didn't think that babies were really my thing . . . but Leila . . . different class.'

Rebecca smiled. They talked about her daughter for a while, then Jeff's family and siblings – his childhood had been difficult. A couple of drinks in they got onto work and Rebecca's Paris plans, her conversations with the partner organisations that they were going to be working alongside once they got there. Jeff spoke passionately about the need to make the network as broad-based and international as possible; Rebecca had heard some of this before, but it was particularly powerful when it was just you and him, face to face. From there he moved seamlessly to the school strikers and how brilliant it was that Rebecca had managed to get Planet Action so involved in this new movement.

'So much energy and potential. It's huge for us, Rebecca, and it's almost all down to you.'

She accepted the compliment and was grateful for it but now was the time to ask.

'I was at the Downing Street demo the other day actually.'

'Were you? I didn't know you were planning to go.' He looked at her across the table. 'You should've said . . . because I was there too.'

'Yes, I saw you.'

'Really? Why didn't you—'

'You looked busy.' She took a gulp of her drink and then told Jeff what she'd seen, how it had seemed a little strange. He nodded as she spoke.

'God, yes, I'm not surprised. I wish you'd come up and said hello, I could have explained. Plus of course I would've liked to have seen you. And Leila.' He explained now. Why he'd been there. Who he was with. Why they were kitted out the way they were. 'Those guys are . . .' He hesitated. '. . . I'm not quite sure how to put it. Let's just say they're at the slightly more active end of Planet Action's activism.'

'I didn't recognise any of them from any of our meetings.'

'No, you wouldn't. Some of them started out there but they . . . or rather *we*, don't tend to meet like that any more.' He told Rebecca that a few of this group were proposing to use the school-strike demo as an opportunity to ratchet things up a bit. To get close to and maybe even into Downing Street. 'That's the debate we were having, that's what you saw. In the end me and one of the other guys talked them out of it. I thought the demo as it was, was enough. I mean it was brilliant, beautiful, and so doing something different, creating a lot of aggro, would just distract. There's a time and a place for everything but the other day wasn't the right time for that.'

Rebecca nodded as Jeff spoke. Taking it all in. His explanation made sense, the situation as he described it tallied perfectly with what she'd seen. It was completely plausible. The only trouble was, she didn't believe him.

52

VICTORIA TERRACE, MIDSUMMER COMMON, CAMBRIDGE, UK

Professor Walston stood at her study window, waiting for her one-time student, sometime employer, and fellow cloud enthusiast to arrive. Her '*foul-weather friend*'. Edith didn't make many jokes, but she'd made that one. Winner had loved it; he'd had two T-shirts printed with the phrase on – one for each of them. Edith had never worn hers, but she'd kept it. Clive was a great one for present-giving – from small tokens to extravagant, unasked-for gifts. Edith Walston had been on the receiving end of several.

Winner's visits had become few and far between in recent years. Edith had come to consider them – even describe them to others – as rare treats. Today would be different. Clive would come with his questions, scientific conundrums that he hoped Edith might help him solve. But today she needed to ask some questions of her own.

She was unsure whether to show him the envelope of articles she'd collected as soon as he arrived, or wait. She was still pondering this when she saw what she guessed must be his car draw up to the kerb – it was an S-Class Mercedes with tinted windows. It was seven-thirty a.m., and he was on time, which was unusual. Also unusual was the fact that there was a second, identical vehicle drawing up just behind the first. A couple of heavyset fellows in dark suits got out of the first car and looked around. One stayed by the Merc while the other went for a stroll, wandering up Victoria Terrace, past her house, checking out people's front gardens, glancing inside the parked cars. She hoped that none of her neighbours were watching this. The chances were, they'd call the police. Maybe these men were police? Reccy complete, the man signalled to the driver of the second car who got out and hurried round to the rear passenger door holding un umbrella – it was raining, but only lightly. Winner waved him away. He was wearing a smart-looking black raincoat and carrying a package.

Edith went to the door, opening it just as Winner was about to ring the bell. He looked tired and on edge – unusual for Clive – but upon seeing Edith, he smiled and gestured skywards.

'Is this weather foul enough for us, d'you reckon?'

'It will have to do. Who are your friends?'

'Yeah, I'm sorry about that. Fucken' ridiculous . . . excuse my language. Ridiculous and embarrassing.'

'But necessary?'

'For now. Yes, I think so.'

Edith ushered him inside. He hung his coat on the rack by the door and followed her into the study.

'I'm sorry about the early start as well, prof. I've gotta do a whole day of back-to-back meetings in London later. Pain in the rear.'

'I don't mind. I prefer the morning. It's good of you to drive all the way out here.'

'Are you joking? I love coming here.' It was true that he appeared to have already relaxed a little. 'We got to Cambridge early, so I had these guys drive me around for a while. All the young scholars on their rickety black bicycles . . . it's like taking a mini break to 1958.'

He walked around the study, checking things out.

'I'm pleased to see you're still doing that crazy back-to-front thing with your books.'

'I am.'

'I dunno why you think you need to test yourself. You're still the sharpest knife in any cutlery drawer I've ever come across.'

'Thank you.'

'I brought you a book in fact.' He handed her the parcel he'd been holding. 'Thought you might like it. You don't have to open it now; I know you don't like opening presents in front of people. Do it later.' She thanked him and put the parcel down on the coffee table. 'Like the new bobble hat by the way . . . bright colours suit you.'

'Thank you. I made us some coffee; shall we sit?'

'Good idea.' Clive sat down briefly before standing up again and pacing the room. 'So how about you go ahead and tell me what you made of the cloud data we sent you, prof? I got so freakin' excited when you said it was worth talking about, I changed all my plans.' Edith nodded. She decided that she would wait and ask the questions she needed to ask later on. If she could calm Clive down, help him out and gain his confidence then there was a better chance of him being honest with her anyway.

'I had a good look at the data. I ran it through one or two new programs I've been working on.'

'That's brilliant.'

'For proper modelling, the numbers need to be reliable, and the data sets have to be clean and complete.'

'I know what I sent you is partial but I'm gonna get more. I've got a plan.'

'I did what I could with what you gave me.'

'Thank you.'

'Please sit down, Clive, you're making me nervous.' He sat. 'As you're aware – no models are right, but some models are useful.'

'Tell me about it. I married two of them.' Edith gave Clive a scolding look. 'I'm sorry, professor; bad joke. Continue please.'

The professor talked Winner through what she'd found as a result of modelling the Spanish data. Sulphur dioxide particles were more effective at reflecting sunlight than saltwater spray. Powdered aluminium and titanium were better still, but it depended on the size of the particles and how evenly they were distributed.

'The initial research proposal you sent through talked about diamond particles too; but there were no numbers.'

'I know. That was always a bit of a Hail Mary Shot – as the Yanks say – anyway.'

'You didn't attempt those tests?'

'We attempted them; we didn't complete them . . . it's a long story.' Clive could feel the professor's eyes on him. 'Anyway, far as you're concerned it's the fine-grained aluminium and titanium that come out on top? That's the bottom line.'

'That's one single finding, it's not the bottom line.'

'Okay. What is?'

Edith sat back in her chair, her thin hands folded in her lap.

'We come up against the same problem that we always come up against, Clive. We still have no idea whether cloud modification can work on a large scale . . .'

'Sure, but—'

'And, more importantly – we have no clear understanding of what might happen if we get it wrong. That applies to clouds, the reflective screens in space, spraying aerosols around in the stratosphere – all of it. Hurrying into a dramatic, world-reshaping technology in a rush is simply a bad idea.'

Winner was back on his feet, striding up and down in front of the bookshelves. He turned and smiled.

'Who's hurrying?'

'You are.'

'Yeah, I suppose I am. But it's not always out of choice.'

Edith paused.

'Feel free to push back against this, Clive. That's why we're here.'

'Okay, here's why I think you might be wrong . . .'

Clive and Edith batted the argument to and fro. Their conversation jack-knifed around between philosophy and physics, pure maths and biology. They talked about the organising principle in nature and strange attractors. Winner talked about the new generation of super computers, which he believed were getting close to understanding random events. Edith spoke about chaos theory and the fact that strange, jagged, twisted-looking shapes were now being identified inside all sorts of things that we thought were simple and predictable – the most basic pendulum, a bouncy ball.

'But the computers I'm talking about are making a quadrillion calculations per second. I've seen them in action. They take something truly random, a physical thing like radioactive decay and the computers generate numbers from that data. Once they can do that it's a skip and a jump before they can predict things that right now, we think of as random.'

'A skip and a jump?'

'Maybe a skip and a triple jump.' He grinned, then told Edith about an idea he had. 'I'm gonna put a thousand lava lamps in a room in my lab in Melbourne and watch them with camera-equipped computers for twenty-four hours a day. If we do that for long enough we'll start to see patterns. We'll begin to understand that what appears random, isn't random at all.'

The professor nodded.

'Okay and after however many weeks or months or years it takes for you to understand how one thousand lava lamps behave, what then? You take your computers outside and let them watch the weather?'

'That's right.'

'How long do you think it will be before they start to understand that?'

Clive smiled. 'Hopefully not longer than we've got.'

'We?'

'Me. You. Everyone.'

Edith went and stood at her window, staring at the grey clouds hanging low over Midsummer Common.

'Weather is unpredictable.'

'I know that.'

'Are you sure? People have forgotten what unpredictable means. It doesn't mean that something is hard to predict or that it's odd or erratic. Unpredictable means impossible to predict. The weather behaves in ways that can't be foreseen or foretold.'

'Okay. But even if that's true, it doesn't mean we can't make changes.'

Edith nodded. 'You're right. We can make changes. But the effects of those changes are going to be unpredictable too. Geoengineering can shuffle the deck and deal us a new hand but there's no guarantee that the new cards will be any better than the ones we had. They could well be significantly worse.'

Winner gave a mirthless laugh.

'You can't compare geoengineering to shuffling a deck of cards, Edith.'

'I can. And I am. Say you get the degree of cloud brightening just right – or the stratospheric shrouding or the positioning of these sun-reflecting mirrors – maybe you can slow global warming.'

'Exactly! We think we can reduce global temperatures by point one degree Celsius per year and—'

'But if you get it wrong, even a little bit wrong, then you alter rain patterns, reduce crop growth, you damage the ozone layer. Perhaps you manage to increase rainfall and lower temperatures in China but at the expense of India or parts of Africa. You'll see weather wars, famine, flooding, wildfires, mass migration, extinction.'

'What do you think's happening now?'

'Geoengineering isn't the only option. We should use what we've been given – the wind, waves, the sun. We should be using anything and everything that we know might help us rescue this poor planet. All the birds, beasts, plants . . . and people on it. I always thought we had that in common, Clive.'

'We do. Course we bloody do. I've got a dozen different renewable projects on the go, they're doing well but—'

'But the people who are interested in you, aren't as interested in that work, are they, Clive? They want to believe that some act of geoengineering magic will come along and allow them to keep doing what they're doing. Or they want the rest of us to believe that anyway.'

Winner put his thumb and forefinger to the bridge of his nose.

'Wind . . . wave . . . solar . . . I'm working on all of those, the work is going well. I'm trying to argue for them too. But I need . . .' He paused.

'What is it you need, Clive? From me, I mean? Why did you come here today?'

Winner stared at his feet.

'If you were able to write this Spanish data up in some way, Edith. Just a short paper saying that what we have here is interesting?' He gave her a hopeful glance. 'Or perhaps that cloud brightening is heading in a hopeful direction. That'd really, really help.'

'Help you raise more money?'

'In part. But the stakes are slightly higher than that right now.'

'Meaning?'

Winner shook his head. 'I'd like to level with you, prof. Believe me. But . . . I can't.'

Edith looked at him.

'I'll write something for you.'

'That's amazing.'

'I'll place it somewhere prominent.'

'Thank you.'

'But I want something from you in return.'

'Anything. *Literally anything*.' Edith took the envelope of newspaper and magazine cuttings from her pocket and handed it to Clive.

'I want you to look at these and tell me what they mean.'

53

JUBILEE STREET, HOUNSLOW, LONDON

Carver had told Naz that he'd let her know as soon as possible when her lessons with Patrick and Jemima McCluskey would begin. In the meantime, she should keep her mind on the Clive Winner case and any leads they might have missed. With this in mind, once she'd cleared the backlog of chores she'd promised to do for her parents Naz turned again to the latest issue of *New Scientist* and started flicking through it once more. Carver thought he'd seen either page thirteen or eighteen on the floor of Edith Walston's study, but she'd read every word on those particular pages. They both had.

'Turn every page.' That was what Carver had taught her back at the school of journalism. So that's what she decided to do – read every word of every page. She was halfway down page thirty-one when she noticed something. It was one line in a long feature comparing how much money various European countries were spending on scientific research. She'd read about France, Germany, Italy – boring scarcely did it justice – then came the section on Spain. The journalist was explaining the Spanish government's policy of matching private investment with public money, especially if these projects could benefit the poorer regions of the country. This policy plus the availability of large swathes of military land had encouraged 'at least one well-known company to take some of their more ambitious geoengineering projects to Andalucía'. As Naz read this, she felt something. A slight shift in her stomach. She thought about calling Carver immediately, then changed her mind. She would show some initiative; really impress him. She folded the magazine in half, shoved it into her tracksuit pocket and sprinted downstairs.

Naz decided to use a different internet café from the ones she'd used previously; she paid for half an hour and sat down at the terminal closest to the back of the shop. She started by simply googling 'big Spanish newspapers'. Then she selected the ones that seemed to her to be most serious, the most newsy. The *El País* website was the second one she looked at. She opened another search window, selected a few different words and combinations of words from the *New Scientist* article and translated them into Spanish. After that it was surprisingly simple. She typed the words into the *El País* search engine. A list of half-a-dozen articles appeared, the first one on the list was the one that she – they – had been looking for.

Avión perdido . . . La compañía de Winner dice que están haciendo todo.

Naz translated the sentence.

'Doing everything you can are you Clive Winner? Well, me and William are going to do everything we can too.'

54

VICTORIA TERRACE, MIDSUMMER COMMON, CAMBRIDGE, UK

Clive had taken the collection of cuttings that Edith had given him and spread it out on the coffee table. He was sitting studying them when he felt the phone buzz in his pocket. He was grateful for the interruption. Looking at the screen he saw that it was Jennifer. He glanced up at the professor.

'I'm sorry. This is my right-hand woman. It's about that round of meetings I'm going to after this, I have to take it.'

'Do you want me to step out of the room?'

'Course not . . . hey there, Jen.' He turned away from the coffee table and gazed at a wall of back-to-front books. 'Yeah, I'm still in Cambridge . . . fine . . . I'll be there, on time or close to. How many of these people am I seeing? . . . Sweet Jesus. And what will that mean in terms of money? . . . Okay, that's good. You're in touch with Daryl, yes? . . . He's happy with the security inside the hotel? . . . No, I don't like it either but this is the way it's going to have to be for a while, so try and play nice. I gotta go . . . bye.'

Clive shuffled Edith's collection of cuttings around on the table, reading a few of the headlines, skim-reading the content of others.

Certain names and details jumped out at him. He sighed several times but he said nothing.

Eventually Edith spoke.

'What do you make of those?'

'I don't know, Edith. It's a pretty random collection, isn't it? Pretty depressing too. How about we make papier mâché?'

'Don't joke with me about this, Clive. Quite a few of these names are familiar to you, aren't they?'

'A few, yes.'

Edith bent down and rearranged the articles, pushing a few closer to Clive's side of the table.

'I've been collecting things like this for a while. This is just a small selection. Stories of funding being withdrawn, prominent scientists changing their minds all of a sudden, people we respect having years of careful work discredited, newspapers attacking people's reputations . . . physical attacks. Strange-sounding accidents.' She pointed at an article from the *International New York Times*; there was a picture – in the foreground a fresh-faced young man, in the background a volcano. Alongside it was a map of the eastern Caribbean with one tiny island highlighted. Next to that she'd placed a news article from the *Telegraph*: 'Tributes pour in for Greenland's *Ice Woman*.'

'Like I say . . . a weird collection.'

'These people work in our field. Some of them worked for you or for your rivals.'

'It's a small world . . . lots of people work for lots of people. Where are you going with this, Edith?'

She shook her head. 'I don't know. Not really. I just wanted to show you these articles and to see what you said.'

'Great. So, we've done that now. I should go, I need to be back in London for these God-awful meetings in . . .' He looked at his watch. '. . . an hour. Me and those goons out there should get out of your hair.'

'Why do you need all the security? Who are you scared of?'

Winner laughed. It was unconvincing.

'Right now? You.'

He bent down, gathered all the cuttings together and pushed them back inside the manila envelope. He handed them back. 'You want to know what I think you should do with these articles? I think you should burn them. Burn them and forget about them.' He started walking towards the door.

'What went wrong in Spain, Clive? Why did you stop testing before the research was complete?'

He stopped.

'I had no choice. Something happened . . .' Edith watched him weigh something up in his mind. '. . . Prof, please, don't ask me any more of these questions.'

'Why?'

'Because I care too much about you to give you the answers. I need to go.'

55

THE MANDARIN ORIENTAL HYDE PARK, KNIGHTSBRIDGE, LONDON

The hotel was fancy as hell and hiring a suite for the day was costing a small fortune. But Clive had insisted. 'If I have to spend twelve hours talking to drongos then I wanna do it sitting in a decent room . . . view of the park, a fruit basket, all of that.'

Jennifer wasn't sure whether the fruit basket comment had been a joke or not, but she'd ordered one just in case. When the bellhop delivered it, together with the invoice for her to sign, she almost sent it back.

'That's nearly two hundred bucks for a basket of fruit. Did you have it flown in from Kenya business class?' The kid didn't know.

A great many things were testing Jennifer's patience today – the extortionate cost of the room, Clive's unpredictable mood and uncharacteristic jumpiness but most of all the fact that she was having to deal with Daryl Tread. Clive had asked his head of security to oversee everything and this meant that Jennifer was having to speak to him on a half-hourly basis and – even worse – do what he said. Daryl wasn't in London himself, but he was taking a very hands-on approach from wherever the hell he was. He'd arranged for four Armani-clad gorillas from a high-end security consultancy to look after things at the hotel while another two were acting as Clive's personal security detail. The best London-based security team money could buy, apparently. Daryl had told Jennifer to make sure his team at the Mandarin were happy with the set-up of the room.

Looking at the suit who was doing the security sweep it seemed unlikely that he'd ever been happy about anything. Daryl had ordered her to send him pictures of the suite too. Her phone pinged and she read the latest WhatsApp message: *Pictures unclear. Does room have means of access and egress to corridor in two locations?* Jennifer sighed and typed: *It has two freaking doors if that's what you're trying to say.* She deleted the message and tried again: *Yes.*

Send better photos.

In retrospect she'd preferred it when Daryl was saying very little. Or even better – nothing. At the same time as all this was going on she was having to sort out a problem back in Boston involving her son and her useless ex-husband. He'd suggested to Ryley that they stay at Lindy's house for a couple of days. Ryley had agreed, not wanting to upset his dad but had no clean underwear, extra clothes, his hay-fever medicine – nothing. He'd asked Jennifer to transfer some money into his account so he could go to the mall and get these things.

'Why don't you ask that id . . . why don't you ask your father?'

'Because . . .' He paused. '. . . just because. Please, Mom?' She'd sent the money. There was a knock at the door. Jennifer went to answer it.

'Miss Prepas, I'm Verity, the duty manager. I wanted to make sure that you and Mr Winner had absolutely everything you need.'

'We do. Thank you.'

'I'm so glad. It's a lovely suite this one, a clear view of the park, great light. This is where Mrs Ono stays when she's in town.'

'Yoko Ono. No kidding?'

'She loves it here. She has a couple of rather wonderful wild strawberry-scented room diffusers installed when she stays. They perfume the room beautifully. We could have those brought in for you if you like?'

'Would that be included?'

'Er, no, those would be extra.'

'We'll leave it. The room smells fine. If it starts not to, then I'll open a window . . .' She glanced across at the security guy who shook his neckless head. '. . . or I'll think of something else. Thank you, Verity. I'll walk down with you and see how my people are getting on.'

She'd flown in two of the most presentable members of her team to meet and greet the individuals who were paying big bucks to talk about their environmental conundrum with Clive face to face. She also had one of her tech people in town to make sure that the live link-ups went smoothly.

On the way down in the lift she looked again at her list – the New Orleans city council, an Amsterdam-based company that manufactured artificial reefs, some small mammal charity that must have blown a good part of their annual marketing budget on twenty minutes of Clive Winner. She hoped he'd read the notes she'd had prepared for him properly and that he had something useful to offer them. There were a dozen down-the-line conversations and twenty-seven face-to-face encounters; if it went to plan then Clive would clear just north of three million dollars. Enough to keep the show on the road until Clive's involvement in the Brits' science park project was signed and sealed.

She looked at her phone. She'd sent a WhatsApp message to Jeremy Cunis yesterday. She'd kept it short. *My guy is in town for a couple of days. How about we try and make this face to face happen, elephant traps allowing?* She could see that Jeremy had read it, but there'd been no response.

56

THE HIGH STREET, HOUNSLOW, LONDON

'So a plane involved in one of Winner's pet projects disappears into thin air and no one outside Spain reports it. Flipping heck.'

'Yeah, that's what I thought.' Naz had locked the internet café computer and stepped out onto the street to call Carver.

'This *everything* that Winner's unnamed spokeswoman says they're doing. I wonder what that involves. I also wonder how much of this our mate Edith Walston is aware of.'

'You think she knows?'

'Somehow I don't think so.'

'You think we should tell her?'

'Maybe. But not yet.'

He paused.

'We might be able to find out more if we go even more local, we check out the Spanish regional and local Andalusian papers too. How easy is it to use this translation software you used?'

'It's not software, it's just a website. It's easy as anything; you just—'

'How about this? I'll get my stuff together and we meet in an hour at the Charing Cross Library.'

'Is that the place you go to when you're not at work?'

'It's one of them.'

'Cool.'

'I'll most likely get there before you do. I'll get us two computer terminals together.'

He was checking he had his library card and everything else he needed inside his plastic carrier bag when his phone rang again.

'Never bloody rains but it pours . . .' He looked at the number. The code appeared familiar. He answered it.

'William?' A woman's voice.

'Er, yeah.'

'It's Henrietta. Henrietta Allen.'

57

THE MANDARIN ORIENTAL HYDE PARK, KNIGHTSBRIDGE, LONDON

Winner's security detail brought him into the Mandarin Oriental through the service entrance. The guy who had checked the hotel suite took Jennifer down to the basement to meet him. As they waited outside the cacophonous hotel kitchen they were joined by yet another man, one who she hadn't previously met. He was tall, huge in fact. He looked like that English soccer player that had tried to make it in movies. Mainly by playing cockney gangsters. He spoke like him too. Jennifer couldn't remember his name. The way both her guy from the hotel suite and the two goons that arrived alongside Clive deferred to this man suggested that he was the boss. He nodded at the two goons before offering Clive a huge ham-sized hand to shake.

'Good to meet you in person, Mr Winner. Don't worry, I've had a full briefing from Daryl – we've worked with him and his associates before – you're in good hands.'

'Thanks.'

'Any individual with ill-intent, anyone posing any threat at all, they're not getting past us.'

'Good to know.'

'Most of our work these days is with oligarchs. It'll be nice to deal with someone who speaks the Queen's English.' He smiled. 'Or an Aussie version of it anyway.'

'Right.' Clive retrieved his hand. 'I'd like to get going if that's all right with you.' He pointed at Jennifer. 'Are me and my colleague okay to head up?'

'Absolutely. I'll walk you to the lift and one of my blokes will meet you on your floor.' He lifted his lapel and issued instructions to that effect.

Inside the lift, Jennifer waited until the doors were shut before speaking.

'What's all this about, Clive?'

'Precautions.'

'Four bodyguards?'

'Four here. Don't forget the two that I've got following me everywhere including the shitter. I don't like it any more than you do, Jen, but it's what Daryl thinks is necessary. Have you spoken to him?'

'Every ten or fifteen minutes.'

'How is he?'

'The last time we spoke he was happy. He says these guys are good, ex-British Army, they all served in Afghanistan.'

Clive snorted. 'Right, and that's going so well, isn't it?'

Jennifer said nothing. Clive usually returned from his trips to Cambridge invigorated and excited. Obviously not this time.

'Do you want to tell me how it went with Professor Walston?'

'*Curate's egg* is I believe how the Poms like to put it. Good in parts. She's agreed to write something that'll give our cloud-brightening work a boost. She'll have it published somewhere prominent.'

'That's great news.'

'Yeah.'

'So can I let Downing Street know that?'

'Sure. Tell your man Jeremy Cunis that.'

'Just him? I sent him a message suggesting we try and arrange a meeting between you and the PM while you're here in London. I've had nothing back. There are other people in Downing Street I could approach.'

Winner was shaking his head. 'Leave it with Cunis for now. Let's see what happens.'

Jennifer glanced sideways at Winner. His brow was furrowed, he was staring blankly at the metal lift doors in front of him.

'Are you all right, Clive? Do you want me to get you something before we get started? A coffee?'

'No, Edith gave me coffee. Coffee . . . and some food for thought.' The lift doors opened, there was another booted, suited bodyguard waiting to walk them twenty feet down the corridor.

Clive turned and smiled at Jennifer. 'I'm fine, Jen. Absolutely fine. Talk to me about this fresh fucken' hell you've arranged for me. Who are we starting with?'

'I've put the artificial reef guy in first.'

'Bowling me a soft one to start, huh? I'm guessing I'll get the googly later?'

'The googly?'

'It's a cricket thing. A particular sort of ball. You've probably got something similar in baseball.'

'A fast ball.'

'No. It's more complicated than that.' He smiled. 'I was fucken' miserable in the car on the way here. You've cheered me up. You always do. Okay, tell me about this first guy.'

'Richard Heenbakker is the name he flew in with from Amsterdam last night. He's already inside.'

They paused outside the door to the suite. Clive passed his raincoat to Jennifer, took a couple of deep breaths, and pushed the door open.

'Mr Heenbakker, I've been looking forward to meeting you. This reef work you're doing looks incredible. I need to hear all about it . . . can I call you Richard?'

Jennifer sat in the corner of the room, out of anyone's eye-line and took notes.

'You know what Darwin called coral, Richard?' Winner didn't give him time to answer. 'He called them *God's architects*. Good, huh? So you asked what I did – I invited all of God's little architects to an orgy. Who could say no to an invite like that? We had it in this big fucken' water tank that I had built way outside Melbourne and all the coral came. I added a little of this special sauce of mine . . . a kinda coral Viagra. And like I said before . . . *all the coral came*.'

Heenbakker laughed a big Dutch belly laugh.

'Then we took the roughest, toughest most hairy-chested coral – the evolutionary winners – back to the Great Barrier Reef. And the rest is history. But before you get to make history, you have to do the chemistry. And the biology. We can do the same for your people, or at least help you down the road a bit. Tell me where you're building this reef of yours.'

By the time his twenty minutes were up, Mr Heenbakker was Richie and he and Clive were going to visit a reef in the Dutch Antilles together early next year. More importantly, Richie was going to buy a batch of heat-resistant coral spores for a sum still to be decided upon.

The second meeting was one of the ones Jennifer was most apprehensive about – the small mammals' charity that she suspected had spent a large part of their budget in order to ask Clive a few questions. The charity had sent through a list of endangered animals they wanted to discuss but Winner quickly steered the conversation around to genetic rescue. 'Have you guys done any work around Emma's giant rat or the gloomy tube-nosed bat? Great names huh?'

The woman from the charity admitted that they hadn't, mainly because the mammals he was talking about weren't endangered – they were pretty much extinct.

'In theory, yes, but I've got a handful of cells from both of those mammals suspended in liquid nitrogen waiting for a genetic rescue if I can get the backing.'

The chair of the charity promised to raise it with her board and Clive moved on to the list of endangered mammals she'd sent through. It included giant, spiny and soft-furred rats, endangered guinea pigs and a variety of dormice. Clive had some ideas about how these animals' habitats might be tweaked to give them a better chance. He also had the names of some rewilding projects across Europe and South America that he thought could be good homes for some. He'd draw up a full list and have it sent over. 'I reckon we could save most, if not all of those little fuckers if we put our minds to it. Excuse my language.' The chair was full of thanks. She was halfway to the door when Clive called after her. 'Deborah, looking at this list again . . .' He waved the piece of paper. 'One more thought. You could tell the edible dormice that they might want to think about changing their name.'

By the time lunch arrived – roast beef and horseradish sandwiches and one extremely well-polished apple from his nearly two-hundred-bucks fruit basket – Clive's mood had improved. He and Jennifer ate together.

'This is better than last time. Not as good as being back in the lab but at least I'm talking about science.'

'I'm glad.'

'I've been thinking some more about my meeting with Edith. That and other stuff. When you message Jeremy Cunis about the cloud thing, push him again on the face to face with the PM. Tell him I can do it whenever and wherever works for them.'

'Okay.'

'And ask if there's a way that I can get some more Paris speech ideas to them in the meantime – a secure way.'

'Right. I'll do it as soon as we're through the next lot of these.'

'Great. Who's up next?'

Next Jennifer had scheduled in a few 'down-the-line' meetings with individuals and organisations based on the East Coast of

America. First up was the representative of a group of Virginian chambers of commerce who were hoping to plant a thousand acres of pine trees right across the state.

'I've had a look at your proposal, alongside some weather projections for eastern America over the next ten to twenty years.'

'Great, thank you, Mr Winner.'

'What you're planning there basically amounts to planting a thousand acres of *vertical matches*.'

'Er, Clive, I think . . .'

'Don't worry, Jen.' He smiled. 'It's Jen's job to jump in and stop me before I start telling the truth. That is the truth – but it's okay, I've got a better idea for you. Are you familiar with the coast live oak?' They weren't. 'It's big, green, pretty, and – most importantly given where we're all heading – fire retardant.'

Clive then told them about some other green initiatives that they might want to get behind. 'While I've got my foot in the door, let me send you some recent stuff we've been doing on wind, wave and solar. I know you've got things going on over there in Virginia . . .' Four round, healthy-looking faces nodded back. '. . . and as a friend of mine was reminding me earlier, we should really be making the best use we can of everything the Good Lord has given us.' The nodding increased. When the call finished, Jennifer walked over, smiling.

'What the Good Lord has given us? I'm pretty sure Professor Walston didn't put it that way.'

'She would've done if she'd been speaking to the Virginian chambers of commerce.'

The only awkward conversation, and unhappy customer, arrived just before they broke for coffee in the form of a down-the-line conversation with the mayor of New Orleans city council. Jennifer could tell it was going to be difficult from the off. The mayor was an overinflated pink balloon of a man in a loud shirt.

'My people said you did a pretty incredible job with some coral reef and on a few other things and that you were worth twenty minutes of my time.'

'I'm flattered, Mr Mayor. Can I call you Earl?'

'Sure.'

'I've been reading about your town.'

'Our city . . .'

'Apologies. Your city. New Orleans is fifteen feet below sea level.'

'Yep. But we're always findin' new and better ways to pump all that water that gets in – back out.'

'Sure, but the more you pump the deeper it sinks. The more it sinks, the more you'll need to pump. Can you see where I'm going with this, Earl? The state of Louisiana has shrunk by . . .' He looked at his notes. '. . . two thousand square miles in the last hundred years. You're losing the equivalent of an American football pitch every couple of hours.'

'So what do you suggest?'

'A sensible, planned, retreat.'

The mayor laughed. 'Retreat? You're shittin' me? I don't understan' this. My people said you'd have some smart ideas for elevated roads, bigger sea walls, some clever tech fixes for this problem. Medium to long-term.'

'I could talk to you about those kind of things. But they're not a solution, not really.'

'I gotta tell you, Mr Winner. I've spoken to other people in your field and they were a lot more positive. I spoke to a company last week, very impressive. Optimistic – you get me?'

'Then you should go with them.'

'Perhaps I will . . . the main man over there told me that if the council work with him we were gonna put the "can" in Canute.'

'The dick in dickhead more like.'

'I beg your pardon?'

'Nothing. If you want to live in New Orleans, Earl – medium to long-term – my advice? Grow gills.'

The mayor laughed.

'I've paid a lot of money to talk to you, Mr Winner. I've got to tell you I don't feel I've got my money's worth.'

'We'll refund you.'

'Hold on just a minute. How about if I said we wanted to protect certain parts of the city, but that we could consider retreating from some other parts.' Winner nodded. He had an idea where this was going. 'Did you look at that map my people sent through?'

'I have it here.'

'Let me walk you through the geography – acquaint you with the different wards and such . . .'

Winner let the mayor talk. He muted himself and glanced over at Jennifer.

'Can you believe this guy?' It was said in a ventriloquist's mumble.

She whispered back. 'Be diplomatic.'

Winner pulled a face.

'I'll try.' He unmuted himself and listened, growing increasingly impatient, while the mayor explained which districts of his city might be sacrificed and which must be saved. When he finished, he looked up, a broad grin on his balloon face.

'What d'you think, Mr Winner?'

'Why didn't you say so at the beginning?'

'Say what at the beginning?'

'That it's not the whole city you're trying to save. It's the rich people, the real estate, your tourist trade, the financial centre.'

'Well, that's not exactly—'

'That is exactly what you just told me – whether you intended to or not. And do you know, if you'd asked for our help yesterday then I probably would've said yes. But not today.'

58

CHARING CROSS LIBRARY, LONDON

Carver was aware that he wasn't being as productive as he should have been. His main contribution so far had been scaring the school kids sitting at the tables by the window into silence and fetching Naz a hot chocolate from the vending machine. She was better at this sort of stuff than he was; more than happy to have half-a-dozen windows open on her computer at the same time and switching between them at speed – searching, copying, pasting, translating from Spanish and searching again before either making a note or sending stuff to the printer over by the librarian's desk. That was the other thing Carver was proving useful for – standing by the printer and picking up the sheets of A4 it was spewing out before the nosey so-and-so could read them. Carver noticed a couple of members of the Silver Surfers eyeing him and Naz jealously – possibly under the impression that he'd paid for one-to-one tuition. He stood at her shoulder, trying to look like he was in charge.

'The way you do this you'd think you'd invented the internet.'

'Naz Zuckerberg – that's me.'

'Naz Berners-Lee you mean. Zuckerberg is one of the blokes busy messing the whole thing up. I'm going to try a couple of searches of my own.'

'Cool.'

Carver sat down at his own terminal and turned to his notes. The truth was his mind was on other things, namely – Henrietta Allen. Although Leonard had said that his wife would be in touch, her call had caught him off guard. She'd wanted to know when the so-called 'kitchen dinner' that her husband had invited Carver to could happen. Replaying the conversation in his head he feared he'd come across as a complete fool. He'd started by explaining how busy he was, which was true – he was due to see McCluskey tomorrow, he'd promised Naomi he'd show his face at the office on at least a couple of days that week.

Henrietta was undeterred. 'So you're busy all week?'

'Er, I think so, yes.'

'So then, come on Sunday. Sunday's perfect. We'll have Sunday lunch.' She paused. 'Do you want me to say Sunday a few more times?'

'No. But . . .'

'Come on, William. Leonard is desperately keen that we have you over and you know what they say about *all work and no play*. Not that anyone could ever describe you – or the work you do – as dull; but you take my point.'

'Well, yes. I suppose.'

'Excellent. Do you remember the address, or shall I send it again?' He remembered the address. 'Lovely. Come early, we'll have a walk before lunch. How's eleven?'

'Eleven it is.'

Carver was drawing meaningless swirly circles in his notebook when Naz tapped him on the shoulder.

'I've found a couple of names that might be useful in the *Diario de Cádiz*. The missing pilot's mother is called Francesca Galinda.'

'Okay.'

'And there's a quote from a bloke called Carlos Quintana, I think he might be the boyfriend.'

59

THE MANDARIN ORIENTAL HYDE PARK, KNIGHTSBRIDGE, LONDON

During the coffee break Winner started to apologise.

'Sorry about that. You can give Earl a refund if you like.'

Jennifer waved this suggestion away.

'No refunds. He wanted your advice; you gave it to him. I most likely won't get that all-expenses-paid trip to Mardi Gras he was promising now, but we all have to make sacrifices.'

'That's the spirit.'

'It's gone well.' She looked at her laptop. 'A couple of dozen hits; one miss. Your average is good.'

Clive smiled, he stood and looked over Jennifer's shoulder at the grid she'd created.

'Is that the finishing line I can see there, Jen?'

'Yep, we're nearly done.'

'Just as well, I never thought I'd say it, but I'm tired of hearing myself talk.'

He went and got himself and Jennifer glasses of fizzy spring water.

'So, who's next? We're back in the room, aren't we?'

'We are. This one's a late addition, they paid a packet for us to squeeze them in. They're called Propitus . . .'

'Sounds like a hedge fund to me.'

'London based. They want to talk to you about . . .' She read her notes. '. . . investment opportunities in a time of environmental change.'

'Straightforward enough. The kind of thing I can talk about in my sleep in fact – maybe I will. Who am I speaking to?'

'His name's Collins.'

The guy's clothes weren't right for a *hedgie*; not expensive enough. He was carrying one of those big black leather document cases. Clive wondered why that was necessary. He also wondered about the eye patch – it was hard not to stare. Accident or affectation? Clive stood and the two men shook hands, Collins' hand felt like ice.

'Right, good to meet you, Mr Collins, sorry if I kept you waiting.'

'Don't worry, I'm not in a rush.'

'Okay, but I'm afraid we only have twenty minutes?' He looked at Jennifer.

She nodded. 'Yes, twenty minutes or so.'

'Twenty should be enough.'

Collins sat down on the couch opposite the armchair where Winner was sitting.

'So . . .' He clapped his hands together and sat forward. 'What's Propitus? A hedge fund I'm guessing.'

'More of a consultancy.'

'Okay.' He smiled. This guy was odd. 'Jen tells me you're looking for . . . what was it? Investment opportunities in a time of environmental change. I was just speaking to a gentleman from Louisiana and while I was it occurred to me that one way to make money would be to buy the rights to deep-sea diving tours of New Orleans.' He grinned. 'Miami too for that matter. Some clever person has probably already bought the domain name *Dive Venice*. Maybe it was you?'

'Not me, I like Venice though, I've done some work there. It'll be a shame to see it go.' Clive was pretty good with accents, but he couldn't place this one – not socially or geographically. It wasn't London, nor northern. Somewhere in between?

'Yes. So why does a consultancy want to consult with me? How can I help?'

'Good question. Probably the best thing is if you just sit and listen.'

Clive glanced across the hotel room at Jennifer, but she was busy on her phone. He looked at the oversized black case by Collins' knee. It appeared new.

'I can do that.'

'You've been busy today.' Clive nodded. 'Meeting all these potential new customers, helping them with their problems.'

'Yes, Mr Collins, now about—'

'Be quiet.'

'What the—'

'I told you to sit and listen. So – sit and listen. I represent your existing customers. Unhappy customers. People you made certain promises to. They're concerned about the company's direction of travel. Concerned about your behaviour more generally.'

Jennifer had pocketed her phone and hurried across the room. She stopped at Clive's side.

'I'm going to have to ask you to leave, Mr Collins. Right now. If you don't then I'll order one of our security team to remove you by force.'

Collins shook his head. 'That's not going to happen.' He looked away from Jennifer and back towards Clive. 'We know that your accountant, Mr Yeoh, has already raised these concerns with you. That makes this your second warning. There won't be a third.' His unpatched eye looked down in the direction of his black case. 'The people I work for wanted me to tell you that – face to face.' Jennifer reached for her phone then changed her mind and strode towards the door. The eye followed her. Collins smiled.

'There's no one out in the corridor, Miss Prepas. There are no bodyguards anywhere in the hotel; not that work for you or Mr Winner anyway.' He paused. 'I think Clive understands now. Don't you, Clive?'

Jennifer was holding the door handle. She stopped and turned to look at her boss.

'Jen.' He paused. 'Do me a favour and give us a few minutes, will you? Everything'll be fine. Me and . . . Mr Collins here just need some time in private, to figure a few things out.'

'But—'

'Please Jen . . .' He stared at her. The look on his face was one that she hadn't seen before. 'Please?'

'Okay.'

'And that message to Downing Street we talked about earlier.' He glanced across at Collins. 'Hold off on that for now.'

Jennifer left, pulling the door closed, slowly, behind her.

She wasn't sure what led her to stop outside the hotel-room door. However, once she had, there was no question in her mind as to what she'd do next. Collins was right, the hotel corridor was empty. So much for the best security money could buy. Jennifer had a teenage son. She'd had plenty of practice standing outside bedroom doors, eavesdropping on conversations taking place within. She'd heard some disturbing stuff down the years, either from Ryley himself or from his hormonal pals but no previous act of eavesdropping had the same effect on her as this one. Initially it was just fear that she felt. Then anger.

Jennifer listened until it became clear that Winner and Collins were concluding their conversation, then she walked swiftly and quietly down the corridor in the direction of the emergency exit at the end. Then she walked down eleven floors to the ground. There she stopped. She considered walking straight out of the hotel and taking a taxi to the airport. She considered waiting by the lift and confronting her boss – asking Clive to explain what she'd heard. Because there had to be an explanation. In the end, Jennifer walked through to the hotel bar. She took a table at the side with no line of sight between her and the lobby. The place wasn't busy, the waiter came straight over.

'A brandy. A large one. The most expensive you've got.'

60

CAVERSHAM, BERKSHIRE, UK

The car-cleaning brigade were out in force. On the walk from the bus stop to McCluskey's house Carver had to nod a greeting or exchange a couple of weather-related clichés with several elderly gentlemen out hosing down or polishing up their vehicles.

'Saharan sand.'

'I beg your pardon?' Carver stopped and stared at the man. He was wearing golfing clothes but holding a hose and a very big sponge. He held it up for Carver to appreciate.

'You see that? It's red.' The sponge had a slightly red tinge to it. More ochre than red, strictly speaking. 'That's from the sand, blown in from the Sahara.'

Carver nodded. 'Right.'

'That's not normal, is it?'

'I suppose not.'

'Like something from the Bible.'

'Indeed.'

Carver tried to remember his Bible and the bit about plagues. If the car-washing golfer was right and this was blood, then it would be frogs next. After that lice. Or was it locusts? The bloke was going to need a bigger sponge. Carver thought about telling him this, but it was clear from the man's demeanour that he'd said what he wanted to say, and anyway he didn't want to be late. McCluskey was expecting him.

Arriving outside her two-up two-down, the first thing he noticed was that there was now a second heron standing next to McCluskey's fishpond. This one was slightly smaller than the original, wrought-iron heron and made from clay. Carver smiled, he walked up the path and rang the bell.

'I told you having one heron would attract others.'

'Very funny. That first one wasn't realistic enough, this one's better.'

'Not much. There's a taxidermist shop I know down in Streatham. I could try to get you one from there?'

McCluskey looked interested.

'D'you think they have herons?'

'They seem to have stuffed everything else. There are bears, dogs, cats, flamingos in the window.'

'It would have to be weatherproof.'

'I could ask them to varnish it for you.'

McCluskey stood back from the door and ushered Carver in.

'I'm starting to think you're more interested in taking the piss than helping me look after my fish.'

'Not at all. I think you should persevere. It's bound to work eventually. If you get enough of these fake herons then the real ones won't be able to get past them to eat the fish. It'll be like a heron fence. Made of herons.'

'Shut up and come in. I've got you some of those cakes you like.'

They sat in the living room, eating fondant fancies and drinking tea.

Carver told McCluskey about Naz. The tug of war he'd been having with Naomi over her journalistic future.

'You really think that offering her a bit of help from me with the shorthand and some coaching from your man Patrick will persuade her to stick with you?'

'I know it will.'

'You've already told her that I'll help, haven't you?'

'Sort of.'

'And she's giving up the chance of a proper job, more money, all a'that . . . to study with us and work for you? I only met her the once but she seemed smarter than that.'

Carver ignored this.

'Naomi is going to hold her job offer open.'

'That's awful decent of her.'

'I suppose. But Naz won't end up needing it, I'm certain of it. She wants to do the real stuff, proper journalism. She's got a nose for it.'

'And Patrick has said he'll help?'

'He will if you will.'

'Sounds like a classic Carver fait accompli to me. Fine, I'll do it. I guess that brings us to the favour I need from you.'

From above their heads, there was a scuttling sound.

'What's that?'

'That's John. Old Caversham colleague I told you about. He's upstairs. This Pegasus thing has thrown up something rather interesting. There's a chance you might be able to help.'

Upstairs in the spare room, Carver was introduced. McCluskey's friend looked more like a bloke who'd come to fit a new carpet than a computer and communications genius. Not that he'd have been able to fit a carpet – most of the floor was covered, either with wobbly-looking piles of newspapers or packing boxes. The walls were similarly busy. McCluskey's investigation had expanded. Her ex-colleague John had thick-lensed glasses, a Father Christmas beard and was wearing a pair of denim dungarees with knee protectors. Either he'd arrived knowing that he was going to be crawling around on McCluskey's floor a lot or the pair of them were planning to go roller-skating later.

'Carver, This is John. John Smith.'

'You're joking?'

McCluskey shot him a look.

'That's his name. His real name. John, this is Carver. William to his friends, although he doesn't really have any. Tell him what you told me.'

John Smith didn't just look like Father Christmas, he sounded like him too. A deep, jolly-sounding voice that was pleasant to listen to, even if you didn't completely understand what on earth he was talking about. He repeated some of what McCluskey had told Carver about Pegasus, but in a lot more detail. He spoke about the malware he'd sent back to the so-far still-unknown group or individual who'd bugged his phone. He talked about the progress they'd made in finding out more about the other individuals that had been targeted. Among these were human rights activists and lawyers working in Mexico and Morocco, a member of India's political opposition . . .

'We've even got the estranged wife of this Gulf sheikh who seems to have been bugged because her ex-husband was feeling jealous. Crazy huh? But increasingly it's looking like the majority of what we've got are people who're involved in one particular field.'

'Which is?'

'Green stuff . . . the environment.'

'I see.' Carver looked across at McCluskey.

'I'm sure you can probably guess where we're going with this, Billy. We need Clive Winner's mobile phone number. I was hoping you could help us get it.'

61

HEATHROW TERMINAL 5, HOUNSLOW, LONDON

Jennifer had waved her colleagues off in the direction of the departure gates at Heathrow. She'd see them on the plane. Usually, she would have stayed with them, despite the fact that she was flying business and they were in coach, but she wanted some time to herself. Her head was still pounding – too little sleep and too much brandy. She found a quiet corner of the executive lounge and got her phone out. She called Ryley. Her son didn't pick up but she hadn't really expected him to. He was at school – hopefully. She messaged him, giving him her timings before rereading the several text messages she'd received from Clive. She'd ignored his calls – the first time ever – and as a result received the longest message she'd ever had from him. He'd told her not to worry about that weird encounter with Collins, he'd cleared it all up, turned out it was no big deal. They should talk as soon as she was back in Boston. Leave the Downing Street thing with him for now.

She stared at her phone, put it back in her bag. Then got it out again. She knew that if she was going to do something about the conversation that she'd heard from outside the hotel-room door then she needed to do it now – before she left London. If she spoke to Clive, then she'd end up changing her mind and she didn't want to do that. For her own good, and for his. She'd thought long and hard about who she might call and what she could tell them. There were no obvious choices but for some reason, in that moment, one choice seemed like the correct one.

She went to her emails, selected the one that her colleague had sent her the previous week and opened it. She opened the attached sound file, pressed the phone firmly to her ear and listened again to the messages left on Clive's Downing Street answerphone. When Naziah Shah started to speak, she took a pen from her bag and scribbled down the mobile phone number the young woman had left on the back of her boarding pass. She heard her flight number being called on the airport tannoy. They were boarding. She still had time. Jennifer dialled the number.

62

LA BARROSA, ANDALUSIA, SPAIN

Carlos had all but given up hope. There was nothing on Alma's phone. Nothing he could find anyway. Loli was coming over later to take one more look but if that came to nothing then he'd agreed that they would go to see Alma's mother. Mrs Galinda had left yet another message asking him to visit and – as Loli said – it was her daughter's phone and she should have it, not him. In anticipation of this Carlos had forwarded some photos from Alma's phone to his own. Several dozen in fact. He would get some of these printed. He knew which ones. It would be something. Not enough, but something. He rubbed his eyes, got up from the table. He paced around his living room; it was no good getting emotional again. He went over and stared out of his top-floor window in the direction of the sea. It was a clear early autumn day, the sky cobalt blue. The clumps of irregular-shaped white chimneys shone in the sun. He was hungry and there was next to nothing in the fridge. He needed something to eat now and something he could make for Loli later – food and beer. He went to get his keys and coat.

*

Jennifer slept for most of the flight – physical exhaustion, emotional exhaustion, every conceivable sort of exhaustion. The stewardess woke her as they were beginning their descent into Boston; she put her seat back up but kept her eye mask on and tried to sleep some more. She couldn't. She made a mental list of what she'd do once home instead. She would – in this order – hug her son until he begged to be let go. Check out the granite worktop and the new induction hob, which had finally freakin' arrived. After that she would pour herself a modest-sized glass of cold white wine (her head felt better) and phone Clive.

Carlos bought a loaf of freshly baked bread, tomatoes, cucumber, tuna fish and Manchego as well as a bottle of Rioja and some Cruzcampo. He'd make himself a sandwich when he got back and a salad that he and Loli could eat later. He was almost back at the apartment block when the plastic bag with the drinks in it split; the bottle of wine hit the pavement but miraculously did not break. Carlos was bending down and repacking his other carrier bag when he saw the guy, standing on the opposite side of the road, staring at him. He'd been relieved when the shaven-headed goon in the Toyota had disappeared, but the truth was he'd never felt that threatened by him. This guy was different. He finished packing the food and drink back into the bag and hurried in the direction of the apartment. Once inside, he called Loli.

It was an odd-sounding noise – a muffled bang. The slam of a car door? Or maybe a neighbour's door. But then nothing. Silence. He stayed sitting in the kitchen and shouted. Maybe it was her, she was due around now.

'Hello?'

He stood up from the kitchen table, scraped his half-finished sandwich into the bin so the place didn't look too messy, then stepped into the hall.

'Hi?'

Walking to the door, he stopped then stooped and put his ear close to the keyhole. Still nothing. And yet he was sure that he'd heard something. Sure, now he thought about it, that there was someone still there on the other side of the closed door. He turned the handle and pulled the door open. She fell in, almost falling on top of him. Her head landing alongside his feet.

'Mum?'

Ryley crouched down then sat, cross-legged on the wooden floor. 'Mum, what the h . . .?' He lifted her by the shoulders and pulled her head gently up onto his lap. He pushed his mother's hair back from across her face. And then he saw the wound. A scorch-marked bullet hole in the side of Jennifer Prepas' head. '*No.*' He covered the hole with the palm of his hand and rocked his mother gently in his lap. 'Mum? Mum . . . wake up. Please?' Ryley felt a catch in the back of his throat, a sob that quickly became the most dreadful, pain-filled scream.

PART THREE

STRATUS

stratus – flattened or spread out

Stratus are the lowest-lying cloud type and can exist in a variety of thicknesses – sometimes opaque enough to darken entire days, allowing for little light to pass through.

63

NEW BROADCASTING HOUSE, PORTLAND PLACE, LONDON

'I screwed up.'

'Not your fault.' Carver was doing his best to reassure Naz. 'A missed call from a number you didn't know. I'm not sure I would've done anything different.'

They were sitting in the café in the piazza next to Broadcasting House drinking coffee.

'You'd have listened to the . . . flipping message.'

'Maybe. Or maybe not. You were busy. Either way, it's too late to do anything about it now. We should focus on what we've got, not what we haven't.'

They had the Spanish newspaper articles from *El País* and others that Naz had discovered. A plane accident in southern Spain involving a pilot working for Clive Winner. The female pilot missing and almost certainly dead. The story, tragic and intriguing in equal measure, had gone largely unreported. That by itself was interesting to Carver but more importantly the pilot had been part of Winner's crazy cloud-altering work, which provided a link to Professor Walston. Carver had left messages for Edith Walston but so far heard nothing back.

The other thing that he and Naz had – or half had – was the phone message from Jennifer Prepas, one of Winner's most senior people – his consigliere according to some. She'd tried to call Naz just nine hours before being shot dead outside her own house. This story had been covered – comprehensively. It had been the lead item on the main American news networks for the best part of a day – the tale of a top executive and attractive single mother being gunned down in a well-heeled part of Boston ticked all the boxes as far as Fox, ABC, and all the others were concerned. Watching the coverage, Naz had been surprised and a little shocked at how graphic the coverage had been. Close-ups of the bloodied step outside the dead woman's house, intimate details of Jennifer Prepas' past and endless photos of her, her ex-husband and her teenage son. Photos of Clive Winner too of course. It was the son that Naz couldn't help thinking about. The footage of him being escorted from a Boston police station while a dozen reporters shouted idiotic questions was particularly upsetting. She'd mentioned it to Carver.

'Yeah. That's what happens when there aren't any rules. Things aren't brilliant here, but we haven't plumbed those depths. Not yet anyway.'

A robbery gone wrong. This was the police's explanation of what had led to Jennifer Prepas' death, and every single news outlet – American and international – appeared to have taken that at face value. Maybe that was what had happened?

Naz drank her coffee.

'If I'd just listened to the message. If I'd phoned her back . . .'

'Try not to be too tough on yourself about that, Naz. We're still on the story, we're making progress, largely because of you. I've got a good feeling about Edith Walston, she'll be watching what we're watching and drawing her own conclusions. Let's give that time.'

'Okay, I hope you're right.'

'In the meantime, while we're waiting, I think you should try to concentrate on the National Certificate work. When are you seeing Patrick?'

'At the weekend. Sunday he said.'

'And your first shorthand session with McCluskey?'

'That's tomorrow. I'm a little nervous.'

'Yeah, she still makes me nervous, and I've known her for twenty-odd years. So, when you go and see her, one word of advice . . .'

64

WASHINGTON STREET, BOSTON, MASSACHUSETTS, USA

Winner had the car drop him at the end of the street. He walked the last block, past the tall ash trees, the neat front lawns until he reached Jennifer and Ryley's house. Barely a fortnight had passed since his last visit, yet everything had changed – including the house itself. The grass in front of the powder-blue triple-decker was all churned up, no doubt by the cops and forensics people who had been working there. Them plus those vultures from the press. There were scraps of police tape still attached to the front fence and one of the pillars that flanked the front door. The yellow tapes fluttered in the wind like party streamers. Clive noticed that the front door had been repainted.

He untied the tape from the pillar, and after failing to find anywhere else to dispose of it stuffed it into the pocket of his raincoat. He was just about to press the bell when the door opened and a man in a green polo shirt greeted him with an outstretched hand. Clive remembered meeting Jennifer's ex-husband once before, at a company get-together of some sort. The man had come across as a little too easily impressed, too eager to please and not very clever. Clive was unsurprised when Jennifer told him they'd separated. She could do a lot better.

'Mr Winner . . . Clive, it's so good of you to come all this way.'

'Not at all. Good to see you again.' He'd reminded himself of the guy's name just before getting out of the car, now it had gone again. 'How are Ryley and you holding up?'

They sat in the living room. There were flowers everywhere, lilies mainly. Winner himself had sent a lot of them. The place stank of lilies. There was a row of condolence cards on the mantelpiece. No doubt Clive's was in there somewhere although he didn't know which it was; someone in the New York office had bought, signed and sent it on his behalf. He chastised himself for that now. He had a cheque in his pocket for a very large sum of money. He would have liked to have simply handed it over and left but he couldn't do that. He needed to stay a while. Perhaps Ryley was around? He'd like to meet Ryley; the cheque was meant for him after all. It would pay for the rest of his schooling, for four years at any American college he cared to choose. There'd be money left over after all that was paid for too, unless Ryley's dad got his hands on it. Clive made a mental note to speak to his accountant about how that could be avoided. He'd been avoiding Tony Yeoh but would make an exception if it meant that the guy sitting in front of him wouldn't be able to chuck Ryley's inheritance up the wall. Jen would've been furious if that happened.

The doorbell rang and Jennifer's ex got to his feet again.

'That'll be Detective Sergeant Hass.'

'Beg your pardon?'

'He wanted to meet with you, let you know exactly where the investigation is at.' Clive sighed. This was meant to be a brief hello and goodbye with the family, not a big production number with police briefings and fuck knows what else.

'I don't think my people knew about this.'

'Really? I'm sorry. The detective asked me when you were comin' to visit and I told him. I thought they'd been in touch with people at your end.'

Winner shrugged. Maybe they had.

'Never mind. It's not a big deal, let's hear what he's got to say.'

While Jennifer's ex went to answer the door, Clive got up and walked around. The kitchen finally finished, the granite counter and hob looked pretty good. There was a pile of dirty dishes in the sink, including a half-eaten bowl of Froot Loops – Ryley's he guessed. Clive felt a strong urge to roll up his shirtsleeves and do the dishes. He managed to resist this temptation – it would look weird. It was weird.

'Hey there, Mr Winner. Good to meet ya.'

The barrel-chested Boston cop was wearing one of the nastiest suit and tie combinations Clive had seen in a long time. He had a partner with him who had better taste in suits but not much else to recommend him. They got the introductions out of the way quickly. Clive refused refreshment on everyone's behalf. The four men sat and Winner invited the detective to bring him up to speed.

'Far as we can tell this was a straightforward robbery. A mugging gone wrong, like I said in the press. We've had other cases that've been similar but not so . . .' He looked for the right word. '. . . extreme. There are a couple of local gangs who work these streets; it's a ritzy area, they know this is where the money is. Sometimes it's a burglary, sometimes it's a stick-up on the street.' He looked at Clive. 'D'you say *stick up* in Australia?'

'Sometimes. I understand what it means.'

'Great. So our best guess is the guy was parked out there on the street. He sees Miss Prepas arriving at the house, likes the look of the bag she's carrying. Coach it was . . . high end. He follows her up the front walk as far as the stoop. Tries to grab the bag, she fights back, won't give it to him. He panics, takes out a handgun and shoots.' Detective Hass took a small notepad from his jacket pocket. 'Instrument of despatch is a Glock. Calibre . . . 22.'

Clive waited to see if there was more. It appeared not.

'"Instrument of despatch."'

'Yeah. A Glock.'

'Is that the kind of gun that muggers tend to carry?'

'To be honest with you, Mr Winner, these days, everybody carries everything.'

'I see.'

Ryley was hearing all of this from the top of the hall stairs. It was taking all the willpower the teenager had to just listen and not run down the stairs and tell the cop what a dick he was. He and his friends had had some run-ins with the local police. He could just about believe that they might be stupid enough to believe that this was what had happened to his mother. But what about this guy Clive Winner? His mum hadn't told him too much about the man she worked for, but she'd told Ryley repeatedly that he was clever – some kind of genius in fact. Surely Winner wasn't buying this bullshit? But judging by what was going on now down in the living room – he was. The four men were exchanging polite goodbyes. Winner was saying something to his father about some money.

Ryley turned and walked silently back up to his room. He lay on his bed. He remembered every single detail of that day. There hadn't been a struggle. Up until the bang, there was nothing – silence. Silence followed by a single gunshot. That was all. If there'd been a struggle or a fight, then he would've heard it. His mum would've yelled – she was good at yelling when she needed to. She would've shouted Ryley's name and he could've . . . he . . .

Clive handed Ryley's father the cheque in the hall, he asked him to open it later. To speak to his son, and call his people if there were any questions. He bid the two cops farewell: thanking them for their work. And then he left. There was a black Lexus waiting for him at the kerb; sitting in the back with the window down was Tony Yeoh. Disappointing but not, Clive supposed, any real surprise. His accountant had offered to come along to the meeting for 'moral support'. Winner had refused. Tony had been offering to help Winner in all sorts of ways recently. He waited until Clive was in the car and settled before speaking.

'So, how'd that go? Did you get what you needed?'

Winner shrugged. 'I dunno. I got a special report on the police enquiry from two of Boston's finest.'

'Is that right? What did they have to say?'

Clive shook his head.

'If you ever get bored with accountancy, Tony, you should think about acting.'

'I'll never get bored of accountancy. Spending all day surrounded by money; playing hide and seek with the taxman – best job in the world. Are the police making progress?'

'They're just dotting the "i"s and crossing the "t"s and then they'll close the case. A run of the mill mugging gone wrong is what they say.'

'Right . . .' Tony glanced across at Winner, but the stony face was giving little away. 'Well in that case I think we've probably done everything we can then, mate.' He placed a fleshy hand on Clive's arm.

'Have we? What've we done?'

Tony removed the hand.

'The kid's got more money than he could know what to do with, his college is sorted. He's got his dad. He'll be fine.'

Clive looked out of the window then back at his accountant. Tony Yeoh seemed to have acquired yet another chin since he'd last seen him. That made four.

'I'm guessing that you and your mum weren't that close?' Clive said.

'We were normal close. There were lots of us kids. I was closer to my old man I guess; on balance. But then he went and croaked.'

Clive nodded. 'Ryley's dad's a dick. Or he has dick-ish tendencies anyway. Can we do something to make sure he doesn't piss all that money away before Ryley gets to benefit?'

'Sure. I can have something drawn up. I'll put a stop on the cheque until he's signed off on that.'

Clive watched as Tony took three phones from his jacket pocket, found the one he was looking for and sent a message. His thick fingers were surprisingly dextrous.

'Done.'

'Thank you. So, do you want to tell me why you're here, what you want? Or do you want me to guess?'

'I'm here with good news. We took another look at your schedule, and we've managed to free some time up. How does a couple of weeks in the Melbourne lab sound? Your happy place.'

'Who's we?'

'Me and your new diary secretary.'

'I didn't know I had a new diary secretary.'

'She's excellent, very experienced. She'll be operating out of the New York office.'

'Why?'

'Time zones work better than Sydney. It makes sense. She's going to iron out anything that needs ironing. The aim is to take some of the weight off your shoulders, let you get on with being your brilliant self. Have a look at this.' Tony handed Clive a single side of A4. On it was Winner's schedule for the next month – a couple of flights, half-a-dozen meetings, one hotel. It was the emptiest diary Clive had ever seen.

'I'm getting snow-blindness looking at this, what's going on?'

'Like I said, we've managed to free up some time.'

'What about London?'

'What about it?'

'I'll need to get back there to tie down the science park thing. Talk to the prime minister and his people about how we're going to make the cloud-brightening research work for them.'

'We don't need you to do that. It's all in hand. Credit to Jennifer really, she did an amazing job.'

'Who's going instead of me?'

'Yours truly. Don't worry, I won't fuck it up, and I'll bring back a nice fat cheque for you to start spending on other interesting things.'

'*You're* going to meet with the British prime minister?'

'That won't be necessary. I'll meet some of his people.'

Clive stared out of the car window.

'Who? Jeremy Cunis?'

'Not him, no.'

'Why? Has he been put on light duties too?' They were on the outskirts of Boston now and heading for the airport. It was semi-industrial, dull browns and greys. The rain didn't help.

'I can't believe you're calling lab work light duties. You're always telling me how it's the most important thing you do. There'll be plenty of other chances for you to meet with politicians, trust me.'

'After Paris.'

'The climate conference? Well, you're going to be pretty busy right up until then.'

'I might be back in harness, Tony, but I'm not a fucking idiot. Don't patronise me. At least let me go and see Professor Walston before Melbourne. I need to see how she's doing with that article she's writing, find out when it'll be published. The Poms will want to see that before they sign on the line . . .' He glanced at his schedule. 'I could fly straight to London from here, get to Cambridge on Wednesday for the day and then on to Melbourne.'

'No.'

'Why?'

'It's not necessary. From now on your diary secretary will deal with Professor Walston.'

Winner slammed his hand against the car headrest in front of him.

'Fuck that. Edith is my—'

'Trust me on this one, Clive, it's better we do it this way. For you. And for her.'

65

LA BARROSA, ANDALUSIA, SPAIN

They kept Carlos in a cell for three nights before releasing him. Assaulting a police officer and damage to property they said. In the end the alleged victim decided not to press charges. Of course he did – he wasn't even a serving police officer, he was retired but unsurprisingly the Guardia Civil believed everything that he'd said and nothing that Carlos said. He'd told the cops that this guy had clearly been following him, he told them that he'd been the second bloke who'd been doing this. He gave them a description of the shaven-headed guy in the Toyota and suggested that maybe the pair were working as a team. The police weren't interested. The man Carlos and his friend had attacked was a respected ex-officer. He did security work at the nearby military base. He'd been sitting in his car, minding his own business, when Carlos and the thus-far unidentified friend had started attacking the car with baseball bats.

As he got his clothes out of the washing machine – he'd washed them twice in an attempt to get the jail cell smell out – Carlos couldn't help smiling to himself. It had been Loli's idea. Together they'd smashed both side windows and put some serious dents in the bodywork before the guy was able to start the car and move off. They'd chased him down the narrow street, Carlos hurling abuse, and Loli a well-aimed baseball bat that had taken out the car's back window as well. Carlos had refused to tell them who his accomplice in the baseball cap had been.

He'd felt a sense of euphoria in the immediate aftermath and even now he felt good that he'd done something. He had no idea what the connection between the two men tailing him and Alma's disappearance was, but he knew they were connected. His mood changed as he remembered the promise he'd made to go and see Alma's mother. He had nothing to say. No hope to give her and nothing to take apart from her dead daughter's phone. He decided that at the very least he needed to do something about that. Flowers or maybe a cake?

In the local supermarket he took his time, walking slowly up and down the aisles. None of the cakes on display were appropriate; he put some Magdalenas in his basket, some bread and milk for himself and then set about looking for a small gift for Mrs Galinda. He paused at a small selection of scented candles, potpourri and stuff like that. A young woman standing next to him turned and smiled. Turning back she accidentally knocked a tray filled with bags of potpourri to the floor. He helped her pick them up. They exchanged a few words. He felt guilty for some ridiculous reason. As though this, a meaningless interaction – a nothing – was in some way a betrayal of Alma. At the checkout the henna-haired till assistant swished the items, including one rose-scented candle, across the scanner. It came to twenty-three euros. Carlos reached for his pocket. Then the other pocket. Then every pocket in his trousers and jacket. A look of absolute panic filled his face. The woman on the till shook her head.

'Don't worry . . . if you've left your wallet, just pay me later.'

'No. I have my wallet. It's not that . . .' He checked all his pockets again but nothing. His phone. And Alma's. They were both gone.

66

CAVERSHAM, BERKSHIRE, UK

It was just before ten when Naz arrived outside Jemima McCluskey's house. She was early – as Carver had advised – and had brought a small present which was his other piece of advice. It was a grey, overcast day and the only sign that there was anyone at home was a light in one of the upstairs front windows. Naz rang the bell and waited. And waited. A couple of minutes passed. She rang again and heard steps from somewhere inside. McCluskey opened the door dressed in a green quilted jacket and tweed skirt.

'I hope you're not going to be as impatient as that when it comes to studying your shorthand.'

'No, sorry. I wasn't sure you were in.'

'I told you that I'd be in, didn't I?'

'Yes.'

'So. I'm in.' She held the door open for Naz to enter, which she did, somewhat nervously. McCluskey's hair reminded Naz of fairground candyfloss and she had the hugest pair of ears she'd ever seen. They'd met once before, briefly, but the ears had escaped Naz's notice; looking at them now, she was at a loss to explain why.

'What's that you're carrying there?' McCluskey was pointing at the present that Naz was holding in her hand; inexpertly wrapped in recycled Christmas paper.

'Oh, yes. This is for you.'

'Why?'

'I'm sorry?'

'Why is this for me?'

'Well, Mr Carver said . . .' She stopped herself.

'Mr Carver said what?'

Naz didn't want to repeat what Carver had told her but lying to this woman seemed like an even riskier option.

'He said you *have to take a dragon a gift*.'

'Cheeky bastard.'

She took the present and unwrapped it – it was a glass snow globe, inside was a beautifully detailed model of the Taj Mahal.

'William mentioned that you collect snow globes. I've had this one since I was a kid. Me and my brother went there with my mum and dad.'

McCluskey looked at Naz. She still looked like a kid.

'You shouldn't give your stuff away willy-nilly.'

'It's been gathering dust at the back of a cupboard for years. I promise I won't miss it.'

'Well, if you're sure. I've got one Taj Mahal already, but this one's better.' She examined the miniature version of the white mausoleum more closely. 'There's some proper craftsmanship gone into this. The one Carver got me had "Made in China" stamped on the bottom – not what the Mughal Emperor would have wanted. Come on through . . . I've set you up in the kitchen.'

On McCluskey's kitchen table there was a new spiral-bound notebook, several black biros and a hardback Teeline textbook that looked about a hundred years old. Naz unshouldered her rucksack and put it on a chair.

'I've got my own textbook.'

'Bully for you. But while you're here we'll be using this one. It's tried and tested. Take a seat.' Naz sat. 'The best way to learn shorthand is to write to dictation. I'll do that with you on your next visit maybe, but not today . . . I've my own work to do. So I've recorded a few five-minute radio news bulletins on this.' McCluskey lifted what looked like a small brown leather suitcase with a tattered shoulder strap from the floor and plonked it down on the table next to Naz.

'What's that?'

'It's a UHER. As it happens it's one of the ones that Carver used to cart around the world.' It was clear from the look on Naz's face that she was still none the wiser. 'It's a reel-to-reel recorder. Very simple to use, excellent sound quality and almost impossible to break. The only downside is they weigh a bloody ton. This fellow here is probably the reason that Carver walks like the missing link. Just press play when you're ready, stop when you're finished and try to get as much of each bulletin down in the best Teeline you can manage. I'll be back in half an hour to mark it. This'll give us an idea of what level you're at now and how much work we've got to do.'

'Okay. Er . . . thank you.'

'No worries. The bathroom's in the hall, the tea and kettle are on the side. Water's in the tap.' She turned to leave.

'Thank you.'

'You're welcome. Thank you for the Taj Mahal.' She paused. 'We'll do an hour or so on this . . . then maybe you'd like to come and have a look at what I'm working on?'

Naz nodded vigorously. 'I'd love that.'

'Good. My old Caversham pal is away on his holidays with the grandkids for a few days, so I could use another pair of hands – or more importantly an extra pair of eyes.'

'Course, amazing. William said you were working on something interesting, but he warned me not to be too nosey.'

McCluskey shook her head.

'That's rich coming from Carver. And poor advice to give an

aspiring journalist as well. Let's make some progress with the shorthand and then see if you can make yourself useful in any other way.'

Naz watched while McCluskey read and marked her shorthand. Her hand moved quickly across the lines of Teeline that Naz had painstakingly written and the red pen she was holding was never inactive for long. When she'd finished, she looked across the table at her pupil.

'How d'you think you did?'

'Badly.'

'No, not badly. Not brilliant but not badly. You're not that many marks away from a pass.'

'I'd like to do better than that.'

'Good for you. If you get a marker with a sense of humour then you might even pick up a couple of extra points for comedy.'

Naz gave McCluskey a questioning look.

'That bulletins story about Alexander Litvinenko. You've written here that the judge is halfway through a *pubic inquiry*. As if the poor man hasn't suffered enough.'

Naz made an exasperated sound.

'Chin up. Work to do but you'll get there. How about a cup of tea? We can take it upstairs. Are you hungry?'

Naz was hungry. She watched as McCluskey moved around her kitchen making tea and sandwiches – doorstop-sized pieces of bread carved from a brown loaf, heavily buttered and filled with thick slices of Scottish cheddar 'better than English' and Branston Pickle. Naz watched with interest, especially when McCluskey wrapped a dampened tea towel around the base of the plate of sandwiches.

'Stops them drying up and curling. I sometimes get distracted when I'm working. Let's take these up to command and control.'

Inside the spare room, Naz stood and stared. There were piles of newspapers and boxes everywhere. On the wall were lists of telephone numbers, hundreds of them, some ringed with red marker pen and connected to photocopied newspaper articles and agency copy in a variety of languages. McCluskey glanced across at Naz.

'Impressive, eh? Will there be a question in your exams about investigative journalism, do you know?'

'It might be one of the optional questions. It isn't always there is what I've been told.'

'Shame. Well, if you want to know the secret to investigative reporting? It's a good filing system.'

Naz looked around the room.

'Is this a good filing system?'

'Yes, it bloody is. The best. It's straightforward once you know what you're looking at. My pal managed to pinch all of these numbers from the people who were trying to spy on him. Reverse ferreting, he called it. Our job is to find out who they are – good guys? Bad guys? Somewhere in between? If we're lucky, one or two of these numbers might be for someone who's doing the bugging, not just the people being bugged.' McCluskey put the plate of sandwiches down and walked towards the wall. 'It turns out that a lot of them have some involvement in green issues of one sort or another.'

'Is that why you were after Clive Winner's mobile number?'

'Carver told you that, did he?' Naz nodded. 'Winner is a person of interest. He has been for a while. At least a dozen of the people we've identified have done some kind of work for Clive Winner or have a connection to one of his slightly odd projects.' She pointed in the direction of a particular group of numbers. 'I've put them all together over here. But we don't know if that's coincidental or not. We need his number if we're going to work that out.'

Then it occurred to Naz.

'His. Or someone very close to him? His consigliere for example.'

'Er, well that could well take us a few steps further in the right direction.'

'Then I can help.'

She reached for her phone. Naz would never know what Jennifer Prepas would have told her if she'd been able to answer her call, but she did have a record of her number.

67

TATE BRITAIN, MILLBANK, LONDON

Carver's hunch about Edith Walston proved to be correct. The professor called him just after seven a.m. from a withheld number; she didn't talk for long. She could meet him later that day. It was either then and at the time and place of her choosing or not at all. He agreed immediately. Naz was with McCluskey and that was unfortunate, but he'd been supposed to spend the day at New Broadcasting House and anything that meant he didn't have to do that was music to his ears. He called Naomi and explained the situation. She was too tied up with work to be angry. He promised he'd be in to see her soon.

Edith Walston's instructions were precise. Carver was to meet her at noon at the bottom of the main central staircase, inside the main entrance to Tate Britain. 'Britain NOT Modern.'

He arrived just before twelve and found the gallery busy, with several school groups arriving and leaving simultaneously. Despite the bustle, Professor Walston was hard to miss, her trademark bobble hat a colourful beacon among all the dark school uniforms. As he approached, Carver offered his hand, which she took and shook in a distracted fashion. She was more interested in the shoals of school kids moving around the gallery entrance.

'Is this an acceptable place to meet? I assumed that busy would be preferable.'

'Busy is good . . .' Carver looked around. 'This is fine.'

'Excellent. I thought as much. Also . . . there's a painting here I'd like to see.'

'Okay.'

'So, even if our conversation comes to naught, I shan't feel that I've wasted an entire day.'

'I'm sure our conversation won't come to naught.'

The professor shot Carver a sideways look.

'Don't be so sure. I haven't decided what, if anything, I'm going to tell you yet.' She picked up her Cambridge University Press tote bag, turned and set off up the stairs. 'The picture I'm looking for is up here.'

Before following her, Carver scanned the gallery entrance once more. The reason he'd arrived late – not later than the agreed time, but not as early as he'd wanted – was that he'd had to change tubes and double back on himself a couple of times on the way here. He wasn't sure that he was being tailed, but he had a suspicion. He'd decided not to mention it, concerned that it might put the professor on edge and make her less inclined to tell him whatever it was she was considering telling him. Having said that, Edith Walston didn't seem the sort who scared easily. He turned back around to find her glaring at him from the top of the stone staircase.

'Are you coming, or aren't you?'

'I'm coming.'

The picture the professor was looking for was hanging in a small, dimly lit gallery at the back of the Tate's top floor. At the entrance to the room were a pair of overlapping thick red velvet curtains that you had to shuffle in between to gain entry. Once inside it took a while for Carver's eyes to adjust to the gloom. When they did, he saw half-a-dozen large Velázquez paintings in ornate gold frames distributed around the walls. Each picture was individually lit with a gentle buttery-yellow light emanating from spots in the floor and ceiling. Edith Walston had headed straight for one particular picture and he went to join her. He read the information card next to the painting: *Immaculate Conception, Diego Velázquez, Oil on Canvas, 1617.* The picture featured a long-faced and beautiful Virgin Mother, hovering above the earth, surrounded on all sides by puffy grey-white clouds. Edith Walston studied the Velázquez in silence for what seemed like an age before finally speaking.

'Incredible.'

He nodded.

'Very nice.'

'Doesn't it make you feel inadequate? Standing in front of this sort of perfection.'

'No more than usual.' Carver's mind had wandered away from the picture, he'd had half an eye on who else was entering or exiting the underlit gallery. Now he looked at the painting again. 'I'm guessing you wanted to see this one because of all the . . .' He took a guess. '. . . cumulonimbus going on.'

'More cumulus than cumulonimbus I'd say. That's certainly part of the appeal.'

'Velázquez paints a good cloud, does he?'

'Not bad.'

'But not the best. Who'd win that prize? I bet Turner's probably the main man, is he?'

Edith shook her head.

'Not for me. Turner's better at sea than sky. John Constable is the fellow when it comes to clouds.' She turned and met Carver's eye. 'Clive Winner recently gave me a book, a new collection, featuring every cloud picture Constable ever painted. A beautiful book.'

'That's kind of him. He had it couriered it over, did he?'

'He brought it himself. He came to Cambridge.'

'I see. Was that . . . a productive meeting?'

'Not as productive as I'd hoped.' The professor sighed. 'Give me a little longer to look at these other Velázquez pictures, will you, Mr Carver? Then we will talk.'

'Of course.'

There was a long, low bench in the middle of the gloomy gallery, which Carver discovered by cracking his knee against. He swore, then sat down and waited. Before long, Edith joined him.

'As interesting as it was having you come to visit me in Cambridge, Mr Carver, I had hoped that I'd be able to throw away that business card of yours and never see you again.'

'Yes, I get that a lot.'

'But I'm afraid my meeting with Clive failed to allay some concerns I've had. In fact, it raised new ones.'

'What sort of concerns?'

In response, the professor gave him a potted history of all the work she and Clive Winner had done together; right back to when he'd studied under her. From the early cloud-seeding work – persuading high-flying, fast-moving clouds to slow and rain on parts of Africa that they usually ignored.

'Clouds are capricious, but we had some success.'

'Managed to create some of those fresh showers for thirsting flowers that we talked about when we last met?'

'Indeed. And more importantly crops and reservoirs and people. Although even the early work we did, Clive and I . . . it posed moral problems. In giving one group of people water, you inevitably take it away from someone else. Then there are the less worthy causes . . .' She mentioned the work they'd done encouraging clouds to drop their cargo the day before a military parade or an Olympic opening ceremony and not on the day itself. 'Sometimes we'd have to sit down with questionable people. We used to joke that we'd always sup with a long spoon . . . we convinced ourselves that the good we could do outweighed the bad. But it's a slippery slope.'

'And Clive Winner lost his footing?'

'Something like that. After that work he did on the Great Barrier Reef – quite brilliant work by the way – suddenly he was everybody's favourite scientist. The man who could save the world. Perhaps he started to believe his own publicity. That's always a mistake.' She was staring straight ahead at something only she could see. 'A number of things happened. Several things were worrying me, that's why I asked Clive to come and see me, to put my mind at rest.' She paused. 'He couldn't. And then there was that dreadful news about Jennifer Prepas.'

'You knew her?'

'We'd met. I knew that she was Clive's loyal lieutenant.'

'And you don't believe that what happened to her outside her house was an accident?'

'Do you?'

'No.'

Carver shuffled closer to the professor who appeared to not even notice, lost in her own thoughts.

'My colleague Naz . . . it was her that contacted you originally.'

'Naziah. I remember.'

'Jennifer Prepas left an answerphone message on Naz's mobile. She didn't say what she wanted to talk about, but it sounded serious. I can play you the message if you like. Ten hours later she was dead.'

The professor lifted her tote bag and put it on the bench.

'I wasn't sure whether I was going to let you see these or not. Now I believe I will.' She reached into her tote bag and pulled out the manila envelope as well as several more recent articles that appeared to be about Jennifer Prepas.

Carver took the envelope and opened it. He had to hold the newspaper clippings close to read them in the gloom but it seemed safer to be doing this in an almost empty gallery than anywhere else. It was an eclectic collection, gathered from a wide range of publications – specialised scientific journals and more familiar newspapers both domestic and international. Carver skim-read a few. They ranged from rather dry stories about scientists he'd never heard of having their funding taken away, to more tabloidy articles accusing some better-known scientific figures of dishonesty or hypocrisy. There were several references to Climategate – Carver thought that story had disappeared but it appeared that it rumbled on. Then there were the obituaries, people in Winner's and the professor's world who had taken their own lives as well as several who'd died in accidents. He came across the piece from the *New Scientist* – the article he'd suspected the professor of hiding from him when they last met. It was the article that Naz had identified.

'I've read this already. The article that mentions some geoengineering project in Andalusia? I take it you were involved in that with Winner?'

'From a distance. He sent me the data to look at, I'm still looking at it in fact. But he shut the project down, half-finished. I still don't know why.'

'I might be able to help you with that; Naz and I found some more detail in the Spanish press.'

'I'd be interested. Whatever happened in Spain really shook Clive. I tried to get him to talk to me about it, but he wouldn't. Or couldn't.'

68

LA BARROSA, ANDALUSIA, SPAIN

Francesca Galinda had rehearsed what she was going to say to Carlos time and time again. She would tell him what Alma had told her. She would apologise for not telling him sooner. It would be hard, painful for both of them but maybe it would bring them closer. Her daughter had loved Carlos, adored him in fact. Despite her mother's reservations.

Carlos put the scented candle in a bag, gave his shoes a polish with a piece of dampened toilet tissue and went downstairs to wait. Loli had offered to go with him and he'd jumped at the offer. He'd always been intimidated by Alma's mum; whenever they'd visited her he came away with the same feeling – that she disapproved of him but not that strongly. She was happy to wait until her daughter's infatuation with him passed. On the way over to her house in the old part of the town they were going to buy some proper cakes – not Magdalenas. Loli had insisted. Here she came now. She studied Carlos with an appraising eye. 'Are those the only black trousers and white shirt you've got?' Carlos nodded. 'Then they'll have to do. Let's go. We need to get the cakes. And buy a comb, we can at least do something about the hair.'

Francesca's little bungalow – Alma's childhood home – was famous locally for its flowers. They were everywhere – in pots fixed to the whitewashed walls, planted in beds next to a tiled patio and in large terracotta pots either side of the ornately grilled, wooden front door. Regardless of when you visited, there would be bright-red geraniums everywhere you looked, although as they turned the corner and Carlos saw the house, he noticed that the flowers looked a little less resplendent than usual. Under-watered perhaps. Maybe he could water them while Loli and Alma's mother chatted? He suggested this.

'Forget it.' Loli took his plastic bag, handed him the cakes, knocked firmly on the door and stepped back, leaving Carlos standing there, cakes in hand. He was shuffling backwards to stand alongside Loli when the door swung open.

'Good afternoon, Mrs Galinda, we brought you these.' He held the ribbon-tied box of cakes up for her to see. The old lady pushed his outstretched hand to one side, she opened her arms, stepped forward and gathered Carlos in. Her small body was warm against his stomach, her head barely reaching his chest. Glancing down he saw the old lady's shoulders rising and falling, felt her body heave. He realised she was crying and then, immediately, that he was crying too. He let the box of cakes fall and put his arms around her.

Inside the house, Alma's mother fussed over her guests, seating them side by side on the good sofa and demanding they make themselves comfortable while she fetched coffee and found plates for the 'beautiful' cakes. It wasn't easy for Carlos to feel comfortable in Mrs Galinda's small living room; everywhere he looked, pictures of Alma gazed back. School photos, family photos, several communion pictures, there was even a picture of her sitting straight-backed and proud in the cockpit of the flying fried egg. Alma had always been well celebrated in her family home; after his first visit, Carlos had wondered out loud why her mum didn't just have Alma's grinning face made into wallpaper and be done with it? Alma had laughed.

'I'm sure your mother has pictures of you.'

'Not as many as she has of the dogs.'

Mrs Galinda returned with the coffee and a plate of slightly squashed cakes. Once they all had a cup and plate in their hand, she pointed out the new additions to the Alma Galinda gallery. She'd had the pictures of her daughter that she carried around in her wallet enlarged and framed, she'd also found wall space for a not very good portrait of Alma that the old boardwalk artist had done. Picasso de la Playa mainly did sunsets, but he'd produced this picture unbidden and unpaid for and given it to Alma's mother, explaining that her daughter was 'too beautiful not to paint'. Carlos kept his eyes away from walls and surfaces and instead focussed on the rug or whichever of the two women was talking. He sipped his coffee and ate his cake and waited. He would have to tell Francesca about the phone, but he wanted to tell her everything else that he had done first. At the next lull in conversation, he launched into it.

'I'm sorry I haven't been to visit for so long. I have been doing everything I can think of to find Alma, Mrs Galinda. Perhaps Loli has said?' The old lady nodded. Encouraged by this, he continued but before long he realised he was babbling . . . he talked about being shown the huge fish with a bellyful of diamonds, the deserted fishing village near the Portuguese border where the tide had started to wash all sorts of things ashore. There was something called the Canary Current – like the islands – and it was flowing in a way it hadn't flowed before. He mentioned the waterlogged tower. Glancing up he saw a look of confusion on her face and realised that what he was saying sounded more like a fairy tale or a children's story than a credible explanation of why he had ignored her pleas that he visit her. He cut to the chase.

'I found her phone.'

'You found Alma's phone?'

'Yes.'

'Where is it? Can I see it?'

Carlos stared down at his hands, folded in his lap.

'I don't have it any more. I lost it. A pickpocket I think, possibly when—'

'A pickpocket?' There was a look of disbelief on her face. Then more questions: how long had he had it for? Had he shown it to the police? Was there anything on it that could tell them what had happened to Alma? As he spoke, he realised how inadequate his answers were, how stupid he'd been. Finally.

'Why didn't you bring it to me? I am her mother!'

'I know. I was going to, I swear that I was but . . .'

'The pickpocket.'

'Yes.'

The conversation petered out. The awkward silences grew longer. Eventually Loli suggested that maybe they should leave Francesca to rest and she agreed that would be best. She walked them to the door. Once there, she spoke.

'After she disappeared, I would call Alma's phone number sometimes . . . just to hear her voice.' Carlos nodded. The missed calls. 'Yesterday I tried again but the message was gone. Her voice was gone.' She paused. 'That was the last piece of her that I had.' Carlos stared down at his feet. He tried to think of something to say but there was nothing. 'My daughter loved you, Carlos.'

'I know, and I loved her.'

'But you did not deserve her.'

Francesca sat in her living room in silence for a long time after Carlos and Loli had left. It took a while for the anger to leave her. Once it had she realised she hadn't told Carlos any of what she had planned to. None of the apologies she'd rehearsed or the information she'd been keeping from him. Perhaps now she would not. What was the point? Her daughter was gone. For all his faults she knew that Carlos had loved Alma and grieved her. Why make him sadder still? Francesca had kept secrets before and she would keep this one too. About Alma's boss.

69

TATE BRITAIN, MILLBANK, LONDON

Once he'd finished looking through the collection of newspaper articles and cuttings Carver turned and looked at Professor Walston.

'What did Winner say when you showed him these?'

'At first, he tried to dismiss them. Later, he told me to burn them. That was more or less the last thing he said before he left.'

'"Burn them."' Carver stared at the pile of cuttings. 'So, either he thinks these pose a threat to him, or maybe to you?'

'To both of us I imagine. And he's probably right.'

'Can you explain?'

She sighed. Not for the first time, Carver got the impression that he was testing her patience.

'How much do you think the fossil-fuel industry is worth? Globally I mean.'

'Billions?'

'Trillions. Currently around six trillion pounds – give or take.' Edith smiled.

'Right.'

'What do you think happens when countries and companies – entire industries in fact – when groups of powerful people with a large stake in fossil fuels begin to feel threatened?' The question was rhetorical. 'They react in the same way that anything threatened reacts. Sometimes they back off, sometimes they try to negotiate. But when you're this powerful and there is this much at stake – mainly you fight back.'

'I can understand that.' He pointed at the pile of cuttings. 'And perhaps that can help explain some of what is going on here. But why would Clive Winner be considered a threat? I thought he was these people's favourite scientist, their blue-eyed boy.'

'He was.' She paused. 'Clive isn't perfect. He's light years away from perfect in fact, but he's a good scientist – he was that before he became a famous, feted figure and he's still that now. He keeps an open mind – like all good scientists, like all sentient human beings should.'

'Okay.'

'I think Clive is changing his mind – about geo, about renewables, about lots of things. That would be bad news enough as far as these powerful people I'm talking about are concerned. But I think he's interested in changing other people's minds too. And that makes him dangerous.'

Carver suggested that he and the professor leave the gallery separately. He went first but rather than heading directly home, he crossed the road and found a bench with a clear view back towards the gallery. The professor took her time, so much so that Carver began to wonder if she'd found another exit. Eventually she appeared, holding a gallery carrier bag as well as her own tote. He supposed it was a good sign that Edith was so unfazed by their conversation that she'd decided to do a little shopping afterwards. She pulled her stripy bobble hat down a little lower against the chill wind, used the banister on her way down the Tate's stone steps and set off in the direction of Pimlico. Carver saw no sign that anyone other than himself was watching her, and once he was sure that was the case and she had disappeared from view he set off in the other direction, walking down Millbank and towards Westminster.

The feeling of being followed is an odd one. You know – even if you don't know how you know. At least that was Carver's experience. He stopped once at a convenient bollard to retie a shoelace that was already tied just fine. Near St James's Park he stopped again, this time outside a posh tailor's shop; the well-polished windows gave him a good view of who'd been walking behind him for the last twenty or thirty yards on both sides of the street, but he saw nothing untoward. Either his instincts were off or whoever it was that was tailing him was extremely good at it.

70

HIGHBURY FIELDS, LONDON

Rebecca had dressed the baby and was in the bedroom getting dressed herself when the doorbell rang.

'Patrick? You got that?' No answer. She went to the intercom.

'Hello?'

'Hi, it's Naz. I'm here to see Patrick for my, er . . . class?'

'Sure, come on up.'

She went and banged on the bathroom door. 'Patrick, that's your woman Naz.'

'She's early.'

'Well, she's here.'

There was a rapid tapping at the flat door. Naz must have run up the stairs. Sure enough when Rebecca opened the door the young woman standing in front of her was red-faced and breathing heavily.

'You look lovely.'

Rebecca smiled. She didn't feel lovely. She pushed a hand through her blonde hair. It felt a little greasy. She was going to wash it but there hadn't been time. She was a million miles from lovely. But it was nice to be told it anyway.

'Thank you. It's good to meet you, Naz. I've heard a lot about you.'

'From Patrick?'

'From Carver mainly. He's a fan.' Naz was tempted to ask what it was that William had said about her but she managed to resist. 'Come on in. Place is a bit of a mess, I'm afraid.'

Naz waved this apology away. Rebecca led her through to the living room and offered to make her a cup of tea. While she was gone, Naz surveyed the room, checking out the various knick-knacks, the pictures on the mantelpiece of Patrick and Rebecca on a couple of happy-looking holidays, at a family Christmas and a more recent photo of the two of them sitting either side of a hospital cot, both grinning like crazy. There in the cot was a purple-faced bundle of a baby. When she returned, Rebecca was carrying the same – significantly larger and less purple-looking – baby in her arms.

'Do you think you might be able to hold this one while I sort your tea? Patrick's still in the bath.'

'Sure.' Naz reached out and took the baby, holding her with some confidence. Rebecca looked on approvingly. 'You're used to babies?'

'Big family, loads of cousins. All shapes and sizes.'

Rebecca got Naz a tea, took Leila back and put her down in her pram. The baby seemed happy to lie there wriggling while Naz waited for Patrick and Rebecca got herself together. She and Leila were going out for the day.

'We're going to give you and Patrick some space to work. Space and peace and quiet. We're going to the park.'

'I assumed you'd be catching up with your Planet Action gang? Jeffus and co.?'

Patrick was standing by the door, bathed, and dressed and unsmiling.

'Not today, no.'

Patrick said hello to Naz and began bringing several lever-arch files and some textbooks through from the spare room-stroke-nursery and setting them down next to the coffee table. There was clearly an atmosphere in the flat, it seemed like Naz might've interrupted a row of some sort. Or perhaps she'd caused one?

'You know we don't have to do this today, Patrick? I can come back some other time if you'd like to spend the day with Rebecca and Leila? I don't mind at all.'

'No, it's fine. I promised William and, anyway, you're here now.' He turned to his girlfriend. 'I'm guessing this will take a good bit of the day. I can look after Leila later if you like so you can have a break.'

'Okay.'

'When are you leaving?'

'Half an hour or so.'

First Patrick read through some of Naz's portfolio, a selection of articles she'd written while working at the local newspaper. He suggested she reorder them before presenting them for examination.

'Why did you start with this one?'

Naz grinned. 'That was the first time I got a byline.'

Patrick took the article from its clear plastic folder and read: '*Innovative Hounslow business initiative* – that's boring as a whole sentence and boring word by word.'

'It gets better as you read on.'

'They'll never know.'

'What do you mean?'

'Because they'll do what I and every other sensible person would do after seeing that headline and stop reading. Put it at the back of the folder or take it out completely.'

His manner was brusque but the advice he gave her was good. When he heard Rebecca getting ready to leave, Patrick got up and went next door, closing the living-room door behind him. Naz could hear their conversation anyway.

'How's it going?'

'Okay I guess.'

'You could be a little more encouraging with her, Patrick, she's young.'

'We've got to get through almost the entire National Certificate syllabus. I'm just trying to do it as efficiently as possibly. She's not exactly miss charm school herself.'

'Maybe because you're not giving her the chance.'

'Plus, there's the fact that she'd clearly climb over my dead body to get my job.' The couple said their awkward goodbyes, Patrick asked when they'd be back and Rebecca said she'd message him and let him know. She asked him to say goodbye to Naz. When Patrick walked back into the living room, Naz was doing a reasonably good impression of someone who'd been entirely absorbed in their work.

'Becs said bye.'

'Ah, thanks. She seems great. Leila too.'

'Yeah.'

They worked for another hour then broke for lunch. Naz had brought crisps and sandwiches from her parents' shop and Patrick made tea. While they were eating Patrick asked how things were going with McCluskey.

'My shorthand's getting better, I think. Jemima seems happy enough.'

'Has she told you about Keir Hardie teaching himself shorthand with a piece of chalk on a coalface wall yet?'

'No.'

'She will.'

Naz smiled.

'I'm helping her with some of her own stuff too.'

'Oh yeah?'

Naz told him about Pegasus. About how there might be a link between that and the Clive Winner investigation that she and Carver were involved in. She realised that she was trying to impress Patrick, to show off. She tried to stop herself but for the first time that day he seemed to be genuinely interested in what she was saying. He asked questions. Where did McCluskey think the malware came from, when was it developed, what was it capable of? Naz answered when she could.

'McCluskey did mention that you and Carver had had experience of this sort of thing . . . in Egypt was it?'

'Egypt and elsewhere during the Arab Spring. But I saw more of the sort of thing you're talking about in . . . er . . . Hong Kong. But the stuff we were seeing there wasn't as sophisticated as this Pegasus thing sounds. It's evolved.'

'So it's harder to detect – but Jemima and John Smith have detected it already. They're trying to work out why the people they've identified are being spied on and by who.'

'So motive is the obvious clue. But there are other things you can look for in the data.'

'I'm sure McCluskey would love it if you were able to take a look. You might see something she hasn't. She mentions you all the time – Patrick this, Patrick that . . .'

He shook his head. 'It's not my job any more. Anyway, it sounds like she's got all the help she needs.' Naz was about to challenge this assertion, but Patrick stopped her. 'We should get back to the revision. I'd prefer it if this didn't take the entire day.'

'Sure, yeah.'

The rest of the afternoon was productive if not pleasurable. Naz made lots of notes, Patrick gave her more good advice on how to approach the various modules, clues to what the examiners would be looking for. As it got later, he became more distracted, surly in fact. He checked his phone repeatedly. When Naz suggested they stop for the day he jumped at the idea.

'Yeah, that feels like enough. I guess we could do another session another time. If you like.'

'Okay, thanks. Although I've heard people sound more enthusiastic.'

'I'm doing this as a favour to William, Naz. Not for the fun of it.'

'I understand.'

She packed up her papers, put her tracksuit jacket back on and walked to the door. He followed her. At the door Naz turned and looked Patrick square in the eye.

'You're absolutely right by the way.'

'Eh?'

'That conversation you had with Rebecca, I overheard it and you're right . . . I would climb over your dead body to get your job.'

'Okay, thanks for confirming that.'

'So, maybe you should stop playing dead?'

Rebecca had a few errands to run. She wanted to buy a present for a friend she'd made at National Childbirth Trust classes. The woman was her favourite, she'd had a rough time during the birth of her baby and was having a belated baby shower that Rebecca wasn't going to be able to get to because it clashed with Paris. That was if she was still going to Paris. She was no longer sure she could. She wandered Upper Street popping in and out of shops looking for something for both her friend and the baby. A classy piece of old costume jewellery – a necklace – was an easy choice, finding something for the kid was more difficult. There was no shortage of shops, but they all seemed to be stocking the same range of gear – tiny Ramones T-shirts, Ziggy Stardust babygrows and the like. The shop assistant in one shop tried to interest her in a T-shirt featuring a cartoon baby wearing sunglasses and holding a guitar singing 'Nobody Knows the Snuggles I've Seen'.

Rebecca shook her head. 'Have you got anything that isn't . . . cool. Or sarcastic?'

'We've got a giraffe mobile.'

'I'll take that.'

The woman wrapped it for her, and she took it to the post office to send. On the way to the play park Leila fell asleep in her buggy. Rebecca got a cappuccino from the 2CV that had been converted into a coffee cart near the fields and found a bench in the sun. It was good to be out of the flat and with some time to herself to think. She'd put the trip to the pub and the awkward conversation she'd had with Jeff to the back of her mind but it wouldn't stay there forever. She needed to talk through the stuff he'd told her with someone. It couldn't be anyone from Planet Action; she ran through her list of friends trying to think of who might be most appropriate. And understanding. And available. There were a couple of people.

She finished her coffee just as Leila was waking up. The baby blinked away her sleepiness, gazed up at Rebecca and smiled. She looked so much like Patrick when she was waking up. An endearing combination of sleepy confusion and optimism. Patrick was the only person Rebecca wanted to talk to about her concerns over Jeff and Planet Action. She was sure it was the last thing in the world he wanted to talk about, but stuff it, she wasn't going to give him any choice. They would go out tomorrow night. All she needed to do was find a babysitter.

71

STOCKWELL ROAD, LONDON

A walk then lunch. That was what Henrietta had said. How the hell were you supposed to dress for that? Her and Leonard lived in the countryside – more or less – so presumably a walk would mean a muddy trek through fields or woods or suchlike? But then lunch. Their house was pretty posh. Carver briefly thought about taking a change of clothes before realising how ridiculous he'd look turning up for lunch with an overnight bag. He settled on his usual black trousers, white shirt and blazer, all of which he'd had dry-cleaned, but with some sturdy walking boots that he'd had forever but only used once, and a raincoat. He had a paisley tie in his blazer pocket in case the Sunday lunch turned out to be more formal than his conversation with Henrietta had led him to believe.

Carver checked himself over one more time in the bathroom mirror before he left. Moving in for a close-up he noticed a grey nose hair.

'God, that's depressing.' He managed to pluck it out with his thumb and forefinger although it hurt like hell.

He wasn't due in Haslemere until eleven a.m. but set off just after eight. That vague feeling that he was being followed had stayed with him ever since his meeting with Edith Walston at the Tate, and he was planning to take a very roundabout route to Charing Cross to make sure there was no one tailing him. He took this circuitous route to the Overground but quickly became sure there was no one taking any interest in his movements today. The vague feeling had gone, and it was a relief that it had.

On the train he tried to relax. Part of the problem he thought was that although this was a social visit he would need to find a moment when he and Leonard could discuss Clive Winner and the new information that he had. He wanted to know what Leonard had made of Jennifer Prepas' murder and get an update on any contact between Winner and Downing Street.

In the event, all Carver's work-related plans proved pointless. Arriving at Haslemere station he was met by Henrietta. She had bad news.

'I'm so sorry, William. Leonard has been called in to work. Some emergency or other. Your train here probably crossed with his heading back in. I thought I'd meet you and give you the option of changing your mind before you got all the way to the house.'

It took a while for Carver to process the new information. When he did, he realised that he was actually pleased that there would be no work involved in his visit and not too upset that Leonard wouldn't be around. He told Henrietta that he would be happy to stay.

'Excellent news. In which case I propose that we start our walk right here. There's a nice little rambling route that takes us all the way around the town. It might prove a little too gentle for you mind – by the looks of those boots you've got on you're a proper walker not a part-time *flâneuse* like me.'

Carver assured her this wasn't the case.

The route Henrietta had in mind began just behind the local church. As they walked past, the vicar appeared – Carver remembered him from Leonard and Henrietta's Christmas drinks party.

'Good morning, Mrs Allen, what a beautiful morning. A blessed relief after the rain we've been having.'

'Indeed it is.'

'I didn't see you in church this morning.'

'No, vicar. That's because I wasn't there. I was preparing lunch for Mr Carver here.'

'Ah, I see. Pleased to meet you, Mr Carver. Are you a civil service man as well?'

'No, I'm afraid not.'

'Mr Carver is a public servant though. And a very dutiful one. You met him at Christmas drinks a couple of years back.'

'Oh yes, I think I remember.' It was clear from the look on the vicar's face that he did not. Henrietta put her hand on Carver's arm.

'William is hungry and I'm making him do the Haslemere hike before I feed him so we should go.'

'Of course.'

'By the way, your Union flag is flying upside down again.'

The vicar glanced up at the flagpole.

'Not again. I'm sorry. I'll have another word with Balloo.'

'I beg your pardon?'

'Balloo. He's the assistant Cub Scout leader, he looks after the flag-raising ceremony.'

'I see.'

'We'll get it right next week.'

'My breath will be bated.'

The walk was enjoyable. The lunch was delicious. Henrietta's four sons joined them at various points but only to carve themselves off some chunks of lamb and fill their plates with roast potatoes, buttered broccoli and mint sauce, before taking their food to the games room where a winner-stays-on round of pool was taking place. Henrietta explained that they weren't often all at home together, all four were weekly boarders at the school they went to but usually at least one stayed at school for the weekend to play rugby or cricket depending on the season.

'Four boys at a fee-paying school can't be cheap.' Carver regretted this the moment he'd said it, fearing that it would sound either impolite or judgemental, but Henrietta didn't seem to mind at all.

'It's a king's ransom . . . absolutely ridiculous. It's one of the few things that Leonard and I disagree on. There's a perfectly good local state secondary but Grove Hall has been educating Allen boys for six generations and blah blah blah.'

Carver smiled. 'Yes, I think I met the schoolmaster when I was here last.'

'Poor you.'

'You rescued me.'

Carver had planned to get some work done on Sunday evening. To reread the articles that Edith Walston had given him before he and Naz went to see McCluskey. In fact he didn't leave Henrietta's house until after nine, the train back to London took forever and he had trouble staying awake. It was nearly midnight when he fell into bed – full of good food and wine and feeling happier than he remembered feeling for a long time. He had a good few messages on his phone that he hadn't bothered reading properly. It buzzed again just as he was falling asleep. He picked it up and squinted at the message; it was from Henrietta. He put his glasses back on.

Just checking that you got back okay?

He answered: *I did. Thank you.*

Then he waited. He was about to take his glasses off when another message arrived.

It was my pleasure. H x.

Carver stared at this single line until the screen went dark. He put the phone back on the side table, took his glasses off and fell asleep.

72

CAVERSHAM, BERKSHIRE, UK

Hailstones the size of peas were ricocheting off the sill outside McCluskey's kitchen window and back up onto the glass. The sound reminded Naz of making popcorn with her mum. It was getting on McCluskey's nerves.

'This is going tae kill off my hydrangeas for good.' She gave the weather a glare. 'Plus, I can hardly hear myself think. Where had I got to?'

Naz glanced at her notepad. Until recently she would have welcomed any interruption as a chance for her shorthand to catch up with McCluskey's dictation, but her Teeline was improving. She was up to speed. She read the last sentence Jemima had dictated.

'*My love is like the melody that's sweetly played in tune.*'

'Very good . . . *As fair thou art.*' She paused. 'Is it – *thou art* or *art thou*?'

'Can I just put – *you are*?'

McCluskey grudgingly agreed that she could.

Naz had asked if she could come early so she could do some extra shorthand practice before the other two arrived and they all started work upstairs in command and control. Carver was bringing the newspaper and magazine articles that Edith Walston had given him. They were going to see if they could match any of the names mentioned in those pieces with the mobile phone numbers on the spare-room wall. McCluskey's old Caversham colleague John Smith was back from his holidays and so he was coming too. Naz sensed that McCluskey was excited at the prospect of all this activity.

'Feels like a double tea-bag day tae me.' She took a second tea bag from the jar next to her kettle and dropped it into her mug. She looked across at Naz. 'You want yours stronger?'

'No, one is fine, thank you.' You could almost stand a spoon up in the mugs of tea McCluskey made as it was.

'What about the toast? I've got orange marmalade or Marmite.'

John Smith arrived first and was fed. He talked enthusiastically about his holiday, a camping trip to North Yorkshire with his grandkids. Naz listened politely to the Father Christmas lookalike in the denim dungarees but she had half an eye on the kitchen clock. Carver was late. This wasn't like him. They had another round of buttered toast. McCluskey suggested they give him ten more minutes. Then another five. Naz wondered out loud if she should message him but was advised against it.

Carver eventually arrived half-an-hour late and needing some cash to pay the taxi driver. John Smith obliged. Carver apologised for keeping everyone waiting and explained.

'I was followed from the flat, all the way to Paddington. I doubled back a couple of times on the tube but I couldn't get shot of him.'

McCluskey shook her head.

'Sounds like the fellow knew what he was doing.'

Carver nodded. 'I thought I'd lost him when I jumped off the train at the very last moment at Reading. But there he was again outside the station.' Carver told them he'd come close to giving up and heading back to London at that point, but he had the articles they were planning to work through, so it would've meant wasting their time as well as his. He gave up on the idea of a bus and jumped in a cab for the last leg. 'I got lucky with the cabbie. She'd been waiting to be asked to follow someone or shake off a tail her whole life. She was good at it but it took a while.' He made eye contact with Naz. She looked apprehensive.

'So with all that, I guess you got a proper look at him?'

'Yeah.'

'And?'

'Jeans, blue hoodie, light-brown boots and . . . sunglasses.'

'That's the same man who came to the shop. It must be.'

'I think you're right.' He paused. 'I'm sorry.'

Naz absorbed this new, unwelcome information. When she spoke she tried to sound braver than she felt.

'Why are you sorry? That idiot is hassling you now, not me. I'm delighted.'

Carver smiled.

'That's the spirit. Unfortunately if what Edith Walston told me is correct then the people we're dealing with have the resources to follow *all of us all of the time* if they want to. Was your trip out here okay?'

Carver had warned Naz to keep an eye out. He'd taught her some of the tricks he used – loose shoelaces and shop windows and so on.

'All fine I think, I travelled out pretty early to do some extra shorthand. I was going against commuter traffic so the train was almost empty. So that was fine and no one got on or off the Caversham bus when I did.'

McCluskey, John Smith and Carver nodded approvingly.

'So . . .' Carver took a manila envelope out of his plastic bag. 'Shall we get cracking? See if any of these leads the professor gave me are useful?'

It didn't take long for them to realise that they were. Carver read through the articles looking for names and highlighting them. Most of the individuals mentioned were scientists or researchers of one sort or another. Naz and John Smith used a couple of secure laptops that the former Caversham man had set up in the upstairs hall to comb the internet looking for contact numbers for these people. McCluskey then checked to see if any of the numbers appeared on the wall and if there was a connection with others they'd already identified. It was a painstaking business. They worked at it for the best part of the day with one break for lunch.

By five p.m. they'd established that at least eighteen of the scientists mentioned in the articles had been bugged using Pegasus. All of these had experienced some sort of misfortune; from having their work discredited, to being sacked for misconduct, two had committed suicide and three more had died in accidents. One young guy had fallen into the volcano he'd been studying. The corner of the spare room given over to environmental scientists who'd been spied on had spread. Still the question remained – spied on by whom?

McCluskey stood back and looked at all the material she'd taped to the wall.

'I had no clue that climate science was such a dangerous profession.'

She took Jennifer Prepas' name and contact number and stuck it at the top. 'I know she's not a scientist but I think we have tae put Jennifer Prepas' name in this group, don't we?'

John Smith walked in from the hall, laptop in hand.

'So we've got Winner's right-hand woman who was just about to double cross him . . .'

Carver shook his head. 'We don't know for sure that that was why she was calling Naz.'

Smith continued. 'Then underneath that we've got a load of Clive Winner's rivals – in one way or another?'

'Associates. People working for him or in the same field – not necessarily rivals. We're a long way from being able to prove that Clive Winner was responsible for the spying. If what Edith Walston told me is correct then this could go much wider than Winner.'

'If you'd been able to get hold of Clive Winner's number as promised . . .'

'I never promised that. I said we'd try.'

As the discussion veered away from a reasoned argument and in the direction of a row, McCluskey intervened.

'I think we should call it a day. Pick it up again tomorrow.' She looked across at Naz. 'How far into that envelope of articles are we?'

Naz had a look.

'Just over halfway.'

'Okay. So we do the other half tomorrow – there'll be some more leads in there I'm sure. Perhaps something will jump out at us.'

Naz nodded and stared at the wall. Then an idea occurred to her.

'When I was speaking to Patrick about this he said something about it not just being motive that you should look for, but that the data can contain other clues.'

McCluskey nodded. 'Sounds interesting. Maybe one of us should try to contact him?'

Carver nodded. 'I guess I could. I mean it's probably easier for me.' He paused. 'In fact, I'm seeing him later.'

'You are? How come?'

'Well, I'm kind of babysitting.'

73

LA BARROSA, ANDALUSIA, SPAIN

Carlos pushed the heavy metal shutters up and wound down the green- and white-striped awning, not that it looked like the Che bar customers would have much need of it today – the sun was up but invisible behind blankets of grey cloud.

'Hey you! Are you hiding from me?' Pepe was walking slowly up the boardwalk, his fishing rods in one hand and his cool box in the other. His pipe was clamped between his teeth, but it didn't stop him from talking. Or rather shouting. 'Eh? I'm talking to you, you *puta*! Have you been hiding?'

'I don't know what you're talking about, old man.' He knew exactly what Pepe was talking about. The old fisherman had come to his apartment three or four times in the last few days and rung the bell endlessly. Carlos had ignored him, putting his headphones on and waiting until he went away.

'Anyway. I've found you now.'

'Yes, you have. What is it? You want a free beer? Isn't it a little early? Even for you.'

'Go fuck yourself. I don't want a beer, I want to talk to you. Sit down.'

'I'm working.'

'There's no one here, you idiot. Sit down.'

Carlos grudgingly sat. Might as well get whatever this was over with, Pepe wouldn't leave until he'd said his piece.

'Have you given up?'

'What?'

'I want to know if you've given up, after your fuck-up with the phone. Is that it?'

'Pepe. Please, give me a break.'

'No, I won't.'

'What do you want me to do?'

'Well, you could start by getting the phone back, Francesca would like to have it.'

'How do you propose I do that, Pepe? Call the police? Lost property?'

'Of course not . . .' He paused. '. . . maybe you have given up. Maybe I'm wasting my time.'

'I haven't given up. There's just nothing I can do.'

'Course there is. There's always something you can do. Alma knew that. I taught her that when she was little. Not that she ever needed much teaching . . .' The old fisherman proceeded to tell Carlos a story about Alma and her kind nature, her brave character. Carlos had preferred it when Pepe was hurling insults at him.

'I'm still not clear what it is you want me to do, Pepe?'

'Alma's phone. You paid that kid in Cádiz to open it for you, yes?'

'Yeah, at the place you recommended. The place where you go to sell false teeth.'

Pepe ignored this. 'So then you go back and ask him for it.'

'For what?'

'The copy of Alma's phone that he undoubtedly made.'

'What makes you think he copied it?'

'He's a horrible little pervert – just like his father. Of course he made a copy.'

'And what if he refuses to give it to me?'

'Then you tell him that you and me are going to drive up there on your bike and beat the living shit out of the pair of them.'

Carlos laughed.

'Okay, you win, I'll go. Is there anything else?'

'That'll do for a start.' He paused. 'Oh, and maybe that beer.'

'The beer you didn't want?'

'Yes, that one.'

74

HIGHBURY FIELDS, LONDON

Carver still wasn't sure how he'd got himself into this situation. How had Rebecca managed to talk him into it? No doubt she'd tried a dozen other people before asking. All of them must have said no. He should've said no too. But he hadn't. In fact, now that he came to think of it, Carver remembered that he'd actually agreed to babysit quite readily. Naz had given him what he assumed she intended to be a pep talk on the train back from McCluskey's: babies were easy, Leila would be sleeping, Rebecca and Patrick would not leave their daughter for long, nor venture far. He and Naz had caught a train from Twyford rather than Reading. It seemed unlikely that the sunglasses-wearing thug would have spent the whole day hanging around Reading station on the off-chance that Carver returned there, but better safe than sorry. He was going straight from Waterloo to Patrick and Rebecca's place, and he didn't want to take any chances.

Rebecca's suggestion of a night out – she might even have used the words *date-night* – had taken Patrick by surprise. Not that they couldn't both use an evening out of the house, away from parental duties and parental conversations and parental everything. Nevertheless, something about the timing of her proposal or perhaps the way she'd suggested it had made him nervous. He consoled himself with the thought that as nervous as he felt – William Carver must be feeling ten times that. He couldn't quite believe that he'd said yes. He showered and dressed first – selecting a shirt that he remembered Rebecca liking. Then he took Leila and got her to sleep while Rebecca got ready.

Carver arrived a little early. Patrick opened the door to find him holding a bottle of red wine.

'Who's that for? Leila?'

'Er, well no. I wasn't quite sure what to bring. It felt wrong turning up with nothing.'

'I don't think you're supposed to bring anything when you babysit. Apart from a responsible attitude and perhaps a negative drugs test.'

'I think I can tick both those boxes. Is she er . . . asleep?'

'She is.'

'Great.'

The restaurant was busy. At least it was when they first arrived. Arsenal were playing at home and their favourite Greek place was packed with football fans, feeding and watering themselves before heading off to the game. They were playing Liverpool and you could almost hear the nerves jangling. They ordered a mixed mezze and some wine to start. The food took a while to come. While they were waiting Rebecca chatted with a group at the neighbouring table – four middle-aged men all wearing Arsenal scarves.

'Big game tonight, huh?'

'Big as they come.'

'Exciting. Have you got a good feeling?' After a brief conflab the four men agreed that they did not have a good feeling. 'I see. That famous Gooner optimism. Just as long as it's a good game though, eh?'

'I suppose.'

Their first few dishes arrived and the restaurant began to empty as the majority of customers headed off to the game. Before long the place was quiet enough that they felt they could talk more openly. They chatted about Leila for a while and their families. When the time felt right, when it seemed like Patrick had relaxed a little, Rebecca asked the question she'd been wanting to ask.

'I need to talk to you about something.'

'Sure.'

'Something difficult.'

Patrick took a gulp of his wine. 'Okay.'

'It's about Planet Action.'

'You mean it's about Jeff.'

Rebecca frowned. 'Well, yes. But maybe not in the way that you think.'

There it was again. The same noise. Carver picked up the baby monitor and studied it. He'd definitely heard a squeak but there was no sign of any movement on the screen. Maybe she squeaked in her sleep? The slightly grainy, black-and-white image of Leila – thumb in mouth, bum in air – appeared normal. He was beginning to wish he'd never agreed to this. Rebecca and Patrick were only down the road; they'd told him they could be back in five minutes if necessary – but God this was stressful. Who knew what a baby could get up to in the space of five minutes if they put their mind to it – especially a wilful one like this one undoubtedly was?

He glanced at the bottle of red wine he'd brought, standing unopened on the dining-room table. He didn't want to risk a glass now, but he intended to have several as soon as they got back. There was another squeak. That didn't sound like a sleeping squeak. Carver lifted the monitor up again and squinted at the image. Who's to say that it hadn't been hacked? You could hack almost anything these days. Then there was the whole area of 'deep fakes'. Patrick had shown him some of these videos in the past. If you could create a convincing-looking Tony Blair, apologising profusely for taking the UK into Iraq, then you could certainly fake a small baby sleeping. He decided to go and take the briefest of looks.

Rebecca told Patrick what she'd seen at the demonstration – Jeff in conversation with a group of other tracksuit-wearing individuals. He asked her for as much detail as she could give him – how many of them, any sign of cameras or walkie-talkies, were they close to any sort of vehicle? After she was sure she'd told him everything about the day in question she told him about the meeting she'd had with Jeff subsequently – the trip to the pub. Patrick's mood changed. But not for too long. Rebecca apologised for misleading him and explained why she'd done it. He believed her.

'Based on everything you've told me I think you're right to be suspicious. I don't think he was in Downing Street because he and his mates had a mind to cause trouble. The opposite in fact.'

'The opposite?'

'I think he's a policeman. Or similar. Or perhaps a paid police informer. That's what you were thinking too, wasn't it?'

'I didn't want to believe that, but yes.'

She told Patrick about Jeff's interest in the school strike and how keen he'd been that she collect as many names and mobile numbers from the young people involved as possible. About the concerns she had about what was being done with that information. Who it was being handed on to and for what reason.

When Patrick and Rebecca arrived home Carver was on the sofa, *Newsnight* was on the TV but the sound was turned down. He had his feet on the coffee table and was leaning so far back that he was almost horizontal. Leila was asleep on his chest. The sound of Rebecca's laugh caused her to shuffle slightly, then she settled again. Carver lifted a hand in greeting.

'I popped my head in to check that she was all right. Maybe I got a little too close. She woke up.'

Rebecca nodded. 'No kidding. Schoolboy error. Are you okay?'

'Fine. We walked around for a while. I did the bobbing up and down thing that she likes. Turns out she likes staring out of the window at the streetlight across the road as well.'

'Does she? I'll have to try that.'

'We did that for a while. Quite a long while. She finally fell asleep as soon as *Newsnight* started.'

'It has the same effect on me. Shall I take her?'

Rebecca removed the white sleep-suited bundle from Carver's chest and took her next door. Patrick stayed. He pointed at the wine.

'You didn't want a glass.'

'I thought I'd wait. It's probably too late now. I should head off.' He hauled himself to his feet. 'How was your night?'

'Good, I think. It was what we needed. We're both really grateful.'

'Not at all. Anytime . . .' He paused. '. . . or possibly never again. I'll let you know once I've recovered from tonight.'

Patrick smiled. 'Okay. When you next see Naz, will you tell her I'm up for another revision session whenever it suits. I was a bit of an idiot the last time I saw her, I'd like to apologise.'

'I see. You could apologise to her tomorrow if you like.'

'Tomorrow? I've got some time tomorrow. You think she'd like to come over?'

'Not exactly . . .'

75

CAVERSHAM, BERKSHIRE, UK

Patrick arrived at McCluskey's in time for lunch – the homemade vegetable soup and one of McCluskey's doorstop-sized cheese-and-pickle sandwiches. He was quiet, letting conversation go on around him and saying little. McCluskey tried to bring him out of himself.

'Tell my mate John here about the sort of bugging operations you were seeing during the Arab Spring and out in Hong Kong, Patrick.'

'Okay.' He pushed his soup bowl to one side. 'It seems like an age ago.' He looked across at Carver. 'Maybe William would remember better?'

Carver shook his head. 'No, you always had a much better grasp of that stuff than me.'

'The anti-government protestors we met there were pretty savvy about it. Especially in Hong Kong. They changed phones regularly, used burners all the time. They communicated face to face whenever possible and when they did communicate by phone, it was always using end-to-end encryption.'

John Smith nodded. 'WhatsApp, Signal?'

'Yep, and Telegram and Confide and . . .' He paused. '. . . there were a couple of others – the names will come back to me. They knew that the spyware usually arrived embedded in a suspect email or text, so they'd ignore any kind of message they weren't expecting.'

'Sensible. The thing about Pegasus is the delivery mechanism is even subtler. You can infect your phone just by answering a regular audio or video call.'

'From an unknown number?'

'Sure, or from someone you do know and who's decided they want to know more about you. Everything about you in fact. Pegasus can read all messages, conversations, copy photos, passwords, access the microphone, geolocator . . . basically it can access the lot. I've seen a phone switch itself from *very definitely off* to *on* and start recording a conversation taking place within eavesdropping distance of where it had been left.'

'That's . . .' He hesitated. Patrick's mind turned briefly to something Rebecca had said recently about her phone behaving oddly. 'That's scary.'

'It scared the pants off me. To begin with anyway.' John described how he managed to copy the malware onto a burner phone and send a bug back in the other direction.

'That's impressive.'

'What did you think we used to do up on the top floor at Caversham? Sit around and twiddle our thumbs? Shall I show you what we've got?'

'Sure.'

Upstairs, the old Caversham man took the lead in explaining what Patrick was looking at. Patrick could sense Carver's growing impatience. Eventually he interrupted.

'In short, we've got shedloads of data – the names and numbers of lots of people who've been bugged but we're still not sure who is doing it. Nor exactly why.' Carver looked at Patrick. 'You told Naz that motive is important but that there are other ways that we might be able to read the data.'

'That's right.' Patrick moved closer to the wall. Stopping in front of the long list of climate-scientist and researcher names and mobile phone numbers.

'The other thing that might help you figure out who's doing the spying is to look at *when* the spyware was installed. In Hong Kong a load of students were bugged the day before there was going to be a big demo at the John Lennon wall.'

John Smith nodded. 'That could help.'

Patrick looked closely at the wall of numbers. He glanced back at his four colleagues, squeezed inside the too-small room. Was he really the only person who'd noticed it? Perhaps he was.

'Is this how the numbers appeared as you downloaded them, John?'

'Yep.'

'Obviously to us they're phone numbers . . . but here they're just a long series of large numbers . . . in numerical order. Whatever software you used to steal them decided to arrange them logically.'

John Smith was standing next to Patrick now.

'He's right.'

Carver cleared his throat. 'Interesting, but I don't understand how that helps us.'

Patrick smiled. 'If John removes the ordering and goes back to the raw data then there's a fair chance that the numbers will be grouped in bunches. Each bunch will be the numbers that one individual or group asked to be bugged at the same time.'

John Smith was rocking backwards and forward on his heels in excitement.

'Genius.'

It took John less than half an hour to retrieve the raw data, another hour to print out the numbers in this new, hopefully more helpful, order. They pinned these to the wall, then stood back and looked. There, grouped more closely together now were the scientists and researchers that Professor Walston had alerted them to, also there was Jennifer Prepas' mobile number and several dozen other American mobiles. There was a similar number of Australian contacts and then a surprisingly long list of contacts with the 34 prefix. Carver was particularly interested in these.

'Three four is—'

'Spain.' This was Naz.

'That's right. Edith Walston said that whatever it was that happened in Spain, that missing plane, it had unsettled Clive. He wouldn't or couldn't talk to her about it.'

McCluskey went over and stood next to Carver; she counted the Spanish numbers.

'That's the motherlode of mobile numbers.'

John Smith joined them.

'All tapped en masse. Most likely on the same day.'

Carver turned to look at Naz.

'When are your exams?'

'The end of next week.'

'Then we'll need to move fast. I'll book us two seats on the first available flight to Seville.'

'Really? When?'

'Tomorrow.'

76

WINNER LABORATORIES, BENDIGO, VICTORIA, AUSTRALIA

'Happy as a clam.'

Martha Tobi turned and looked at her boss.

'I beg your pardon?'

'That's what I am – as *happy as a clam* although I have no idea where that fucken' phrase comes from or what clams have got to be so happy about. Perhaps that should be the next experiment. We'll figure out what it is in a clam's DNA that makes it so bloody happy and then see if we can't gene-edit other shellfish to make them happy too. After that, people.'

'How would you identify or quantify happiness?'

Winner laughed. 'You're right, Marth. Stupid idea. Better stick with this work we're doing on oysters and scallops, focus on what we're good at.'

'Yes. Although I think we should be finished soon. The latest tank results are good.'

'Don't bury the fucken' headline, Marth. Tell me.' She told him. Her and Clive's work on making east-coast oysters and scallops more resilient to ocean temperature change appeared to be working. 'Hurray for us – *Mr and Mrs Crispr*. So, what next? I think I've still got that list you drew up . . .' Winner reached into the top pocket of his white lab coat and found a piece of paper. '. . . swine flu, more coral spores . . . I'm bored with those . . . burp-free cows, American chestnut trees. Can I choose?' Martha Tobi shrugged. 'I'm the boss, Marth, surely I can fucken' choose?'

'Some of the detoxified cane toads have retoxified themselves.'

'Okay, so we should do that.'

His colleague nodded.

'Now, or after lunch?'

'Lunch first.'

'Okay, I also need to return a call I got from fucken' Tony Yeoh. I don't know what it could have been that reminded me of him.'

Clive's diary secretary had told him to be ready to receive a call from Tony Yeoh at half-past one Melbourne time. Both the timing and the content of their conversations were dictated not by Winner but by his accountant these days. His computer made a bright and breezy pinging sound and there Tony was – the fat, ugly bastard.

'Hello there, Clive, 'pologies for keeping you waiting.'

'No worries.'

It seemed to Winner that his accountant had had his hair dyed since he'd last seen him. There was an odd hennaed tinge to it.

'You're looking well.'

'Thanks.'

'Being back in that lab suits you.'

'I suppose so.'

'From what I hear, you're thriving. Up at sparrow's fart, working till midnight, doing all sorts of interesting stuff inside that air-locked box of yours.'

'You've got spies everywhere, haven't you, Tony?'

'No need to be like that, Clive. I'm calling with exciting news.'

'What?'

'You're about to receive a VIP invite to the stratospheric aerosol-scattering conference.' Winner said nothing. 'All the big players are going to be there. A lot of your old friends. Did I mention it was a VIP invite?'

'You did. What's this? A reward for good behaviour?'

'You're being welcomed back into the fold, mate.'

'Right. And what if I don't want to go and play the prodigal son?'

'It's not the sort of invitation that you say no to.'

'I understand. Where's the meeting?'

'Riyadh.'

'Of course it is.'

77

RYANAIR 8363, STN TO SVQ

Carver hadn't flown for a while. He was planning to allow himself one whisky and ginger – partly as a stomach settler but also as a reward for making it through check-in and airport security without losing his mind.

'That'll be eighteen euros.' The air steward's badge boasted that he spoke Romanian as well as English.

'You've got to be joking. You just announced that you're selling a litre of whisky for fourteen quid.'

'That's right.'

'Okay, then I'll take one of those and you can sell me the ginger ale separately.' The steward muttered something under his breath. Carver gave him a questioning look. 'I'm sorry, I missed that. My Romanian is a little rusty.'

'I'm afraid I can't allow you to drink duty free on the plane. If we did that, then there would be great drunkenness.' Carver settled for two packets of Pringles and a truly disgusting latte. He and Naz were sat in the middle seats with Carver on the aisle and Naz next to a young Spanish couple who were heading home from holiday.

He offered Naz a Pringle. 'Just when you think flying can't get any worse – it does.'

The air steward was making another in-flight announcement. Carver scowled. 'This plane's more like an airborne souk than a short-haul flight. Fourteen pounds for a litre of spirits, three euros for a packet of cigarettes . . .' He stopped and listened to the steward who was making an announcement about the range of cosmetics they had on board. Carver shook his head. '. . . Our eyelashes are selling like hot bread. That's not a sentence I was expecting to hear when I woke up this morning.'

Naz smiled. 'What did flying used to be like? Before it was like this I mean?'

'When I first started flying, and for a while after that, it was good. Magical even.'

He tried to sleep; a jumper draped over his head. Naz chatted with the Spanish couple. When Carver woke, she appeared to have learnt Spanish and made a couple of friends for life, all in the course of a two-and-a-half-hour flight.

Seville airport was not busy and picking up the hire car was straightforward. Carver drove and Naz navigated as they made their way around and out of the city before picking up the motorway that would take them towards Cádiz and the coast. The fields they passed looked scorched, the Spanish summer just gone had set new heat records and it wasn't much cooler in mid-October. They drove with the windows down and a dry air blowing through the car. Naz took big breaths and tried to identify what it was she was smelling.

'Lavender?'

'Probably.'

'Horses.'

'No doubt.'

She'd been on holiday to Spain twice with her family, but this was different and a thousand times more exciting. The family holidays had been to the coast around Marbella. Marbs as the legions of British ex-pats referred to it. She and Carver were heading for a different coast – the coast of light. Altogether more interesting. They'd booked a guest house between La Barrosa, where the missing pilot's mother lived, and a place called Old Sancti Petri. Carver had booked the first place on the BBC-approved list of local accommodation; this basically meant cheap, safe and more-or-less clean. As they drove up the pothole-strewn road towards the sea and the address he'd been sent, Carver wondered whether he shouldn't have looked a little further down the list.

The guest house amounted to one small brick house belonging to the owner and four small outhouses that looked more like beach huts than proper accommodation. The owner gave them each a key attached to a painted seashell and issued instructions in a rapid Andalusian-accented Spanish that Carver could make neither head nor tail of. Naz had more success but only after asking the man to repeat a few things. After he'd finished, she thanked him and turned to Carver.

'We have to come to the house by nine if we want breakfast. If we'd like to eat tonight, then there's a restaurant down at the beach. He doesn't have Wi-Fi, but the restaurant does. Then there was a long list of things we can't put down the toilet and something about "arañas"?'

'Oranges?'

'I'm not sure, I can look it up.'

'I'm sure we'll figure it out. Let's dump our stuff and get down to the restaurant, I'm starving.'

There were only a handful of other people in the restaurant and Carver and Naz had their pick of tables. They chose to sit at the edge of the deck, facing the sea and with a clear view of what was going to be an impressive sunset. The waiter came and put a new paper tablecloth down on the plastic picnic table, together with a basket of bread and cutlery. He ignored Naz's attempts to practise her Spanish a little more, speaking to them in fluent English. The kitchen would close soon so they should order quickly, they only had a few things left – grilled tuna, locally caught, another fish similar to red snapper, prawns in garlic and a meat stew that was a local speciality. He scribbled their order on the paper tablecloth, got the beers they'd ordered and then disappeared into the kitchen; it seemed as though it was just him and one chef running the place. The beach looked quiet too. Carver took a long sip of cold beer and sat back in the picnic chair.

'It all feels a bit end of the season, doesn't it?'

Naz nodded. 'Yeah, I love it. Whenever I've been in Spain it's been too hot and heaving with tourists.' She looked down the beach. There was a group of Spanish kids – one of them on crutches – playing football. There were a few families sitting on the sand on towels or on folding chairs, waiting for the sunset. A beach-seller walked by, carrying armfuls of tie-dyed wraps and towels, and wearing maybe a dozen hats; he made eye contact with Naz who smiled. He started to move in their direction then changed his mind when he saw the waiter returning from the kitchen.

They'd ordered most of what the limited menu had to offer. It was delicious – the fish as fresh as the waiter had promised, the prawns in garlic so good that Carver polished the brown terracotta bowl to a shine with chunks of white bread in his attempt to get the last of the sauce. In between mouthfuls of food, they spoke about what they needed to do the following day.

After a good deal of work on Naz's part, Francesca Galinda had agreed to see them. Naz had found a landline for the pilot's family through Spanish directory enquiries and after doing half an hour of prep, transcribing certain sentences and potential responses using an online translation site, she'd called her. Naz had explained who she and Carver were and said something about the radio programme they worked for. She'd mentioned the World Service and that had helped. Mrs Galinda had been suspicious at first, but Naz stuck at it.

'I've got the address and she's expecting us at eleven. It's a fifteen-minute drive.'

'Good, well done. I'd like to tell you that I'd had as much success with Alma's former employers . . . but I haven't.'

Winner's cloud-brightening project had operated out of an office on military-owned land and military-level security seemed to surround the project. It had been difficult getting hold of a phone number for the office and when Carver eventually found one and phoned it, he was connected to someone who spoke good English but refused to give her name. He'd asked to speak to the project leader, Señor Romero, and was told that was impossible. Could he leave a message? If he wanted but it was extremely unlikely that Romero would respond. He left a message anyway and his secretary, or whoever this was, took the details before repeating that Señor Romero wasn't talking to anyone, especially journalists.

'I asked her for Romero's mobile number so I could text through a proper explanation of our request.'

Naz smiled. 'I'm guessing she didn't fall for that?'

'Unfortunately, no.'

'Worth a go. I'd bet a million euros that Señor Romero's number is on that list of ours somewhere.' Carver nodded. McCluskey had made them a copy of all the hacked phone numbers that might have any connection to Clive Winner.

'Maybe after we've seen Mrs Galinda we drive up to the military base and see if we have any more luck face to face.' He finished his beer. 'What's face to face in Spanish?'

'Er . . . cara a cara?'

The waiter brought the bill and Carver paid it and left a good-sized tip. In return they got a couple of frozen shot glasses containing the most delicious lemony-flavoured liqueur Naz had ever drunk. Carver had a message from Naomi asking him to call her back as soon as possible. He'd do that once he was back in his room. They waited so that Naz could see the sun set. She asked Carver to take a photo of her with the setting sun behind her so she could send it to her parents. He took several. He briefly considered asking Naz to take one of him too, before dismissing the thought as ridiculous. Who would he send it to?

Back at the guest house, there was a gangly teenage kid standing outside Carver's room holding a Tupperware box.

'*Hola. Arañas?*'

Carver frowned.

'Oranges?'

'Not oranges. Spiders.'

'What are you talking about?'

'I will make the spiders go away for a euro.' The kid explained that spiders were a particular problem at this time of year. Most of the bedrooms had them and it was his job to dispose of them. Carver could do it himself if he wanted but it was difficult. And they were big.

Carver nodded. 'Okay. Go for it.'

The boy was in and out of the room in ten minutes.

'Five euros.'

'You said one euro.'

The boy carefully peeled back the top of his Tupperware box for Carver to look inside. 'Five spiders. Five euros.'

It was hard to fault the logic. Carver paid him.

'Where are you going to put those?'

The kid smiled. 'I will give them freedom.'

'Yeah, in some other poor bastard's bedroom. Just make sure they don't find their way back into mine.'

The boy shook his head. 'They will not. You have paid.' He gave a thumbs-up sign. 'We're all good.'

78

NEW BROADCASTING HOUSE, PORTLAND PLACE, LONDON

Naomi was trying not to lose her temper.

'You've been watching us work for how long – a couple of weeks?'

'We've studied the programme intensively for over one hundred and forty hours.'

Naomi quickly did the maths.

'For less than a week then, and you're telling me you think I could lose two posts.'

'Possibly more. We haven't quite been able to complete all of the time-and-motion studies yet.' The management consultant in front of her frowned and looked serious. Naomi had the strong suspicion that this particular look had been practised in front of a mirror.

'I thought all those . . . studies were in.' Somehow she had resisted the urge to include the word 'ridiculous'.

'There's one reporter we haven't seen.'

'Right.'

'I mean we haven't seen him at all. He's not listed as being on leave, but he's not been into the office either.'

'No, the reporter you're talking about is more . . . free range.'

'We could go to him in the field.' The young fellow smiled,

clearly pleased with himself for remembering the proper terminology.

'I don't think that would be much fun for anyone involved.'

'The consultancy process isn't meant to be "fun", Ms Holder.'

'Okay, well at least it's delivering in that respect.' She felt her phone vibrate in her pocket. 'I should take this.' Whoever it was, it had to be better than talking to *Captain Bumfluff*, as Naomi's team had dubbed him.

'Hello?'

'Hi, it's Carver.' Or maybe not.

'Hello, William, were your ears burning? . . . I'm busy, but talk to me anyway, what's going on?' She smiled apologetically at the man sitting opposite her. 'Yes, I remember. That's an important story, I'm glad to hear you're making good progress. Impactful journalism, that's what we're all about. So where are you? . . . You're where? You better not have taken . . .' She stood up, her face red with fury. 'I didn't authorise that. I don't care if you think it's a fait accompli – you can just fucking un-fait it . . . Where exactly in Spain are you Carver? Carver?'

Naomi attempted to call him back, but the phone was switched off. She sat back down. 'Any chance that we can pretend that didn't happen.'

The fresh-faced consultant made his serious face.

'I thought not.' She smiled. 'Well, on the plus side I've just thought of one person I might be willing to sack.'

79

HIGHBURY FIELDS, LONDON

Rebecca and Patrick had gone around and around with this. Rebecca could stand up at the next Planet Action meeting and accuse Jeff of infiltrating the group – based on a vague feeling she had and no evidence. She could just walk away from the group, forget about it. Remove herself from the list of Planet Action people going to the Paris Climate Conference as well. The trip she herself had organised, and that she had been genuinely excited about.

'There must be another option?' She was sitting down at one end of their sofa, Patrick was lying with his feet hanging off the other end, his head in her lap.

'You could go to the police.'

'Very funny.'

She took the can of beer out of Patrick's hand and took a gulp.

'I've read some stuff about other groups – anti-foxhunt campaigners and other green groups that were spied on, infiltrated in some way. There are some dreadful stories – women getting married to these guys, having families.'

Patrick nodded. 'What happened when they were found out?'

'Yeah. That was the interesting bit. Most of the time, as soon as their cover was blown, or it looked like it was about to be, they just disappeared. Obviously, that's despicable, horrendous, especially for the women and families, but it did get me thinking.'

'Of a subtle way to let Jeffus know that someone was on to him. See if he scarpers?'

'Yep.' She handed the tin of beer back to him.

Patrick was quiet for a while.

'There is something I could do. It wouldn't be completely journalistically ethical, but it might work.'

'How unethical?'

Patrick explained. They could send an email to the Metropolitan Police's press office, a vaguely worded enquiry saying that the BBC were looking at allegations that a climate campaign group in London had been infiltrated by police.

'I could get a mate of mine in local radio to send it so there wouldn't be any obvious connection with you.'

'It sounds pretty unethical to me.'

'Not really. If you're right about Jeff then it's a story, an email like that is a legitimate journalistic enquiry. We're just going about things in a slightly unconventional way.'

'That's what you'd say if it ended up in front of you at BBC complaints, would you?'

'No, if that happened then I'd probably have to recommend that I be sacked. Hopefully it won't come to that. And on the plus side, if that happens at least Naz won't have to kill me to get my job.'

Rebecca grinned. 'Okay. And this isn't . . . dangerous at all, is it?'

'I don't see why it would be. We keep it vague, we don't name him. If he is a policeman, then he'll probably just disappear like you said has happened before. If he isn't, then no harm done.'

80

LA BARROSA, ANDALUSIA, SPAIN

Carver woke at seven, unsure at first what it was that had woken him. Another peal of clanging church bells cleared that question up.

'What a bloody din.'

The owner of the guest house served them breakfast on the patio outside his house. Strong coffee and *pan con tomate* – chunks of toasted white bread served with olive oil and a homemade paste of tomatoes, garlic and salt. Naz waited until Carver had eaten several helpings and drunk two cups of coffee before risking conversation.

'Nice waking up to the sound of church bells.'

'Are you kidding? It sounded like someone hitting a safe door with a shovel.'

They finished their breakfast and thanked the man. With time to spare, Carver told Naz that he was going to walk to the beach and see if the water looked swimmable. It was clear from the way he put this that he would prefer it to be a solo outing. Naz said she'd take a walk in the direction of the nearby port and check that out. They agreed to meet back at the guest house in an hour and drive to Mrs Galinda's house from there.

Naz headed in the direction of Old Sancti Petri but quickly

became bored with walking up the side of a dusty road. She turned back and headed for the beach; it was long enough for her to walk there without feeling that she was cramping Carver's style. The restaurant where they'd eaten the previous evening was deserted; a little further on an old man was strolling up and down in between the fixed sun umbrellas collecting cigarette butts using a green nylon fishing net on a long bamboo pole. Out in the sea – far from the shore – Naz saw a lone swimmer. He had goggles on and was doing a slow but rather graceful front crawl. She looked again; surely not?

She walked for another twenty minutes up the beach before turning round and heading back. As she reached the restaurant she took another look out to sea. There was Carver, wearing goggles and a pair of canary-yellow swimming shorts wading out of the water. The shingle was clearly causing him some discomfort. He saw her and nodded a hello but stopped some twenty feet from where she was.

'My stuff is behind you.'

Naz turned and saw an untidy pile of clothes and what looked like one of the guest-house bath mats on the restaurant deck.

'Do you want me to fetch those for you?'

'No. But maybe . . .' It was a toss-up which of them was more embarrassed.

'I'll just go back up and wait for you at the guest house.'

'Good idea.'

They drove to Mrs Galinda's house – or as close as they could get; the road narrowed to little more than a car's width fifty yards from where the sat nav wanted them to be and so they walked the last part. Standing in front of the little white bungalow was a skinny old fellow sweeping the courtyard with a bunched-up bundle of sticks for a broom. There were bright-red geraniums growing out of pots on the walls and most of the available patio. The place looked like a postcard and Naz was tempted to take a photo to send to her mum. She resisted the temptation. Maybe when they left.

Mrs Galinda had made coffee for her guests; she sat them on her good sofa and asked that they wait. Alma's friend Loli was coming to translate. They waited; the only noise was the soft click of the ceiling fan as it turned slowly, cooling the room. Everywhere you looked in the living room, Alma Galinda was gazing back at you. Family photos, school portraits, an interesting oil painting. Most notably was the photograph of her sitting in the cockpit of a little yellow-and-white plane – beaming with pleasure. Francesca arrived back with a plate of pink wafery-looking biscuits. She saw Carver staring at the picture.

'*Ese es el huevo frito volador.*'

He smiled and nodded before turning to Naz for an explanation.

'I'm not sure . . . something about an egg. We might have to wait for Alma's mate to arrive to get to the bottom of that one.'

Loli arrived full of apologies for being late. Naz and Carver heard her out in the hall, loudly kissing and being kissed by their host. In the living room Loli sized them up.

'You are the journalists?' They nodded. 'The BBC journalists?' More nodding. 'I thought you would be dressed differently.'

Naz gave an apologetic smile.

'No. Sorry.'

'It is not important. What is important is that you are here. I googled both of your names.' She looked at Carver. 'You are a little bit famous.'

Carver shifted in his seat.

'I suppose; not really.'

'So, what is it you want me to translate? What do you want to ask Mrs Galinda?'

Before Carver could frame a response there was a knocking on the front door. Francesca went to answer it. More introductions were made. The young man's name was Carlos Quintana. Naz recognised it from one of the articles she'd read in the Spanish local press. She leant over and whispered to Carver.

'This is Alma's boyfriend.'

Carlos took a chair in the corner and Francesca asked Carver to continue. He had the impression that the boy's presence here was a conciliatory gesture on Mrs Galinda's part. An olive branch of some sort.

'My colleague and I work for a news programme in the UK, we are investigating Clive Winner. We know that your daughter was working for him when she . . .' He hesitated. '. . . disappeared. We think Winner and his company might know more about the missing plane than they've said so far.'

Loli translated this for Mrs Galinda but it was Carlos who responded first and quite vehemently.

'*Veras?* Winner *es el diablo*.'

Naz whispered a translation to Carver.

'Yeah, I got that one.' He glanced at Carlos before concentrating his attention again on Francesca.

'I wouldn't say that Clive Winner is the devil, we don't know exactly what he is yet. That's what we're trying to find out. But I do think he and his people know more about your daughter's accident than they have said so far and I think we might be able to find out what that is. With your help.' He waited for Loli to translate this and for Francesca to respond.

'What kind of help?'

'We'd like to talk about what happened that day, about Alma's work more generally. Really anything that you think we might find useful.'

Before this could be communicated to Alma's mother, Carlos spoke again. Naz didn't catch all of it, but she got enough.

'He said "*Dale el teléfono*." I think he's suggesting that they should let us see a mobile phone.'

'Whose phone? Alma's?'

'I guess so.'

'The boy is growing on me.'

*

Loli explained how Carlos and Alma's Uncle Pepe had found the phone washed up on a beach near the Portuguese border. She told them that they – Carlos himself, Loli and more recently Alma's mother – had studied the phone thoroughly but found no clues as to what could have happened to Alma. Francesca had the phone now, or rather a new phone with the contents of her daughter's old mobile downloaded onto it. Loli explained that the original phone had been stolen – pickpocketed while Carlos was looking after it. Carver's ears pricked up at this.

'The fact that someone went to the trouble of stealing it suggests that there's something on there that they didn't want you to see. Or at least they thought there was.' He paused. 'Do you think we could take a look at the phone? Just briefly.'

After a short consultation Alma's mother went and got the mobile phone in question and handed it over. She turned to Loli and said something which the woman translated for Carver.

'She asks that you be very careful not to delete or change anything.'

'Of course.'

Carver shuffled closer to Naz and they scrolled through Alma's most recent emails, texts and WhatsApp messages. Nothing caught their eye but then it was unlikely that anything would. Naz looked over at Loli.

'All of these most recent messages, they're all just normal, yes? Nothing out of the ordinary?'

'No.'

Naz glanced at Carlos.

'They are all boring.' He clearly understood English even if he was reluctant to speak it. 'I read them a hundred times. The photos I looked at a thousand times.'

Carver could sense that Mrs Galinda was becoming impatient. Unhappy about having these two strangers handling the only thing she had left of her daughter.

'I will give this back in a moment, but can I take a quick look at the photographs Carlos mentioned?'

Her mother reluctantly agreed. Carver moved away from Naz so that they might appear less conspiratorial and clicked on the gallery.

'These last few shots. The sky and clouds and such. Have you any idea what those are?'

Loli answered.

'Just nothing. We think maybe she took them lying on the beach. Or even by accident.'

Carver shrugged. He turned to Naz.

'Do you know how to do that thing? The time code thing where you can find out when a picture was taken? Patrick showed me once.'

Naz took the phone. 'Like this . . .' Her fingers danced around the phone for a few moments. She handed the device back for Carver to see.

'So these last few pictures were all taken on or around seven p.m. on the 9th of September.'

Loli shook her head.

'That's not possible.'

'Why?'

'That is the evening Alma disappeared. She was already up in the plane at that time.'

'Then she was taking photos while she was flying. And not by accident. The question is what was she trying to photograph?'

He passed the phone back to Francesca who studied the images in question.

'*No hay nada, solo cielo.*'

Carver nodded.

'Just the sky and some clouds. But she was trying to take a picture of something. I'm sure of it.' He smiled apologetically. 'Could I have one more look?'

The phone was handed back. Carver held the device close to his face and squinted.

'Maybe if the image was brighter . . .' He brightened the screen.

Squinted again. Then shook his head. 'No . . . I thought I saw something. But maybe not. You look.'

The phone was passed back to Francesca, then Loli, finally to Carlos. While this was happening, Naz noticed Carver quietly taking his notebook from his plastic bag and scribbling something down.

They spent another half an hour asking Francesca questions about her daughter, what sort of woman she was, how long she'd worked as a pilot on the cloud-brightening project, whether she liked the work. Were there any problems with the project, was there any conflict between Alma and the team or even with Winner himself? Both Carver and Naz sensed some discomfort at this question. Naz noticed Francesca's eyes flick in Carlos' direction, but she said no more.

Back in the car it became clear that Carver had made the most of the extra minute or so that he'd been allowed to study Alma's phone. He had glanced briefly again at the photos before moving quickly to her contact numbers.

'Clive Winner was in there?'

'Not by name. But there was a number for someone called Loco Australiano. My Spanish isn't great, but it strikes me that that's as good a nickname for Winner as any. So we've got a mobile number for him plus Alma's own number.'

'We're about to make McCluskey's mate John a very happy man.'

'It's what I live for.'

81

THE FOUR SEASONS, RIYADH, SAUDI ARABIA

Clive Winner disliked Riyadh. He could appreciate that it was an accomplishment – building a major city in one of the most inhospitable corners of the world – but once you'd given the Saudis some credit for that you were still left with the question: why? Why not choose somewhere else? Somewhere less dusty. Somewhere where the mercury doesn't hit fifty quite so frequently. It was insane. The Saudis had all the money in the world, why didn't they relocate? Buy Sweden or something like that. He looked around the enormous conference room looking for someone to suggest this to but there was no one he wanted to talk with. He was only there because he had to be there. He had delivered one talk about his cloud-brightening work to a roomful of eager ears but mainly he was there to be seen. Tony Yeoh had put it succinctly: 'You don't go to the party – you don't get the goody bag.'

The fourteenth Conference on Stratospheric Aerosol Scattering was a lousy party, but the goody bag would, Tony promised him, make it all worthwhile. He'd had several offers of funding already

– significant offers of six- and seven-figure numbers. His company was back in the black and Clive Winner was back in favour, all he had to do was keep playing by the rules.

82

LA BARROSA, ANDALUSIA, SPAIN

'It looks like Araña-Boy is planning to rip us off for another five euros. I hope he's planted the spiders in your room this time.'

But the boy didn't have his Tupperware with him. He was waiting to deliver a message instead.

'You know Pepe?'

Naz shook her head. 'No, sorry.'

'He is part of the family.'

'Part of which family?'

'Galinda. He's waiting for you at the restaurant. At the sea.'

Naz counted the number of empty Cruzcampo bottles on the old man's table. Seven. How long had he been waiting? Pepe greeted them with a raised bottle and a gap-toothed smile. He had a white polystyrene picnic box next to his chair, the top was half off and there was something moving inside. The ugliest-looking fish Naz had ever seen. He waved at the seats opposite him, inviting them to sit. His battered-looking fishing rod was leaning against one and Naz moved it, leaning it carefully against a nearby wooden pillar.

'*Cerveza?*'

'Thank you.'

Pepe shouted something in the direction of the bar. Naz wasn't sure what he'd said or that the waiter had actually heard but before long he returned carrying two silver buckets filled with crushed ice and bottled beer. The old man drank, and in between long gulps of beer spoke in quickfire Spanish. Carver tried to match him in the drinking stakes while nodding along and understanding almost nothing. Naz slowly managed to tune her ear to Pepe's heavy Andalusian accent and rapid delivery and before long was getting at least a few words in each sentence.

'I think he's mainly talking about fish. And tides. There was something about Lawrence of Arabia.'

'Yes, I thought I heard him say that.'

'I have no idea why.'

'No, nor me. Could you ask him to say why he wanted to see us? And to say it slowly?'

The next time Pepe stopped to open another bottle of beer, Naz tried this.

The old man nodded. '*Sí, sí. Muy importante.*'

He took a pipe from his pocket and a box of matches from the other and lit the tobacco-stuffed bowl with a slightly shaky hand. This done he began to talk. It took a while before Naz felt confident enough of what the old man was saying to try communicating it to Carver.

'He says he spoke to Mrs Galinda after we left. He thinks that you are right, that the photos on Alma's phone are significant. She was trying to photograph something.'

'Okay.'

'He says there were other people taking photographs that day, lots of them. And with expensive cameras. He thinks maybe they were able to photograph what Alma could not?'

'What sort of people?'

'Yeah . . . that's where it gets tricky. I think he's saying *bird people*.'

'Sweet Jesus.'

After a couple more beers, and with the help of the waiter, Pepe managed to make himself understood. The week that Alma disappeared was a big week in the birdwatching calendar. The spoonbills were migrating, quite a sight apparently, and twitchers from all over Spain and across Europe had come to see them. At least a dozen birdwatchers had been camped out at Torre del Puerco with high-powered binoculars and long-lensed cameras on the day that Alma went missing.

'It's not the most promising lead I've ever had. But it's the only one we've got.' He looked at Naz. 'What do you think?'

'I think I can do something with that.'

Naz thanked Pepe on their behalf. She tried thanking him for the beers too until it became clear that they were paying for those. Before he left, he put the two or three that were still undrunk into the cooler along with the fish. He shook hands with Carver, bowed to Naz and set off down the beach – cooler in one hand and fishing rod in the other. They waited until he was a small figure in the distance before they spoke again. Carver first.

'So, if you're going to see whether the birdwatchers managed to see something that Alma missed, the question is, what am I going to do?'

'We've still got to drive up to the military base and see if Señor Romero wants to talk to us.'

'Yes. There's another long shot. Pound to a penny Winner or his people have told them to talk to no one.'

'I guess so.'

'We'll go anyway, but I've been thinking . . .'

'What?'

'We'll send McCluskey's mate Clive Winner's mobile number. And Alma's. So he can go ahead and do whatever he can with those but in the meantime . . .' Carver met Naz's eye. 'We've got Clive Winner's number. It seems to me that the sensible thing is to ring it. What have we got to lose?'

83

THE FOUR SEASONS, RIYADH, SAUDI ARABIA

A handwritten note, slipped under his hotel-room door. Clive thought it might be his room bill at first, before he remembered that someone else was picking up the tab both for the room and for anything else he could possibly want for the duration of his stay in Riyadh. Food, drink, entertainment. He opened the note and read. It was an invitation to meet an unnamed individual at the National Museum at three p.m. that afternoon. It was written in careful capitals on hotel notepaper. Clive knew what the clever thing to do was – tear it up and bin it, or, even safer, flush it down the lavatory. That's what he did and once he'd finished and every scrap of paper was gone from the toilet bowl he looked at his conference timetable.

Winner caught a cab on the street – not from outside the hotel – he asked the taxi to drop him at the Murabba Palace and told the driver that he was visiting the fort, not the museum. It was hardly a fail-safe security measure, but it was something. He'd visited the National Museum a couple of times before – as far as he knew it was one of only two or three things that tourists could do in Riyadh. A sign inside the door said that admission was free for conference delegates upon presentation of a pass. He paid in cash. The note hadn't said where to meet, just when, and as the place was large he decided to wander. He'd seen the re-enactment of the Prophet Mohammed's battle of Medina before but it was interesting. The same went for the history of the Sauds. He was standing staring at a *kiswah* cloth that had once covered the Kaaba in Mecca when someone came and stood next to him.

'I didn't think you'd come. In fact, I probably would have bet quite a lot of money on you not coming.'

'I'm a scientist, I'm naturally inquisitive.'

'Inquisitive but not clever.'

'I guess so. What's your excuse?'

'I'm loyal.'

'Who to? If you don't mind me asking.'

'The prime minister.'

'It's Jeremy, isn't it?'

'Yes, good memory.'

'Can we do this quickly, Jeremy? I'd like to give myself the best possible chance of not being *suicided* the moment I get back to my hotel room.' Jeremy Cunis gave Clive a copy of the speech that the prime minister was planning to give in Paris.

'He doesn't like it. He's hoping that you might be able to help him write a speech that he does like.'

'Okay. How? I'm assuming the brains trust, face-to-face idea is out of the question.'

'Absolutely. There's a non-official, private email address written at the bottom of the speech.'

'How private?'

'As private as we can make it.'

'Fair enough. Is that it?'

'That's it.'

'You're doing this because you're loyal. Remind me why I'm doing this.'

Jeremy Cunis shrugged. 'I'm not sure. I'd like to think that it had something to do with what they did to Jennifer.'

Winner nodded.

'I suppose that's right. For Jenny. And others.'

84

LA BARROSA, ANDALUSIA, SPAIN

Naz and Carver had adopted something of a routine. They ate breakfast together, Naz walked while Carver swam, they did their own work in the morning and then met again at the restaurant on the beach for lunch. Quite often they were the only customers. Naz usually had the grilled tuna, Carver invariably ordered the *gambas al ajillo*.

'How're you getting on?'

'If I ever meet a real live spoonbill face to face, there's a chance I might want to throttle it.'

'Aren't they endangered?'

'You could've fooled me. I've got close-up photographs of about a thousand of the little so-and-sos on my laptop.'

'Maybe it's lots of pictures of the same spoonbill. Or the same flock anyway.'

'It's not. Do you want to know how much of a saddo I've become? I can tell spoonbills apart now.'

Carver smiled. 'You're a fully fledged member of the birdwatching community.'

'They are nice. It is amazing how helpful they've all been.'

'Yeah, well most of them probably don't get a lot of emails from real live women.'

'I think that's unfair.' Naz opened her laptop. 'Do you want to look at some of these? I've just had another batch from a bloke in Hamburg.'

'Absolutely not. Let me know if you get sent a picture that explains why a plane could disappear into thin air, other than that – feel free to keep me fully uninformed.'

Carver's phone pinged inside his pocket and he got it out and looked. 'It's one of those idiot voice things people send you, what's wrong with either actually calling someone or just a regular message? How do you listen to these?' He passed his phone to Naz. She put it down on the table, turned on the speaker and pressed play. There was a clicking sound and then . . .

'William Carver, this is Clive Winner. You called me . . .'

85

CANONBURY SECONDARY SCHOOL, HIGHBURY, LONDON

The Planet Action meeting was at six. Rebecca was outside the school gates at five to, arriving at the same time as a couple of other members of the Paris delegation. As they walked across the rain-drenched playground, they exchanged some small talk about the weather, about their excitement ahead of Paris, what a great job she was doing organising everything. Rebecca answered their questions, tried to engage in the conversation but she felt nervous. The letter that Patrick had drafted had been sent to the Metropolitan Police press office and acknowledged. He'd said it was unlikely that anything would happen quickly, but who knew? It was chilly inside the high-ceilinged main hall and Rebecca kept her coat on. She wheeled the whiteboard squeakily across the wooden floor, took a marker pen and wrote: 'Congress of the Parties, Twenty-One'.

'We'll wait for Jeff and then get going.' She wondered whether anyone could hear anything resembling a tone in her voice.

They waited. And waited. No Jeff. Someone phoned him but got no answer. Eventually the group agreed that they should go ahead without him. In his absence, Rebecca took charge. The delegation members made notes and questions were asked. The meeting ran on past the original seven p.m. finish, past seven-thirty. She eventually wrapped things up just before eight when it seemed like all questions had been asked and answered. She thanked everyone for coming. A small group stayed on to put the chairs away and tidy the hall; as they did this, they speculated about what might have happened to Jeff. How unlike him it was not to be there. How they hoped it wasn't anything serious. Someone had to find the caretaker and tell him they were done and that he could lock up. Rebecca lived nearest, she said that she'd do it. The rest of them should get on home. She went to find the caretaker.

86

MAESTRO DE LA MER, CONIL, ANDALUSIA, SPAIN.

It was a lot of security for a restaurant. Albeit a very posh one. It turned out that the three bodyguards outside were for Carver's benefit only. They recognised him from twenty feet away. Carver watched them converse; deciding something. The shortest and stockiest of the men spoke in Spanish-accented English.

'Evening, Mr Carver, your host is inside but we'd like to do a quick pat-down first? It is routine.'

The pat-down was the least-routine, probably the most thorough search Carver could remember having. After they'd frisked him they examined his wallet – card by card, squinted at his collection of small change, asked him to remove his watch. This done there was another conversation.

'Can we see your phone, Mr Carver?'

'I don't have one.'

'No phone?'

'Not with me, no.'

The man shrugged, then they patted Carver down again to make sure. Eventually he was given the all-clear and allowed to walk through the door into the restaurant. It was a small place, just eight tables in total, most of them occupied by couples dressed up for a special occasion – honeymooners and older couples celebrating a big anniversary Carver guessed. Clive Winner was sitting at a corner table talking to a man in chef's whites. There was a half-full bottle of white Rioja on the table but only Winner was drinking. Carver walked across.

'William Carver, I presume? Thank God you're here, my stomach thought my throat had been cut.'

'Your message said seven.'

'Yes, but I'm hungry. Can I introduce you to Felipe? Mr Maestro del Mer himself.'

Carver shook the man's hand; he had a good grip. He talked his guests through the menu, hoped they'd enjoy themselves and thanked Winner for those very interesting ideas, he'd keep an eye out for an email. As soon as the *maestro* was gone, Winner grinned and leaned in towards Carver.

'He's a bit of a dick but the stuff he does with food is insane. I was pitching him an idea.'

Winner obviously wanted Carver to ask, so he did.

'Food-related?'

'Course . . . the one thing we humans are really good at is consuming things. I wanted to see if he'd help us persuade people to tuck in to stuff we've got too much of and need to control.'

'For instance?'

'It's a long list – Asian carp, locusts, rats, seagulls – not the nice little ones. Those big fuckers that want to steal your ice cream and shit on your car. We could eat a few of them.'

'Doesn't sound very appetising.'

'Cook it properly, give it a French name or cover it in chocolate and people will eat it. Felipe could make it work, he's a fucken' alchemist.'

Carver looked at the man sitting opposite him. Clive Winner was handsome. Square-jawed, blond hair expensively cut, a healthy, suntanned complexion and easy smile. If someone told you you were looking at some up-and-coming Aussie politician or even a former surfing champ then you wouldn't question it. But he wasn't those. What was he? Carver remembered the various descriptions he'd heard applied – a snake-oil salesman, a bad egg, a genius. All of those might conceivably apply to this man. But a murderer? Or an accessory to murder? Carver wasn't sure.

'Felipe wanted us to try the taster menu. I hope that's okay.' The question expected no reply. 'Here comes round one . . .' The waiters moved around their table quickly, placing his and Winner's first course down simultaneously. Dressed entirely in black, they looked to Carver more like some kind of modern dance troupe than a group of waiters serving food. It was an extremely small meringue with a dribble of something sticky on it. Half a mouthful at most. Winner wolfed it down too.

'Sea honey.'

'Eh?' Carver was wondering whether all the courses were going to be this small.

'It's a salty honey. The bees make it from the pollen of this plant that grows right by the seashore. There's salt in the flower and so you taste it in the honey. Clever, huh? He does all sorts of smart stuff with plankton too.'

'Plankton?'

'Yeah.'

'Do they get a lot of humpbacks eating here then?'

'That's quite funny. I wasn't expecting you to be funny.' Winner smiled. 'So . . . I guess you have questions. Most journalists have questions.'

'I do have questions.'

'Okay then. Why don't we say one question per course. That gives you twelve. Now I bet you're glad we're having the taster menu?' Carver nodded; he was trying to work out how to talk to this man. It seemed that Winner's mood could change within the space of a single sentence. 'Most journalists I've met have been wood from the neck up. That's why I don't do interviews. It'd be great if you could try and make the questions interesting.'

'I'll do my best.' He eyed his glass of wine but ignored it and had a sip of water instead. 'This seems like a pretty laid-back part of the world. Why d'you need so much security?'

'Eh?'

'All the bodyguards.'

'Oh them. Just because they're here with me, doesn't mean they're mine. You need to be more scientific. Appearances can be deceptive, and things can change. Today they're bodyguards . . . tomorrow they're eyewitnesses. Or worse.'

'I'm not sure I understand.'

'Then try harder. Did they search you?'

'Thoroughly.'

'Well, they searched me too. Did they take your phone?'

'I didn't bring one.'

Winner nodded. 'Smart move. They've got mine.'

'Really?'

'I didn't put up much of a fight over that one. I wanted us to be able to talk honestly and openly to each other. If that's what we decide to do.'

Carver met Clive Winner's eye. 'I'd like to . . . talk honestly I mean.'

'Let's try that then. Let's hear your open, honest second question.'

'Edith Walston showed me a collection of articles, the same articles she wanted you to look at.'

'That's not a question. That's a statement.'

'The question's coming . . .'

Mentioning Edith Walston's name had had a quietening effect on Winner. It had been the right thing to do, but Carver was unsure what he was going to say next. The waiters had delivered another bite-sized course. Carver ate it. 'The professor didn't want to talk to me at first . . .'

'Is that right?'

'She was reluctant. But she decided to do it anyway. She wants to work out why so many people in your world . . . people working for you . . . have been having accidents or experiencing various misfortunes recently.'

'Still no question.'

'Why are they?' Carver looked across the table at Winner. He was smiling. 'Christopher Baylor . . . Carla Jensen . . . Alma Galinda . . . Jennifer Prepas . . .'

Winner's smile disappeared.

'When did you meet with Edith?'

'A week or so ago . . . at Tate Britain. There was a painting she wanted to see. By Velázquez.'

Winner nodded. 'I know the picture. Edith has wanted to see it for years. I was gonna suggest we go together but then . . . I couldn't.' Winner paused. 'I don't suppose she mentioned a book. A collection of Constable pictures?'

'She did. I think she liked it.'

'That's good. It's a beautiful book . . . not that you'll know it once Edith's stuck it on the shelf in that mad fucken' study of hers. You've seen that too?'

Carver nodded. 'Edith's a good woman.'

Another course arrived. A flavoured foam. Carver stopped one of the dancers and asked for some bread.

Winner glanced around the restaurant. 'You mention Alma. I brought her here. I liked her. I think she liked me. A little bit anyway.'

'Okay.'

'You think that I had something to do with the plane going missing? That I killed her?'

'I don't know.'

'What about those other names you mentioned. Jennifer, Chris Baylor . . . what evidence do you have that connects their deaths with me?'

'As yet, nothing. But we're—'

'Really? Nothing.' He paused. 'It sounds like some people on my side might've overestimated you.' A thought entered Carver's mind and stuck, like a dart. Looking across the table at his dinner companion he saw that he was smiling. Clive Winner hadn't come here to tell him something, he was here to find out what Carver knew. Winner watched this knowledge sink in.

'Good to see that you're catching up . . . albeit slowly. So, now that we've established what you know – which is the sum total of fuck all – what do you suggest we do for the remaining nine courses?'

'We could continue talking honestly to each other.'

Winner paused. 'Perhaps.' He helped himself to the bread Carver had ordered. 'Did you really think I'd be here unless they had wanted me to be?'

'Who are they?'

'Ah, there's the trillion-dollar question. The *seven-and-a-half-trillion*-dollar question. Maybe Edith mentioned that to you too?'

'She did.'

'Well, then you know.'

87

CANONBURY SECONDARY SCHOOL, HIGHBURY, LONDON

The school caretaker was nowhere to be found. Rebecca had checked every classroom, staff room and the man's office. She had no phone number. Perhaps he was hanging around outside, although in this weather it was more likely he'd popped around the corner to the Compton Arms. Maybe he'd done that and lost track of the time. She'd check the playground first.

Outside the school reception building she pulled her coat tight around her. It was starting to rain again, that cold piercing rain that stings your cheeks. She walked around the building once but there was no sign. The pub it was. She strode past the waterlogged long-jump pit and across the running track – a shortcut of sorts. She was at the tall iron gates and pushing at them to open them before she realised. They were shut. Padlocked.

'What the . . .?'

Rebecca gave the padlock a useless shake before turning and looking around at the school grounds. How had the others found their way out? There had to be another exit somewhere. Unless the main gate was locked after they'd left? She went back the way she'd come and walked round the huge red-brick building again looking for the other exit. She was sure there was one. Eventually she gave up and walked back to the reception. All the lights were off now. This made no sense. She looked around, then back towards the dark windowed reception. She put her bags down, leaned forward and put her head against the cold glass. She peered through the window into the empty foyer. There was no one. Standing upright she saw him. Standing directly behind her, his face reflected in the dark glass. She swung around.

'What the fuck? You scared the hell out of me.'

'Really? I thought you were un-scareable. Super brave.'

Jeff was grinning.

'What do you want?'

'Just a chat. A chance to straighten some things out. Why don't we go back inside?'

'It's locked. And I'm late. I need to get home.'

'I've got the key. It won't take long, promise. Let's get in out of this weather.' He moved past her, brushing against her shoulder. He opened the door and walked in, switching on the lights while holding the door open.

'I need to get home, Jeff. Patrick and—'

'Becs!' And there he was, walking from the rear of the school, walking briskly and pushing the buggy and shouting, 'Hey there, Becs!'

As he approached, he looked past his girlfriend and towards Jeff. 'Hello there, Jeff, horrible night, huh?'

He stopped and smiled at Rebecca. 'Leila fancied a late-night walk. We figured we'd come and pick you up. The front gate's locked but there's one around the back. Are you good to go?'

88

MAESTRO DEL MER, CONIL, ANDALUSIA, SPAIN.

More food arrived and they ate it. The plates were removed. Carver had lost count of the courses and of how many questions he'd asked. It seemed as though Clive Winner was asking most of the questions now.

'You met with Alma's family?'

'With her boyfriend and Alma's mother.'

'What's she like? How are they?'

'You should go and visit her. Find out for yourself.'

'Perhaps I will.'

'If they let you.'

Winner gave a mirthless laugh. They ate another course in silence. Carver had the sense that Clive Winner was making his mind up about something.

Eventually Winner spoke; more quietly now.

'I didn't kill Alma Galinda. As I told you before – I liked her. We talked about things. In retrospect we shouldn't have.'

'Shouldn't have talked? Or shouldn't have liked each other?'

'Both. I tried to stop what happened from happening. But I couldn't. I've been trying to protect the family too.'

'If you weren't responsible, who was?'

'People that I work for . . . one of them or maybe a group of them.'

'Why?'

'Hard to know for sure. The most likely thing is that I was being taught a lesson.'

'A woman died in order to teach you a lesson?'

'To bring me back into line.'

'What about Jennifer Prepas? Christopher Baylor?'

'I don't know.' He glanced up at Carver. 'I honestly don't know. But the people I'm talking about, they're capable of anything. They're also very good at finding what it is that you care most about – and using it.'

'You're scared of them?'

Winner laughed. 'Course I'm fucken' scared of them. You should be too. I'm useful to them because there's still a chance that I could be their *Get Out of Jail Free Card*. You haven't got that going for you. All you've really got going for you is that you know nothing.' He took a swig of wine. 'You should be hoping it stays that way.' He put his glass back down and stared at Carver. 'But you're not, are you?'

'No.'

Carver had gone easy on the wine but he'd drunk several glasses of water – this was one of the saltiest and least satisfying meals he'd ever eaten. He needed the toilet. 'Will you excuse me a minute?'

'Sure. Hey, Carver, while you're up, do me a favour and go ask the guy . . .' He gestured in the direction of the bodyguard standing at the door. '. . . ask him if he knows what time we need to leave here for the airport, will you?'

'Sure.'

Carver asked on his way to the toilet. The minder was clearly unhappy about the question but said he'd go and find an answer. Mr Winner would be told. When Carver got back from the bathroom more food had arrived. Two waiters were standing by, ready to unveil it. As soon as he'd sat down the pair lifted a brass cloche from above each plate and a cloud of peppery-smelling smoke emerged. Once that cleared, Carver saw a piece of fish in a green sauce. It reminded him of a boil-in-the-bag dinner he used to eat as a child.

'Did Professor Walston . . . Edith . . . talk to you about her religious beliefs?'

Carver shook his head.

Winner seemed pleased; he had re-established himself as the professor's friend and confidant.

'She thinks that earth's just an interesting experiment that some higher intelligence set running a few million years ago in some dark corner of the lab. They pop back and check on us every now and then.'

'When they need a good laugh?'

'Or a good cry. Edith reckons the only reason this higher intelligence hasn't binned the experiment and flushed us down the intergalactic toilet is that they haven't worked out why clouds do what they do yet either. That and maybe the fact that human beings learned how to make music.'

'It's an interesting idea.'

'Yeah. A hypothesis that's hard to test, let alone prove.' He ate his piece of green fish. 'I was thinking about things while you were having a pee.'

'Okay.'

'We have a few things in common you and me. You wouldn't know it to look at us but we do.'

'What are they?'

'Are you familiar with the term *useful idiot*?'

'Of course.'

'That's you.' He smiled. 'Don't take offence. The term applies to me too. Although technically speaking, I'm a *useful genius*. I'm not sure whether being one or the other is more or less embarrassing or forgivable. Either way, I've decided to help you out. To provide you with some useful information.'

'Why would you do that?'

'You'll have to work that one out. There could be several reasons. Could be I'm trying to make amends. Some weird fucken' lapsed Catholic thing. Maybe I'm settling a score. Perhaps I'm just trying to put something on the other side of the scales. I've been thinking quite a lot about that recently.' He took his napkin from his lap and placed it on his plate. 'I'm not exactly sure how many courses we've had but I think I'm done.'

'Okay, but . . .'

'When I leave, the goon squad will go with me. You stay, finish the meal. I've left something underneath the tablecloth just in front of me. My gift to you.'

'Er . . . thank you.'

Winner grinned. 'Don't thank me. And my advice – think twice before you decide to do anything with it. For your sake, not mine.'

'Right . . . can I just ask—'

'Nah. That's enough questions. This is why I don't do interviews, too many questions. When you read it, you'll understand.'

Winner poured the last of the white wine into his glass, lifted it in a half-hearted toast, drank it down and left. Carver waited until he and his entourage were gone and he was sure that no one was coming back before retrieving the piece of paper. And he read it. And he understood.

89

LA BARROSA, ANDALUSIA, SPAIN.

'I have done you a dozen favours. Here I am asking you for one. One lousy favour!'

Carlos was going to have to say yes, if only to stop the old fisherman from repeatedly leaning across the bar and yelling at him with his dreadful breath.

'Okay, Pepe, I'll take you up there again, but not till after work. It'll be getting dark by the time we get there.'

'That's fine by me. What's the problem? You scared of the dark?'

'No, I . . . forget it. Whatever treasure it is you think might've washed up there I hope you're not going to sell it to that crook in Cádiz.'

'I couldn't if I wanted to. I'm banned. We both are.' Pepe glanced in the direction of the fridge. 'I'd take another one of those beers if you've got one.' Carlos sighed and served him.

'That's three Euros.'

'Don't be stupid.'

Carlos handed him the bottle.

'What is it you think you're going to find up there?'
'I will show you when we get there.'

Pepe rode pillion again and told the same stories again, either forgetting or not caring that he'd told Carlos about the place that used to rear the bulls for the big fights in Ronda, the freshwater fish the size of a small man, teaching Peter O'Toole to ride a camel. This at least was a new story, albeit almost certainly untrue. The bike's engine grew increasingly loud and its driver increasingly crotchety. It took them nearly four hours to reach Lepe, another ten minutes on the dirt track. When they finally got to the place where they'd stopped before, Carlos suggested that Pepe go ahead.

'I need to rest for a while, you go. If there's anything you need help with, you can come back for me.'

'No. You need to come. After that drive you should stretch your legs anyway. Come on.'

They walked through the dusk. First on a reasonably well-worn path that took them through the reed-covered nature reserve to the point where the sand dunes started. The old man kept walking and continued chatting away, checking back over his shoulder now and again to make sure that Carlos was keeping pace. 'We're close now, I'm sure. I can't believe how hard it is to find this place, no matter how many times you come. Or how. Boat, bike. It's easier by boat of course . . .' Carlos was barely listening any more. He spotted the waterlogged tower first.

'There it is.'

'Ah, so it is.' He patted Carlos on the arm. 'Good lad.' Pepe kept walking straight towards the tower. Carlos caught up and stopped him.

'You said it's too muddy. We'll sink in that bog. We need to go around, remember?' The old man was a danger to himself and others.

'No, it's fine. I put down some old wooden pallets. You can walk across now.'

'I don't understand.' He followed Pepe a little further, across the boggy ground to a point where, as promised, a makeshift bridge of wooden pallets had been laid down across the waterlogged stretch of land. And then Carlos saw it, from inside the tower; in the only window visible – a light.

'What? What's going on here Pepe?'

The old man would not meet his eye. He gazed down at the ground.

'I wasn't sure what to do. There is no good thing.' He paused. 'But it is right that you should see her first, before anyone else. You loved her. She loved you.'

'She?'

'I have done what I can. Candles and some flowers.' He hesitated. 'She has been in the water for a long time, but she is still Alma . . . Still beautiful.'

Carlos shook his head. Tears sprung to his eyes.

'How?'

'I told you before . . . the sea takes away. But sometimes it gives back.'

PART FOUR

CUMULONIMBUS

cumulus – heap
nimbus – rain cloud

The King of Clouds, more commonly known as thunderclouds, cumulonimbus is the only cloud type that can produce hail, thunder, and lightning. They often sit just a few hundred feet above the earth's surface and represent huge powerhouses, storing the same amount of energy as ten Hiroshima-sized atom bombs.

90

GREEN'S CLUB, ST JAMES'S STREET, LONDON

Carver disliked gentlemen's clubs in general and judging from first impressions, Leonard Allen's St James's Street club was no exception. They'd arranged to meet at six, although Leonard advised William to arrive at least ten minutes early. This was rush hour in clubland, and Green's was breaking in a new doorman. 'A nice enough young fellow but no clue of who's who.'

When Carver arrived, sure enough there was a long queue of red-faced men at the entrance, waiting to be admitted. The new fellow was doing his best, he had a large ledger open on the desk in front of him and he'd dialled the obsequious levels up to eleven. 'Thank you so much for your patience. Can I ask whether you're a Green's member yourself or whether you're meeting one of our members?'

Eventually it was Carver's turn. The new man looked him up and down. The yellow plastic bag seemed to be of particular interest.

'Thank you for your patience, sir. I assume you're meeting one of our members here this evening?'

Carver decided not to take it personally. He was invited to go and wait for Leonard in the 'second reception room'. If there'd been a third reception room, then Carver was pretty sure that was where he would've been directed to. The high-ceilinged room was draughty, and the furniture worn; perhaps because of this the reception room was all but empty and that suited Carver. He picked a high-backed armchair in the corner and sat in it, his bag at his feet. The walls were filled with pictures, a haphazard mix of black-and-white etchings and oils, all extravagantly framed; most of them depicting ships, stately homes, or horses.

Leonard arrived, dressed in a dark, chalk-striped suit and smiling. 'I don't frequent this corner of the club too often. It seems to be where all the old, unwanted pictures have ended up . . .' He gestured at an old fellow asleep by the window. 'And the old, unwanted members. Are you happy here or would you rather move somewhere a little livelier?'

Carver shook his head. 'I'm happy here.'

'I suspected as much. In which case, I'll fetch us some drinks and nuts and whatnot. Whisky?'

Carver nodded.

Once they were sat facing each other in a couple of raggedy armchairs with a table of drinks, nuts and olives in between them, Leonard spoke first.

'You went rather quiet on me for a while.'

Carver shrugged. 'I was working on the story . . . investigating Clive Winner. Your original suggestion as I recall?'

'Yes, so, I have something of a confession to make.'

'What's that?'

Leonard was embarrassed. He was worried he might have sent Carver off down the wrong track. Some of his fears about Clive Winner had proved to be unfounded. He'd been reassured more recently that the Downing Street title was more honorific than real. Leonard's Foreign Office friend assured him that Winner had stopped playing footsie with dodgy hedge funds and questionable regimes and was very much committed to UK plc. There'd be more detail at the Paris conference, but things were definitely moving in the right direction.

'Don't get me wrong. I still think the man's as unreliable as all hell – genius and snake-oil salesman in equal measure. But for now, he's inside the tent, urinating out.' Leonard smiled. 'Rather than the other way around. What have you made of him?'

'I met him.'

'Really?' Leonard didn't play surprise as well as he played embarrassment. 'Well, that's an achievement in itself. He hardly ever speaks to journalists. Were you able to get anything out of him?'

'I don't know that I got anything *out of him.*'

'No, he's slippery. No doubt about it.'

'But he gave me something.'

'What's that?'

'You, Leonard. He gave me you.'

91

LA BARROSA BEACH, ANDALUSIA, SPAIN

Carlos had emptied his bank account to pay for this. The grumpy old British journalist – Carver – had offered him some money towards it but Carlos had wanted to pay for this himself. He was still not convinced that it would achieve anything, or that anyone would pay attention, but it felt good to be doing something positive, something that he hoped Alma would understand and approve of. The beach was filling up now – nothing like as busy as during the height of the season but there were still a good few tourists around – heading down in time to see the sunset. More importantly there were a couple of journalists and a photographer from the local paper in attendance. Carlos tried to recall the word Naz had used, he remembered it had made him laugh . . . *a snapper*. That was it. Loli had translated the rest of Naz's instructions and made sure he understood. Timing was important.

'All you need is one or two local journalists and a decent snapper. I can help you with the rest. I'll be logged in at my end when we do this, and we'll put it out on social media straight away. Trust me, it'll work.'

He'd had the banner printed at the place that Alma used to use and they'd done it for cost. He saved a bit more money by helping the pilot roll and load the banner into the plane – he'd done it often enough with the supermarket ads and birthday greetings that Alma used to fly from the back of the 'flying fried egg'.

Here came the plane now, flying from the south. Carlos got his phone out and got ready to take some pictures to send to Naz. He nudged the newspaper photographer to make sure he was ready too.

92

GREEN'S CLUB, ST JAMES'S STREET, LONDON

Leonard Allen looked like he had aged ten years in as many minutes. He was leafing through the documents that Carver had given him. His face was grey. Carver watched him read.

'We've got dates and places, meetings you've attended that have nothing to do with your remit. My partner and I have found confirmed hotel bookings, your name on flight manifests. When you add it all up it seems to confirm that you are what Clive Winner says you are.'

'Which is?'

'Somewhere between horribly compromised and seriously corrupt. We haven't worked out exactly how much money you get from the fossil-fuel people or how it reaches you . . . but we will.'

Leonard looked again at the documents Carver had given him.

'Maybe. Maybe not. Until then it's still one fellow's word against another's. And I'm guessing there's not a hope in hell of Winner going on the record.'

'I don't need him on the record. I've got this too.' Carver took an A4-sized full-colour photo from his bag and handed it to Leonard.

'What's this?'

'I think you know what it is, Leonard. It was taken by a German guy, a birdwatcher. He was trying to photograph a spoonbill, but he got this instead . . .'

93

LA BARROSA BEACH, ANDALUSIA, SPAIN

The pilot did not fly as well as Alma – neither as low nor so recklessly slow. The banner was waving a little in the wind, but it was easy enough to read and people on the beach were looking up and reading it. Spanish on one side, English on the other. The photographer started snapping away.

Alma Galinda fue asesinada. Aqui hay pregunta . . .

At the stone tower the plane turned a wide loop, slowed and flew back the way it had come. Carlos read the English version as it fluttered by: 'Alma Galinda was murdered. Here is our question . . . the drone that killed her was made by the British and bought by the Saudis. What do these two countries know about our friend's death?'

Around him on the beach, Carlos could sense other people beginning to sit up and pay attention. A few individuals were taking their own pictures and presumably sending and sharing them with others. Carlos remembered something that Naz had said to him: '*A lie is usually halfway around the world before the truth has put its boots on* . . . it's one of William's favourite quotes. If we work together and we get this right then we can help the truth do some catching up.'

94

GREEN'S CLUB, ST JAMES'S STREET, LONDON

Carver pointed at the picture that Leonard was holding in his hand.

'This is the attack drone that brought Alma Galinda's plane down. It was British made; we sold it to the Saudis, and you were involved in brokering the deal – it's the sort they've been using in Yemen but this one went elsewhere. It was used in Spain on the 9th of September.' He paused. 'But I think you know all this already, Leonard, don't you?'

Carver watched the civil servant squinting at the picture, looking for any sign that the photo might be fake – or that you could make a case for it being fabricated.

'We've got several similar pictures, all digital, all high definition, all time- and date-stamped. The wing and tail you can see in the top right of the picture belongs to Alma Galinda's plane. We've got a picture of her sitting in the same plane. We have the autopsy on Alma's body too. Everything matches. Everything points in the same direction.'

Leonard Allen finished his whisky, the ice rattling against his teeth. When he looked across at Carver the smile was still there, but it lacked conviction.

'What do you want?'

'What do I want? Well, I'd like you to be able to tell me that you weren't trying to use me. That I wasn't supposed to be your useful idiot. Another way to bring Clive Winner back into line. But I don't think you can tell me that can you?'

'I made a mistake.' He paused. 'I've made a series of mistakes.'

'These aren't mistakes, Leonard, this is corruption. It's illegal. And immoral. You're a public servant.'

Leonard laughed. 'And I've been a good one. For a long time. But haven't you heard, William? Haven't you been watching? Public service isn't really a thing any more.'

Carver shook his head. 'I don't believe that. I'm going to go now.'

'How long have I got?'

'Before I put this on the radio? A few days. If you want to comment, or a right of reply then let me know but I should tell you that the story – or some of it anyway – is already out there in the world.'

'Where?'

'Spain.'

'How? I mean in what form?'

'I suspect you'll find out soon enough.'

Carver stood and picked up his bag. Leonard stood up too, but with some difficulty. He appeared to be shaking somewhat.

'William, I'm begging you. There's not just me to consider here, there's my family. There's Henrietta . . .'

Carver shook his head.

'Don't do that, Leonard. Please don't do that.'

He turned and left.

95

JUBILEE STREET, HOUNSLOW, LONDON

Naz heard her mother calling her name. She walked downstairs and found her mum sitting at the kitchen table with a cup of tea and her latest thousand-piece jigsaw in front of her. She glanced up at her daughter and smiled.

'I have something you want.'

'What?'

'First you have to help me with this jigsaw.' She lifted the half of the box with the picture up for Naz to see. It was a waterfall . . . Niagara perhaps. 'Your Auntie Meena sent me this one. It is her revenge for the Chelsea Flower Show puzzle I gave her last Christmas. It is very difficult – nothing but blues and whites. Even the edges are impossible. Come and help me. Ten pieces of jigsaw and I will show you what I have.'

'Five?'

'Okay.'

Her mum propped the photo of Niagara against her mug of tea and began shaking the box of jigsaw pieces, like a prospector panning for gold. It didn't take Naz long to find five edges and put them together. Her mum nodded approvingly.

'You are a jigsaw genius. Shall we see what else you are good at?'

'What do you mean?'

Her mum took an envelope from her lap and held it up for Naz to see. Brown. Official-looking. Naz felt her pulse quicken. 'Exam results?'

'I think so.' She handed her daughter the envelope. Naz ripped it open, scanning its contents.

'*Yesssss*. Get in.'

'What does it say?'

'I got ninety-two per cent.'

'Ninety-two? Really? That's amazing, I am very proud.'

'It's incredible. Unbelievable.' She paused. 'You know what else it is?' Her mother shook her head. 'It's one more point than Patrick got.' She got her phone out.

'Naziah! You are not going to telephone him and gloat.'

'Course not.' She smiled. 'But he'd want to know.'

'I thought you said that Patrick was on holiday.'

'He's in Paris. But not really on holiday. He's looking after the baby while Rebecca is working. I'll send him a message. I need to call McCluskey too. And William of course.'

96

THE YORKSHIRE GREY, FITZROVIA, LONDON

Carver wouldn't take no for an answer. He'd insisted that he and Naz celebrate her exam result in style.

'I'll book us a table at the Yorkshire Grey. We can see if McCluskey will make a trip up to London for it too.'

So here they were; a slightly unlikely-looking party of three, sitting at what Bernard the landlord claimed was his best table, and eating and drinking and talking shop. Carver had ordered a bottle of champagne. Then another. This took Naz rather by surprise until he happened to mention that their boss Naomi had offered to pick up the tab for the booze. He proposed several toasts – to Naz. Then to McCluskey. To Naz and McCluskey. To journalism. The late afternoon turned into early evening. Bernard had the Christmas decorations up and the log fire going and when Naz returned from a trip to the loo and stopped briefly to take it all in, she really couldn't remember when she'd been happier. She felt like she had been initiated into something very special. The only shame was that Patrick couldn't be with them. Naz had tried to reach him on WhatsApp, but it was a big day at the Paris conference, and they were not surprised when he didn't answer.

McCluskey asked for an update on the Alma Galinda story.

'I've seen some bits and pieces out of Spain; that plane stunt certainly got people's attention, plenty on social media and in the Spanish press. So, when do you go with what you've got?'

Carver and Naz explained that the lawyers wanted to give the main groups with accusations levelled against them longer to respond.

'That's who? Couple of UK government departments, your civil servant fellow and the Saudis. I wonder which of those the lawyers are most concerned about?' McCluskey shook her head. 'Bollocks to that. You should get your story out ASAP. Those bawbags are just biding their time and assuming people will lose interest.'

Carver nodded. 'I know but . . .' He hesitated.

McCluskey studied him.

'You don't mind waiting?'

'No.'

'Why? You think it goes wider?'

'Wider, without a doubt. But also higher. The question is . . . how much higher?'

97

THE HOLIDAY INN, CHARLES DE GAULLE, PARIS, FRANCE

The hotel that the Planet Action delegation were staying in was out near the airport. It was a drag having to travel in every day, but Leila seemed to love the hotel, love the train ride into the centre of Paris and love being with both her parents somewhere new and exciting. She was also obsessed with the Eiffel Tower – pointing a fat little finger in its direction whenever it came into view.

Rebecca had gone in early that day to work and they'd agreed to meet at the Arc de Triomphe at their regular spot as soon as she and the Planet Action group had watched the prime minister's speech and issued a statement in response. Pre-briefing had raised expectations. The press had been told to expect far-reaching announcements on coal, the removal of fossil-fuel subsidies, sustainable farming, rewilding and more besides.

Patrick carried Leila's buggy up the stairs at George V Metro and walked towards the monument. The area around the Arc de Triomphe was a sea of bright, colourful banners representing green groups across Europe and the world. A group of teenage girls from Rebecca's placard-making class had worked together to design and paint the banner that Planet Action brought with them. It was an updated version of the classic recruiting poster from the First World

War with a haunted-looking man being quizzed by his children – *What did YOU do in the Great War Daddy?* In this version, one of the sides of the father's armchair was on fire. So were the living-room curtains. The children were asking their dad what he did in the Great Climate War. He was as unwilling to answer the question in this version as he was in the original but in this poster the father was holding a glass of thick, black oil, which he was about to drink from. When Patrick and Leila arrived at the banner, Rebecca was already there. She looked angry. Simultaneously furious and upset.

'Did you see it?'

'The speech? No, we were on the train. Tell me.'

'It was dreadful. The same old, same old. Clichés and empty promises. "We must not name and shame, we should engage with and gently encourage the fossil-fuel industry." That's an actual quote. He even mentioned the bloody huskies.'

'I'm sorry.'

'It was meant to be ground-breaking, a *speech for the ages*. What do you think happened?'

'Politics happened.' Rebecca shook her head. She reached down into the buggy and retrieved her daughter. Holding her close to her chest, feeling Leila's warm body against her own she felt better. But only briefly. She looked at Patrick again.

'It's not just that, Patrick. There's something else.'

'What?'

'I saw him. He's here.'

'Who's here?' But Patrick knew. 'You saw Jeff?'

Rebecca nodded.

'Did he see you?'

'I don't think so. Why is he here?'

'I don't know but I would guess he's trying to pick up where he left off in London. Making contacts, gathering information on this new generation of campaigners, giving it or selling it to whoever it is he works for. The difference is . . . now we know. We can do something about it.'

98

THE LONDON EYE, SOUTH BANK, LONDON

Carver had been half-expecting Leonard's call, but the request to meet took him by surprise. He'd told him that it'd be better for the civil servant or his lawyer to email or courier any statement he had to make – that was how *right of reply* usually worked. But Leonard had persisted; he needed to meet Carver face to face, the things he had to say could only be said in person. Both Naz and McCluskey had counselled caution but eventually a combination of curiosity and guilt got the better of Carver and he agreed to a rendezvous back where it had all begun.

There was no sign of Leonard at the foot of the London Eye or among the people queuing for tickets. Carver looked up at the pods, turning slowly against the grey sky. Inside one of the ascending capsules there was a man in a familiar-looking fawn-coloured mackintosh. He was standing, straight-backed and still while a gaggle of tourists – one large family perhaps – moved around the pod posing for pictures. Carver saw several camera flashes. He joined the queue in front of the ticket office. The line shuffled forward. *Trip of a lifetime! Soar through the air at a height of 440 feet . . .* etc. Glancing up from the familiar information board he caught the young ticket attendant's eye. She smiled at him from behind the Plexiglas screen. Eventually it was his turn. The intercom crackled.

'Hello again, how're you doing?'

'Not too bad, thanks, Iris. How about you?'

'Good. Very good in fact. It's my last week sitting in this horrible little box. I finished my hairdressing course.'

'Congratulations.'

'Thanks. I start work at a salon next week. A little place down in Stockwell.'

'Really? That's my neck of the woods.'

'Small world. The pay's rubbish but it's a start. First step on the ladder and all that.'

'Of course.'

There was an awkward silence.

'Your . . . er . . . brother's up there already.'

'Right.' Carver paused. 'He's not actually my brother.'

'No, I sort of guessed that. For one thing you don't look or dress anything like each other.'

'Right.'

'Also . . . he's so polite, it's kind of rude.' Carver nodded. 'Whereas you're the opposite.' Carver glanced away, towards the wheel.

'He's a friend. Or rather . . . a colleague.' Neither of these descriptions rang true. He had once considered Leonard a friend. Or an *almost-friend*. Now he wasn't a friend, nor a colleague. Not even a contact; not any more. He was just a man whose life Carver was about to destroy. 'I guess I'd better buy a ticket and go and see him.'

Iris smiled.

'I guess you might as well. Seeing as how you're here. You know in all my time working here you're easily the *least enthusiastic* customer I've ever had.'

'I do my best.'

*

Carver waited at the foot of the Eye. Several pods arrived, emptied, refilled, and left. Once at the front of the queue he stood to one side, waiting for Leonard's capsule to arrive. He stared out at the river, more black than brown in colour today. A broken tree floated by; one branch reaching out from the water like an emaciated arm. By the time Leonard's capsule reached the platform all the other occupants had gathered at the door, waiting for it to open. When it did, they streamed out, brushing past him. The figure in the fawn raincoat remained standing, stock-still, both hands on the silver railing at the edge of the pod. Carver felt the skin at the back of his neck tighten. He swung around and scanned the group of people who'd just left but their backs were to him. He turned back.

'Leonard . . .' Carver walked towards the figure. '. . . hey.' He put a hand on the civil servant's shoulder.

Leonard jumped.

'What the . . .' He turned and looked at Carver. 'Oh, William. I'm sorry.' He attempted a smile. 'I was miles away. Miles. And several decades.'

'Right.'

'Trying to remember how and when I managed to bugger things up so badly.'

The two men sat on the lozenge-shaped seat in the centre of the pod. There were half-a-dozen other people in the capsule, a group of Dutch tourists, but they stayed close to the windows, misidentifying various London landmarks.

Leonard spoke first, thanking Carver for agreeing to meet.

'I was sure you'd say no. Plenty of reasons for you not to want to, that's for sure. Henrietta had no such doubts.'

The mention of Leonard's wife troubled Carver.

'Before we go any further, I think I should make it clear that the story I've been working on, everything we've found out about the fossil-fuel industry's influence and tactics . . . it'll go out at 8.10 on the radio the day after tomorrow. That'll happen regardless of what you say to me today. If you have a statement to make, your right of reply, then I'll include that as part of my report . . . but that's all.'

Leonard looked chastened.

'I understand. I didn't come here to beg or bargain with you.' He smiled. 'Of course, I would do either . . . or both . . . if I thought it might do any good, but I know we've gone beyond that.'

'That's right. So why are we here, Leonard?'

'I want to explain. I'm not sure why, but I need you to understand why I did what I did.'

Some of what Leonard Allen told him, Carver already knew. Other details he had guessed at – specifically the financial pressures that had pushed the old public servant to betray everything he'd previously believed in. But alongside this information – relayed in the sort of detail one would expect from an old Whitehall man – there were several surprises.

Leonard had entered the civil service at his father's insistence. 'My old man was at the Foreign Office, his father Ministry of Defence. Signing up for the service was tantamount to joining the family firm.' Leonard had thrived at first, rising steadily through the ranks. 'Hard to believe now but I was considered to be a good prospect, a high-flier, destined for great things.' Then something had changed; posts he would have been expected to have been given had gone to others. 'I became stuck. *Overlooked* – in every sense of that word.' With Henrietta's help he attempted to charm his way back into favour, but the Christmas parties and dinners did nothing to persuade Leonard's superiors that he had changed. He'd been characterised as something of a stickler, inflexible and old-fashioned at a time when those things were increasingly unpopular. 'Once someone puts you in a pigeonhole, it's the devil's own job to wriggle your way out.' As Leonard's career stalled so his family grew – four boys to put through an expensive private school. They remortgaged the house once. Then again. 'A silly deal that we should never have signed. The Bank of Scotland basically owns eighty per cent of anything we recoup when we sell it.' When a PR company with a Mayfair address and impeccable credentials got in touch with the offer of a perfectly legitimate work trip which also happened to include business-class flights and ten nights at a seven-star hotel for the whole Allen family, Leonard said yes. The invitation arrived at a time when a holiday of any sort had seemed impossible. 'That old slippery-slope cliché proved correct in every respect – I slipped and slid. The only surprising thing now that I look back upon it is how quickly it happened and how little resistance I put up.'

'Right up to the point where you recruited me to do some of the dirty work for you.'

'I've done much worse than encourage a journalist to dig into the affairs of Clive Winner. He's no angel by the way.'

'I'm sure.'

Leonard stood up, took his coat off, folding it carefully before sitting back down.

'What I've come to realise is – nowadays, everyone lies to everyone else.'

Carver shook his head.

'I don't.'

The civil servant glanced at Carver.

'No. You probably don't.'

'And I don't believe that most other people do either. I admit that lying is a lot more fashionable than it used to be. I remember it being more of a *last resort* thing than a habit or a political strategy. But most people still want the truth. They try to be truthful, and they want to be told the truth in return. They know when they're being lied to.'

'God, I wish I believed that, Carver, I really do.'

The glass pod they were sitting in had reached its highest point. Carver looked out, the grey clouds had thinned and just then a splash of light hit one of the office buildings opposite, turning it briefly beautiful.

'It's never too late.'

Leonard laughed.

'That's the sort of thing Henrietta says. In my experience – it's often too late. I am destined to be remembered – if at all – as a walking cautionary tale.' Carver said nothing. 'However, I might yet decide that I'd like to take some people down with me. That was the other reason for asking to see you. If I were to write down everything that had happened, chapter and verse, I take it that you might be able to find a use for that?'

'Of course.'

'Then I'll think about it.' The remainder of the time was taken up with slightly strained small talk. Leonard told Carver about his boys, their progress at school and sporting achievements. When the pod finally reached terra firma, both men were relieved and they parted politely but quickly. Leonard headed off in the direction of Waterloo station and so Carver loitered a while, trying to decide on an alternative route home. Before leaving he walked over to the ticket booth to say goodbye.

'I'm planning to steer clear of the London Eye for a while . . . although I suppose you are too. Good luck with the new career.'

Iris smiled. 'Thanks. I've been thinking . . . you should take one of my cards.'

'Why?'

'I've worked out what you should do with your hair. I wasn't sure the first time I saw you, but I've got an idea now.'

'Really?' His hand went instinctively to his head. 'There isn't exactly a lot of hair to work with.'

'I could make it work – *mates' rates*.'

'Mates' rates?'

'Cheap. Take one of my cards.'

She slid a card under the plastic glass divide. Carver took it and read: *A Breath of Fresh Hair*.

'I know, crap, isn't it? I hate all these funny – not really very funny – hairdresser names. When I get my own place, it'll have a simple straightforward name. No silly word games or double meanings.'

Leonard looked across the Waterloo Road, willing the red man to turn green. If he could make the next train, then he'd be home before Henrietta and could have a hot shower and a drink. He needed both. The crowd of commuters waiting impatiently to cross the road had grown, the lights were taking an age. He shuffled a few inches backwards, away from the kerb and the fast-moving traffic. The man behind him moved back a little too. Leonard half turned and muttered a polite thank you. He checked his watch. If the lights would only change, he could make this train. The blow was low to the small of his back. Not enough to hurt but more than enough to send Leonard stumbling out into the road. The red transit van had accelerated to make the lights. Leonard had time to turn and face the driver, to make eye contact in fact. He saw the man's panic-stricken face. And then his wife's face. And that was all.

Collins had killed this way before. It was not his favourite. Too much risk and very little satisfaction. The key was to hold your upper body still, you did not push with a hand – that would be too obvious to the crowd around you. You used the knee. And you did not leave straight away either. You stayed – making the same horrified sounds and mimicking the shocked-looking faces of those around you. After four or five minutes had passed, once you heard the sirens, then you could go; fade into the crowd and leave. The only fly in the ointment had been the speed camera that had flashed at around the same time that Leonard Allen had staggered into the road. Triggered by the same red van that killed him perhaps? But this was an annoyance rather than a serious concern. The people he worked for could fix that.

Epilogue

STOCKWELL ROAD, LONDON

Carver spent nearly half an hour sitting on his sofa tapping at his phone. Writing. Deleting. Writing. Deleting. He wanted the message to Henrietta to be an honest one – it had to be that – but also kind. Comforting even? He could not apologise for what he'd done . . . the journalistic textbooks all told you that it was impossible to defame a dead man but he knew that this was exactly what his and Naz's report had done. Still, he could not apologise, but he could offer to explain. If she'd be willing to meet him, then he could do that. In the end that was what he sent – a couple of lines, hoping that she was well and offering to meet.

She messaged straight back: *I appreciate the gesture, William. I know it is well meant. But . . .*

He left the rest of her message unread. Perhaps he'd read it later. He turned the phone off and went to fix himself a drink. It was too early really but what the hell. He was drinking his whisky and soda when the doorbell rang. He ignored it. It rang again. He went to the window and stared down onto the street. As he did he saw a small, bobble-hatted figure step back from the downstairs door and into view. Edith Walston looked up, saw Carver and nodded a greeting. He waved back, feeling rather ridiculous doing it. Carver indicated that he would come down but Edith shook her head. She pointed in the direction of the door then turned and left. Maybe she smiled. Or maybe not.

The envelope she'd put through Carver's letterbox contained a printed-out copy of an email exchange – an exchange that had taken place in recent weeks. The emails were dated but the two correspondents' addresses had been blacked out. It didn't matter as far as identification was concerned, the two men referred to each other by name, the tone of their messages as they exchanged ideas and played with different phrases was warm. It was obvious to Carver what this was, it would be obvious to anyone that read it. Carver turned to the last page – Clive Winner had added a handwritten note:

> I heard the radio report about Alma on the World Service. It made me glad. Here's something else. Something me and Edith thought you might find useful. It's the speech your man didn't give. But he wanted to. Something else for the other side of the scales. With regards . . . your fellow idiot.

REUTERS . . . COP 21 PM SPEECH LATEST

Downing Street are refusing to confirm or deny that a document leaked to a British journalist contains a speech which the UK prime minister originally intended to deliver at last month's climate conference in Paris. The address, which calls for the phasing out of coal, an immediate switch to renewables, a ban on non-electric vehicles as well as comprehensive reforestation and rewilding has been hailed by green groups, and there is increasing pressure on the UK Government to explain why – if the prime minister penned the speech – he did not deliver it.

Acknowledgements

The following books were particularly helpful in researching this book: *Under A White Sky* by Elizabeth Kolbert, *The Planet Remade: How Geoengineering Could Change the World* by Oliver Morton, *The Future We Choose* by Christiana Figueres and Tom Rivett-Carnac, *The New Climate War* by Michael E. Mann, *Chaos* by James Gleick, *The Water Will Come: Rising Seas, Sinking Cities and the Remaking of the Civilized World* by Jeff Goodell, *Kill Chain: Drones and the Rise of High-Tech Assassins* by Andrew Cockburn and *The Cloud Collector's Handbook* by Gavin Pretor-Pinney. I would like to thank the Dolce-Barden family for putting up with a strange man living at the bottom of their garden, wandering around talking to himself for so long. Thank you to Matilda Harrison for the early reading, keen eye and excellent suggestions.

Huge thanks to Jade Chandler for her unerring editorial good sense and patience as this book took shape and to the whole Baskerville team, in particular Alice Herbert, Ellie Bailey, Megan Schaffer, Drew Hunt and Zulekhá Afzal. Thank you to John Saddler – agent, friend and poet.

Finally to Vic – there's no one I'd rather sit alongside as the waters rise.

About the Author

Peter Hanington is the author of *A Dying Breed*, *A Single Source* and *A Cursed Place*, which star old-school radio journalist William Carver. Peter worked as a journalist and radio producer for over twenty-five years, including fourteen years at Radio 4 on the *Today* programme as well as *The World Tonight* and *Newshour* on the BBC World Service. His field work has taken him around the world, from Russia to Hong Kong, Lebanon, Liberia and South Africa. He currently lives between London and New York and still travels frequently as research for his novels.